P9-CQX-870

Praise for *USA TODAY* bestselling author

CHRISTIE RIDGWAY

"Kick off your shoes and escape to endless summer.
This is romance at its best."
—Emily March, *New York Times* bestselling author
of *Nightingale Way*, on *Bungalow Nights*

"Sexy and addictive—Ridgway will keep you up all night!"
—*New York Times* bestselling author Susan Andersen
on *Beach House No. 9*

"Ridgway's feel-good read, with its perfectly integrated,
extremely hot, and well-crafted love scenes,
is contemporary romance at its best."
—*Booklist* on *Can't Hurry Love* (starred review)

"Sexy, sassy, funny, and cool, this effervescent sizzler
nicely launches Ridgway's new series
and is a perfect pick-me-up for a summer's day."
—*Library Journal* on *Crush on You*

"Pure romance, delightfully warm and funny."
—*New York Times* bestselling author Jennifer Crusie

"Christie Ridgway writes with the perfect combination of
humor and heart. This funny, sexy story
is as fresh and breezy as its Southern California setting.
An irresistible read!"
—*New York Times* bestselling author Susan Wiggs
on *How to Knit a Wild Bikini*

"Christie Ridgway is delightful."
—*New York Times* bestselling author Rachel Gibson

Dear Reader,

This California girl invites you to a very special California place...your own cottage, right on the sand, where the Pacific Ocean races forward to give your bare feet its cool kiss. The keys to Beach House No. 9 are at your fingertips. Turn the page and you're in!

Some years ago, the title *Beach House No. 9* popped into my head. Busy with other projects, I scribbled it on a piece of paper and pinned it to my office bulletin board. And there it was, waiting for me, after I took a jaunt up the coast and found a very special cove that became the inspiration for the Crescent Cove in my back-to-back-to-back trilogy. Yep, the next two books in the series, *Bungalow Nights* and *The Love Shack,* are coming right up—and offer more No. 9 magic. The romances are sexy and fun, but I expect a tear or two may be shed...making the happy-ever-afters all the sweeter.

In this book, heroine Jane Pearson is everything I love in a woman—she's talented and she's no pushover, not even for a gorgeous man with a chip on his shoulder. Griffin Lowell tells himself she's all wrong for him... enjoy watching him find out how right she really is.

Here comes the sun!

Christie

CHRISTIE RIDGWAY

BEACH HOUSE NO. 9

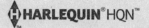
HARLEQUIN® HQN™

Recycling programs
for this product may
not exist in your area.

ISBN-13: 978-0-373-77740-2

BEACH HOUSE NO. 9

Copyright © 2013 by Christie Ridgway

Printed in U.S.A.

www.Harlequin.com

Acknowledgments

I sold my very first book to Harlequin
and it's with great pleasure that I continue our
association. Many thanks to Margaret Marbury,
who showed such enthusiasm for the idea and
made it happen. Another round of the same to
my editor, Margo Lipschultz, who has taken the time
to get to know me and my books and
who has made this trilogy so, so much better.
Last, I must raise my glass to Harlequin's
art department. The beautiful covers for this series
perfectly capture the enchantment of Crescent Cove.

BEACH HOUSE NO. 9

To the brothers in my life:
my own, my husband and his brother, my two sons.
I've seen what's underneath those all-guy exteriors—
deep family bonds and strong yet tender hearts
that are reflected by every hero in my stories.

At last we are in it up to our necks, and everything is changed, even your outlook on life.

—Ernie Pyle,
Pulitzer Prize-winning war correspondent

Love makes your soul crawl out from its hiding place.

—Zora Neale Hurston, 20th century author

CHAPTER ONE

THE SALT AIR, Jane Pearson realized, was hampering the success of her impending mission. First, it made her normally normal hair fuzzy. Not such a big deal, she supposed as she picked her way downhill, taking the narrow track of crushed shells that led from the coastal road to the picturesque cottages of Crescent Cove, but it was also wilting the white linen dress she wore.

At home, the garment had seemed perfect I-mean-business wear for a June late afternoon. It had short cap sleeves and a collar she'd buttoned tight to the neck, but the swing hemline no longer moved crisply about her knees, instead clinging damply to her thighs. By the time she reached Beach House No. 9, she feared she wouldn't appear the no-nonsense professional. Kleenex ghost might be a better comparison, the kind that kids made at Halloween—this one spritzed with water and topped with frizzy blondish tendrils.

No matter, she thought. Her determination remained firm. Despite the state of her attire, she wouldn't soften when facing the man she was here to confront. Griffin Lowell had been ignoring her calls—all eleven of them!—and she wasn't willing to wait any longer for a response. According to his literary agent, the writer was way behind on his memoir. Jane had been hired to cure his critical case of deadline denial and then help shape the pages she prodded him to produce. It was time to get started.

He needed her.

You need him too, Jane, a little voice in her head added.

She ignored the unwelcome reminder and focused instead on her surroundings. Crescent Cove wasn't a hardship to visit. It was actually an amazing find in this Southern California county notable for the recently built, oh-so-alike housing developments and shopping malls that sprouted like beige-stuccoed fungi along the Pacific Coast Highway. About those red terra-cotta tile roofs... didn't anyone realize that too much of a good thing made a bad thing?

By contrast, this beach colony was straight from another time. The fifty or so unconventional bungalows and colorful cottages were prime examples of beach vernacular architectural design—she'd read that—and snuggled the bluffs along a two-mile stretch of sand. Each appeared as cheery and appealing as the bougainvillea that grew like weeds around them in colors ranging from pale salmon to the brightest scarlet. The prevailing sound at the cove was the rhythmic shush of the waves, as the growl of tires on the highway above was screened by a stand of tall eucalyptus. Their medicinal tang mingled with the scents of seaweed, sand and ocean.

A black Labrador in a tie-dyed kerchief ambled toward her, and she smiled at him. Jane loved dogs, though she'd never actually owned one. Growing up, her famed scientist of a father had claimed that pets would distract children from the rigor of their studies. And these days, her hours were too unpredictable to allow for a pet.

"Hello," she called out to the canine, wiggling her fingers in his direction. His moseying pace didn't check, however, and he turned down an alley that snaked between two rows of houses. Well. Just another male wrapped up in his own pursuits.

Continuing forward, she approached No. 9 from the rear, where more crushed shells led to a double garage, its door painted a seafoam-green. A handful of beach cruiser bicycles leaned against the dark brown shingled siding. Six cars were parked nearby, half of them luxury sedans, half in dubious running condition, all with two or more surfboards strapped on top, bright-striped beach towels sandwiched between them.

Did Griffin Lowell have houseguests? The thought made Jane pause while she was still fifty feet from the back door. Surely not. His agent had told her the man in question had gone completely hermit, ignoring phone calls, texts and emails—even from friends and family. Jane knew all too well how effectively he'd snubbed her.

"Before he went incommunicado, I spoke to him about getting some assistance with the book," Frank, the agent, had said. "He agreed. So light a firecracker under him, will you, Jane?"

Of course she would. She was excellent at her job, and after the disaster of her last assignment, it was imperative she prove that again.

Her short-heeled pumps had slender ankle straps and cut-outs like eyelets scattered across the toe cap. She watched them carefully as she navigated another fifteen feet on the unsteady shell surface before pausing a second time. Taking in some deep breaths, she tried smoothing down her wisping-every-which-way hair and palm-ironing the damp fabric of her dress. The stakes had her a little tense.

Not to mention that there was the whole recluse thing to consider. Griffin had spent a year embedded with American troops in Afghanistan. He'd seen things, experienced things—hence the memoir—that without a doubt had impacted him. Was he right now sitting alone, staring out to sea, brooding over the nature of God and man? She felt her uneasiness tick up another notch as she imagined that scene, and then herself interrupting his silent solitude.

But you've been given a second chance, Jane, and you can't afford to balk.

With that mantra echoing in her head, she made it to the mat lying outside the front door. It looked like a Jolly Roger, and beneath the skull and crossbones was written: Abandon Hope All Ye Who Enter Here.

Another woman might add that warning to the eleven disregarded phone calls, her jittering nerves, plus the limp state of her clothing and then decide to tackle the author another day. Jane, however, lifted her chin as well as her fist, prepared to rap on the door.

It swung open before her knuckles met wood. A guy in bare feet, yellow board shorts and bleached blond curls stared down at her. From inside came the unmistakable sound of a party. Rap music, raised voices, the shattering of a beer bottle followed by curses worthy of a sailor. Two women passed behind the beach boy, wearing near-identical denim miniskirts and mini bikini tops too, their long highlighted locks straightened to shiny perfection. They clutched tropical-colored drinks complete with umbrellas and didn't spare a glance for Jane with her fuzzy hair and drooping dress. In the distance, she heard a masculine voice say, "I'm drunk. Smashed. Pissed." Another someone yelled, "Hey, Brittany, how 'bout you and me get naked?"

Oh, the man she was after was *so* not a hermit.

"Griffin?" she said, eyeing the surfer dude.

"Nah, I'm Ted. You want him?"

"Yes." She wasn't sure if she was happy or sad that Beach Boy wasn't the man she was after. "Is he available?" As in, not inebriated and not getting bare with Brittany.

"For you? Sure." He gestured with his thumb over his shoulder. "Inside. Can't miss him."

As she scooted past, the dude yelled, "Hey, Griffin! Guess who the liquor store sent out to deliver the chips and booze? Some little thing from librarian school!"

Ignoring her annoyance at the comment, she took in her surroundings. A party was definitely going on at Griffin's. Twenty or so people milled about a rectangular living room that had a whitewashed brick fireplace on the wall opposite sliding glass doors leading to an ocean-view deck. There, more people were gathered. The rap song gave way to something by Jimmy Buffett as she moved through the crowd, wondering how she "couldn't miss" the reporter. He worked for magazines, so she'd never seen him on television. The black-and-white photo her preliminary research had uncovered depicted a scruffy figure wearing a combat helmet, flak jacket and dusty sunglasses.

The music blasting from the speakers hiccuped, and the Jimmy Buffett song started again from the top just as she reached those rear doors. Her gaze shifted right, drawn to a twirling mobile hanging in the corner that was made from driftwood and worn, mismatched flip-flops suspended with fishing line. Beneath that piece of "art" was where she found him. She didn't know how she knew, but she'd bet a hundred-dollar bill she didn't have to spare that she'd located Griffin Lowell.

In fatigue-green cargo shorts and an unbuttoned Hawaiian shirt, he was tipped back in a distressed-leather recliner, a buxom bikini babe perched on each of its arms. A red bandanna covered his head like a biker's do-rag— or probably a pirate's, because there was a gold earring in one ear and a patch over each eye. A lean, tan hand was curved around a beer bottle resting on his taut belly. He appeared to be sleeping. Perhaps meditating, if buccaneers did such a thing.

She took a breath. "Griffin? Griffin Lowell?"

His free hand slid toward his crotch. She yanked her gaze away, but then realized he was merely reaching for his front pocket. "How much do I owe you?" he rumbled. "You didn't forget the tequila, did you?"

"And the diet cherry cola," one of the bikinis added. "I can't drink tequila without diet cherry cola."

He grimaced but repeated her anyway. "And the diet cherry cola."

Jane just stared at him, shaking her head. It was hard to get a read on the man, what with his hair covered in fabric and his face obscured by those ridiculous eye patches. Peering more closely at them, she could see the black rubber was embossed with, once again, the Jolly Roger skull and bones. "I didn't bring anything at all," Jane said, her voice rising a little as Buffett made way for a band she didn't know. "But, Griffin Lowell, you still owe me."

After a second's hesitation, the chair jumped upright, dislodging the girls. Griffin held out his beer and one of the bikinis took it, leaving him free to strip away his pirate paraphernalia: earring, bandanna, eye patch one and eye patch two. For the first time, she got a real look at him.

Oh, Jane thought, swallowing. *Shiver me timbers.*

He was undeniably attractive, with a lean face as tan as his hand, its bones stark and masculine. There was a grit of black stubble on his cheeks and chin, and his head hair was only a half inch or so longer. A soldier's style, she supposed. But the eyes that studied her beneath his dark brows were a startling aqua-blue that both observed and assessed with a spotlight intensity. Reporter's eyes.

They seemed cold at first, but as his gaze roamed

lower, to her mouth, then to the too-tight collar that suddenly seemed to choke off her airway and on to her clingy dress and now-rubbery knees, the skin he visually explored began to heat, inch by inch. It was like those beacon fires of old, used to signal an enemy's approach. A kindling at one location spurred the lighting of the next and so on and so on until everyone—or in this case, every nerve—was on alert. And then Jane recalled that pirates had used such fires too, but as false navigational beacons that lured ships to dangerous waters where they would run aground or even sink.

She should have been chilled by the thought, but instead another wave of heat tumbled over her body. In reaction, she could actually feel her hair lifting away from her scalp and twisting itself into curls she'd never had before.

Willing herself not to touch them, she cleared her throat and spoke with authority. "You haven't been taking my calls, so I've come here to discuss your book."

At her words, his gaze immediately shuttered, and he shoved back into a reclined position. "I'm not interested." He held out his hand for his beer and drained it in one long draw.

Jane didn't let his closed eyes deter her even as annoyance ignited at his clear—and yes, rude—dismissal. "You signed a contract to write a memoir," she reminded him crisply, then forced herself to soften her tone. "But you don't have to do it alone. That's why I'm here—for you."

When his eyes popped open at that, she even managed a friendly smile. His gaze started running down her body again, causing her lips to flatten and her insides to squirm so her outside wouldn't. As his eyes resettled on her mouth, she bit her bottom lip to hold back the odd little whimper that was slinking up her throat. It was as unusual as the sudden impulse she felt to turn tail and run.

You can't afford to balk, Jane.

That little voice acted like a bucket of ice water. "You have pages due soon," she told Griffin, steady again. "I've been hired to help you meet your obligation."

He cocked his head at her, clearly unenthused.

She continued anyway. "To that end, I'm ready to provide you everything you need." And in her experience, sometimes that meant applying a swift kick to the seat of an author's pants, an option that was sounding better and better by the moment. "Whatever you need."

"Yeah?" One of those black brows lifted, and his voice drawled. "The only things I need, honey-pie, are a couple of shots of tequila, another six-pack of beer and a night of sweaty sex."

The second brow lifted to the level of the first. "You game?"

JANE DIDN'T HAVE TIME to respond with more than a sputter before someone shouted Griffin's name and he was gone, leaving her alone with the empty recliner and the bikinis. "Finally," one said. "I'll bet it's the diet cherry cola." She wandered off, presumably to check.

The second bikini smiled at Jane, who managed to smile back. "Nice, uh, party. A special occasion?"

The sleek-haired woman shrugged. "It's Tuesday?"

"Actually," Jane said, "it's Wednesday."

"Oh." The bikini rubbed a spot between her brows. "I've lost track. Finals week, you know."

Was testing required for the technicians at tanning salons? "You're a student?"

"Graduate work. Marine biology." Then she cracked up. "You should see your face! I'm kidding. I'm in beauty school."

The young woman didn't need to take classes for that,

Jane thought. She was striking in that wide-mouthed, big-breasted way of women who were soap-opera actresses or models in *Maxim* magazine. "You visit Griffin often?"

"It's Party Central, y'know? My girlfriend's boyfriend surfs with him, so we've all been hanging out here. He doesn't seem to mind."

Which seemed to also verify he wasn't hard at work on his manuscript. Figuring he'd had enough time to take care of the liquor delivery, Jane excused herself and went in search of him again. It took a few minutes to determine he wasn't in the galley-style kitchen, any of the bedrooms, the bathrooms or even the garage that housed another gathering of partiers clustered around a table set up for beer pong. On her second search, she discovered that somehow he'd gotten past her and was now stretched out on a lounge in a corner of the deck, his eyes closed once again. His fingers were curled around a fresh bottle of beer.

He might as well have been alone.

Jane didn't let that deter her. Instead, she dragged a molded plastic chair to his side and plunked herself onto its seat, tucking her wild hair behind her ears. Not a single male muscle twitched.

With a huff, she sent him a pointed look, but that didn't appear to pierce the bubble he'd erected around himself either. Though she supposed waiting him out would give her the upper hand, she didn't have that kind of patience. His deadline was at stake. Her reputation.

She huffed again. "Griffin."

Only his lips moved. "Honey-pie."

Her back teeth ground together. "Look, I'm here because you told your agent you were interested in someone helping you with your manuscript. That's what I do."

When Griffin didn't respond, she raised her voice. "I'm a book doctor," she said. "My name is Jane."

That prodded him a little. His eyes opened a slit. They closed again as one corner of his mouth ticked up. "Of course it is."

She ignored his amused tone. It wasn't an unusual reaction, after all. She looked like a Jane. Her brother Byron—as serious and renowned a scientist as their father—had the wild and dramatic appearance corresponding to his literary namesake. Her other overachieving brother, Phillip Marlowe Pearson, could pass for a hard-boiled detective, though as a medical researcher he was much more interested in running DNA tests than running down criminals. Just like them, her name matched her exterior. Her dishwater-blond hair, her pleasant but unremarkable features, her plain gray eyes all said—in a restrained, ladylike hush—*Jane.*

If her mother hadn't died when she was still an infant, Jane might have asked her why she hadn't made a more exotic choice for her only daughter's given name. Would she have looked different if she'd been called Daisy or Delilah?

However, Jane had an inkling that Griffin Lowell would be attempting to ignore her even if she looked like Scheherazade. And the one who had stories to tell was the man on her left. "About your book…" she started.

"I can't talk about that at the moment," he said.

"Why? You don't look busy."

His lashes remained resting on his cheeks. "I have guests."

"Who have found their diet cherry cola," she pointed out, inexplicably annoyed as she glimpsed that particular woman at the other end of the deck. When she bent over to brush some sand off her calf, her bountiful chest nearly escaped its triangular fabric confines.

"She doesn't look like she needs to watch her weight, though, does she?" Eyes wide open now, he was looking in the same direction as Jane.

"I wouldn't care to opine," she said.

He snorted. "You even sound like a governess."

She smiled at him. Thinly. "All the better to get the job done."

"Yeah?" The picture of nonchalance, he folded his arms over his chest and crossed his legs at the ankle. "I think your luck would improve if you'd loosen up a little. Why don't you go inside and track down a swimsuit. Pour yourself a drink. Then we'll talk."

She narrowed her eyes at him, willing, for the moment, to play along. "And you'll be right here when I return? I have your word on that?"

His gaze slid off to the side. "Let's make an appointment for next week."

As if. After meeting him and seeing the setup he had here, she was only more determined not to allow him another inch of wiggle room. His agent was right. The man was in serious denial. "You've got to get to work immediately, Griffin, or you won't make your deadline. The first half of the book is due at the end of the month."

He ignored that, his gaze fastened on the label of the bottle in his hand. "Book doctor, huh? You know your way around vocabulary and grammar?"

"Yes, though I do more than—"

"So you really know your stuff?" he asked. "Can you spell humulus lupulus? Do you have a familiarity with Saccharomyces uvarum?"

She held on to her patience. "Unless you're writing a

treatise on beer, specifically lagers, I don't think either of those terms will come up."

He paused as if vaguely surprised, then he gave a slight shake of his head. "Fine. Let's talk serial commas, then. Please state your views on their usage."

Really, the man could make a woman start to consider serial murder—beginning with him. "The serial comma, also known as the Oxford or Harvard comma, refers to the punctuation mark used before the final item in a list of three or more. It's the standard in American English—"

"According to who?" He bristled.

"Whom," she corrected. "And it's according to *The Chicago Manual of Style.*"

"But—"

"Though that's for nonjournalistic writing," she went on, ignoring his interruption. "I'm aware reporters like yourself follow the *AP Stylebook,* which recommends leaving out the comma before a coordinating conjunction."

He was silent at that.

She waited a beat. "Did I pass the test?"

"Look." He sounded exasperated. "I just want to be left alone."

She gazed around her, taking in the half-dressed beautiful beach people who were drinking his booze and crowding his deck as the sun slid toward the horizon. "Your need for solitude would be a bit more convincing if you weren't surrounded by a crowd. If your guests didn't call your place Party Central."

Something flashed in his eyes. "That's none of your business."

Oops. Though clashes between herself and a stalled client were to be expected, downright hostility was not her friend. Jane scooched her chair closer, twisting it to face him. "Griffin…" she said and, like a good governess with a recalcitrant charge, put out a placating hand to touch his leg.

Weird happened when fingers met shin. An electric spark snapped, a tingle shot up her arm, their gazes collided, veered away, crashed again. As yet another glow of heat radiated across her skin, she was paralyzed, still touching him, still staring at him. Confused, she couldn't seem to pull away. Members of the opposite sex didn't produce such strong physical reactions in her. She was above all that, she'd always assumed, her interest more in a man's mind than in his…manliness.

"Griff!" someone said in the distance, then became more insistent. "Griff!"

"What?" He didn't move. Their stares didn't waver.

"Sammy says he's going to jump," the voice answered.

"Fine," Griffin responded without emotion. "Tell him to watch the rocks."

"He says he's going for the record. He says he's going to beat you."

Griffin jerked. The movement broke Jane's paralysis, and she snatched her hand from his leg. His head swung around to address the man who was standing right beside them. "What did you say?"

It was Beach Boy from the front door. Ted. He pointed to the bluff at the south end of the cove. Even from here, Jane could see a handful of men scrambling along a path up its side. "Sammy says he's taking off from a spot five feet above your last leap."

Griffin glanced over his shoulder. "Sammy's drunk."

Beach Boy's curls bounced when he nodded. "It's why he's talking trash. But I think he means it. I think he's going to outdo you this time."

"Outdo me? Like hell he will." Griffin was already

standing. Then he gripped the railing of the deck and swung himself over and onto the sand below. "Get your camera ready," he advised the other man as he stripped off his shirt and ran toward the outcropping.

Jane realized she'd spent too much time with English majors and MFAs. They preferred Frisbee golf and strolls through farmers' markets. They didn't splash through surf that rose to their knees and then ascend a steep hillside, the muscles in their backs shifting and their strong arms flexing as they reached for each handhold.

They didn't shout something indistinct and then hurl themselves off a jutting boulder into the roiling ocean.

Several of Griffin's party guests did just that, from various heights. Jane found herself holding her breath as each man launched himself into space. Her initial reaction could mostly be summed up by "Why?" but after the first couple of men made it back to shore, she could admit there was a certain...exuberance in the activity.

Ultimately there were only two men left on the bluff. One, she guessed, was the drunken Sammy. The other was Griffin. They stood beside each other, the wind tugging at the legs of their shorts.

"Griff should talk him out of it," one of the partygoers lining the deck railing said. They all wore dark glasses or had their hands up to shade their eyes from the lowering sun. "He'll have the record if he takes off from there, but Sammy's just pickled enough not to realize that height means he has to jump farther outward into deeper water."

But if Griffin tried to talk sense into the other man, it apparently didn't work. Those on the deck gasped in unison as Sammy bounded from the rock. The others followed his descent, but Jane kept her gaze on their host, who instantly scrambled even higher.

"Is Griffin trying to get a better look at his friend?" she asked Beach Boy, who was still beside her.

"No," the dude said on a sigh, as Griffin stopped at a sharp nose of stone. "He's upping the ante. Nobody's ever attempted a jump from that height. It could be…" He didn't finish, but the expression on his face did it for him.

It could be dangerous.

Appalled, Jane closed her eyes, squeezing them tight. Though she'd been concerned about her latest author's uncooperative attitude and then his penchant for crowded beer bashes, she'd remained confident in her ability to help him mold his memoir. She'd been taught long ago that failure was not an option, after all. But clearly the task of aiding Griffin Lowell was going to be more complicated than mentioning deadlines and being available with red pen in hand.

This man was more than a stalled writer. Clearly he was also an impulsive risk taker with an overblown competitive streak.

Or a full-fledged death wish.

CHAPTER TWO

THE TV WAS DRONING at a dull level when Griffin woke up, just as it did every morning. Without opening his eyes, he fumbled for the remote and edged the volume higher. It didn't register whether the broadcast was news or cartoons or something in between, because it didn't matter—the noise was only necessary to block out the voices in his head. He wasn't schizophrenic, he was just hyper-memoried. They had the tendency to play in the background of his brain unless he supplanted them with the sound of twenty-four-hour news or hard-driving music or an alcohol-infused social gathering.

Being Party Central had its benefits.

And another man besides himself was reaping them, he realized as he made his way toward the kitchen a few minutes later. One of his surfing buddies, Ted, was sacked out on the living room floor, a beach towel thrown over him. In his hand, he clutched a bikini top.

Griffin didn't see a sign of the bottoms or the female body that the D-cups belonged to. He shrugged and prodded the guy's shoulder with his flip-flop. "Hey."

Ted batted at the annoyance, thwapping the bikini strings against Griffin's ankle. "It's not a school day, Mom," he murmured.

Though Griffin could hear the television from here, Ted's mutter sucked him straight to a sandbag-and-timber hooch in a remote northern valley of Afghanistan. Soldiers slept within inches of each other, and someone was always talking in their sleep. To their mom.

Or to their demons.

With a sharp shake of his head, he dislodged the thought and then jostled Ted again. "Kid." The surfer was in the same age range as the nineteen-to-twenty-seven-year-olds with whom Griffin had spent his embedded year. Those young men had grown up fast. Griffin, at thirty-one, sometimes felt as if he was twice that after those three-hundred-sixty-five days.

"Kid," he said again. "Get up. Stretch out on the couch. Better yet, take a bed in one of the guest rooms."

Ted blinked and slowly rolled to a sitting position. He looked down at his naked chest, the beach towel and then the half a bathing suit tangled around his fingers. "Did I get lucky last night?"

"Don't know."

The other man lifted the fabric he held and stretched it between both hands. "I was dreaming about that librarian."

That librarian? Griffin tried not to scowl. Ted could only mean the small stubborn woman who'd arrived uninvited to the party. She was the only bookish female around last night. He'd done his best to ignore her, but she wasn't easy to avoid, damn her pretty eyes. Jesus, now she had Griffin's surf buddy thinking about her in his sleep!

"You called her 'Mom,'" he told Ted.

"Nah. That was my second dream. In my first, you take her with you off the cliff, and her clothes sorta melt to nothing on the way down."

"Huh." Griffin tried imagining it, but all he could picture was her mouth flapping at him. The mouth was pretty too, soft-looking. Tender. But it flapped all the same. *You signed a contract. You've got to get to work.*

Ted looked from the bikini to Griffin. "Which reminds me. I took some good shots of your jump. And also of you pulling Sammy to shore. I think he drank as much seawater as beer last night."

"He puked up both." Griffin felt guilty about it. He shouldn't have let the guy take that leap. He'd tried reasoning with him, but he'd recognized the mulish light in his eyes. Griffin had never managed to talk his twin, Gage, out of anything when he looked like that. And Erica had worn that same intractable expression the last time they'd spoken.

A warm furry body bumped against his knee, and he reached down to pet his dog, Private. "You need to go out?" he asked the black Lab. "Okay, I'll let you take a turn in the garden before breakfast. But for God's sake, stay off Old Man Monroe's property. The last time you did your business there he threatened me with citizen's arrest."

Private didn't seem worried about their cantankerous neighbor or his owner's fate, but just ambled through the back door, his craggy teeth in an anticipatory smile. As Griffin swung the paneled wood shut, a small blue espadrille placed itself in harm's way.

The canvas, embroidered with multicolored flowers, was attached to the librarian.

Governess.

Jane.

He'd been so sure he'd gotten rid of her yesterday. After all, she'd been gone when he got back from his jump. "What the hell are you doing here?" he asked, using his body to block the opening.

Her answer was to slip a venti-sized cup through the narrow gap, from a coffee place that was a twenty-minute car ride away. Crescent Cove's isolated location meant you had to commute for your four-buck fix of fancy Seattle caffeine.

"I thought you might like this."

He narrowed his eyes at her. Her jeans were rolled at the ankle, and she wore a pale blue oxford shirt that seemed to leach the gray from her big eyes. They were as silvery as the morning overcast and looked a little spooky with her dark lashes surrounding them. Her mouth wasn't scary, though. A rose-petal pink, it had the puffy, swollen look of one that had been kissed all night long.

That was what was so arresting about her, he decided. It had caught his attention the day before too. Though she walked around all buttoned up, there was that contradiction of the making-out kind of mouth.

It gave him this insane urge to check her for hickeys.

Jane sent him a bright smile. "You look like a caramel macchiato kind of man to me," she said. Then added, "With extra whip."

"Goodbye." He didn't give a damn about her toes.

"Wait, wait, wait," she cried, but her words turned muffled as he closed the door firmly between them.

"I would have taken that caramel macchiato," Ted complained, drifting into the kitchen.

Griffin ignored the insistent knocking on the back door. "You don't know this sort of woman like I do, Ted." His instincts were on red alert, had been since he'd slipped off his eye patches to find her in his place. That silvery gaze had seemed to look right through him. He didn't appreciate being that open. "You take her coffee, she takes your soul."

"I don't know. She looks harmless to me."

"Her looks…" Griffin let the thought die off. He wasn't going to get into Jane's looks with Ted, who'd been dreaming of her naked. Griffin couldn't really imagine there was anything interesting under those clothes she wore. He *wouldn't* imagine there was anything interesting under there. She had the mouth, and the demands that came from it were all the reason he needed to pretend she didn't exist.

She'd stopped knocking.

The relief he felt at that had him almost smiling at Ted. He clapped his hands together. "What are we going to do today?" The other man was a part-time county lifeguard. His leftover hours seemed to revolve around surfing and partying, both of which made him the perfect companion in Griffin's eyes.

Ted's expression turned troubled. "I don't know, Griff. Maybe I should take off."

"What? Why?"

"You'd probably like some privacy."

It wasn't exactly panic that shot through him at that last word, but it was close enough to make Griffin's voice tight. "I would hate some privacy. What's going on?"

Ted shifted one shoulder. "The librarian. You're supposed to be writing, she said."

"The librarian doesn't know what she's talking about." Glancing over his shoulder, he checked the view out the window. She wasn't there. The tightness around his throat eased. "I don't owe anyone anything," he lied.

Ted's hands were worrying the scarlet bikini top. "Yeah? But still…there's something about what she said.…"

"There's something about her!" Griffin interrupted, glancing over his shoulder again. "You're dreaming she's naked, her mouth is annoying the hell out of me, and—" He broke off as the woman in question came into sight through his window.

"—she's stealing my dog."

He stalked closer to the glass. Sure enough, she had threaded what looked like a belt through Private's kerchief-collar. Though he couldn't hear her words, it was clear she was coaxing the dog to follow her. He rapped on the glass with his knuckles.

"Hey!" he yelled, cranking open the window. "Leave my pet alone. Besides being a party crasher, are you a dognapper too?"

She froze, those lips of hers turning down in a frown. She looked from Griffin to the animal, then back to Griffin again. Her eyes narrowed.

"Hell," he muttered, knowing what was coming next. He'd just given her the damn idea himself.

Jane put her free hand on her hip. "Come out and get him."

"You don't want me to do that." He assumed his fiercest expression, the one that had caused a gunman to hesitate a crucial second at a Taliban-manned checkpoint, thus saving Griffin's life.

Jane, however, merely tapped a toe. "Is that supposed to be a threat? Are you going to come out here and just do-nothing me to death? You can't meet a deadline, let alone mete out some kind of punishment."

Rage burned in Griffin's belly. "Ted," he said, with a jerk of his head. "Go out there and get Private."

"No way. I'm afraid of the dog."

Griffin shot his friend a look. Ted let Private share sandwiches with him, alternating bites. "Bullshit."

"Okay. I'm afraid of *her*."

Jane apparently heard the exchange because she was laughing. "You're not the only one," she called out.

Griffin saw red again. He strode to the back door and threw it open. Then he advanced on the governess, determined to get back his dog and get her on her way, never to return.

"Stealing's pretty low, lady," he said in a menacing voice. "You think it's okay to purloin man's best friend? Abscond with an innocent animal?"

She laughed again. "Purloin. Abscond. You're good with synonyms, at least. Maybe there's hope after all that you can meet your authorial commitment."

This close he could smell her. It was a sweet, feminine scent, and it almost dizzied him as he made to snatch the impromptu leash from her hand.

"Don't touch her!" a cranky elderly voice snapped.

"What?" Griffin glanced over to see Old Man Monroe approaching, his beetled brows and stabbing cane making clear he was on another of his tirades. "What's got you riled now?"

"I won't allow you to hurt that young lady."

Hurt her? He had never wanted to hurt a woman in his life, which was probably how the thing with Erica had gotten so out of hand. He hadn't even wanted to wound her with the truth. "I'm not touching the young lady. What's she to you anyway?"

Old Man Monroe, who had likely been bad-tempered for all ninety-four years he'd been on the planet, looked at Griffin with undisguised dislike. It didn't bother him a lick. It had been the man's attitude toward both Griffin and his brother every vacation since they'd begun running around the cove on their own as kids.

"She saved me from calling county animal control. Your mangy mutt was in my garden again. Wouldn't budge an inch, even though I was throwing my old GI boots at him."

"Couldn't hit the side of a barn," Jane murmured under

her breath, "but I thought I should get your pup out of there anyway."

"Would have cost you three hundred bucks to spring him from the shelter," Old Man Monroe said.

"Or you could just have picked up the phone instead of your army boots and called me. You know the number."

Monroe continued as if Griffin hadn't said a word. "So you owe the young lady."

Jane shot him a triumphant smile. "Haven't I been saying just that?"

Ignoring them both, Griffin detached Private from the improvised leash and then began walking the dog back toward the house.

"Don't you have something to say to her?" his curmudgeonly neighbor demanded.

"Yes," Jane echoed. "Don't you have something to say to me?"

"Sure," Griffin answered, not looking back. "Go away. And don't think you can traipse into my house again. I'm putting everyone at Party Central on notice. Nobody looking like a governess or a librarian is welcome at Beach House No. 9."

JUST LIKE THE dognapping, Griffin had given Jane the idea himself. *Nobody looking like a governess or a librarian is welcome at Beach House No. 9.*

She was determined to get inside the place again. Beyond that? Her plan went hazy there. But she figured if she could make her way into Party Central once more, then he would understand she wasn't letting him off the hook. Her fortitude might be the prod that would get him sitting down to start those pages.

Unlike this morning, this time she approached the house from the front. It meant trudging through the sand in a pair of strappy wedge sandals, but she plowed forward, passing other cottages and winding around happy beachgoers. Though the month of June often meant coastal overcast in the late afternoons, the Crescent Cove sky was a brilliant blue as the sun sank toward the horizon. The long sweatshirt she wore over her party outfit made her too hot, and she paused in front of the small bungalow numbered "8" in order to slide down the zipper.

A slender woman was tapping a For Rent sign into the ice plant growing beside the front porch steps. Unlike Jane, she must have been immune to the sun, for over her capri jeans she wore a fisherman's knit sweater that reached her knees. Turning, she let out a frightened bleat. Her hand clutched at her chest. "Sorry," she said. "I didn't see you standing there."

"I should apologize," Jane said. "I didn't mean to scare you."

The woman pushed her long dark hair away from her forehead. "Not your fault, really. I startle easily." Her gaze took in Jane's outfit, her high shoes, the hair that she'd salt-air-armored with a palmful of styling product and her flat iron set on High. "Visiting Beach House No. 9?"

"Ha!" Jane said, smiling. "I look like I'll fit right in, do I?"

"Um, yeah. Are you a friend of Griffin's?"

"Sort of. I'm Jane Pearson."

"I've known Griffin all my life. I've always lived at the cove, and the Lowells summered here every year." She gave a shy smile. "I'm Skye Alexander. Nowadays I manage the rental properties in the area."

"Nice to meet you." Jane's gaze lingered on the For Rent sign as she filed away the thought that Skye might be a helpful resource regarding Griffin.

Skye glanced over her shoulder. "No. 8 had a leaky

roof, among other things, that kept it unavailable for a while. Griffin actually wanted it, but he had to take the place next door."

They both turned to look at Beach House No. 9. A kite attached to a fishing pole was whipping above the second-floor balcony. People were crowded on the first-floor deck, and Jane could make out a Beach Boys tune that changed to something from the Beastie Boys. A nubile female in a string bikini and nothing else climbed onto a table and began gyrating, to the hoots and applause of the rest.

"Has the makings of a rowdy one tonight," Skye said.

Jane sent her a weak smile. "I can't wait."

The short trek to the front door of Party Central gave her time for second thoughts. Not that she was necessarily afraid of a little hedonistic celebrating—she had a friend or two who might say she was past due for some of that—but she wasn't exactly comfortable with the idea or with her costume.

It wasn't Jane-the-governess wear. Of course, that was entirely the point, but still, she shivered as she let the sweatshirt slide from her shoulders on her approach to the front door. Her exposed skin prickled as the ocean breeze tickled her flesh. Taking a page from the bikini girls of the day before, she'd put on her own suit. The black two-piece had appeared fairly modest in the Macy's dressing room, and she'd snapped on a mid-thigh-length black jean skirt over the bottoms as well. But the deep plunge of the halter top and the hip-hugging waistband of the skirt left a lot of bare flesh revealed. Her wedge shoes made her legs feel miles longer—which was good until she realized that meant miles more nakedness too.

She thought about swamping herself in the fleece sweatshirt again. She considered turning around and coming up with another plan for a different day. Then she remembered Ian Stone and how he'd trampled her pride *and* her reputation. Her inner resolve stiffened. With a deep breath, she knocked on the front door.

As she'd hoped, it wasn't Griffin who opened it. If yesterday was any indication, he was tucked in some secluded corner. The guy on the other side of the threshold wasn't familiar to her, though he was dressed in the common male uniform of board shorts and a tan. His smile was white, and a dark blue tattoo over one pumped pec showed the silhouette of a surfer carrying his board under his arm.

"Babe!" he said, as if they were old friends. His warm palm cupped her shoulder to draw her inside. "You need a beverage!"

It was that easy. She figured the layers of mascara she'd applied had done their part, as well as the raspberry gloss she'd pinkied onto her mouth. Once she had an umbrella drink in her hand, Jane decided she could introduce herself as something more exotic with an entirely straight face. Jana. Janelle. Jezebel.

As she walked across the deck, a man grabbed her wrist, and dragged her near to dance to an old B-52s tune. He put his hands at her waist and she used the shuffling circle they made to search for Griffin. If she spotted him, she wasn't sure what she'd do. Wave? Stick out her tongue? But both seemed childish when all she wanted was to remind him of his obligations, one professional to another.

She glanced down at her naked skin and skimpy outfit with another wave of misgiving. Perhaps this had been a bad idea after all. The urge to cover up had her edging away from her dance partner. His fingers tightened on her waist.

"Where you going?" he asked.

"To get my sweatshirt." She made a vague gesture toward the front door where she'd left the thing on a bench.

"And hide away all that creamy skin?" the guy protested, leaning close to her ear. "That would just be so… wrong."

Her smile was halfhearted. "Yeah, well, I'm a little chilled." *Please, please don't offer to warm me up.*

He took her hand and started boogying across the deck. "Okay. Where'd you leave it?"

"At the entrance." Gratified that he hadn't followed with the obvious line, she let him lead her through the crowd. Even with her wedge heels, her lack of height meant she didn't see much more than the shoulders, chests and backs of the male guests. If there was one thing she could say about the surfer crowd, their upper bodies were very well developed.

When her dance partner finally stopped, she stuttered her steps to prevent her nose from ramming into his spine. He spun around and pressed her against a nearby wall. Jane realized he'd drawn her into a small side room that held a washer, a dryer and a wooden contraption draped with a handful of beach towels.

"This isn't the entrance," she pointed out. "That's where I left my sweatshirt."

He smiled at her. "Let me be the one to warm you up."

Oh, damn. "You just had to go there," she muttered. Then she raised her voice. "No, thanks."

"Please," her dance partner wheedled. He was a nice-looking guy, and for a second Jane considered it. She hadn't been kissed since the Ian disaster and she was all Jezebel-ed up, wasn't she? Why not take a little walk on the wild side?

Someone strolled by the open door, and the man called

out. "Jer! Come in here and convince this pretty little thing that I can rock her world."

"Jer" paused, stretching muscular arms to grip the doorjamb on either side. Jane's pulse tripped, then started accelerating. The new guy was big enough to block a lot of the light. The room's walls started to contract—in her mind anyway.

The second man's smile seemed sinister. "Ricky's good, but I'm better. You want to take a turn with me, pretty lady?"

She swallowed. "I don't want to take a turn with anyone. Excuse me." But Ricky still had hold of her wrist.

"She's with me, Jer."

"Aaah, she'll share, won't you…?"

"Jane," she said, in her most quelling tone. To heck with Jana, Janelle or Jezebel. Her real name had turned men off before. Like Griffin. "I'm Jane, and I want to go now."

"Me Tarzan," Jer said, thumping his chest, and then moved into the small room. "Want to make Boy with me, baby?"

She was never wearing a bathing suit again. Or wedge heels. Or so much mascara—though with her gold-tipped lashes, she couldn't give it up entirely.

"Get out of my way," she said, yanking her wrist free of Ricky to give him a push. When he stumbled away, she was left with Jer between her and the exit. Though she told herself she wasn't in any real danger, her heart was pounding against her breastbone, and her blood was running ice-cold under her suddenly hot skin. "I'm leaving now."

"Ah, babe—" Jer started, and then he was yanked backward, into the narrow hall. "Hey!"

Griffin Lowell pushed the man farther down the passage, then took his place in the doorway. Another pair of shorts hung on his hips and a wedge of bare chest showed between the sides of his half-buttoned shirt, which was decorated with pineapples and busty, half-naked hula girls. His whiskers were grittier than they'd been that morning and only called attention to his—frowning—mouth. "What's going on?"

Ricky moved closer to Jane and slid a proprietary arm around her. "Have you met the new girl?"

Griffin's turquoise eyes slid toward her. Her exposed flesh prickled all over again, and her blood turned as hot as the surface of her skin. Was that a hint of appreciation in his eyes? "She's my girl," he said with a straight face.

"Nice try." Ricky laughed. "You haven't had a woman in the three months you've been living here."

"I've been waiting for this one."

Ricky frowned now. "Well, you can't have her. I saw her first. Squatter's rights and all that."

Squatter's rights? She sent the guy a baleful look. Now that Griffin stood two feet away, her sense of impending danger had evaporated.

"Let go of the lady, Rick."

"I won't." He yanked Jane close to his side, and when she struggled to escape his grip, he wrapped an arm around her front too. "Just because you want her doesn't mean you get to have her."

"But she wants me right back," Griffin said, his eyes glittering. "Don't you, honey-pie?"

With her bare skin, bathing suit, straight hair and several coats of mascara, she hadn't been entirely sure he'd recognized her. The "honey-pie" made clear that he definitely had, and she wasn't too proud to accept help. She answered him in as sweet a voice as possible. "Of course I want you, chili-dog."

His gaze zeroed in on her face. "Chili-dog."

"I just love our little names for each other." She reached out a hand toward him.

Ricky was frowning. "I'm not buying any of this," he said, his attitude bordering on belligerent.

Griffin's fingers closed over hers. A zing of heat flamed up her arm and that sense of impending danger returned tenfold. Uh-oh. Maybe playing along with him had been the riskier choice. "Then believe this," he said.

A quick jerk had her free of the other man and pressed against Griffin's hard chest. Then his mouth slammed onto Jane's.

CHAPTER THREE

"SHUT THE PARTY down early last night, eh?" Old Man Monroe called to Griffin as he monitored Private's morning sniff-and-pee. The front of the nonagenarian's upslope property bordered the side yard of Beach House No. 9.

Griffin grunted in response. He'd shut down Party Central for good. The crabby coot currently frowning at him might have managed to do that himself by complaining about the nightly noise, but without his hearing aids he was apparently stone-deaf. When he saw the crowd gather at Griffin's, he said he just removed the "fiendish devices" and turned on the History Channel's closed captions.

What had prompted Griffin to kick everyone out the night before hadn't been concern over his neighbor. He'd been furious that— No, there'd been no fury about it. He'd been ice-cold when he'd cut the music and ejected the partygoers from the premises, starting with that bastard Rick. The man had mumbled something—an apology, an excuse?—but Griffin had shoved him so hard down the porch steps that he'd landed on his dumb ass. After that he'd been smart enough to scramble to his feet and run.

Griffin had done a lot of shoving last night.

Guilt rushed into his gut at the memory, and he pinched the bridge of his nose to refocus his thoughts. Jane had exited as fast as Rick—though staying on her feet—and that was good. He wouldn't be bothered by her again.

He wouldn't be bothered by anyone, for that matter. After last night he'd made it clear he wasn't into playing the happy host any longer. The act hadn't worked for shit anyway. He'd have to find some other distraction to keep the events of the embedded year from invading his mind.

"So what's the word on your brother?" Monroe asked now. "Is he in a safe place?"

Worry sucked as a diversion, Griffin discovered. Private must have sensed the emotion, because the dog whined, then rushed to his owner's side, butting his leg. Griffin slid his palm along the warm crown of the animal's head and then caressed his butter-soft ears. It made his breath come a little easier.

"Gage is in his element." Smack-dab in the danger zone, snapping photos with his camera. But he'd know if Gage was threatened, he reassured himself. The twin connection had always been strong. Still, it was only shallow comfort. Griffin knew firsthand that safety in war-torn places was a moment-to-moment thing.

"Is he—"

"I don't want to talk about him, old man," Griffin said. It was unkind, but, hell, he didn't owe Rex Monroe politeness. Their neighbor had more than once ratted out him and Gage to their mother, including the first time he'd spied them climbing from their bedroom window after lights-out. As seventh-graders, they'd been busted with girls about to enter high school.

He shot Monroe a dark look. "Were s'mores with a couple of older chicks on the beach against the law?" he groused. "I was planning on getting some hands-on education that night."

The old man's laugh was rusty. "You forget the two of you juvenile delinquents had toilet-papered my car earlier that day."

Oh, yeah. He had forgotten. He and Gage had gravitated to trouble that summer and every other. Those annual months at the cove had offered a freedom they didn't have in their suburban life and were likely the seed from which had grown their need for adventure.

Maybe that sense of freedom was what had drawn Griffin back. After a year of teetering on the brink of death, maybe here he could figure out how he was supposed to go on.

Private's nose jerked out of a patch of weedy grass. His body quivered for a moment, and then he bounded off with a short, happy bark. Griffin groaned. The dog loved company almost as much as chow time, which was saying a lot for a Lab. Probably some former guest was dropping by, one who hadn't yet gotten word that his doors were now locked. No more midmorning margaritas, afternoon beers, late-night lambada contests.

He headed for his back door. "Be your usual rude self, will you, Rex, and whoever that is—get rid of 'em."

The old codger squinted, peering over Griffin's head. "If it was one of your usual ruffian playmates, I'd be happy to."

Oh, hell, Griffin thought.

"But this is that nice young woman again."

Who was probably after an apology. On a sigh, he turned.

As he'd suspected, it was the governess, in her animal-rescuer guise, her fingers looped around Private's collar. Today she was back in Jane-wear, shell-studded flip-flops, knee-length orange shorts, an oversize T-shirt that proclaimed "Reading Is Sexy," and her hair curling every which way. His pet gazed on her with tongue-lolling devotion. "Did you lose your dog again?" she asked.

He'd lost his mind, kissing her last night. She'd shown

up uninvited again, which was hardly a surprise. He'd already guessed the woman didn't like taking no for an answer. What *had* surprised him was the way she'd dressed, all beach-sweetie with skin showing, hair straight, some nice—yet not overblown—cleavage. If it had been a disguise, it was a piss-poor one. From his perch on the deck railing he'd noticed her immediately and kept his gaze on her, following behind when she'd been pulled off the dance floor.

No matter what she wore, she still had those eerie, see-through eyes. They scared him a little, just like mirrors did these days. And then there was The Mouth. That primmed-up, puffy-lipped mouth that always looked as if someone had been sucking on it before he got there.

As effing Rick had been about to do.

Though the other man was more talk than action, meaning Jane could have handled him herself, Griffin had still gone territorial. Seeing the jerk move in on her, he'd thought, *Damn it, I'm tasting her first!* and then he'd been doing that. Tasting her.

What had come across his tongue had been berries, rum, surprise and…heat. Shit. All that heat.

And didn't he know that the last thing he needed to add to the mess of his inner life was high temperatures. Or a woman.

Galvanized to get her out of his world—for good this time—he stomped toward her, taking control of his dog and the situation. "I suppose you want to hear me say I'm sorry."

She ignored him to peer around his shoulder. "I thought your name rang a bell when we introduced ourselves yesterday morning, Mr. Monroe. It came to me later. You are *the* Rex Monroe, yes? The famous reporter?"

Without looking, Griffin could feel the cantankerous

antique behind him preening. "Well, young lady, I don't know about famous…"

Griffin rolled his eyes. "Don't get him started."

"It's an honor to meet you, sir," Jane continued, still ignoring Griffin. "I devoured a compendium of 1940s war journalism about ten years ago. I enjoyed your pieces so much."

"Why, you must have been just a baby," Monroe said, sounding pleased.

Jane smiled. "I was a bookworm from birth."

"You bug the hell out of me, anyway," Griffin muttered.

She'd never smiled at him like that. She'd worn a clearly fake one upon their introduction two days before. Last night, after he'd wrenched his mouth from hers, he'd shoved her off and spun away—not knowing if he'd left her spitting fire or beaming with pleasure.

Yeah, he'd pushed her away. And yeah, he supposed she hadn't been too pleased with either that or the way he'd taken it upon himself to lock their lips first. Hers had been as soft as they looked, pillowy like he'd imagined, and they'd opened on the smallest of gasps when he swiped across the seam with his impatient tongue.

Once inside, he'd stroked deep for her flavor, not acting with his usual finesse. He'd just claimed every centimeter of that wet heat as lust had shuddered across his skin in waves. What had he been thinking? She was a pest.

She was governess Jane, the librarian look-alike.

Certainly she was here to slap him.

Resigned to it, he turned his face to the side and tapped his cheek with the hand not gripping Private. "Go ahead. Hit me."

She took a step back, blinking. "What are you talking about? I don't want to hit you."

"You should seize the opportunity," Old Man Monroe advised.

"Can it, you decrepit coot," Griffin called over his shoulder.

Jane blinked again. "Don't you know who you're talking to? This man won major awards for his war reporting. A Pulitzer. He's one of the best of the best."

"Yeah, yeah, yeah. Greatest generation and all that. It doesn't change the fact that he's been a pain in my ass since I was seven years old."

"A mutual sentiment," his neighbor put in.

"Surely it's time for your daily dose of *The Golden Girls,*" Griffin said, turning his head to glare at the grizzled grouch. "Or maybe you need a nap, old man?"

"If I take one, then that's my prerogative. I'm retired from deadlines, unlike yourself. Don't be lazy."

"Lazy?" His temper yanked its chain like a mad dog glimpsing the mailman. "I spent a year without running water or electricity. A year with flies and firefights and my own filth. A bullet went through my helmet when I was lying on my bunk, and it was hooked on a nail fourteen inches from my own damn skull."

"So sit your keister down and write about it."

"I did, though I suppose you're too senile to read the words. I gave the magazine that sponsored the embed assignment an article every month."

"But now you have the time, the space and the security to analyze the events. Put them in context. Describe how they've changed you. Sex and booze aren't going to take the experiences out of your head, boy."

Boy? Most days Griffin felt a thousand years old. And not that he'd confess to Monroe or anyone else, but booze had fallen off his "Might Work" list. As for sex…that drive had been neutralized after what had happened to

Erica. Even before then, when they were bunking with the platoon, there'd been too little alone time and too many strung-tight nerves to find a reprieve in that kind of release.

Okay, and he'd also been trying to get some distance from her.

"I'm going inside," he said, turning toward the back door, Private close to his thigh. "Sweet dreams, Rex."

"Griffin."

His feet stopped moving. He'd almost convinced his brain that Jane wasn't still standing there. Those three-hundred-plus days in Afghanistan had demonstrated the power of the mind. During his stint with the troops, on occasion he would swear he smelled hot water—and it did have a scent. Other mornings he'd woken, and before he'd opened his eyes he would hear Gage humming his favorite Lynyrd Skynyrd tune. He could feel his brother just a few feet away.

Once, after an incident like that, he'd managed to reach his twin via sat phone. He'd asked him what, if anything, he'd been singing to himself as he washed up for the day. "Free Bird." Yeah, it had felt really, really real.

But Governess Jane was really, really real as well. So he turned to face her. "What is it? You rethinking that slap?"

Her lips were in their primmed state. "About what happened last night…you should know I don't scare off so easily."

She thought he'd had a motive beyond her mouth? "Clearly."

"And if you come near me with that purpose in mind again, it won't be your face that feels the pain."

His brows rose. He didn't plan on ever seeing her again, let alone kissing her, but he decided against clue-

ing her in. And for damn sure he wasn't going to confess
that kissing her had been only about impulse, not intention. "Fine."

She started to move off, and it was then he noticed the
medium-sized piece of luggage in her hand. His hackles
rose. "What do you have there?" he asked, gesturing to it.

"I believe it's called a duffel bag?"

Goose bumps were forming along his spine. "You're
out of here, right?" Please, God, she was leaving.

"I'm out of here, but not going far," she said smugly.
"I'm moving into the vacant bungalow next door."

It took little time for Jane to get situated in No. 8. It was
much smaller than Griffin's place, and she'd brought only
a few items from her apartment. That was a small space
too, and a long commute—even by SoCal standards—
from here. She didn't feel a particular attachment to it.
Often her job had taken her away from the one-bedroom
for weeks at a time when a client had wanted her closer.
Of course, in this case her client wanted her anything *but*
closer, but he'd thank her for her dedication in the end.
She was sure of it.

The idea had come to Jane as she'd picked her way past
the empty cottage after leaving the party—after that kiss.
If Griffin was pulling out all the stops to chase her off, her
solution was to place herself even more underfoot. Following this morning's first cup of coffee, she'd found Skye
Alexander's phone number and made the arrangements.

The only flaw was how distracting Jane found the endless view of ocean and the ever-changing play of waves
against sand. If Rex Monroe hadn't stopped by with a
leather-bound volume of plastic-sheathed pages, she might
have succumbed to temptation and spent the afternoon

concerning herself with nothing more than the freckles a sunbath might bring out on her nose.

Now, though, she laid Rex's book on the small dining table situated between the galley kitchen and postage-stamp living room. To the right of the album, she set her sweating glass of iced tea. Her pulse picked up as she drew out a chair. She had a feeling she'd find the key to achieving Griffin's cooperation here.

A knock sounded on the front door. With a pat and a promise for the book, she turned toward the entry. It was the property manager, Skye, on the other side of the threshold. Today the brunette had her hair in a tight French braid, revealing the fine bones of her slender face. She didn't wear a stitch of makeup and was dressed in baggy chinos and a T-shirt. A sweater-vest that must have been the discard of a male relative concealed more of her shape.

She held up a red glass plate piled with cookies and covered by plastic wrap. "I thought you might enjoy these. Are you settling in okay?"

Jane gestured her inside and led her toward the small couch and adjacent easy chair that sat across from a small fireplace. "I should be bringing *you* treats. Thank you so much for giving me the oh-so-reasonable rental rate."

Shrugging, Skye perched on a cushion. "We're doing each other a favor. Most vacationers have already secured their places for the season, not to mention the lousy economy that's affecting bookings…plus, I like it when I know a little something about who's living here. It makes the cove feel…safer."

Safer? "It's like something out of a fairy tale," Jane said. "The cove seems almost magical."

Skye slid the cookies onto the narrow coffee table in front of her. "It definitely felt that way when we were kids. We ran around like a tribe of lost boys and girls in Neverland."

"That's right. You said you grew up with the Lowells."

"Every summer." She hesitated. "That's why when you said you wanted to keep an eye on Griff, it added another good reason to let you have No. 8."

Uh-oh. Did that mean Skye had a special interest in him herself? A romantic interest? Maybe she saw another woman as some kind of threat and wanted a catbird seat on what she imagined might take place between Jane and the man next door. "I, um, there's nothing between…" She shut down thoughts of that kiss the night before. "My business here is just that—purely business."

Skye's expression blanked, and then she laughed a little. "There's nothing between me and Griffin either, if that's what you're thinking. His twin brother, Gage…"

Twin brother? Good Lord, there were two of them? The other woman's rising blush told her even more. "Oh, it's *him* you're involved with," Jane said.

"No." Skye gave a violent shake of her head. "Not that either. Never that. It's just that we…that Gage and I correspond. He's a photojournalist on assignment in the Middle East, and he worries about his brother."

Maybe it was the voracious reader in her, but Jane thought there might be a story in the "not that either" that was going on between the brunette and Gage Lowell. Her curiosity was piqued. "Would you like a glass of iced tea while we chat?"

"No, thanks." Skye jumped to her feet. "I won't take up much of your time. I just wanted to welcome you to the neighborhood."

Jane trailed the other woman to the front door. Skye paused there, the doorknob in her hand. Then she turned, her pretty face serious. "Don't forget that in fairy tales…

well, there's almost always a wolf or a dragon waiting to capture the fair maiden."

A chill skittered down Jane's spine as the property manager slipped out. She had to shake herself to get rid of the dark mood that tried settling over her. With a look toward the sunny vista out the windows, she headed back to her seat and the album waiting there.

She'd just settled onto the chair when another knock sounded. This time, she heard a curious scrabble against the door as she pulled it open. Private, the black Lab, widened the space with his muscular shoulders. Curly-haired Ted, fingers wrapped around the dog's kerchief, was yanked inside behind the eager canine.

The dog swiped her fingers with a wet tongue before heading straight for the red plate of cookies on the table beside the couch. He sat, staring at them.

"Sorry," Ted said. "I'm on pet patrol, and he must have smelled those as we came by. He has a nose on him you wouldn't believe."

The man looked at the treats with the same hopeful expression as the animal he was tending. Jane laughed. "I take it you both like oatmeal raisin?"

"If it's a baked good, I think we both like just about anything," Ted confessed.

Jane found a paper napkin, then removed the clear wrap from the plate. "Would you like some iced tea with that?" she asked.

Ted fed the dog a cookie before helping himself to one. "I'm good, thanks," he said, between bites.

Jane watched him split a second treat with the dog. "Are the festivities at Party Central beginning early? I got the impression No. 9 didn't start rocking and rolling until late afternoon."

Ted shook his head. Swallowed. "Ah, nope. Last night, Griffin declared the parties are over, over there."

"Oh." She slid her hand along Private's fur as the dog leaned against her legs. "I must have missed that announcement."

"It was after you left. He went on a tear and had everyone out in less than thirty minutes. Paid for a bunch of cabs to take home those people too drunk to drive themselves."

What, had kissing Jane put him out of a celebratory mood? "Does he ever have a good time at those parties he throws?"

Ted shrugged. "Truth? Since he moved to the cove, I don't think Griffin has had any good times at all."

But he'd changed up the circumstances, Jane mused. Without the diversion of booze and bikinis, maybe he was ready to settle down to work. Optimism made her hungry, she realized, and the cookies looked so good. She grabbed one and, as she felt the hard press of Private's body, broke off a hefty piece for him.

Ted watched the dog gobble it down. "We should probably keep the canine treat-sharing sorta secret, okay? Our furry buddy here eats that low-cal kibble, and Griffin's always after me when I feed him scraps."

"Oops." She made a face. "He won't hear it from me."

"As a matter of fact," Ted continued, "you won't tell Griff we visited at all, will you? We're under strict instructions to avoid No. 8, but Private isn't so good with orders."

Jane sighed. So much for optimism. "I suppose that means I shouldn't expect Griffin to start cooperating with me anytime soon."

The surfer shrugged, his expression sympathetic. "Well, he did close down Party Central."

Hope lightened her mood a little. "Does he look like he's buckling down to work? You know, sitting at a table with a laptop or a pad and pen?"

Ted ran his hand over his hair. "He's in a chair. Like you said, at a table."

Ha! Jane felt herself smiling. "That's good! That's very good."

"But there's no computer. And I haven't seen a scrap of paper or a writing implement anywhere in the house."

Jane considered this. "Do you suppose he's working it out in his head? Making mental plans, might you say?"

"He's got his iPod blasting so loud that I don't believe he can hear himself think," Ted replied. "And he's playing cards. Hand after hand of solitaire."

Man and dog left soon after that, and their visit made Jane dispirited enough that she ate two more cookies— pessimism apparently made her hungry too—while staring morosely into the distance. First it was the warning of wolves and dragons, she thought as she munched. Next it was news of a recluse firmly ensconced in his cave. This did have the feel of a fairy tale.

She took up the glass plate and set it beside Rex's album on the dining table. Then the front door reverberated with yet another round of knocking, and she turned to trudge toward it. "What now?" she muttered, as she pulled it open. "A troll?"

Griffin narrowed his eyes at her. "My mood is a lot uglier than that."

She stepped back to avoid the brush of his body as he barged inside. Though she realized she should welcome him onto her turf, there was a disturbing aura about him. He moved into the small living area, his wide shoulders and simmering temper making the room feel a lot smaller and a lot...hotter.

A memory from the night before burst in her head. His hard hands gripping her bare shoulders. The sandpaper feel of the whiskers edging his lips. The thrust of his tongue, the clack of his teeth against hers, the almost violent edge to the unexpected kiss.

Her stomach muscles had contracted, and though she'd been quaking beneath his touch, she'd opened her mouth wider, succumbing to the insistent demand of his. Beneath her bikini top, her nipples had stiffened, and she'd pressed closer to ease the ache.

When his fingers had tightened on her skin, she'd thought his touch might be tattooed there forever, and her only regret was all the other places he'd yet to make contact.

Then in a move as aggressive as the kiss itself, he'd put her away from him. She'd staggered back, dazed, her gaze on his stiff back as he'd stalked off.

It had taken two hours and a cup of black coffee to realize he'd been using sex to scare her away. Well, not exactly sex…okay, it was exactly sex. A kiss, she realized now, a kiss from Griffin, could be as intimate as any full body connection she'd had with another man. Her nerve endings were still smoking from it.

"Don't look at me like that," Griffin barked.

She felt a blush rise up her neck. "I don't know what you're talking about."

He rolled his eyes, then stalked farther into the room and threw himself down on the couch. "What will it take to get you out of here? You're making me nuts. I can feel you all the way at No. 9."

"That's ridiculous." Lust couldn't travel that far, could it? A governess's lust surely didn't have that kind of power. One spoke Jane's name in a hush, and heretofore her sexual desires had been fairly muted as well. "It's just your guilt talking."

He rocketed to his feet. "You deserved that damn kiss, walking around with all that skin, and especially with that...that..." His vague gesture seemed to indicate her hair.

She put a hand to it. "I can't help that it's fuzzy," she said in a defensive tone. "And anti-frizz serum makes it sticky."

"What the hell are you talking about?"

"I don't know." It was true. With him in this small room, the air crackled with an energy that was messing with her brain synapses. "I thought you were complaining about my hair."

"It's not your hair." He glared at her. "It's your mouth. Can't you do something about that?"

She put her hand over her lips, embarrassed all over again. Ian had once commented on it as well. "A former boyfriend called it a silent-movie-star mouth," she heard herself confess. At the time, she'd pictured photos of famous actresses of the era with their waiflike features and bow-shaped lips and been uncertain what to think.

"God knows I want to tie you to some railroad tracks," Griffin muttered.

She imagined his hands on her, winding rope around her wrists and ankles, and another flare of heat shot over her skin. Her palms were sweating, and she buried them in her pockets. *Oh, Jane,* she told herself, looking away from his tight jaw and angry eyes, *we're definitely not in the library stacks anymore.*

"This is ridiculous." He was muttering again, and now he began to pace about the room. "There's got to be some way for me to get out of this."

Thoughts of bondage fled. Jane was here so Griffin

wouldn't get out of this! If he ducked his obligations, she'd lose her chance to recoup her reputation. Worse, some might misconstrue his failure as a result of something she'd done. If she left Crescent Cove without seeing Griffin through to his deadline, her good standing would be further harmed. Irretrievably, maybe. No doubt Ian Stone would be the first to proclaim that she'd left yet another author in the lurch.

Alarm refocused her mind on important matters, and she crossed to the album that Rex Monroe had delivered to her. "Griffin's tear sheets from Afghanistan," he'd told her, meaning copies of every article published during his embedded year. She'd been eager to read through the pages, figuring that by familiarizing herself with what he'd written she'd be better able to help shape his memoir.

"The only way to get out of this," she told Griffin in a firm voice, "is by getting to your contractual obligation. By telling this story." With that, she flipped open the volume.

On Our Way, the first magazine article's headline read. Beneath it was a photo of Griffin, clean-shaven, smiling, his arm around an exotic-looking, dark-haired, dark-eyed woman. The caption identified her as Erica Mendoza.

"On *our* way," Jane repeated. Puzzled, she looked up.

Griffin's gaze swept over the photograph, then settled back on her. "You didn't do your homework like a good governess should, did you, Jane?"

"Uh… Maybe not." His agent had phoned, and she'd leaped at the opportunity, then rushed to Crescent Cove once she'd realized Griffin wouldn't take her calls. She touched a fingertip to the lovely face so close to his in the picture. "Who's this?"

"The original book deal was supposed to be like the

articles themselves," he answered. "A 'he said, she said'–style account of our embedded year."

"He said, she said," Jane repeated. "Our embedded year."

"Right," Griffin agreed, his voice impassive. "Our embedded year. He said, she said."

She waited, watched him take a breath.

"But now…" Griffin said. "She's dead."

CHAPTER FOUR

GRIFFIN WATCHED Jane rock back on her heels as shock settled on her face. Such an expressive face it was, those big eyes wide, her soft lips parting on a sudden breath. She had a baby's skin, fair and fine-pored, molding the delicate bones of her cheeks and the clean edges of her jaw. Despite her bluster, her fragility didn't stand a chance against him.

Hell, he bet he'd have her running by nightfall.

"What happened?" she asked.

"That story you're so eager for me to write, honey-pie?" Griffin gestured at the album of collected magazine pieces, though he avoided glancing at the photo of Erica. "I better warn you, it's got blood and gore."

Jane flinched. For a second he thought he might have scared her off with just that, but then she drew out one of the dining chairs and took a seat. A cool cucumber once again. "Why don't you tell me about it?"

A sudden urge to bolt cramped his gut, but he rode out the impulse. This was one of two memories of that year he didn't have to stave off with rock 'n' roll blasting through a pair of earbuds or the monotone chatter of news from his big-screen TV. While an auto's backfire could have him crouching to protect himself from small-arms fire, or the cry of a seagull take him straight to the nights when the monkeys shrieked from the craggy mountains surrounding the base in Afghanistan, thoughts of Erica raised a wall between him and the rest of the world.

"We each had a different sponsoring magazine, both owned by the same publishing company," he said, moving back so he could lean against the nearby wall. "The newsweekly was paying my way. Erica was the first embedded war journalist on assignment for what's generally considered a women's fashion publication."

Jane glanced at the collection of tear sheets. "Brave lady."

"Dogged." He didn't want to examine too closely right now what, exactly, she'd been so determined to accomplish, so he pushed the question away. "It's a man's world out there. Every ten or fourteen days, we rotated to a slightly larger base for a chance at a hot meal and water to wash with, but the rest of the time it was MREs and our own sweat. The guys pissed into PVC pipes stuck in the ground."

Griffin eyed Jane, trying to picture her among the soldiers in his platoon. Erica had been bold and bawdy, coping with the almost-adolescent sexual bravado of the young men by telling jokes so dirty they could almost make him cringe. Jane, on the other hand… She'd probably faint dead away.

As if reading his mind, the blonde straightened in her chair, her eyebrows drawn together and down. "Don't stop on my account. Three summers in a row my dad hauled my brothers and me out to the Arizona desert while he conducted fieldwork studying an elusive reptile. One of my first jobs in this business? I assisted a man ghostwriting the autobiography of a notorious metal band's lead singer. To get 'color,' I rode with them on their reunion tour bus for a month. I might look sheltered, but I assure you that's not the case."

Her annoyance bemused him. "What elusive reptile was that?"

She didn't blink. "The Black-and-Green Spotted Hootswaggle."

"You made that up."

Her little movement might well have been a flounce. "So? I've forgotten its real name. My father always says I have no head for science."

Yet she'd survived those arid summers and then four weeks with the kind of band infamous for debauchery. "Did you, uh, date any of those band members?"

"Well, I did make sure I had all my shots up to date before the tour—you know, rabies, distemper, smallpox and the like—but no, tempted as I was by scrawny men wearing leather pants and hair extensions."

She made him smile. Not only was she funny with her dry way of delivery, but for some reason it pleased him to know some ancient lecher with a groupie list a mile long hadn't touched the baby skin, kissed the tender mouth.

That mouth that was part silent star, part very bad girl.

"But we've gotten off the subject," Jane continued.

Damn it, she made him do that too, Griffin realized. He was supposed to be sending her on her way, not smiling at her.

The governess gestured at the tear sheets again. "We were talking about Erica."

In his mind's eye he saw the women who had populated their remote outpost. It wasn't the single real one he pictured, however. Instead he saw their other female companions—the naked centerfolds taped to the plywood walls, their humongous breasts and big white smiles fly-speckled, their expressions creepily come-hither as their paper selves watched over the boys ever ready to risk their lives. One young man had a morning ritual of kissing the paper nipples for luck.

"Erica…" Jane prompted again.

He ran his hand over the back of his neck. "A patrol was going out to search the valley for weapon hoards and ratlines—foot trails that are enemy supply routes. The night before I'd been on the same kind of mission myself."

"But this time was different?" Jane asked.

"There'd been radio chatter." He looked down at his feet, aware of his own blank tone. Glad that he felt just that way inside. "That day, she shouldn't have gone with them."

"Did someone try to talk her out of it?"

"Sure." He'd thought he'd convinced her not to go, too tired to recognize the set expression on her face and the determined light in her eyes. When she'd left, he'd been sleeping, dosed up on the pills they all swallowed down to find a few hours of relief from the high temperatures and the tension. Until he woke up and found her note tucked between his fingers, he hadn't known what she'd been planning. "She didn't listen."

Erica had only heard what she wanted to hear. About the wisdom of going out that day. About what was going on between her and Griffin.

Jane picked up a cookie from the glass plate in front of her, then put it back down. "What happened?"

"Ambush. Particulars are a little sketchy, as everyone was busy trying to stay alive. They took fire and jumped off the trail. But when they realized she wasn't with them, they headed back, at their own considerable risk. They found her sitting down, holding her arm. She'd been hit in an artery. Bled out in a matter of minutes."

Jane pushed the platter of cookies farther from the

table edge. "Oh." Her voice was tight, as if there was a hand around her throat. "That's terrible."

Griffin gazed off into the distance. "This one kid, Randolph, he put her body over his shoulder in a fireman's carry. Her blood stained his vest from his shoulders to his waist. It was the first thing I noticed when he returned. That, and the way tears had turned the dirt on his face to mud."

Griffin had been sitting against a wall of sandbags, idly watching another guy squeeze cheese onto a granola bar, razzing the man about how the combo made him sick to his stomach. They'd been laughing.

Then Randolph had been standing there. Without a word, Griffin had known. He'd gotten to his feet, then stumbled toward the spot where they'd placed Erica. "I saw her," he told Jane now. "The dirt in her hair, the stiffening wetness of her sleeve where the blood was already drying, the dusty laces of her boots. One had come undone, and as I stood there, Randolph knelt down and retied it for her."

His brain had clicked away, cataloging each of those items and more, as if storing them for some later test. The details had seemed to fill a yawning black chasm opening up inside him—leaving no room for anything beyond those cold, bare facts. Leaving no room for any feelings. He'd gone icy inside then, and three days later become completely—perhaps permanently—frozen.

At the time, he'd thanked God.

He was still grateful.

"I'm sorry for your loss," Jane said.

Puzzled, he looked at her. His loss? It was Erica who had lost everything. But he nodded, knowing it was expected of him, knowing a man who hadn't been rendered entirely numb would be expected to acknowledge Jane's expression of sympathy.

"That's the kind of story you signed up for," he said. The librarian in her would surely back away from it, right?

"No," she answered, calm. "That's the story *you* signed up for."

The reminder tapped at the ice inside him. Why couldn't she leave this alone? His jaw clenched. "Jane—"

"I worked with an author who is a famed outdoor adventurer," she said. "In his book, he related a tragedy that happened to one of his teams on a mountain climb. They'd stopped for lunch. As they finished, she stood up to reach for something—but had forgotten she'd unclipped from the safety line. Just like that, she went off the side of K2. Gone."

Griffin pressed against the wall, his shoulders digging into the plaster. "And?" he said, wary.

"And he wrote it just like that. He put it on the page with as much emotion as if he was describing the wind catching his sandwich wrapper. I had to help him include the emotion. You'll have to do that too."

He didn't have the emotion! He didn't want the emotion!

Shaking his head, Griffin pushed away from the wall. "I don't need your help, lady."

"Aw." She no longer appeared the least bit sympathetic. "And I was just getting used to honey-pie."

Advice, mockery, he didn't need any of it. He set his sights on the door. He only had to pass her and her flapping mouth and nosy manner and governess tone and be gone—his composure, his chilly control, still intact.

As he went by, she caught his arm. "You know I'm right," she said, her voice steady. "And you won't have to do it alone. I told you. I'll do whatever you need."

"And I told you—"

"Griffin, Erica deserves this."

Erica. Despite his best intentions, his gaze dropped to her photo. It was not how he'd seen her last: lifeless, dirtied, bloodied. It was Erica, vitally attractive. Full of expectations.

Deserving.

As if from a distance, he saw himself wrench his arm from Jane's hold. Then he scooped up the ruby-colored plate. In a gesture that betrayed a rage and frustration he could swear he didn't feel, he flung the platter against the wall. Cookies flew. The plate broke, and glass shards rained like drops of blood.

He hurried out of the house, telling himself the mess he'd made was no reflection of his inner self.

AT THE OPPOSITE END of the cove from Beach House No. 9, Jane sat railside at Captain Crow's, a restaurant/bar that was one of only two commercial establishments on the beach—the other being an adjacent gallery that sold plein air paintings and beautiful handmade boxes, frames and jewelry crafted from items of the sea. She'd poked her nose inside, taking in sun-drenched landscapes and rainbow-hued earbobs of abalone and beach glass, but her urge to admire couldn't overshadow her certainty that the open floor plan made it a lousy place to hide.

Now Captain Crow's, that was another matter.

It was as if Party Central had moved north by a couple miles. Pleasure-seekers peopled the open-air tables and sat elbow-to-elbow on stools pulled up to a narrow, westward-facing counter. Dressed in her usual conservative wear—cropped khakis, a thin, bottle-green button-down shirt and a straw hat settled low on her brow—Jane went unnoticed among the rhinestoned tees and short shorts, the boho skirts and macraméd halter tops. The typical California confluence of Hollywood high culture and laid-back hippie fashion. Nearly overpowering the scent of salt air were the mixed aromas of SPF 30 sunscreen, Rodeo Drive perfumes and top-shelf tequila.

She'd collected a glass of white wine from the bar and slipped onto a free stool, unsure of her next move in her goal of getting Griffin to work. The only short-term certainty was her need to steer clear of him for the moment, giving him a chance to cool off following the plate-throwing incident. Seeing her again too soon might antagonize him further, causing him to do something rash, like ordering her from the cove altogether.

As she took a sip of her straw-colored beverage, she caught a glimpse of Skye Alexander strolling through the restaurant, her roaming gaze suggesting she was looking for someone. Jane pulled her hat lower on her brow and fixed her attention on the orange orb in the blue sky, tracking its descent. She figured it was better to avoid Skye too. Jane wouldn't put it past Griffin to send the other woman to scout her out…and then toss her from the beach colony, despite the fact that it was his own agent who had hired her. Slumping in her seat, she tried lifting her shoulders to her ears, going Quasimodo as camouflage.

But the world hadn't gone her way in ages, so she felt the tap on her back with no surprise. Turning, she consoled herself with the knowledge that there wasn't a free space on either side of her. That thought came too soon as well, though, because someone shouted, and the crowd around her scattered, people rushing down the steps to the sand.

Befuddled, Jane watched them gather near a flagpole at the base of the stairs to the beach. Skye perched on the freed seat next to Jane, her gaze also on the excited throng. A man wearing ragged, low-slung shorts and the ubiquitous tan lifted a conch shell to his lips. The blast of sound set the crowd cheering again, and then a blue flag slowly rose on the pole. When it reached the peak, the bystanders saluted the fluttering fabric. Jane saw it was printed with the universal symbol for martini.

"Cocktail time," Skye explained. "Five o'clock."

Jane's brows lifted, taking in the beverages already in hands, including her own half-full wineglass.

"*Official* cocktail time at Crescent Cove. This ritual goes back to the fifties."

"That's when this beach was discovered?" If Jane kept the other woman talking about their surroundings, maybe she could avoid other subjects. Like Griffin. Like how he was likely in No. 8 right this moment, packing her duffel for her imminent departure. "During the wonder years of tiki parties and limbo games?"

Skye shook her head. "Before then. During Prohibition, rumrunners made it a secret drop-off point for contraband liquor. And before *that,* during the silent film era, my great-great-grandfather used it as a stand-in for a South Seas atoll. He had a movie company, Sunrise Studios, and trucked in all the tropical vegetation that flourishes here."

At the mention of silent films, Jane covered her mouth, then glanced down the beach at the colorful residences spilling from the hillside to the edge of the sand. The ocean breeze shivered through the graceful fronds of the date palms shading their roofs and set the long leaves of the banana plants wagging. The creamy faces of plumeria flowers mingled with brighter splashes of hibiscus in yellow, red and pink. The bougainvillea grew everywhere something else didn't.

She could imagine this place as an exotic backdrop to long-ago movies or as an idyllic vacation getaway. "It really does appear out of another time."

For no more reason than that, a person would be reluctant to leave. It wasn't hard for Jane to picture woody station wagons pulled up behind the cottages. She could see the children of the past playing in the surf, riding inflatable rubber rafts instead of the foam boogie boards the contemporary kids were dragging into the water by leashes attached at their ankles. At five o'clock some sunburned man with a crew cut would blow the conch shell, heralding another idyllic summer evening. "Magic," she murmured.

A foolish notion that she'd always wanted to believe in. Just like love. Her father had detected the weakness in her early on, as clear to him, apparently, as her lack of aptitude in the sciences. "So silly and emotional, Jane," he would say, shaking his head at her. "Just like your mother."

Pushing the memory aside, she tuned back in to Skye's conversation. The crowd had returned to their places, and Jane was forced to lean close to hear over their rowdy chatter. "The earliest houses go back to the 1920s and '30s," the other woman was saying. "My great-great-granddad built some of them, my great-grandfather more, but it wasn't until my mom was pregnant with me that my parents moved here. They live in Provence now, and though I live at the cove full-time, most habitants are seasonal." She paused. "Like the Lowells."

Griffin. Their last moments together replayed in Jane's head, his flattened voice describing what had happened to his colleague Erica in Afghanistan. The neutral tone to his words had been belied by the stiffness of his posture. Even now, Jane could feel the tense muscle of his forearm under her hand and the way he'd wrenched from her hold in order to heave the cookie platter against the wall. It reminded her that she owed Skye a plate…and her client an apology?

Jane didn't think an "I'm sorry" would change his mind about her. By insisting he'd have to touch on that tragedy, she'd become the object of his wrath. She had the very bad feeling he would absolutely refuse to work with her now. On a sigh, she met Skye's gaze. "Did Griffin send you to find me?"

"What? No."

"Oh." The denial eased Jane's worry better than another swallow of wine. "Good."

"But I *was* looking for you." She hesitated. "Your name rang a bell…and then when I put it together with what you said about helping Griffin with his memoir…"

Jane's belly tightened. How widespread was the smear on her reputation?

"I have all of Ian Stone's novels," Skye said.

Jane nodded, tensing further. "I'm not surprised."

The other woman gave a little smile. "I know, I know, me and everyone else. Number one *New York Times* bestseller several times over. Many of them were made into movies."

"The last five."

"I'm one of those people who likes to reread books, poring over them from the dedication page up front to the author's note at the back." Skye hesitated, then the question she'd obviously been dying to ask burst out. "What was it like to work with him? Because that's you, isn't it? I figured it had to be when you told me you work with writers. He dedicated *Sal's Redemption, The Butterfly Place* and *Crossroads Corner* to you, right?"

"Yes." For three years, she'd worked almost exclusively with him. He'd been the focus of her career.

Then he'd become the focus of her life.

"So," Skye prodded. "Will you dish? Is he as handsome as he appears on book jackets and in TV interviews?"

"Handsomer." She sighed inwardly. Ian's good looks didn't reflect his inner character, but she couldn't blame Skye for not recognizing that. Look how long it had taken Jane to figure it out. She'd wanted too much to believe.

So silly and emotional, Jane.

When it came to Ian Stone, that's exactly what she'd been. A lesson had been learned, though. She'd been a fool for love in the past, but she would never again make the mistake of caring for a man who couldn't love her back.

"Gorgeous, huh?" Skye leaned closer. "But then is he like so many really attractive guys? Tell me he's the size of a pickle."

The demand surprised a laugh out of Jane. "You want me to talk about his—" She gestured toward her lap.

"No!" Skye flushed red. "I wouldn't talk about that. I don't like to think about that. I meant his height. The height of his body. His whole self."

Skye's deep fluster struck Jane as odd, but she got another laugh out of imagining Ian's horrified reaction to even a moment's consideration of that particular body part in gherkin terms. Then another picture of him blossomed in her brain, her own version of Pin the Pickle on the Donkey.

Perfect, she thought, because the man was such an ass.

She couldn't hold back a fresh burst of laughter.

"You're in a good mood," a voice said from behind her.

The chuckles drained away as Jane tensed again. Busted.

With a slow pivot, she turned to face Griffin. Ian Stone was handsome in a spoiled, well-tended sort of way. By contrast, Griffin looked as if he'd buzzed his hair himself and he'd nicked his chin while shaving—a couple of days before, if she was any judge of stubble. But his was a wholly masculine face, all the edges hard and those incredible turquoise eyes sharp. Her breath quickened, even though she tried pretending she was all cool control. There was no denying that something about the man had found a previously hidden chink in her, an opening that allowed his male energy to worm its way under her armor, heating her up, loosening her muscles, almost... preparing her.

The thought made her blush, and his gaze narrowed, skewering her now. She wiggled on her stool. "Um...hey."

He nodded absently at Skye, then returned his ominous gaze to Jane. "I've been looking for you."

"Oh?" Her belly fluttered, and she barely registered the finger wave Skye sent her before leaving. From the hard expression on Griffin's face, Jane didn't expect he'd sought her out to deliver good news. What would she do once he declined her services for good? Word would surely get back that yet another author found her unsatisfactory. She sighed, bowing to the inevitable. "What is it?"

He opened his mouth, and then his gaze shifted over her shoulder. The incredible eyes flared for a moment, narrowed again. "Shit."

She glanced around. In the distance a woman was trudging through the sand, a baby balanced on one hip. Three other kids trailed behind her, but she didn't look the least bit matronly, with her long legs bared by a white cotton skirt and a scarlet tank top clinging to her curves. Expensive sunglasses covered her eyes, and her dark hair was glossy and cut in a trendy fashion that had delicate pieces curving around her cheeks and jaw.

Jane turned back to Griffin and could swear he'd gone pale. "Old flame?"

"More like the devil," he muttered, then cursed again. "You've got to do something for me, Jane."

She didn't think this was going to be about his memoir. "Like what?"

He hunkered down, so that he was semishielded by her body. "Hide me."

Wasn't hiding what she'd been after herself?

"I don't think that's going to work," she said after a moment, her attention still on the beach. Was it bad of her to take pleasure in noting that the dark-haired beauty had homed in on the man half concealed behind her? She was waving her arm, her focus clearly settled on his face. Two of the little kids were jumping up and down as well, pointing and waving.

"The children seem to know you. Who are they?"

"The devil's minions." As they continued waving, he rose to his full height on a loud sigh. "There's only one thing for it, then."

"What's that?"

Griffin clamped his hand around Jane's upper arm and pulled her from her stool. "Come on." With an arm slung across her shoulders, he urged her toward the steps leading to the sand. "This way, honey-pie."

She struggled to keep up with his brisk stride. "Tell me what's going on, chili-dog."

He shot her a look, then shrugged. "Our little endearments will do the job just fine, I guess."

"What job is that?" Jane asked warily.

"A minor bit of role-play. You can manage that for the next few minutes or so, can't you?"

She thought of protesting. This definitely wasn't about his memoir. She considered turning back toward the bar and cutting her losses right there and then, given the bad luck that had been dogging her lately. But another few minutes…the optimist inside her wondered what might happen during that time. If she went along with whatever he was planning, perhaps he'd be convinced that she was a handy person to have around, and they could salvage their working relationship. That's what she needed more than anything.

"I guess," she said.

"Great. Consider yourself hired." He hitched her closer to his side. His body was hard and warm and solid enough to prop up her weight if she was the kind of woman inclined to lean on a man. She wasn't. She didn't trust them for that.

He cupped her upper arm, his palm sliding up and down in a caress she could feel through the sleeve of her cotton shirt. It made her flesh prickle, and she shivered.

Griffin's feet halted, stopping their forward movement. Jane glanced up. He was staring at her, an odd expression on his face. His caressing hand moved over her again, and she couldn't stop a second shiver.

"Jesus, Jane," he murmured, stroking her once more. "Jesus."

Her mouth was dry. "Jesus, Jane—what?"

He shook his head as if he was shaking off an uncomfortable thought. His fingers slid away. "Don't look so serious," he told her, his voice gruff.

She frowned at him. "How should I look, then?"

With a careless hand, he chucked her under the chin. The strange moment had clearly passed. "Try smiling, honey-pie. For this to succeed, you have to look and sound the part."

"The part of what?" she asked, suspicious.

Griffin grinned down at her. His blue gaze seemed almost tender, and she felt his testosterone twisting toward her like smoke, seeking that crack in her protective shell. His hand found hers. "The part, sweet Jane, of my lover."

CHAPTER FIVE

THEY DIDN'T GET to introductions right away. The moment she and Griffin appeared on the beach in front of the lovely brunette, the woman launched herself into his arms, causing him to let go of Jane. "You don't know what I've been through!" the beauty said.

One of her young entourage was a girl who looked as if she'd just crossed into her teens. "I'm going to die of boredom here," the teen said. "I can smell the lack of cell phone coverage." She blinked lashes of beyond-natural length and thickness. "I'm probably going to get pregnant just for something to do."

Though Jane was somewhat alarmed when the teen turned to peruse the beach as if seeking out potential baby daddies, no one else commented on her offhand remark. Perhaps no one else had heard it. Griffin and the woman were already walking down the beach in the direction of his cottage, she hanging on to his arm while still carrying the little guy, who looked to be nine or ten months old. One of the baby's sandals slipped off his foot, and Jane swooped it up as she drifted behind them.

"Let's go," the teenager said to the remaining two. They were boys—five and six? Seven and eight?—and were poking at a clump of stinky kelp with a stick.

At the girl's prompting, the smaller of the two ran ahead, brandishing the piece of wood, while the other threw sand at his back, yelling, "Your face looks like monkey poo!"

At that, the teenager tossed a glance at Jane. "My life," she said in a theatrical tone.

"It seems adding an infant of your own to it would only complicate matters," Jane pointed out. "Cute baby bump to monkey poo? A blip in time."

Her extravagant eye-roll made Jane grin. It reminded her of—

Griffin. Good God, was the brunette his ex? This tribe his children?

"I'm Jane," she said to the girl.

The teen slid her a sidelong look. "Of course you are."

Griffin's exact words! "What's your name?"

"Rebecca." She flung an arm in the direction of her presumed siblings. Four inches of braided string and rubber bracelets circled her wrist. "Those are my brothers, Duncan, Oliver and Russ."

Before Jane could pry more out of her, they'd reached Beach House No. 9. The entire party assembled in the living room, the two boys dropping to the floor to wrestle, Rebecca slumping onto the couch in another dramatic move, her mother pushing her sunglasses to the top of her head and hitching the baby higher on her hip. Jane hung back, reluctant to enmesh herself until she knew more.

"Now, Tess," Griffin said. "What's this all about?"

Just like that, the woman burst into tears. The little one she was holding immediately followed suit.

Over the racket, Rebecca let out a gusty sigh. "Pregnant, I tell you. I'm definitely getting pregnant."

Her mother responded by passing over the tearful little guy. Not a bad idea, Jane decided. Birth control by baby brother.

Griffin didn't appear affected by the woman's distress

or the child's. He crossed his arms over his chest. "Tess, what the hell are you doing here?"

"I've left him, Griff," she said. "I've finally left my husband!"

At the outburst, he groaned, offering not an ounce of sympathy. His hands ran over his head. "Geez, Tessie. This matters to me how?"

Tess's sobs redoubled. Jane could only hurt for the woman. Clearly she'd come to Crescent Cove without the expectation of rejection. Jane edged farther away, thinking she'd head to her own cottage.

Her movement caught Griffin's eye, however, and in two strides he had her by the hand and was towing her toward the crier. "I can't deal with this, Tess. And here's why. I've got a new lover now." He put his hands on Jane's shoulders and pulled her back against his chest.

His body heat transferred to Jane and pooled low at the base of her spine. She glanced over her shoulder, and his hands tightened on her. He focused on her mouth, and she felt it like a touch, her lips warming too. The company, the room itself, seemed to drop away, leaving Griffin's intense gaze and Jane's unsteady heartbeat.

Then, jerking his gaze off her, he cleared his throat and pushed her forward a half step. It left inches of cooling air between them. "Meet Jane."

The other woman sniffed, the back of her hand against her nose. She raised lovely, tear-drenched eyes to take in Jane, and then her gaze moved on to Griffin's face. "You've met someone?"

The heartbreak in her voice told the story, Jane thought. And as someone who'd been supplanted by another woman in a man's life, she didn't want to play this scene again, even from the other side. "Look…"

Griffin's hands found her shoulders again to squeeze a warning. "Honey-pie—"

"Chili-dog," she said, turning to glare at him.

"Honey-pie!" The woman—Tess—cried out. "Chili-dog! You really found someone!"

"Isn't that what you're always telling me to do?"

"When I was married," she started, sniffling back more tears, "it seemed like a good idea. But now that we're heading for divorce…"

Jane couldn't continue this way, deceiving this poor woman who'd apparently left her husband for Griffin, who in turn was exhibiting more than his usual detachment. "I'm sorry, but—"

"Jane." An even clearer warning.

Breaking free of his hold, she turned to shoot him a look. "Listen—" But her next words got lost in a loud crash. The little boys had knocked over a small table by the window. The base of a lamp was on the ground, shattered against the hard wood. The shade lay crumpled beside it.

The baby started wailing again.

As if she'd reached the end of her rope, Tess clapped one hand over her eyes. The little boys began shoving each other anew, putting more furniture at risk. Rebecca mouthed something—likely another pregnancy threat—and jumped from the sofa to hand her smallest brother over to Griffin. As the teen stalked out of the room, he held the child at arm's length, then turned to Jane in mute appeal.

"Oh, for goodness' sake." Helpless with his own children! Surely that had to be the case, that they belonged to him, because each one had his dark hair, and at least some of them his distinctive blue eyes, not to mention his ability to be appealing and get on her nerves at the very same time. She took the baby from him and jiggled the child as she grabbed the back of one little boy's shirt. It was a winning technique, because the other automatically followed as she led him down the hall. A small guest room had a TV and remote. She held it out to the larger of the two. "I assume you're familiar with this device?"

In a blink, it was snatched out of her hand. In two, they were seated on the bed, their eyes glued to the screen. Private, the Labrador, appeared from somewhere and wiggled his way between them on the mattress. The show they chose wasn't a cartoon, and she could only hope it wasn't X-rated—a distinct possibility, she figured, in this house—but, given the kids' snarled domestic arrangement, maybe they'd seen it all before.

The baby was now snuffling against her shoulder and gnawing on his fist, so she headed into the kitchen, where she found a cracker. He pounced on it with a show of great delight. As he munched away, she returned to the living room, a box of tissues under her arm.

It appeared as if all was not resolved. Tess had collapsed on the couch cushions, her face in her hands. Griffin, the callous monster, had retreated to the glass doors, his back turned to the woman, his gaze resting on the ceaseless rumble of the surf.

Jane could only hope Rebecca wasn't out looking for a sperm donor.

Without a word, she took a seat on the couch and passed over the tissues. Tess accepted them with a grateful glance. Then she dried her face. Once it was done, she inhaled a long deep breath and took the now-content baby onto her lap. "Thank you," she said, hugging her small son to her. "I'm sorry. I'm so sorry, but I had to get that out of my system."

Then her gaze shifted to Griffin, and she raised her voice. "I want to stay here with the kids."

He swung around, dismay—or panic?—written all over his face. "I didn't even invite you to stay for dinner."

"Griff—"

"Tess. I told you I have a lover. I'm with Jane now."

Not even for the chance to get this job and regain her reputation was she going along with a lie of this magnitude a moment longer. "I'm not his anything," she said, ignoring the fierce frown Griffin turned on her. "Believe me."

"Oh." Tess looked from her to the grim-faced man in the corner. "I don't understand."

"Though he said that we're together," Jane explained, "it's not true."

Tess blinked, and now that Tess's eyes were dry, Jane realized they were the same distinctive and bright turquoise as Griffin's. "That's fabulous news," the other woman replied.

Jane thought it was a little odd to be happy that your ex, the father of your children, had just been lying to you, but she figured Tess's hopes of getting Griffin back had been renewed.

"Because love's a crock and men are beasts," Tess continued in loud tones, and Jane could see from whom Rebecca had inherited her dramatic presence. The brunette sent a pointed look at Griffin. "Even my brother."

Brother?

Oh. *Oh.*

Now feeling stupid, Jane once again glared at the man in the room.

"What?" he asked with a look of aggrieved innocence. But Tess snagged his attention by launching into her reasons for staying at Crescent Cove. "We need a break. The kids will love it here."

He shook his head right away. "There's no available cottage. Ask Skye."

Tess flapped a hand. "There's plenty of room in Beach House No. 9."

He definitely looked panicked now. "I need my privacy."

"You've been hiding from everyone for months," his sister responded.

"No. No, I haven't. Old Man Monroe jaws at me every day. And, uh, I have Jane here. We, uh, have a project to do."

Jane perked up at that. Her spine straightening, she pinned him with her gaze. "So you're committing to working on the book now?"

"As you've been telling me, I have a deadline to meet." He turned to his sister. "See? I can't have all of you underfoot."

"But we won't be any trouble," Tess said. "The kids won't get in your way."

Jane was no longer listening to the other woman, her mind already on the project ahead. She didn't rub her hands together, but she wanted to. "We'll start first thing in the morning."

"Griffin," Tess pleaded. "We need Crescent Cove this summer. Me and the kids. We need it for just a few weeks."

He looked from Tess to Jane, who had no trouble giving him the out he wanted this time. "You need to finish the book, Griffin. That's why I'm here."

His gaze shifted back to Tess, to her, to Tess again. Jane saw a calculating light enter his eyes. *Uh-oh,* she thought.

"All right, sis," he finally said. "You and the kids can stay."

She clapped her hands, and the baby did too. "Thank you."

"You can stay in No. 8," Griffin clarified.

What? Jane mouthed.

Tess frowned. "No. 8?"

"Yes," Griffin answered. "In No. 8, with my assistant Jane, here. Though I'll be busy with my memoir, I'm sure she'll be happy to assist *you* at every opportunity."

WORN PACK OF CARDS in hand, Private padding at his side, Griffin strolled into the small backyard of Beach House No. 9. Okay, *skulked* was a better term, because he couldn't deny the furtiveness of his movements. He stayed close to the side of the house and craned his neck for any sign of the occupants of No. 8. His property provided a view of a slice of the smaller house's rear patch of scruffy grass. When he didn't spy any rowdy relatives or rigid-spined governesses, he picked up his pace toward the nearby picnic table painted sailor-blue.

Once seated on its bench, he tucked in earbuds and thumbed on his iPod. The crashing chords and heavy backbeat of classic Metallica poured into his head as he laid out yet another of his mindless games of solitaire. This was the second day in a row he'd managed to dodge his sister, her children and the woman he'd foisted them on. Or was it, he thought, frowning, the woman onto whom he'd foisted them?

He stared down at his cards for a moment, then cursed the stupid question circling in his head. Damn it! He'd always been lousy at the picky points of grammar and had accepted that fact. But now he was thinking like Jane. Or at least about Jane. Hadn't he been doing a pretty good job of avoiding that too?

With the heel of his palm, he bumped the side of his skull, a little signal to his psyche to move on. For the past forty-eight hours he'd been in the best mood he could remember having in months—the kind of mood a prisoner might experience upon avoiding the electric chair—and though he was still behind bars of a sort, he planned on holding on to this good humor. After all, hadn't he managed to escape his sister, her progeny and the librarian, all in one fell swoop?

Two hands of the card game later, he saw Private jump to his four furry feet. On a groan, Griffin tugged the buds from his ears and quickly scrutinized the vicinity. He groaned again when he realized the one invading his privacy was none other than his elderly neighbor. "What do you want, you old coot?"

Though he was certain he didn't sound the least bit welcoming, Old Man Monroe sat down on the opposite bench.

Griffin returned his gaze to his game. "My dog was right here the whole time, and don't try saying otherwise."

"I'm not here about the dog."

"Yeah? Well, I'm not here to give you your daily senility check. Go home."

"Hear from Gage? Skye said you had mail."

At that, Griffin had to smile, even though he knew the postcard that had been delivered to the cove today—all correspondence addressed to the cottages went to Skye, who then distributed it to the residents—was more than a week old. Seeing his brother's distinctive block lettering pleased him.

"It was one of his own photos." For years, whenever Gage could manage it, he'd find a place that would put an image on card stock and send it across the country or across the world to Griffin. It had started as a friendly twin-to-twin taunt—photojournalist Gage bragging to his brother about the exotic places he found so thrilling. Now, when Griffin had nearly as many faraway locales and out-of-the-ordinary sights stored in his own memory banks, it was a tangible connection. Looking at an image his brother had found through his own viewfinder, touching paper that his brother had also touched, it was as if they were in the same room, at least for a brief moment.

"He's well?" the old man asked.

"As good as he can get, in the kind of places that he goes." Griffin thought about the child Gage had captured on that postcard, in apparent midgiggle. Dirty and thin, he'd still found something to laugh about.

Children had that gift. The thought gave him a guilty prod about his niece and nephews. Angry at himself for letting in the emotion, he slapped down a king in an empty space in the line-up.

Rex Monroe shifted, straightening out his bad leg. Griffin didn't bother looking up. "Don't you have a date with *The Golden Girls* about now?"

"My cable's out. Entertain me."

Instead, Griffin decided to ignore him.

"I have the patience of Job," Rex cautioned after a few minutes had passed.

"You mean you're a job. But not my job. Go harass somebody else."

"Maybe I'll find your sister, tell her you're sitting outside with nothing to do. Looking morose."

The threat put Griffin on his feet, startling Private, who let out a bark. He didn't want Tess or anyone else checking on him, damn it. "I'm not morose."

"You're in a happy frame of mind, then?"

"Sure." He strode to the yard's narrow flower bed and bent over to yank at some weeds, as if he gave a shit about them. "For your information, I'm in a very happy frame of mind."

"Huh," the old guy said, slyness entering his voice. "Does this happiness have to do with Jane?"

Griffin grunted. *Jane.* She'd worn this silly hat the other day, lowered all the way to her eyebrows. For a few moments, on the deck of Captain Crow's, he'd thought she was going to prove cooperative. She'd been close at his side as he'd approached Tess, all compliant and cuddly. That should have been the tip-off. How long could the librarian last like that? But hell, what was wrong with her, having a sudden attack of the truth?

"Jane bugs the crap out of me," Griffin said, ripping a dandelion out by its roots. Its fluffy head reminded him of Jane's fluffy hair. He liked her hair; it twisted and turned, making him want to bury his fingers in it and then... Gah! With a jerk, he tossed the stupid weed away. She was like that, rooting into his head where she didn't belong and wasn't wanted. Messing with his cool equilibrium.

"I guess your sister gets the credit for your good mood, then."

"Oh, right," Griffin said. "Like I want to get involved with her and her domestic dilemmas."

"Looks like you won't," the ancient one said, his voice mild. "Since you've found a way to palm it all off on poor Jane."

"What, you got a spy camera installed around here? And poor Jane, my ass. Poor Jane is actually Annoying Jane who does not follow instructions. If she'd stuck with the program and told my sister that we were...that we had a thing happening here, then Tess would have left me my privacy. She's big on people falling in love."

"Skye says she's had a change of heart about that."

Skye. So she was the codger's source. He'd been nosy and meddlesome from the very beginning, and that hadn't changed, even after all these years. "Did our friendly property manager drop off your monthly allotment of Metamucil today? Followed by a big dose of gossip?"

"Gossip or not, don't you wonder what happened to Tess's marriage?"

Private flopped onto his back on the grass beside Griffin, which required him to perform the obligatory belly rub. "Yeah, I…" he started, then heard himself. "No, I do not wonder what happened. It's none of my business. That's between her and her husband, Deadly Dull David, which right there probably says it all."

"I met him at their wedding reception. He seemed very nice," the old scold replied.

"Gage came up with the name," Griffin mumbled. "You know Gage, he can't imagine anyone enjoying the suburban nine-to-five."

"People change. Grow up. Or down, as the case may be, like when they make their own sister someone else's problem."

Griffin threw up his hands. "Jane again! Why do you keep bringing her up?"

"I'm not the one keeping her around indefinitely. She's a very pretty young woman. Is that why you don't cut her loose?"

Griffin didn't need to explain himself. And not just because the explanation wouldn't put him in a very good light. On second thought, maybe if he disgusted his elderly neighbor he'd go home. "Think about it, old man. If I kicked Jane out of the cove, who would keep my sister out of my hair? This way, Jane is the gatekeeper. I tell her I'm working and she makes sure Tess and her tribe keep their distance."

And it also meant he needn't give his agent some excuse about why he'd gotten rid of her. Frank might legitimately object to that, since he was the one who'd engaged her services in the first place.

"You've kept your distance from Tess and her kids since you returned from overseas," Monroe pressed. "She told Skye you've stayed away from them for months."

"And Skye just had to go running to you with the news," he said darkly. But he couldn't deny the accusation. He looked down at his feet and then muttered the first thing that came into his head. "Russ smells like Afghanistan."

"Eh?"

"The small one is Russ. The one still in diapers. He smells like Afghanistan, okay?" As stupid as it sounded, it was true. "It's the baby wipes—you know those wet cloths people use to wipe a kid's ass? That's what we had between our too-seldom encounters with running water." Upon his return to California, the first time he'd gotten close enough to get a whiff of his youngest nephew, he'd left Tess's house and never been back. Being at her home, breathing in that smell, made it nauseatingly easy for him to imagine Russ—and his siblings—too soon grown. Too soon experiencing that intoxicating cocktail of danger and adrenaline that he'd sucked down with an eagerness that had both ashamed and enticed him. Those were thoughts he didn't want in his head.

There was a moment's silence, and he was sure he'd shut the old guy up, but then his neighbor waved a hand. "In World War Two, I once went seventy-two days without washing up. You ever get lice in your beard? Now, *that's* deprivation."

Annoyed by his dismissive tone, Griffin crossed his arms over his chest. "Let me call the waa-ambulance, old man. You know what was in the best care packages from home? Flea collars. Flea collars for dogs. We fought over 'em to wear around our necks and wind around our ankles."

Monroe's eyes narrowed under his beetled brows. "In my war, our meals *came* with fleas and we were glad for the extra protein."

"Yeah?" Griffin said, scornful. "Well, I can beat that because—"

From the direction of No. 9's back door came the sound of a throat clearing. "Pardon me for interrupting this illuminating pissing contest," Jane said.

The crank ignored her intrusion. "I have two words for you, Griffin: trench foot."

"I…" He wouldn't have let the other man have the last word, except he glanced over and was distracted by the sight of her. She was wearing rhinestone-studded sandals, jeans cut off at the knees and a loose sleeveless top, the hem of which fluttered in the breeze. The wind caught her wavy hair too, setting the sandy tendrils dancing around her face. "You're sunburned," he said. Pink color splashed her nose, cheeks, the tops of her shoulders. Her mouth looked redder too.

That mouth. Every time he looked at the damn thing he got a jolt.

It pursed at him now, signaling she was in a mood. "That's what happens when I spend the day entertaining kids on the beach. Make that two days."

He knew he should feel both guilt and gratitude. But instead he was riveted by the duffel bag in her hand and the soft-sided laptop case that was slung across her chest. She was leaving. From the moment she'd first arrived on the scene that had been his goal—getting rid of her. So this outcome shouldn't surprise him. And Tess or no Tess, it shouldn't bother him in the least either.

He remembered the delicate frame of those shoulders under his hands. Their telltale tremor. Her rosebud mouth parting under his lips in surprise. Her taste heating him up. All that was leaving the cove.

Good. He didn't need the complication...didn't want the connection.

Pinning him with her gaze, she dropped the duffel and placed her hand on her hip. "I should have made something clear two days ago."

"Made what clear?" Her skin had been silky under his hands. That he couldn't forget.

"I'm not a babysitter. Nor am I an 'assistant,' in the way you spoke of me to your sister," she said.

Now guilt did manage to give him a poke. "You said you'd do anything I needed," he reminded her, hating his defensive tone.

She just stared at him, her clear eyes managing to send out a burn.

Oh, yeah, in a mood. He shuffled his feet, shoved his hands into his pockets, tried not to think how cute she looked with that pink nose and silvery glare. She'd kill him if he said that now.

Now that she was leaving.

He took a breath. "Hey, I am sorry about that, Jane. I was an ass." She threw him a *Gee, that wasn't so bad* sort of look. "I understand you're a professional."

"Thank you."

He thought he could add even more to that, now that she was saying her goodbyes. "As a matter of fact, I picked up the phone when Frank called this morning. He was singing your praises."

"That's nice to hear. We go back a ways."

"Yeah. Well, I'm sure he's not wrong."

A smile bloomed on her face. "So, an actual vote of confidence from you, chili-dog? Even better."

He'd miss being chili-dog, just a little. The unexpected pang of sentiment convinced him to give her a bit more. "Frank is sending some packages. I said I'd accept them. A laptop, printer, other supplies. I'm actually planning to set up an office." Not that he was going to do anything inside it, but he figured Jane would take the information as the friendly farewell gift it was. A sign of truce between two former combatants.

Except she wasn't looking at him with gratification. "You don't have a laptop here? No computer whatsoever?"

"Uh…"

She was glaring again. "I thought Ted was wrong, you know. I thought you must have something to write on over here or else you wouldn't have told your sister you needed privacy *two days ago* because *you'd be working.*"

Oh, shit.

"While you were over here basking in slothful solitude, I was out there—" she jerked a thumb over her shoulder in the direction of the sand "—for two solid days building sand castles with your nephews, who might be adorable, but are definitely exhausting."

Old Man Monroe cackled. "You're in the doghouse, boy."

Jane gathered up the bag at her feet, then spun on her flashy sandals, heading back inside his house. The last he'd ever see of her, Griffin thought, was her cute ass. Not a bad way to go, but he didn't like the idea of her going away—forever—mad. "No goodbye?"

Her feet halted. She glanced over her shoulder. "Why?

I'll be back in a minute. I'm just going to put my things in one of the guest rooms."

His jaw dropped. The coot started cackling again.

"Now that you'll have a computer, you're ready to work, Griffin. And since you claim you have confidence in my ability to do my job, it will be much easier for us with me living over here."

"But…but…" Jesus. He couldn't think. Living here? "What, uh, what about Tess and the kids?"

"They'll have more room next door without me under-foot." She started walking again, then took another look back. "Oh, and they'll be coming over tonight for dinner."

The coot's cackling only got louder.

Jane smiled at him. "Why don't you join us, Mr. Monroe? Griffin will be barbecuing."

And the day had started out so happy, Griffin thought, when his reeling brain finally settled. But she'd once again upended him, and he was no longer confident he had the skills to either wait her out or keep her out.

Damn. The enemy had infiltrated, putting the heart of the camp at risk.

FROM HER PLACE beneath the shade of a tropical umbrella, Tess Quincy made a bargain with herself. Twenty more minutes. That's how much longer she'd wait for her husband to meet her as she'd requested. She'd specified "lunchtime" and "on the beach" in her text to his phone, and had—wrongly—assumed he'd show up just minutes after noon. That had been two hours ago. If he didn't appear before the big hand touched the six on her wristwatch—worn in an effort to teach Duncan and Oliver about analog time—she'd retreat back to her cottage. Waiting a second more than that would only be another blow to her ego. It had taken enough hits.

Closing her eyes, she settled more deeply into the old-fashioned beach chair she'd found in a closet at No. 8. A tripod of light wood strung with striped canvas, it didn't lift her rear end off the sand, but it supported her back at the perfect angle for magazine-reading. As a girl, she'd spent hours just like this, paging through *People* and *Us Weekly,* imagining herself as one of the SoCal celebrities so often pictured on the glossy pages.

Nowadays, if she had time for any reading, it was for her moms' book group. They read about tiger mothers and free-range mothers and mothers who managed to start up sexy small businesses. Tess wondered now if she should have been studying up on husbands and wives or how to survive a failed marriage.

A breeze blew her hair across her face. As she fingered it behind her ear, she became aware of someone's gaze on her. At the weight of it, her heart stuttered, then kicked into a rapid beat. Him? Swallowing hard, she lifted her lashes and glanced right.

Her pulse decelerated like a motorboat brought to a sudden halt. It was a stranger who stared at her from his place eight feet away on the sand. A stranger staring at her, she realized now, with a look of blatant interest. Her heart gave another—though milder—kick. And she didn't look away.

Before this week, Tess Quincy, mother of four and wife of more than thirteen years, would have ignored the man. But Tess Quincy, woman with a shambles—or was that a sham?—of a marriage, found herself unwilling to pretend she didn't notice his speculative—and yes, admiring—gaze.

So sue her, it felt good.

The man appeared to be around thirty, which made him a little younger than Tess, and his faint smile topped lean muscles and knee-length swim trunks in bright green. "It *is* you, isn't it?"

For a moment she was speechless, then words spilled easily from her own now-smiling lips. "It depends on who you think I am." With a little thrill, she registered the flirtatious note in her voice and wasn't ashamed of it. It had been months since she'd been noticed as a woman.

"The gum," he said, certain enough now that he strolled closer to her. "Brand name, *OM*. The green tea gum. You're her."

You're her. Another man had said those words to her once. She glanced down at the sleeping child beside her and fussed with the fish-patterned towel covering his napping body. The man who'd said those words originally had hardly looked at her since the precious ten-month-old was born.

The stranger came yet closer and took to one knee, holding out a hand. "Teague White."

She didn't linger on the handshake, but her smile stayed in place. "Tess Quincy. I was Tess Lowell when I made those commercials."

"After all these years, they still play."

Her shoulders lifted, expressing her own surprise over it. She'd filmed them at eighteen, and they'd hit the small screen as she turned nineteen, a long-legged girl in belly-baring yoga pants and a tiny tank, leading a class in meditation. The cause of the ad campaign's sustained popularity wasn't clear. It could have been her nubile teenage body, the gleam of mischief in her eyes when she told the camera that "*OM* will tame a wild mind," or, more likely, the continued heavy airplay. Frequency plus reach had meant success for both *OM* and Tess. She still sank residuals into her kids' college funds.

If she and David divorced, she supposed she'd be using those checks to help support herself.

Teague White's appreciative expression took some of the sting out of the thought. "You look exactly the same."

"I've had four kids since then."

"No," he said, shaking his head.

She felt her dimples dig deep in her cheeks. "Yes." Maybe that last pregnancy hadn't completely taken her out of the realm of attractiveness, after all. She plugged the Pilates DVD into the player twice a week and ran with Russ in the jogging stroller every other day. Night and morning, she brushed, she flossed, she glossed what she could gloss and she moisturized the rest.

Yet her husband, David, didn't look at her the way this stranger did. Her husband, David, barely looked at her at all anymore. This unknown man recognized that eighteen-year-old girl in the wifely shell, and he seemed pretty pleased about it. She cocked her head, the moves not so hard to remember now. "What is it you do, Teague?"

"I'm with the fire department," he said.

"Doing…?" Not that she couldn't guess.

A grin popped out, as if he couldn't hold it back. "I'm a firefighter."

She figured then that he got his own share of appreciative glances with all those manly muscles and the studly occupation. "Day off?"

He nodded. "We wanted surf and sand. You're an added bonus."

It was heady stuff, the attention of an attractive member of the opposite sex. She had plenty of close encounters with males in her daily life, but mostly they wanted to wipe their noses on the tails of her shirt or use her limbs for climbing like a jungle gym at the park.

Down the beach, someone yelled the handsome stranger's name. Both he and Tess looked toward the surf, where a handful of equally muscled men were tossing around a football. They gestured to him and one threw the ball, a perfect spiral that landed at Teague's feet. With a show of reluctance, he picked it up, then clambered to a stand. "You going to be here awhile?"

"I…" If she agreed, she could tell herself she wasn't staying put for David. She could pretend to herself that she was instead waiting for the handsome stranger to return and make her feel desirable again. "Maybe."

His grin flashed on. "And later this week? My friends and I have some time off. We'll be here again."

"I…I have those four kids." Her palm caressed the tuft of Russ's dark hair that was the only part of him visible beneath the towel.

"So? I like kids. And I have a wild mind that maybe only you can tame."

That little thrill buzzed through her veins again. Still… "Four kids and a husband."

She liked him more for not losing the smile. "Lucky guy. Unlucky me." Tossing the football up and down in one hand, he walked backward, his gaze still on her face. "Does that mean you won't run away with me? We could go to Arizona."

"I thought people ran away to Tahiti," she said, laughing.

"The kids'll like the Grand Canyon. Train ride's not to be missed."

Sudden tears pricked the corners of Tess's eyes. Embarrassed, she glanced away. How sad was that? Choked up because a man pretended interest in her *and* her children. David had a lot to answer for. She waved a hand, acknowledging the faux offer.

"Tess?" he called out, prompting her to look at him

again. He'd almost reached his pals. "I always had a crush on you."

Faking another laugh, she waved a second time and watched him rejoin the other firefighters. "'I always had a crush on you,'" she murmured, hearing the wistfulness in her voice.

"He did."

Tess's head whipped around. Skye Alexander dropped to the sand beside her. "You remember him, don't you?"

"'Him'?" She glanced down the beach and then back to Skye. "Should I?"

"Teague White. He used to tag along with your brothers every summer."

Teague White. It didn't ring any bells…then a memory surfaced. Little scrawny kid, around her brothers' age but a head shorter than them. "They called him Tee-Wee. Tee-Wee White." She put her hand over her mouth as a giggle bubbled up and turned her head to stare at the young stud now leaping into the surf. "*That's* Tee-Wee White?"

"Things change. People change."

Husbands. Marriages. Tess glanced at her watch. Two-thirty. But it would be rude to abruptly leave Skye, wouldn't it? She could stay a few more minutes. Blowing out a breath, she forced herself to smile at the younger woman. "Mail from Gage today?"

The property manager wore an old fishing hat on top of her dark hair, a loose, long-sleeved T-shirt and baggy cargo pants. Still, Tess detected the blush crawling up her neck and onto her cheeks. "You know I, uh, correspond with your brother?"

"Griffin mentioned it." Tess recalled what details she'd been given. "Something about wires crossed? He thought Griffin would be here at the cove and you wrote back that he wasn't?"

"Nine months ago. Since then we've kept in touch regularly."

"Nice." Or, not nice, Tess thought, with a sudden pang. Skye wouldn't meet her eyes now, and she had the unwelcome idea that the other woman fancied herself in love with Gage, who lived for thrills and chills. He had more hard edges—if less darkness of the soul—than Griffin, and she couldn't imagine her daredevil sibling with this reserved, almost shy, young woman. *Careful, Skye. He'll break your heart.*

She checked the time. Two thirty-five. Her mood went gloomier. There was no sense pretending David hadn't stood her up. Her gaze shifted to Teague White, playing in the surf. As she watched, he dived dolphin-style into an oncoming wave. God, the guy had a body, long-boned and lithe, covered with wet skin that looked like sculpted bronze sprinkled with diamonds. The sad truth was, the mother in her still worried about all that sun exposure, but the woman she was appreciated the view.

He came up and shook his head, droplets dispersing like she wished her problems would. As if sensing her regard, he looked her way. His smile was white and maybe just the tiniest bit smug.

Careful, Tess. He'll break your heart.

But of course Teague wouldn't. That damage had already been done.

CHAPTER SIX

GRIFFIN PROPPED his feet on the rail at Captain Crow's and sipped from the cardboard cup in his hand. The restaurant didn't serve breakfast, but the prep cook made a pot of coffee in the mornings, and this morning Griffin had made friends with the prep cook. The guy had left for an emergency onion run, giving Griffin privacy and a place to start the day away from the eagle eye of the little dictator.

He still clung to his one and only plan in regards to Jane: avoid her as much as possible—and completely avoid what she wanted him to do.

After moving in two days before, she'd kept mostly to the guest room she'd selected. Though he'd continued blasting music through his earbuds, her close proximity seemed to punch through the wall of sound. He'd felt her presence, the capable and unwavering energy she exuded, despite the beams and plaster between them. She'd brought into his house a new scent too, a light and feminine fragrance that somehow pierced the Pacific's own salty-green perfume.

At dinner that first night, while he'd manned the barbecue and stayed out of range of the conversation between her, his family and Old Man Monroe as much as possible, he'd still been able to chronicle the effect she had on them. She'd managed to surprise a laugh out of his sister, unearth a set of jacks to amuse his nephews, put a book in the hands of his sulking niece and send their elderly neighbor home with a smile after a short stint holding the sleeping baby.

If he didn't keep up his guard, damn it, he had good reason to fear she'd manage to make him start the memoir.

He wasn't ready.

Closing his eyes, he swallowed another gulp of coffee. Caffeine was a necessity, because he was, as usual, sleeping like crap. That sweet Jane smell that had invaded his bungalow didn't help any. With every breath, he was reminded of her—the soft wave of her hair, the spiky darkness of the lashes surrounding her incredible eyes, the tender mouth.

The mouth that would keep on talking and talking and talking at him until she bent him to her will.

No. Wasn't going to happen, though he'd have to find some way to keep her mollified. Maybe he'd scratch a few nonsense words in a notebook or something.

Christ! As if that would satisfy the governess. She wasn't so gullible.

The certainty of that had him groaning aloud. He'd blown it by allowing her to move into No. 9. Dumbfounded by how she'd outmaneuvered him, he'd stayed silent. He could change that now, of course, throw her cute ass out of his place and out of the cove, but he was canny enough to realize she could serve a convenient function for him.

Be a beard, of sorts.

With her settled in his house, it gave the appearance he actually *was* settling into work. As he'd told Rex Monroe, that would keep Tess and company at bay. Better yet, it would appease his agent, who was fifty-one years old, overweight and took daily meds for high blood pressure and high cholesterol. Griffin knew he'd been worrying the guy, a formerly entrenched bachelor who had finally married seven years before and adopted his adoring wife's two small children. Guilt had finally gotten to him two days ago when Frank told him that Griffin's feet-dragging was sending him into a hypertensive state. Dealing with Jane on-site had seemed much more preferable than selecting a funereal spray.

So she was staying in one of the guest rooms and he was staying clear of her.

Except, as he took a deep breath, he could smell her again. Damn it! How did her scent reach him all the way here?

Then he realized, his eyes still closed, that *she* had reached him here. Literally. Once again, she'd broken into his solitude.

"What the hell do you want?" he growled, though he didn't need to ask the question. Everything she did was an attempt to make him mine his *feelings.* Those feelings that he so fucking did not have. She was here to round him up, rope him in and drag him back to the beach house, where she planned to stand over him all day. Likely with a whip.

"I, um, wanted to let you know I'm leaving now. I'll be gone until evening."

Surprise had him sitting up and blinking. Yes, it was Jane standing nearby, he hadn't been wrong about that, but she wasn't wearing her usual resolute expression. She looked, actually, a little unsure of herself.

Curse him for finding it kind of almost adorable.

And definitely curious.

He stared at her, taking in her outfit. It was a short-sleeved, stiff khaki shirtdress that sported a collection of pockets, grommets and zippers. "What's on your schedule for the day? Lion-taming?"

She laughed a little, and one foot moved to twine with

the other, causing his gaze to lower. Huh. The safari suit was paired with perhaps the silliest shoes he'd ever seen. Cork wedges were topped by khaki fabric printed with pink flowers. A paler pink ribbon was threaded through loops in the material and tied in a big bow at the top of her foot. They were…whimsical. A little weird. Very girlie. The complete opposite end of the spectrum from the tailored dress.

Business on top, and *oh, baby* on the bottom.

It made Griffin wonder how closely that described Jane herself. Scratch the professional surface, and what feminine fire might he find beneath? But he wasn't interested in digging for that, he reminded himself as he slouched lower in his seat, any more than he was interested in excavating his own emotions. What would he do with that fire anyway? As much as he hated to admit it, his sex drive had driven off, gone AWOL on him, sometime, somewhere, between Afghanistan and California.

Sure, he'd been a little fixated on Jane's mouth, and they'd shared that single sizzling kiss, as well as that almost torrid moment of awareness when Tess had arrived, but…but, fine, he could admit it to himself. He hadn't had a real, full-fledged, like-a-flagpole erection since before Randolph had come back from patrol drenched in Erica's blood.

As if sensing his disturbed thoughts, Jane made a nervous movement, tucking a strand of hair behind her ear. He frowned. She'd done something to take the wave out of it. It looked…restrained. Contained, like her tight expression.

"What's wrong, Jane?" he asked, sitting up again.

"I love my father!" she said, as if he'd accused her differently.

"Huh?"

She ran her palms along her hips and then picked at a nonexistent piece of lint on the starched cotton fabric. "I mean, he called and asked if I could come for a visit. I haven't seen him in a while, so I think I should go."

"Okay." Woo-hoo. A reprieve for ol' Griff, who had been devising ways to fend her off.

She narrowed her eyes at him. "But don't forget you're getting that delivery from Frank today. All the things you need to set up your home office."

"I can plug a few cords in." As if he would.

"So that's your goal for the day?" She regarded him with a disappointed expression, reminding him of Mrs. Melton, eighth-grade English, who'd thought that Griffin could write a better essay than "I Spent My Summer Vacation Eating Popsicles." He hadn't expected she'd actually appreciate "How I Almost Killed My Brother in August."

Jane crossed her arms over her chest. "I really think you could accomplish more. You *need* to accomplish more."

That bossy tone again. Back to General Jane. He scowled at her. "I *need* another cup of coffee," he said and got up to make that happen.

Once he'd topped it off from the carafe warming in the kitchen, he decided he also needed some sugar. That took him into a back storeroom, where he remembered seeing the dispensers that sat on the tables during operating hours. It smelled good in the small, shelf-filled space, an interesting combination of cinnamon and pepper. He decided to enjoy it along with his freshened beverage. *He* didn't have any place to be today.

Jane would be forced to take off without badgering him again.

Two minutes later, the door that he'd left half-shut creaked open.

"Don't close—" he started, but it was too late. George, the prep cook, had cautioned him that the storeroom door stuck sometimes. Sighing, he supposed this would be one of those times. "—the door."

Jane glanced back at it, then shrugged. Griffin did too. If anyone could circumvent the laws of physics, she could. "Look, I'm not trying to hound you," she said, resting her shoulders against the wood.

His eyebrow rose. "You have me cornered in a store-room. Maybe it's just the zookeeper dress, but you're coming on pretty strong, honey-pie."

"I just want something I can tell my dad." She bit her full lower lip. "He'll ask."

"About me?" Griffin shrugged again. "Tell him whatever. Progress is being made."

That out-of-character anxiousness was back on her face. "I'm a terrible liar."

Likely true. So far, he'd been able to read her with ease. Except he didn't understand why she'd feel compelled to report to her father regarding Griffin's memoir. "Why would your dad be interested in what I'm doing?"

"Because it's what *I'm* doing. Because you're my client." She made an offhand gesture. "Success is the only option."

There was nothing offhand about those words, Griffin thought. A direct quote, he suspected, and something Governess Jane had absorbed to the marrow of her bones. No wonder she carried an invisible whacking ruler on her small, starchy person.

Hadn't she implied the man was some sort of re-searcher?

My father always says I have no head for science.

It got to him, the idea of someone passing judgment on her. Without thinking, he set his coffee aside and stepped nearer. He put his hands on her shoulders and felt their rigidity. His thumbs circled. "Honey-pie, don't go pinning your self-worth on what some man says or does. Or doesn't say or do. You can't depend on 'em."

Her laugh was short. "Don't I know it."

There was bitterness there. Hurt. For a moment, just a flick of a second, the impulse to ride to her rescue flooded him. An urge to take care of her by shoring up all her fragile places.

God knew he had no business acting on it and that he'd disappoint her if he tried. He wasn't made for it—he was too selfish and too detached. *Step back,* he told himself. *Step back now.*

Before he could act, however, she circled his wrists with her small hands. She looked up, her smile lopsided. "Just get started, will you, Griffin? For your own sake."

It wasn't the lopsided smile. It wasn't that soft mouth of hers that still seemed pinker due to her sunburn from two days before. It was the orders that always came out of it and how desperate he was to silence them.

He slid his hands from her shoulders to her face.

She blinked. "Griffin, I'm serious. The work has to be—"

"Shh." He was tired of her talk, talk, talk.

She tried shifting away. "Griff—"

"Stop." His voice hardened. "Stop moving. Be quiet for a moment and be still."

To his amazement, she did. Her eyes widened, her body froze, her breath caught. Had no one ever taken charge of *her?*

Though his sudden power over her was heady, it didn't completely explain his next crazy impulse. "Now let me kiss you," he said, and then he did just that, bending his head to press his mouth to hers. And *pow,* there it was, the sweet blast of heat he'd tasted that Party Central night in his laundry room, when he'd been pissed at Rick and then pissed at himself for stirring up trouble with Jane.

And, oh, yeah, that Jane-trouble was back. Unexpected, though, because it was as if all the starch had gone out of her when he'd taken control. *Be still. Now let me kiss you.*

She was pliant now, her hands falling from his wrists to dangle at her sides. Her head dropped back, and the action opened up those soft lips, giving his tongue entry. She sighed against his mouth, all her defenses gone for the moment as he pressed closer, his body crowding hers.

Again, she didn't protest. A shudder went through her, and he felt it along his chest, along his thighs. He drew his mouth away from her lips, heard her little moan of protest but ignored it to explore the silken heat of her cheek and then the small shell of her ear. He tongued the lobe, felt her breath catch, and then she lifted her hands to grab his waist.

In the small room, their breaths turned loud. The sound was urgent, as urgent as the desire starting to fire in his blood. His mouth found hers again, almost feeding on it, and then his hands went wild, sliding over the crisp fabric of her dress, seeking a way to touch more of her flesh. Frustrated by all the metal apparatuses his fingers found, he slanted his head to take her deeper and yanked at the fabric of her skirt, lifting it to bare the warm backs of her thighs.

She jerked into his palms as he stroked upward. "Shh, shh, shh," he said against her mouth, soothing her, even as the hem rose higher with his wrists. His palms cupped the round globes of her ass over her panties.

Making a noise deep in her throat, she melted against him once more. It lit him up, his blood burning hot and thick, chugging a fire line southward. Causing that heavy, tightening sensation that he'd not experienced in months and months and months. Too long.

Desperate, desperately glad, he slid his hands under the fabric so they were palms to cheeks.

And with that, he was fully erect.

Sweet, sweet mercy. He buried his face in the curve of her neck and shoulder, breathing in that flowery Jane-scent, reveling in the goodness of escalating desire and a solid cock.

The notion that he hadn't, after all, lost this.

The librarian was moving into him now, her pelvis grinding against his stiff shaft, a cute little stand-up lap dance that almost had his rocket launching. But they were in a storeroom. Alone at the moment, but only because of an impromptu onion run. Still, she was eager and he was hard and who could argue against that combination?

His mouth found hers again as he tried weighing the pros and cons of taking this all the way. But his brain was sluggish, what with all the blood his erection—thank God!—was putting to its own use. The decision had to be deferred, he thought, reluctantly sliding his tongue from her mouth. If they'd been near a bed, he knew good sense wouldn't have stood a chance, but they were in that store-room. And an onion run wouldn't last forever.

"Jane," he murmured against her cheek. "Jane, I think we'd better stop."

Her flesh was feverish against his lips. "No."

"I understand." He kissed her mouth. "But, Jane—"

She found his mouth with hers, and her small hands tightened on the sides of his shirt. Maybe it had been a long time for her too, because there was a frantic quality in the thrust of her tongue, the clutch of her hands, the rhythmic pulse of her hips against his.

Flexing his fingers on the globes of her ass, he told himself to be sensible. With a mighty effort, he tore his mouth away. "We have to stop."

"No." Her eyes closed, she rubbed against him, harder, and her lips lifted, seeking his once more.

He evaded her and firmed his voice. "Yes, Jane. I'm saying we stop."

His implacable tone finally got through to her. She froze, and then silver eyes blinked up at him. Her mouth was swollen from his kisses. And from the beginnings of a pout.

He squeezed her bare ass, knowing he would have an aching regret over this for the rest of the day. "You have places to go, remember?" Then, while she was still compliant—because, really, how long could that last?—he succumbed once again to whim and drew her panties down her legs. For a moment they ringed her ankles, a transparent confection of pale pink ruffles. *Oh, sweet Jesus.* Before he pulled her to the concrete floor right then and there, he hunkered down to help her step out of them.

He rose with the ruffles in his hand. "But I don't mind if you leave a little something behind."

She blinked a couple more times, clearly coming out of a sexual daze. "That's my underwear," she said, staring at the little pile of filmy stuff in his palm. Her gaze lifted to his. "Griffin, I'm going to see *my father.*"

In a quick move he stuffed the souvenir in his front pocket, adjusting his erection at the same time. That sign of renewed life made him grin at her, unrepentant. Not only had he found his sexuality again, but he also thought he'd struck upon a way to handle the little librarian who was trying to rock his world. "Have a good time, honey-pie."

CHAPTER SEVEN

FEELING AS HARRIED and anxious as she always did at the prospect of meeting with her father, Jane hurried toward his tri-level executive home. It was boxy and officious-looking, with a flat roofline and dark-tinted windows. A short barbered hedge bordered the brick front pathway bisecting the small patch of grass meticulously cut by the housing association's gardeners to her father's exacting standards. There was a groundskeeper sweeping the bricks at this very moment—Corbett Pearson didn't allow the whine of leaf blowers within the range of his hearing.

She smiled at the gardener in passing, then reached the front door and pressed the bell. There was a house key back at her apartment, but even if she'd had it with her, she wouldn't have used it. Her father didn't appreciate such liberties.

He opened the door, and his chilly gaze swept over her. "Jane," he said. "You look a bit...feverish."

Oh, damn. She thought she'd managed to counteract her flushed state with the air-conditioning set on High during the entire ride over. Damn Griffin! But she couldn't think about him *and* handle her father. "I'm fine, Dad," she said, stepping closer to place a kiss on his cheek. "You're looking well."

He was in his version of casual clothes, meaning he'd gone for a pair of knife-creased khakis instead of the steely-gray slacks he preferred to wear to work. And instead of a white dress shirt, he wore a blue one with the palest and thinnest of olive stripes. Jane had given it to him for Christmas, and she was absurdly pleased to see he had it on.

"Your brothers are here," he said, leading her in the direction of the large family room at the rear of the house. "We're watching baseball."

"Oh, yay," Jane murmured. "All the guys."

Byron and Phillip were seated on the heavy leather sofa placed before the large-screen TV. They didn't look up from their laptops as she entered the room and made only vague gestures with their nontapping fingers as she bussed the top of each of their heads. They were gorgeous creatures, the both of them, but like every Pearson male, no one could call them multitaskers. She glanced at her dad. "You're playing fantasy baseball again this year?"

He'd positioned himself in front of his own computer, set on the bar in the corner of the room. As usual, keeping his distance. "What?" he asked, looking up from the small screen. "Oh, baseball. Yes."

None of them were actually watching the game on the TV. They didn't like sports in the least. Their fantasy league was a statistical challenge the three of them enjoyed. They had bets and side bets and counter bets that were used as mental one-upmanship. Ignoring Jane, they made cryptic remarks to each other as they focused on the computer models they'd probably designed themselves to maximize their chances of winning.

Accustomed to the drill, Jane crossed to the adjoining kitchen and helped herself to a mug of coffee and one of the sweet rolls—possibly her father's only weakness— on the counter. Then she took them both over to the bar and slid onto the stool beside the older man.

"So, Dad," she said. "I'm here."

He continued tapping at his keyboard. "Yes."

Stifling her sigh, she tried again. "You asked me over?"

With a grimace, he hit a key, then turned to his sons. "That was an excellent trade, Phillip." His tone was grudging.

Her brother only grunted at the compliment.

Jane actually sighed this time. What a collection of cavemen.

"I wanted to know about your new job," her father said, half turning on his stool as he finally deigned to address her. "How are you managing with this new author?"

Speaking of Neanderthals... Jane felt a burn crawling up her throat as her mind flashed to Griffin again, and she fingered the brass button fastening her collar closed. Where the heck had that kiss come from, and why the heck had she...well, she'd stood still for it! Remembering her instant surrender was mortifying.

"Jane?"

She cleared her throat. "It's a nonfiction work. A memoir, actually."

"I was asking about the author, not the project," her father remarked. "You know, after the situation with Ian—"

"There's no need to discuss Ian," Jane put in.

"But I still don't understand how you could end that association," Corbett said, frowning. "He seemed to find you talented, and he himself is such a star in publishing that it was foolish of you to—"

"It was time for a change," Jane said. Though, good Lord, taking on Griffin was turning into its own potential disaster. She could feel the imprint of those kisses on her lips, the heat of his hands on her bare flesh. No previous relationship had prepared her for her incendiary response. He likely thought she was easy pickings now. Squirming on the stool, she tried redirecting both her thoughts and the conversation. "What have you been up to, Phil? Byron, how's Caitlyn enjoying her new job?"

He scowled at his laptop. "Caitlyn who?"

Really? "Your girlfriend of three years?"

"Ah. We broke up."

"By!" Jane surged from her stool to take a seat next to her older brother. "I'm sorry. How are you feeling?"

The warm sympathy in her voice appeared to snag his attention. He actually turned his head to gaze at her. "I'm feeling…busy? That's why she broke it off. I have this project that demands a lot of my attention, and she didn't like sharing me with a slide rule, she said, which is ridiculous, because I haven't used a slide rule since I was six and Dad showed us how to do logarithms."

Jane could only sigh. "Oh, Byron."

"I for one think it's good he found out how flighty she is now," their father said. "Before he married the woman."

"Flighty!" Jane protested. Caitlyn had been perfectly nice and had stuck by sensitivity-challenged Byron for years.

Her brother nodded. "She was making rules. No computer at the dinner table."

"You're all hopeless," Jane murmured.

Phil glanced over. "I heard that. I also heard that the real reason Ian Stone's not your client is because the two of you no longer have a romantic attachment."

"Jane!" her father said, disapproval written all over his face. "Is that true? If I'd known you were treading down that path I would have counseled you on the foolishness of mixing the professional and the personal. Your career is much more important than a romance."

She glared at the tattletale in the family. Avoiding a lecture against having a love life was why she didn't tell her father who she dated. "It's water under the bridge, Dad.

Ian and I were done months ago. I've got the new client now." Who was already muddying the waters with another unwise professional-personal mix. She pressed the heels of her hands against her throbbing temples. What was she going to do about it?

"Uh-oh," Byron said. "Jane's got that look on her face."

"What look?" she demanded. "I've got a headache."

"Yeah, the same headache you had when you wanted that kid who lived next door—what was his name...Ed?— to ask you to your prom. It's your love headache. Are you getting silly and emotional with your new client too?" His voice took on an annoying elder-brother teasing slyness. "Does he find you lovable, little sis?"

Silly and emotional. He'd picked that up from their father, Jane thought, now glaring in Byron's direction. It was true that when the Pearson men ate meals they rarely paid attention to the plate and were instead engrossed with their work. Which meant there had been plenty of opportunity in those many years they'd lived together for her to have slipped poison into her brother's mashed potatoes. Damn her for the oversight.

Her father rose, yet another frown on his face. "What's this, Jane?" Corbett came to stand before her, his austere good looks making his expression appear only more critical. "I don't pretend to understand why you chose this field, but in any case, you need to think like a professional."

"Dad—"

"Just direct your attention to doing your job, my girl." He pointed a bony finger at her, the same one that he'd used to point out the errors in her geometry proofs. The sigh he released was the same too. "It goes without saying...."

But he would, she thought, bracing for it.

"It's much better to be competent. You can't count on people, Jane. You can't count on people or the strength of their emotional attachments. So it's much better to be competent than lovable." His frown deepened. "You hear me?"

"Yes, Dad, I hear you." After a minute, she stood to brush another kiss against his cheek. "Thanks."

And the gratitude was sincere. What had been silly and emotional of her was dreading this visit, she decided. Her father's disapproval never failed to motivate her in some manner or other and now was no different. She was going to put the incident in the storeroom with Griffin into perspective. And in the past. It was a brief lapse of judgment best forgotten. She'd direct her attention to doing her job. That was clearly the best way forward. When she returned to the cove, she'd be refocused on business and absolutely immune to any further physical entanglements.

Tess sat on one of four cushioned chairs gracing the small porch that overlooked the ocean at Beach House No. 8. She pretended she wasn't spying on Teague White, who was back on the sand. She couldn't see the Tee-Wee in him; there was no residual sign of small and scrawny in his tall, muscled form. "Big and brawny," she murmured aloud, then, guilty, glanced around to ensure she was alone.

But she was. Alone.

The three older kids were inside the bungalow. Russ, ensconced in the matching lounge chair, was out like a light, curled in a ball on the seat pad. The ocean air and play in the sand had exhausted him. As was his wont, the baby had pulled his blanket around him until he looked like nothing more than a small pile of lightweight fleece.

Squelching another tiny flare of guilt, Tess glanced back at Teague.

He was looking her way. Their eyes met.

Her ego argued with her conscience. If she waved at him, he'd come over; she could see the truth of that on his handsome face. Then he'd flirt a little. Maybe ask her to run away to Arizona again.

Make her feel like a woman, not a wife set aside by her husband.

Pulse speeding up, Tess stood, then crossed the short distance to the rail. She started to raise her left hand, then paused as her wedding set caught the sunlight. On their tenth anniversary, David had given her another ring to wear with her simple gold wedding band. The one-carat solitaire was surrounded by a circle of smaller diamonds. He'd said it reminded him of the brightness of the stars on the night she'd agreed to marry him.

"Tess?"

She whipped around, stumbling so that the small of her back smacked the wooden railing. "David?" Had she conjured him up? Because it was definitely her husband, dressed in business attire, the sun picking out threads of red and gold in his short brown hair. "What are you doing here?"

He frowned. "We made a deal when we signed up Duncan and Oliver for summer soccer. I take them to practices."

She glanced at her watch. "You're early." Even with the traffic he would run into, there was plenty of time. It annoyed her that he'd come now, when he wasn't expected, yet had stood her up two days before. The feeling turned to sarcasm in her throat. "I thought you were so very, very busy."

David's jaw tightened. "I texted you about that. I had

a lunch meeting already in place—yes, I know it was a Sunday, but I couldn't get out of it and you didn't give me enough notification to make other arrangements."

"Arrangements, schmarrangements," she muttered, aware she sounded no more mature than Rebecca. But he could have gotten away if he'd wanted to! He was the head of the accounting department at one of L.A.'s largest and most prestigious talent agencies, Wallis-Downs. That's how they'd met. She'd been on her way to the parking lot following a meeting with her agent. He'd been coming in the door, putting them on a collision course that had landed Tess on her butt with David standing over her.

You're her, he'd said, like Teague had yesterday, recognizing the *OM* girl.

"You're something," he said now, his voice tight. "Upset about where I've been or not been when you're the one who left our home."

You left our marriage! she wanted to shout at him. Sometime when Russ was not long out of newborn-sized diapers, David had left behind his husband and father responsibilities. He used to be so good at them too, coaching Rebecca's rec league basketball team every winter, every Sunday taking a parade of neighborhood kids along with his own to the park down the street. Then, all of a sudden he'd traded those in for weight lifting at the gym and an obsession with spin classes.

Tess's gaze dropped to his favorite cordovan loafers, then moved up to take in the slacks and dress shirt she'd bought him just weeks ago, following the loss of those fifteen pounds he'd been complaining about for years. There was a stain on his necktie, and habit had her stepping forward, ready to sponge it clean. But she forced herself back against the rail.

His eyes narrowed at the movement. "What's going on, Tess?" he said. "When the hell are you coming back?"

He was supposed to sound as miserable as she felt. Not demanding and defensive. "What's wrong with Crescent Cove?" she asked.

"There's nothing wrong with our house. And it's our wedding anniversary next month. I thought you wanted a big party."

That was when she'd still been able to convince herself they had something to celebrate. "I don't think that's such a good idea anymore."

"Because I missed lunch?"

"The boys wanted to see you. No matter where we are, they're still your kids."

"Of course they're my kids," he ground out. Then he huffed a sigh and dropped onto the chair she'd vacated. "I talked to them when I came in. They didn't look up from their Legos. Rebecca was too busy texting to enter into a conversation. How are they?"

The question sounded rote. Or resigned. Tess closed her eyes. "Rebecca seems to be tolerating her mornings at summer school." In the old days she would have told David about their daughter's threat to get pregnant. They would have groaned and laughed together over another episode in what they'd labeled "Teen Theater." But talk of teen pregnancy seemed too awkward a topic right now.

"And the boys?"

"They made buddies with a pair of cousins on vacation up the beach."

David nodded, then scanned the sand and the nearby houses. Tess followed his gaze, though she skipped over the firefighters who were gathering on either side of a volleyball net. "What number did we honeymoon in?" he asked.

A pang stabbed Tess's heart. She'd told herself she had come to Crescent Cove because Griffin was here, but was it really something else? Had she hoped to recapture the magic of those three days and nights following their courthouse marriage? That's all they'd been able to afford, since David had been adamant about saving for a down payment on a house. He'd been so serious, eight years her senior, already settled in his career. She'd been nineteen, unfazed by the brushes with celebrity she'd had as a commercial actress, native Los Angeleno that she was, but simply dazzled by the look on a particular man's face.

Dazzled by him.

You're her, he'd said that morning in the glitzy Century City office building. He'd been in a suit and tie then too, his brown hair cut business-short, his features regular yet unremarkable. But his eyes…oh, his eyes had made Tess quiver, their color a golden whiskey-brown that only little Russ had inherited. Her other children claimed the baby was her favorite, and, like every good mother, she denied it, but his eye color was definitely her favorite, because it was his daddy's eyes that looked out from her smallest boy's face.

"What's that guy doing?" David suddenly rose, then stalked to the rail.

"What? Huh?"

"There's a guy over there on the volleyball court staring at us. Staring at *you*."

Tess pretended she didn't know who he was talking about and glanced over her shoulder. "Oh," she said, shrugging, "that's little Tee-Wee White. We knew him when we were kids. I think Gage put him upside down in a garbage can the first day he showed up on the beach."

David grinned at that, looking more like the man she'd

married. "Speaking of Gage…have you heard from him lately? Is he okay?"

"Griffin says so. He's the one I'm worried about…." Tess frowned, letting that thought die off. In the old days, she would have discussed this with David too. Her concern over how her brother wasn't coping with his year's experience in Afghanistan. But her husband had turned away from her now, and she didn't feel like talking to his back.

She'd spent too much time at their home in Cheviot Hills talking to his back.

"He's still staring," David muttered.

Tess gazed at the stretch of her husband's shoulders beneath the smooth poly-cotton—light starch, she always told the dry cleaner—wider now that he'd become a dedicated gym rat. "I'm thinking of getting back into commercials," she said.

The sudden turn in conversation had him spinning. "What?"

"I've been thinking about it a lot. I could do it. You know my agent calls me up twice a year—"

"Your agent! I never liked him when he worked at Wallis-Downs. He's worse now that he's on his own. That dirty old man calls you up twice a year just so he can drool—or worse—to the sound of your voice."

"Ew!" She glared at him. "That is not true." And his derision only made her more determined to pursue the idea.

David appeared to read the intention on her face. "Who would watch the kids?"

He wouldn't, she thought. "Day care. A nanny, maybe." David wanted distance from her and their children. He'd proved it, with all those weekend work lunches, all those spin classes and bench presses. Then conscience pricked her a little, because he was here, after all, to take Duncan and Oliver to soccer.

"Did you tell the boys to track down their shin guards and cleats?" she asked, her voice warmer, because he had followed through on his promise.

"Yeah." David nodded. Hesitated. "But could you pick them up afterward, Tess? There's this spin class I'd really like to make."

Again, her temper spiked but then was washed cool by a wave of chilly disappointment. She just stared at him, gritting her teeth to hold back her tears. *Where did you go? Where did my wonderful husband and dedicated family man go?*

She tried tracing back the change for the hundredth time. And then she had it. Maybe it took getting away from their home to see the situation clearly. The hinge was his fortieth birthday. Everything had seemed normal until then. They'd bickered over the usual stuff, of course, whether Rebecca planned too many sleepovers, whether they really needed that second fridge in the garage, but they'd still had those quiet moments when one or the other would look over and say, "I love you. You should know how much I love you."

Now Tess didn't know anything. The ocean breeze ruffled his hair. Maybe they should have it out now. She would put it to him, insist he tell her what was going on.

"Dah?"

Both their heads whipped toward the other occupied chair on the porch. Russ was sitting up in his nest of blanket, his whiskey eyes trained on his daddy. "Dah?"

Expressions chased themselves so fast across David's face that she couldn't catch a one of them. "Russ," he whispered. Then he looked over at Tess. "I've got to go. Don't want to be late to soccer."

In a blink he was gone, without another glance at their youngest child.

"Dah," Russ said, his voice rising to a wail.

Tess rushed to him, taking him into her arms for comfort. For both their comfort. "Sweet baby," she said against his soft hair as he snuggled close. His warm weight settled her unsteady heartbeat. "It's okay, it's going to be okay."

For her too, she decided. And it was okay David was gone. She was glad she'd lost the chance to grill him on the great change that had come into his life.

Because she was pretty sure she wasn't ready to hear the truth.

GRIFFIN DIDN'T flinch when Jane confronted him in the kitchen the morning following her visit to her father. He set down the newspaper and gave her his full regard. After that titillating exchange of kisses in the storeroom at Captain Crow's, he figured he knew exactly how to handle her when her badgering became unbearable. When she started nagging him about the writing and about his *feelings,* he had a simple strategy he could implement.

She'd had a day and a night to mull over what had happened between them, and about now he imagined she'd be very wary of any repeat of their lip-to-lip, skin-to-skin contact. Sure, there was definite chemistry between them, but he'd bet she didn't appreciate it in the least. As smokin' hot as they were together, she'd appeared bewildered by the subsequent sexual daze. To be honest, her sweet confusion had surprised him—and was yet another turn-on—but the dazzle would surely put up Jane's hackles.

The minute he started smoldering at her again, she'd go into full retreat. Giving him the upper hand.

He'd had many long, wakeful hours in the dark to convince himself of that conclusion. And to decide that he was right...the best way to keep her out of his head would be by coming on to her.

Her hands were on her hips and her eyes were narrowed. "What are you grinning like that for? Give me one good reason why you didn't do as you promised and set up your home office yesterday."

"You're cute when you're lecturing me," he said, ignoring her question. She was. She had on a prim little pale blue dress, the cotton dotted with sprigs of white flowers. Her flat shoes were white too, with a leather bow over the toes. "Tell me about your panties. Are they another pair with baby-doll ruffles? Or something different? I love those kind with a lot of cheek peek."

Her eyes rounded and her mouth dropped open.

My work here is done, he thought, lifting the newspaper again.

She snatched it from his hands and tossed it onto the counter behind her. "Let's go, buster," she said, grabbing his wrist and tugging him to his feet. "I almost broke my neck on the boxes when I came in the door last night."

With a grimace, he let her lead him out of the kitchen to the entryway. Okay, the delivery did pose a bit of a danger. Jane swiped up the carton that held computer paper, yellow notepads and packages of pencils and pens. Then she tucked a three foot by two foot whiteboard under her arm and turned her expectant gaze upon him.

The remaining boxes were bulky but not heavy, and he could watch her hips sway as he trailed her to the small room adjacent to the living area. Apparently she'd decided that space made the most sense as an office. It held a leather love seat, some bookshelves and had a desk positioned near the window overlooking the beach. At least he'd have something pretty to look at when he pretended to be writing.

"I don't usually do this kind of thing for an author," she said, perching on the love seat and beginning to tear open the package of dry-erase markers. "I'm not the office help, you know."

"Feel free to leave it to me," Griffin offered, setting the boxes on the desk. Getting her out of his hair was going to be even easier than he'd thought. "I'll let you know when I need your services."

"Why do I think that might be on a cold day in hell?" she asked, her voice dry.

He popped open the cardboard flaps of the laptop carton and then struggled to lift the sleek machine from its Styrofoam nest. "It might freeze over before I can get this damn computer free," he muttered.

"Let me help." She tossed down a package of pencils and walked over to grip the edges of the box. "Now pull."

She was close. Too close. He breathed in the fragrance of her shampoo and felt the radiating warmth of her small body. His muscles tensed. When he didn't move, she glanced up. It brought her mouth close. Too close.

They stared at each other.

"We should talk," she suddenly said.

And just as suddenly, Griffin didn't want to. The subject would be the kissing and caressing of the day before. Knowing Jane, her type of "talk" would be to dissect the event. The practical librarian in her would surely speak in terms of hormonal reactions and biological directives. Her governess tendencies would prod her to start spouting rule after rule and the consequences of breaking them.

Prompting Griffin to want to do just that very thing—break rules—as soon as possible.

His glance lowered from her silver eyes to her plump

mouth. He remembered the sweetness to be discovered inside of it. Her instant pliancy when he thrust against her tongue. The rush of blood to his cock, the first erection he'd managed in months.

He was half-hard again just thinking about it, and he didn't want to take away from that common miracle by getting all clinical.

Nothing she said could explain why he had her panties stuffed in the bottom of his right pocket at this very moment. And he didn't want to try justifying it to himself, either.

"My visit to my dad's house brought something to mind," Jane continued. "I'm...I'm worried about your niece."

The non sequitur—at least to his train of thought—rocked Griffin back on his heels. He'd been obsessing about hot kisses and hard-ons and she was thinking about his family?

He yanked the Styrofoam-and-laptop sandwich free of the box. "Not my problem," he growled. Jane was his problem! Her maddening, confounding, unpredictable ways. Buttoned up on top, oh-baby on the bottom. Mouth made for sin, mind bent on meddling.

"You see," Jane persisted. "Rebecca—"

"Why don't you go away now?" he said, stopping her before she got going. "I'll take care of the rest."

She blinked at him. "What's the matter with you?"

He considered smoldering at her, but he thought it wiser to refrain from its overuse. Instead, it would be his tactic of last resort. So he blew out a breath and made some lame excuse about not getting enough a.m. caffeine.

At least she returned to the love seat and continued tearing into the packages of office supplies, giving him a little more breathing room. His gaze wandered out the window. From here he could see his sister under a beach umbrella, that littlest kid of hers playing with plastic blocks on a blanket. The hoodlums-in-the-making were running in circles, chasing each other with clumps of dripping seaweed.

Huh. Maybe he should show them where Rex Monroe parked his car.

Then his niece wandered into his line of sight, dressed in a bikini top with a sarong wrapped around her narrow hips. Her slow movements and put-upon expression made clear she was dragging the heavy weight of teen martyrdom behind her.

Not my problem.

They were all going to grow up one day, from the one who smelled like diaper wipes to the girl with the grumpy face, and make choices or take orders that would put them in harm's way. He couldn't stop that. All he could do was separate from them so whatever happened couldn't hurt him.

Hell, the hoodlums, now belly-crawling on the beach in pursuit of some poor unsuspecting seagull, probably wouldn't make it to twelve.

Not my problem.

"Of course, all girls go through a rebellious stage," Jane said from the other side of the room. "It's not unusual, but…"

"Yeah?" *All girls go through a rebellious stage?* He glanced back at her. "Does that include you? What, you went a morning without flossing? You, gasp, once let your library books go overdue?"

"I would never do that!" She made a face at him. "The library was right next door to my school, so it was easy to return them by the due date."

The little egghead had probably gone to some hoity-toity private school where each student was assigned a private SAT tutor and college essays were critiqued by retired admissions officers. "Where'd you graduate from? Smarty-pants Prep?"

She was focused on picking at the shrink-wrap covering the notepads. "My brothers were homeschooled. I attended the regular public school three blocks away."

Weird. "What? Your parents thought they needed the extra attention and you didn't?"

She made a sound that was suspiciously like a snort. "My brothers have genius IQs. They excel in math and the sciences. When I didn't show an aptitude for those particular subjects…"

My father always says I have no head for science, Griffin remembered.

"…Dad decided the public school was plenty good enough for me."

"Ouch," he said.

Her eyes didn't meet his. "I received a very good education, actually."

"Just not the same one as your brothers."

She shrugged. "I'm not like my brothers at all."

He turned to lean his back against the desk. Because she still wasn't looking at him he had the opportunity to study her face—the gentle curve of her lashes, the generous pillows of her lips. Another arrow of heat shot toward his groin, and he thought of that origami bundle of her panties just inches from his cock. He groaned.

Her gaze shot up. "What's the matter?"

"Uh…" His mind scrambled for some intelligent remark. "Rebellion?" Hadn't they started with that? "You rebelled because you were different than your brothers?"

She shrugged again. "I don't really know. I just think it's important to pay attention to girls Rebecca's age. The impulse to rebel is natural, but they can get into actual trouble if no one's watching."

Griffin pictured the governess as a young teen, as one of their pack of Crescent Cove summer kids. She would have been as big as a gnat and as annoying as one even then. He could see it. A little dab of a thing with those eerie eyes and that puffy mouth. Gage would have bet his twin he could steal a kiss from her first.

Griffin wouldn't have let that happen.

"What kind of trouble did you get into, Jane?" he asked idly, still imagining. There would be a bonfire, and he'd have drawn her just outside its glow, lowering his head to—

"I ran away from home at thirteen. Left L.A. and made my way to San Francisco."

The words jerked him out of his reverie. "What?" he squawked. He couldn't fathom it. "Jesus, Jane." It shook him up to think of it. And he fucking hated being shaken up.

"It's actually kind of a funny story."

His gut didn't believe that for a moment. "I've got to hear this."

She rose from the love seat and paced toward the desk and window. Her gaze took in the ocean view. Griffin took in the clean lines of her profile and the soft wave of her sandy hair. "I decided to take a road trip. I had some babysitting money I used for bus fare."

A shudder worked its way down his spine. Thirteen years old and alone at the Los Angeles bus station. The stuff of any thinking person's nightmares. "Why San Francisco?"

"My mother was from the area. I think I missed her."

"What? She was visiting there?"

"She was dead." Jane turned her head to look at Griffin, her silver eyes mirroring no emotion. "She died when I was a baby."

His hand squeezed into a fist, echoing the sudden tightness in his chest. "Oh, this whole story's hilarious," he said.

"Wait. It gets funny!"

He had good instincts. This was not going to get funny. But she looked so sincere, he couldn't say it aloud. "Tell me when I should start laughing."

"Right about when I changed my mind and turned around and took the very next bus back to Southern California."

He felt some relief at that. Apparently she'd avoided drug traffickers and slave traders. "Go on."

"When I got back to my house…there was nobody home."

Oh, Jesus. "Tell me your family was out searching for you."

"No." She shook her head. "The boys were attending NASA summer camp. I guess my dad thought I was staying with a friend, and he went off on his own research trip. The house was all locked up."

He stared at her. "Is this the funny part?"

She actually laughed. "Yes. I had to run away, but when I went back home, I had to break into my own house. The irony!"

"I don't think that word means what you think it means."

Her eyebrows came together in a frown. "Of course it does. What I just described is situational irony—when the outcome is contrary to expectation. It's all about the reversal, see. I ran away, but when I went back, it was as if, instead, my father ran—"

Shaking his head, he took her face in the palms of his

hands. Her words sputtered out. Her silver eyes lifted to his. It was the storeroom at Captain Crow's all over again. The laundry room, when he'd first been compelled to kiss her. There was just something *about* this woman.

He was smoldering at her. Without even trying. Without even *wanting* to.

His mouth descended toward hers. She stayed where she was, pliant as before, caught in the heat between them. Before he could touch down, she broke free.

Her feet actually scrabbled on the hardwood floor in the hallway. Sighing, he watched her go. Damn woman. Damn, damn woman.

His tactic had been proved to work. He supposed he could feel some satisfaction in that. Going sexy on her had sent her on the run. He'd gotten her out of the room.

But…she'd still made her way under his skin.

The irony!

CHAPTER EIGHT

SHOVING ASIDE a deep reluctance, David Quincy marched down the path that would lead him to the place where his wife had run on her escape from their home. On her escape from him.

After five days without her, he'd come to the conclusion that it only made sense to initiate a calm, reasonable discussion about their situation. He blew out a long breath of air and allowed himself a moment's pause. Tess might ask him to give up her and the kids. Considering the possibility stabbed his gut like a dull knife, but he was a by-the-numbers realist. It's what her absence was leading to, wasn't it? And if that was indeed what she asked of him, he'd find a way to grant her request.

After all, not long ago he'd come to the realization that he didn't deserve any of them.

They'd manage without him, of course. The bigger kids were consumed with their own pursuits. Baby Russ was fine too. Though David hadn't held his smallest son since the day of his fortieth birthday, he appeared to be thriving.

His black dress shoes sank into soft sand. Immediately, grains made their way between his socks and the leather insole. He accepted the petty discomfort with his usual stoicism. Sure, he should have worn something more casual than his business clothes, but he'd been sitting at his desk, staring at spreadsheets without seeing a single column when he'd made the sudden decision to visit.

Looking toward the surf, David caught sight of his daughter. Stretched belly-down on a beach blanket, she wore bug-big sunglasses and was up on her elbows, her nimble thumbs tapping, engrossed in the modern teenager's version of talking drums. It seemed just yesterday she'd been wearing princess tiaras and dipping her digits in finger paints. In a skimpy bikini and with her mother's long legs, she appeared almost full-grown.

Past the need for him.

Her head turned his way, and a smile stretched her mouth, her straight white teeth beautiful. Still, nostalgia squeezed his heart as he remembered those long months when she'd come home from every orthodontist appointment with different colored bands on her braces: orange and black at Halloween, red and green at Christmas, two different shades of blue that time he'd taken her himself.

She'd asked for her father's favorite color.

Now she jumped to her feet. "Dad!" she cried, waving.

He crossed the beach, the soft sand slowing his steps and helping him maintain his newly developed detachment. "How are you, honey?" he asked her. "How was school this morning?"

"I don't know why I'm wasting any of my summer vacation in a classroom."

"The honors history seminar will look good on your college apps."

Rebecca made a face. "Now you sound like Mom. I thought you were on my side. You told her I should get to enjoy my time off."

He hesitated. When they were living in the same house and before his fateful fortieth, it seemed as if the mom-versus-dad debate was perfectly acceptable. But when he and Tess were living in separate places, he figured they should show a united front in things like this. The dull ache in his belly sharpened as he thought about custody again.

It wouldn't surprise him if Tess asked to have the kids 24/7—and he'd grant her wish, of course.

"Dad?"

He cleared his throat. "Mom wants you to maximize your chances and your choices. I can't argue with that."

Especially because he wondered whether Tess's insistence on it was a reflection of her dissatisfaction with what she herself had done post high school. Instead of college or career, she'd married David and devoted herself to him and their children. Was she regretting that now?

She'd left their home. Clearly she was regretting *him*.

The sound of shrieking kids drew his attention up the beach. High-stepping through the surf, all knobby knees and elbows, their skin a golden tan, his oldest sons were racing toward him. Their exuberant expressions were testament to the pleasure they were finding at Crescent Cove.

They probably didn't miss home—or him—at all.

"Dad!" Duncan skidded to a stop in front of him, while Oliver's momentum had him slamming into David. He scaled his father's body like a monkey.

David's arm automatically curved around his boy to steady him. "Hey, kids. What have you been doing?"

Duncan had a new sprinkle of freckles across his nose. "Dad, can I climb up that cliff?" He pointed to the high ragged bluff at the end of the cove. "I want to go up there and jump off like Uncle Griff."

Fear clutched at David's throat. "No!" Jesus. He couldn't bear the thought of something happening to one of his children. That's what had started all this. "It's too dangerous."

"Aah." His older son kicked at the sand. "That's what Mom says."

Relief loosened the stranglehold on his neck. "You listen to her."

"Jane says Uncle Griff's turning into a beach bum," Oliver announced, sliding free of his hold. "So I've decided that's what I'm going to be when I grow up."

"Jane?" David glanced at his daughter.

Rebecca tipped her head, her gaze shifting behind him. David turned to see a quietly pretty young woman walking their way, Russ on her hip, the little guy's head on her shoulder.

The dread he'd been carrying around since his wife and kids had left home redoubled. "Has Mom hired a nanny?" Was Tess already moving on with her life? He understood it was his own actions that had driven her to it, but the idea of actually losing her was still difficult to bear.

"She's not a nanny," Rebecca said. "She's working with Uncle Griff."

"Though childcare experience comes in handy in that capacity too," the woman said as she approached, giving him a wry smile. "I'm Jane Pearson."

He held out his hand. "David Quincy."

At the sound of his voice, baby Russ's head shot up and his body twisted in Jane's hold. "Dah!" he yelled, reaching toward David with chubby arms.

David moved back. "Where's Mom?" he asked Rebecca, ignoring another bellowing "Dah!"

His daughter took her smallest brother onto her own hip, distracting him by swinging side to side. "She's having lunch with some man."

"Oh?" He tried to wipe any expression from his face, though that dull knife was carving at his entrails again.

"It's a business thing, she said," Jane added quickly.

David figured that meant he looked more pained than he had the right to be. "I'm sure."

"Really." She pointed in the direction of the restaurant up the beach. "At Captain Crow's."

Duncan and Oliver were already starting some little-boy game involving sand being scooped into the back of each other's swim trunks. Rebecca was dangling Russ's toes in the wet sand, causing him to squeal.

Jane was the only one still paying David any attention.

"I guess I'll go see if I can have a word with her," he said, already moving away from his kids. Every step felt like a mile, but he didn't falter. The distance from them was what he'd been working on for months. It was also what had pissed off Tess, but he figured it was the only way he could survive.

Love hurt so damn much.

He approached the restaurant from the side entrance. For a moment he was startled by his reflection in the plate glass windows. Less soft now, he looked more like his own father, Lawrence Quincy, a spare and stiff man who had seemed to regard his children like necessary but not-much-wanted accoutrements of modern life. David had not always admired that about him. Now he strove to emulate the emotional aloofness.

He caught sight of his wife, seated at a small table on the deck. Her back was to him, and across from her was a man in beach casual lightweight pants and a short-sleeved shirt—the kind of thing David had in his closet but rarely wore now that he was splitting all of his time between the office and the gym. Tess had her hair in one of those messy knots that appeared to have been put together in a moment and with one pin, but that he knew for a fact could take her up to thirty minutes to perfect.

It was a sexy look he'd always loved on her.

Apparently her companion felt the same, because he leaned forward and reached for the hand she had resting on the table. He covered it, a gesture so proprietary that David had to suppress the vicious urge to rip off the bastard's arm.

But he wouldn't, he promised himself, breathing deeply. The slick dude was the kind of man Tess should have married from the beginning. With a charming manner and affable smile, he would be able to schmooze a room instead of setting everyone to snoring with talk of commissions and expense sheets.

He and Tess had been a mismatch from the very beginning. She should have married another of the talent agency's famous clients instead of the guy who sat behind a desk perusing financial statements. Despite what was said in the press, not everyone in the entertainment business lacked morals.

And boring men who played with numbers all day could be the biggest fuck ups of them all.

As if she heard that thought, Tess turned, her gaze landing on him. Even from a deck away, her blue eyes stood out, and he was transported to that day fourteen years before. They'd collided in the entryway at work. With a sick feeling he'd watched her fly back, then fall to the floor.

He'd rushed to her side, horrified he'd hurt her and, worse, that he'd hurt *her*, the *OM* girl, who had some strange hold over the nation. He'd heard through the grapevine she'd just been booked on Leno, and here he might have broken her tailbone.

But she'd been laughing when he'd helped her up. Next thing he knew, his normally reserved self had insisted he buy her a cup of coffee. They'd walked down the street to the small sidewalk café where there were often sightings of celebrities that made it into *Star* magazine or episodes of *Entertainment Tonight*. He hadn't seen anyone but Tess.

She still captured his attention.

Her hand gestured him near. He threaded his way through the restaurant tables to stand beside her. "I was hoping you had a few minutes to talk," he said.

Her glance took in the empty plates on the table and then swept up to the man across from her. "Uh... Do you remember Reed Markov? He was the head photographer on the *OM* stuff, and—"

"—I call Tess about every two months, trying to convince her to get back in the business. I have the perfect project for her."

David narrowed his eyes. Sure. He knew exactly what kind of "perfect project" the other man had in mind. He recognized Reed now, remembered him from the early days of dating Tess.

"I wasn't sure the two of you were still together," Reed was saying.

David crossed his arms over his chest. "I recall you having trouble with that," he said. Another time, after they'd been married, Tess had invited the photographer to a cocktail party at their place. Reed had mentioned a perfect project then too, one that involved coaxing Tess to leave the house where she lived with her husband for a big bash in the Hollywood Hills that very night.

Classy guy.

The tension in the air, he figured, was what got Tess out of her chair. "Well, thank you, Reed. I'll be in touch."

Reed stood too. "I'd like to help you in any way I can, Tess." Then Mr. Perfect Project leaned over to kiss David's wife. On the mouth.

Maybe it was an air kiss gone awry. Maybe it was a casual kind of Hollywood farewell. Maybe a man who hadn't touched his wife's lips in months shouldn't object when they encountered those of someone else.

That man wasn't David.

His fingers curled into fists, and as the three of them walked across the deck together, a whirlpool of angry heat swirled in his belly. At the exit, Tess turned toward the beach while Reed started for the parking lot. David paused, looking between the two, his heart pumping the caustic burn through his system.

"Are you coming?" Tess asked.

"You go ahead. I just remembered something else I have to do." Then he quickened his stride and found Reed unlocking the door of his classic convertible. "Markov."

The other man leaned against the side of his vanilla-cream Mercedes. His expression no longer held any faux friendliness. "What?"

David got close enough to smell the garlic on his breath. "You have legitimate work for my wife, and if she's interested, fine. But if you pursue her in any other way, I'll tear your head off your body and roll it down the closest alley like a bowling ball."

He didn't wait for a response. Instead he stalked off, heading for his car and not his wife. There was no reasonable discussion to be had. No granting of requests. *To hell with all that!*

To hell with giving her a divorce.

He was a lousy husband and father, and just to prove it, he wasn't going to let his family go. He'd find a way to keep his distance, to keep himself safe from his crushing love for them, but seeing her with another man made it perfectly clear what David *wasn't* going to do.

He wasn't going to let Tess and Rebecca and the boys get away.

THAT EVENING, fog came to Crescent Cove about the same time that Griffin returned to Beach House No. 9 with Private at his heels. Jane heard the door open and shut and called out to him from her place on the love seat in the room that was the designated office.

The office that had been empty of its writer all day long—even though she'd rededicated herself to being all-business.

With that thought, she shot a guilty glance at the trash can beside the desk. At the bottom of it lay the bottle of skinny margarita she'd polished off. When the clock had read five, though she couldn't hear the blow of the conch shell up the beach, she'd decided a drink might smooth over her frustration. Some bikini must have left the partially full "diet" adult beverage behind, and she'd sipped at the lime-and-tequila concoction for the past three hours.

She might be a tiny bit tipsy.

And maybe even lonely. Her work often took her away from home, so she was accustomed to her own company, but tonight…tonight of all nights she wished she'd made arrangements to meet a friend or three.

She did have friends, good ones who had stood by her after the Ian debacle, but their sympathy too often seemed like pity. It was bad enough to feel like a fool without knowing other people considered you one as well. So she'd been declining invitations and keeping to herself for months, not realizing how alone she might come to feel.

Private's nails clicked on the hardwood as he rushed forward with a friendly greeting, pushing his face against her hand. Grateful for the canine enthusiasm, she stroked his head while sending his owner a baleful glance. The man was twelve hours late! He stood on the other side of the threshold, a dark shadow looming in the unlit hallway. "Griffin," she said, peering toward the gloom, "this morning you promised to be back right after lunch. It's dark out."

"My dog had to see a man about a horse," he said.

With a sigh, she ignored the absurdity of that and patted the leather seat beside her. Though the hour was late and she suffered from that slight inebriation, she might as well get some work out of him. That's why she was here, right? "Come sit down now, then. We can at least start thinking about progress."

His steps crossed the floor in the slow meter of a funeral dirge. He dropped to the cushion, and his weight bounced her a little, sending her head on a short woozy spin. When her brain settled, she saw he was sprawled in his seat, his head back, his eyes closed. She'd drawn the drapes against the evening dampness, and the lamp on the side table cast a glow across his face. It warmed his tan skin, but still she could see he was exhausted. Despite her bad mood, concern nibbled at the edges of her heart.

A chenille throw covered her knee-length full skirt and long-sleeved T-shirt, warding off the fog's chill. For a moment she considered tucking the soft fabric around Griffin and then encouraging him to drift into real sleep.

"Are you going to just stare at me in longing all night?" he asked, his eyes still closed.

Her sympathy evaporated, and the residual wooziness disappeared. "You wish," she replied, her voice brisk. "For your information, I was considering calling an embalmer. Frankly, you look ghastly."

"If you're phoning the undertaker, wouldn't that be 'ghostly'?"

Even his wisecrack sounded tired. "Don't you sleep?" she heard herself ask.

At the question, he opened his eyes, then shifted into a

more upright position. "Hey, it's not my fault your snoring registers decibels louder than a power mower."

"I do *not* snore."

"I can't tell you how many soldiers were convinced of the very same thing, honey-pie. But sure enough, come rack time they'd be sawing logs on the bunk beside mine."

She tilted her head. "How did you ever get any rest?"

"Pills. Prescription sleeping pills," he said, stretching his arms along the back of the love seat and closing his eyes again. "Don't look so shocked. Armies have always offered relief to soldiers in combat zones. General Washington gave his guys at Valley Forge rations of rum in an attempt to keep them calm and well rested."

She hadn't realized. "Are you still taking them?"

"No." His eyes opened, and then his gaze shifted away. "Not after—not anymore. Now I count grains of sand."

"Well, that's a task destined to keep you up all night," Jane said. She knew he had the TV going in his room that long, anyway. Since staying at his beach house she'd noted its low drone never subsided from when he went to bed in the evening until he went for coffee in the kitchen the following morning.

Obviously she hadn't been sleeping all that great either. Images kept popping up to disturb her. Griffin in his pirate gear. Griffin jumping off the cliff. His mouth as it descended toward hers in the laundry room. His hands on her in the storeroom at Captain Crow's. That same touch in this very room yesterday.

After that near-kiss, she'd run to No. 8 and played with Tess and the kids until sundown, while a series of warnings ran over and over in her mind. *Don't get involved with the client. It's bad for business. Don't get involved with the client. It's bad for you.* Then this morning, after giving herself another stern talking-to, it was Griffin who'd left, claiming an appointment he couldn't miss.

"But enough about me," he said, starting to rise.

Reaching over, she clamped a hand on his knee to push him back down. "Nice try. We can at least map out some page goals. Let me call up a calendar." Keeping one hand on him, she lifted her laptop from the side table and set it on her lap.

"Could you move up your hand a little bit?" he asked politely.

Already tapping on the keyboard, she didn't look away from the screen. "Sure—" she started, then she broke off and yanked her hand from his leg as if it was on fire. "Stop that."

He was trying to look innocent. "But you had this cute little frown right above your cute little nose. I was only trying to get a cute little hand job—you were so caught up you wouldn't even have noticed."

"Oh? You're that small?"

"Now you're just being insulting."

"So?" He was trying to run her off again, or at the very least distract her from her purpose. "What are you being when you pull stupid stunts like that?" Without waiting for an answer, she scooted closer, tilting the laptop so he had a better view of the screen. "Here's the next few weeks. Why don't we set targets—"

"I can't do this, Jane," Griffin said.

Anxiety gripped her stomach, which did not do good things to the margaritas still sloshing inside. If he came to the point where he flat-out refused to work instead of just doling out excuses, she'd have to face that she'd failed yet again. The flat of her palm pressed her roiling belly. Word would get around, would get back to her father, would have Ian Stone spreading icing on the cakes that were the stories he'd already told about her. "C-can't do what?"

"Can't look at the calendar on the screen. The angle's wrong and the light's crappy."

She let out a silent breath. "Oh. Okay." With the laptop set aside again, she reached for the briefcase at her feet and rummaged for the paper calendar she carried with her. It was smaller than a paperback book, and when she began fumbling through the pages to find the correct month, Griffin pulled it from her hand.

"What's the matter with you?" he asked, giving her a sharp look. His noninebriated self found the correct page right away.

It meant she had to cozy up closer to him so they could both see. As she moved, the throw slipped from her lap, but she let it fall, because she was warm enough now with her bare leg against the soft denim of Griffin's jeans and her shoulder pressed to his muscled one. This close, she could breathe in his scent, a citrus-and-sage smell.

Even without the cushion bounce she went woozy again. Was his a bar soap, she wondered, or was he a man who used body wash in his morning shower? In her mind's eye she could see him squeezing a liquidy gel into his big hand. Then he'd rotate his palms together, spreading the lubricious stuff around. Once coated, he'd smooth them along the sinewy length of his arms and legs she'd noted when he'd climbed the cliff at their first meeting. Next it would be another round of gel, another wet swirl of his palms, and finally he'd run them over his chiseled pectoral muscles and down the rippled abdominals she'd seen those times he'd been shirtless. After that, his hands would move lower, to that place she'd only felt...

"Jane?"

At the sound of his voice, she jumped, yanked from

the impromptu fantasy. Her face went red-hot. *Don't get involved with the client. It's bad for business. Don't get involved with the client. It's bad for you.*

She slid a glance at him. He was staring at her with those X-ray eyes of his.

"What?" Her defensive tone made her wince. "I mean, uh, what?"

"It's your birthday," he said, glancing at the booklet. "I didn't know."

She waved a hand, cursing herself for having written that onto today's square. Silly of her, really. *Silly and emotional.* "Why would you? It's no big deal."

He frowned. "Did you do something special today?"

"Besides waiting around for you to make an appearance?" And drinking a whole lot of margaritas, which now felt like a very bad idea because the effect seemed to be steering her dangerously off course. "No."

Now it was his turn to wince. "If you'd said something—"

"Griffin. I'm a professional with a job to do—and that job is to help you meet your deadline. So whether or not it's my birthday or Private's birthday or even *your* birthday, now is the time for business."

"If it was my birthday I'd want a present."

"I'll keep that in mind. Now, about your due date—"

"Is that why you went to visit your father? Was it for an early birthday celebration?"

"My father doesn't celebrate birthdays." She might be a little bitter about that, which also went to explaining her thirst for the salty, limy beverage she'd imbibed. "He celebrates accomplishments. Accolades. Success."

And what did she have to show for being another year older, she thought, her mood going morose again. Thanks to Ian Stone, her career was a mess and her heart had been battered.

"So how did your visit with your dad go, anyway? You didn't say."

"I was a little late arriving," she remembered, her face heating. Because she'd stopped at a drugstore for a package of cotton underwear. Her car had been in the restaurant parking lot, and she'd decided against returning to No. 9 at that particular moment in case Griffin had followed. She might have jumped him.

"I'll bet he doesn't care for tardiness."

"Yes, well…" She shrugged. "Can we get back to—"

"That's why you should have forgone the underwear. You'd have been distracted and thinking more of yourself instead of worrying about meeting dear old dad's expectations."

Her face went hotter. "How did you know…?"

"That you stopped to replace your panties? Because you're so predictable, Jane."

His condescending tone was wearing on her. "And you aren't? Let me tell you, I was more surprised that you made it back tonight before I was asleep than I was that you didn't keep your word and return after lunch."

His face closed down. "You shouldn't count on me."

"Don't I know it." The only place he'd been reliably showing up had been in the naked-guy fantasies that were occurring way more often than she liked. "We should have been working today."

"I had to see someone, all right?" He snapped out the words. "I told you that."

"A convenient dodge."

"It wasn't convenient at all, damn it." His expression was hard. "A guy from the platoon took a plane all the way out here from Philly. He had five hours in L.A."

Jane blinked. "A layover?"

"He just flew out here to see me, flew back. Can we drop it now?" He was sitting straight, his body tense, and his fingers flexed on his thighs as if he was trying to keep himself still. "Tell you what, let's go out. Do something. Get a drink. Cake and ice cream. Anything you want. It's your birthday."

His sudden agitation made her wary. "You don't need to do that. We're business associates, that's all."

"And friends or something close to it, don't you think?" He sent her a mock leer. "I've had my tongue in your mouth and your panties in my pocket."

Embarrassment now made her hot all over. "Stop that." She started to scooch away from him, except he caught her arm. "That was some weird aberration."

"Is that what they call it these days?" Griffin drew her closer. "C'mon, honey-pie. Birthday girls shouldn't lie."

"Just leave it alone, Griffin." She'd decided to pretend it had never happened, that frantic set of kisses in the restaurant storeroom. "Leave me alone."

"Then you'll go to your room and sit around feeling sorry for yourself. I bet you've been doing that all day, isn't that right?" He lifted her to her feet as if she weighed nothing. "We need to get out of here."

All at once, his mood felt dangerous. He wasn't squeezing her arm, exactly, but when she tried to get loose, he didn't release her. "I don't want to go anywhere."

His eyes were glittering. Tension was oozing from him. And then he smiled, and that was scarier, because it wasn't a lighthearted expression. It looked as serious as a heart attack. "The birthday girl at least deserves a birthday kiss."

"Absolutely n—" The last word was smothered against her lips as Griffin fixed his mouth to hers at the same instant that he released her from his hold. She might have retreated then, escaped the man and his dangerous mood, but instead she stayed where she was. A sound worked its way from the back of her throat. It wasn't a protest or a plea; it was, strange as it seemed, an acknowledgment.

Yes. Here's what I want for my birthday.

His kiss was like a switch. A key. It lit her up, it opened her up, and she felt as if she was in bloom when he touched her. She radiated heat and need, and just like before, her body clamored to imprint on his. With a little sigh, she moved into him.

His forearm clamped like a bar at the small of her back, lifting her into his hips. Her fingers went nerveless and limp as the front of her molded to the front of him. All the starch in her was gone. Were her feet on the ground? She didn't know.

His tongue pressed heavily into her mouth, and she opened for him, taking the thrust and twining her own tongue around his. His arm yanked her even closer, but he still managed to get a hand between them. He used it to cover one breast, gently molding, a stunning counterpoint to the aggression of the kiss.

Her whole body was quivering, her skin supersensitized. She pressed into that caressing hand as she tilted her hips to push against the thick ridge behind the placket of his jeans. His mouth lifted, and she gasped in air, then goose bumps raced everywhere as he slid his wet lips across her cheek to her jaw.

"Griffin." This explosive reaction was new to her, desire so bright and demanding it made a heady, impossible-to-resist experience. "God." She clutched at him now, bringing his head back so their lips were once again aligned.

He said something. Maybe "shh" or, knowing him, probably "shit," but she wasn't worrying about it. His hand

left her breast, and she started to worry about that, until
he ran his palm over her rib cage, her twitching belly and
then down to her thigh. Still kissing her like a madman,
he rucked up her skirt, and then his hot hand was on the
triangle of her panties.

And then he was in her panties.

Two long fingers insinuated themselves between her
plumped lips to brush the throbbing knob of nerves.

A hot shiver speared up her back. His fingertips rubbed
her again. Another molten shiver set her quaking. Pleasure was rising, hot and fast.

His fingers stroked once more, and not knowing if
she'd have the chance again, not knowing if she'd ever feel
such need again, she didn't hold back. Jane pushed into
those stroking fingers once, twice. Sweet bliss swooped
high. Splintered. At the mercy of her orgasm, she bucked
with the undulating pleasure while sucking on his tongue
and clutching his shoulders. When it was over, she buried
her face in his chest.

Griffin was very, very still for a long moment. Then
he removed his hand from her panties and tugged down
the hem of her skirt. A palm stroked the back of her head.
"Jesus Christ, Jane," he said after a moment, a note of
surprise in his voice. "You should warn a man about that
hair trigger."

Someone should have warned her! It must be the margaritas. Or the fact that she was another year older. But
this kind of gift deserved a reciprocal one, right? Her
face burning, she said, "I guess…you…uh, would you
like to…?"

He was already shaking his head, his expression flat.
"I think that would be a very lousy idea."

Which should have been her line. Mortified all over

again, Jane stepped back. "Of course. Anyway…" She made a vague gesture behind her. "I've got to go."

His eyes narrowed. "Go where?"

"You know," she said, shuffling back. "There."

"Jane…"

But she was already on the move, hastening out the back door. She'd go for a walk, inhale some of the chilly, fog-laden air. Take fifteen minutes, twenty, a couple of hours maybe, to sober up. Whatever time she needed away from Griffin to get the tequila and the sex out of her system. Still in a rush, she stepped over the waist-high back fence. Rex Monroe wouldn't mind her taking a shortcut through his yard. He'd understand her need to get away from his neighbor.

She glanced at the steps leading to the elderly man's front door.

Then she was whirling around, dashing back. "Griffin! Griffin!"

He met her at the back entrance, grasping her arms. His touch brought instant comfort, though she knew she shouldn't count on him. He'd said it himself, and hadn't every other man in her life let her down? His grip tightened as her voice went throaty with fear. "Something's happened to Mr. Monroe."

CHAPTER NINE

THE WOMEN WERE hovering. Griffin tried ignoring their chatter, but they weren't just talking among themselves. No, Jane, Tess and Skye were also talking to *him*—offering up advice on how best to shore up Old Man Monroe's stair railing. Pestering him with questions about what he thought had happened the night before.

Why the old coot had fallen.

"How the hell should I know?" he muttered, but the funny thing was they didn't appear much interested in his answers anyway. With barely a pause, they moved on to some other angle. Always talking, talking, talking.

"I need water," he announced, rising to his feet. He left his tools on the wooden porch and didn't bother taking his cell phone, which he'd tossed on top of the T-shirt he'd left on a cushioned patio chair. Rex Monroe's screen door squealed as he pulled it open. It banged behind him as he headed for the small kitchen.

He was filling a glass when he heard his neighbor's voice. "Skye?"

"It's me," he called out, then stepped to the small adjacent den where Monroe was reclined in a ratty chair. The night before, when Griffin and Jane had run to the crumpled form on the porch, the man had already been rousing. Though they'd wanted to call 911, he'd refused any help beyond getting him back to his feet. As of this morning, he claimed no lingering side effects besides a knot on the head and an ache to go along with it. "You want me to get her?"

"You'll do," Monroe said. "Come here."

Griffin hadn't been in the room in ages, if ever. It was small, holding the recliner, a TV-and-cable setup and rows of bookshelves. One wall was paneled and covered with framed photographs. Some of them were clearly shots of the reporter from his foreign correspondent days. Others looked to be—

His glance darted to the old man. "You have Gage's work in here."

Monroe shrugged a thin shoulder covered in a plaid shirt that must have been straight from the dry cleaner, it was so sharply pressed. "He sends me some from time to time."

"Huh."

"Those leather albums? Got tear sheets of your articles in them. Only the better ones, of course, which means they're few and far between."

The insult didn't surprise Griffin, but the fact that his neighbor had collected any of his pieces gave him pause. He ran a finger over a binder and noted it was the same style as the one in Beach House No. 9 that contained his stuff from Afghanistan. "You like me," he said dryly. "You really like me."

Old Man Monroe snorted. "It's sad how your standards lower when you get to be my age."

"Well, clearly your fall didn't soften your tongue any," Griffin noted. "And not that I care, but the females are twittering like you wouldn't believe, so I have to ask. Are you sure you're okay?"

He waved a liver-spotted hand in the air. "Beyond a few minutes I can't account for and the little people with the hammers inside my head, I'm fine."

"It was a good thing that Jane saw you when she did."

"True. And that you were there to pick me up." The old man narrowed his gaze on Griffin. "She said it was lucky—you hadn't been home long. Something about visiting with a man from the platoon?"

"Yeah." He turned to inspect one of his twin's photos. It showed a shirtless soldier from the back, ball cap on his head, army issue on his lower half, strapping a weapon at his hips. His head was bent and across his shoulders was inked a wicked-looking tribal tattoo. A line of barbs circled one thick bicep.

Under the shirt collar of Brian Hernandez, the man he'd met at LAX the day before, Griffin had glimpsed the devil tattoo that crawled up the former soldier's neck. It had been bright red, new-blood red, cherry-red. "Remember when we were cherries?" the kid had asked, touching the thing and using the common term for inexperienced soldiers. "Once I made it to the outpost, I think I was cherry for like thirty seconds."

"Less," Griffin had said. Immediately upon climbing from their Chinook transports, they'd been mortared. A welcome from their adversaries across the valley.

"Griffin?" The old man was speaking again, his voice sharp. "You hear me?"

"Sure," he answered. He'd heard Monroe talking, just hadn't taken in the words.

"I was wondering why your friend came so far for such a short visit."

Griffin shot him a look over his shoulder. "Why the hell would you care?"

"Because I'm nosy, obviously. All good reporters are. You should know that. Of course—"

"I'm not very good, I get it, I get it."

"I was going to say of course I can guess what he wanted."

"Yeah?" Griffin said. "You're a mind reader now? How could you possibly know?" He'd had no clue himself going in, but the agitated tone in the kid's voice when he'd called had taken hold of his insides and wrung them like a washcloth.

"Because it's what everyone who's been in theater asks themselves, wonders about, fixates over." The old man paused. "He wanted to know, what now? We've all asked ourselves some version of that. After the brutal thrill of war, what comes next?"

A long moment passed, then Griffin realized he was holding his breath, waiting. Jesus Christ! Waiting for the effing Ancient Mariner to share the secret of life. Death. War.

Whatever.

"I've got to finish up outside," he said, brusque. "The ladies wouldn't forgive me if your rocky railing means you take another fall."

"Help me out of this chair, then," Monroe ordered. "I like to get some real sunshine on me every day, just in case it's my last."

"We could only get so lucky," Griffin said, crossing to give his neighbor his arm. Then they walked together to the front porch. To free up the extra chair for the old man, he tossed his shirt and cell phone to his sister.

The women, predictably, gathered around Monroe, and Griffin didn't have to check to know that he ate up the attention. Skye, in particular, couldn't stop peppering the coot with questions. Was he certain he was well enough to be sitting up? Had he remembered anything more about the incident? Why had he gone onto the porch at that time of night anyway?

Rex replied in versions of yes, no and he couldn't remember. It was possible he'd heard some strange noise, perhaps a scuffling outside his front door.

Skye's voice rose. "You think someone was trying to get inside?"

Hammer in hand, Griffin looked over from his seat on the first stair only to find Jane was seated beside him. He jumped, dropping the tool. When he reached for it, so did she, and their fingers tangled.

Their gazes met.

He'd been avoiding that, looking at Jane. The only thing worse would be—

"We should talk about it," she said.

—would be talking about it! His fingers convulsed on hers. "Why? I get it. Your defenses were down because you'd been drinking. My libido was up because I'm a guy."

Her fingers jerked away from his to clutch the hem of yet another of her maddening, floaty skirts. Gauzy and delicate, they made his palms itch to rip, to reveal, to ride between her slender thighs. "I don't know what you mean by me drinking."

He rolled his eyes. "Last night you tasted like tequila and lime, honey-pie." Feeling sorry for the birthday girl, he hadn't rubbed it in.

She swallowed. "I turned another year older. So…"

"You don't have to explain." What the hell was the point of discussing it? It would only serve to bring it all up in his mind. He'd been in a hell of a temper himself, on edge from his meeting with Brian, from the memories that were intruding more and more often.

Bright red. Cherry-red. The red of new blood.

It wasn't supposed to be this way! He was cold inside,

desensitized, but nobody would leave him alone. All this talk, talk, talk kept rattling him.

Jane's mouth primmed.

That mouth.

He wrapped his fingers around the hammer and turned back to the task at hand. Nail pierced wood, and he sank it deep, as deep as he wanted to put all the thoughts that kept hammering at him day after day. The war. Erica. Bright red, cherry-red, the red of new blood, Brian.

"Griffin…"

And Jane. Who could have foreseen the fire under that governess guise? And why the hell did he want to touch it so very much? Gage was the real risk taker in the family. But Jane made Griffin want to put his hand in the flame and hold it there.

The burn would make him feel so damn alive.

But he didn't want to feel at all!

"Look," she was saying in her librarian voice. It was hushed but impossible to ignore. "I know that I… Uh, that I…"

"Came like a rocket at the flick of my finger?" He could feel her blush, even with his back turned. "Don't be ashamed, honey-pie. I suppose some men would find it gratifying."

She made a strangled sound. "Do you have to be so… so crude?"

Yes. Because it would be effective in pushing her away, and he needed to do that, he'd decided. Jane was so much sweet damn trouble under her frothy skirts and prim blouses. While he admittedly ached to get into her body, she'd use it as an excuse to get into his head. And though the explosive chemistry between them could knock her straight out of her crazy, girlie shoes, and while he was more grateful than he could say to know that he had a working cock again, he'd learned some lessons through war.

He'd never been armed during his embed year, but weapons had surrounded him all the same. One slow afternoon the soldiers had convinced him he needed to know how to handle every weapon at the outpost. He'd actually touched them many times already—moving a grenade someone inadvertently had left on his pillow or handing a platoon member his M4. But that day he'd learned to load and shoot and had been fascinated by the power in his hands. Maybe it was a man thing, a testosterone-driven interest in a tool, a gadget, but whatever the seductive lure, touching them like that had set his heart hammering. That's when he'd thought better of what he was doing. That's when he'd set down the rifle he was holding and backed slowly away, aware that keeping it too close would change him as a man.

Jane was like that. With her in his hands, he'd be changed…he could see her cracking him open like a nut, and he couldn't risk any of what was in there leaking out.

"I should have known you wouldn't engage in a civilized conversation," she muttered now. "Not even about this."

"You want a conversation?" He swiveled on the step and pinned her with his gaze. She'd been standing out in the sun long enough for the tip of her nose to turn pink. He curled his fingers into a fist so he wouldn't touch her there. Or anywhere. "Jane, here's the bottom line. I don't want you in my bed."

She blinked those silvery eyes and he glanced away from the—what? Surprise? Hurt? Hell.

"It would be bad for me," he continued. "And a disaster for you, because I can't give you what you need…."
Her helpless climax of the night before flared across his

mind, but he dashed water on it, cooling the heat. "What you really need."

"Oh." Her voice was small. Or perhaps insulted. "Thank you for being clear about that. Now I don't need to apologize for leaving you...unsatisfied."

He swallowed his groan. "Jane—"

"Griff!" Tess called his name, and she held up his phone, waving it to indicate there was someone on the line.

"Can you take a message?" he called back. Then he put his hand on Jane's knee. "Look..."

She did, and their eyes caught again. It was like gazing across the water toward the horizon just as the sun left the sky. No obstacles ahead. A silvery slide to forever.

"Griff." The strange note in his sister's voice caused him to jerk. He looked up. She was coming across the porch, a tense expression on her face.

His heart jolted. "Gage?" He jumped to his feet. "Something's happened to Gage?"

"No, no." Tess put both hands out. "Not that. It's your friend. That young man you met yesterday."

"Huh? Brian?"

"That was his mother. She thought you'd want to know...."

Griffin froze. His tongue felt thick. "Just tell me," he ordered his sister. "Say it quick." Like ripping off a Band-Aid.

"He's going to be all right, but..."

"Say it quick."

"After landing yesterday, on the way home, he crashed. He crashed his car into a tree one block from his parents' house. It was raining," she added. "A big storm."

A one-car crash, one block from home. Yeah, it was raining. A big storm. Inside Brian too.

"His mom wanted to make sure that you knew and to thank you for talking with him," Tess added.

Griffin stared at her. "Why the hell would his mother say that?" What had the talking accomplished? Nothing. Not a thing. Dropping the hammer again, he ran down the steps, not wanting to discuss the subject—any subject—anymore.

Talking did nothing—as evidenced by that look on Jane's face and by Brian's latest disaster. Because the fact was, Griffin didn't have the right words to help, to heal, to explain any goddamn thing in the world to anyone, least of all himself.

IT WAS PAST DARK, and David had a simple plan to assuage the loneliness that assailed him every evening in the sprawling ranch house in Cheviot Hills. It was Friday night, and with the weekend ahead, he couldn't face the quiet workless days without a little fix of his family. He was going to watch over them, just until morning. No one had to know about it but him.

He trudged through the soft sand of Crescent Cove, once again in the wrong kind of shoes. Instead of flipflops or those leather things in his closet that his daughter teased him were "mandals," he was in his running shoes. Grains poured into the sides until he felt as if he was wearing lifts. Sloppy lifts that made him stumble a little. He almost dropped the pop-up tent he'd borrowed from his neighbor. The sleeping bags he'd found in the boys' closet bobbled in his grasp.

It would serve him right to fall flat on his face.

Since it was exactly what he'd done with his life.

Between Beach Houses No. 8 and No. 9 was a clear swath of sand. He intended to set up camp there, close enough to his family to ease his spirit, far enough away that they wouldn't be aware of his presence. Though they all needed to become accustomed to Daddy keeping his distance.

It took three tries to set up his makeshift camp. Two times the tent popped up all right but then sprang out of his hold. On the third attempt, he tamed it into submission, but when he crawled inside he kneed over a sharp object that made him roll to his back and cradle his bruised skin. Upon scooting back out and clawing the sand beneath the tent floor, he uncovered a hard plastic shovel. It looked very much like the one that came with the set of sand tools they'd put in the boys' Easter baskets last spring.

"Thanks, Easter Bun," he muttered. Then he tossed it aside and dragged the sleeping bags in behind him.

They didn't have any adult-sized ones at the house. Neither he nor Tess had grown up camping, and the first baby had come too quickly in their marriage to explore it as a recreational possibility. So he'd grabbed the two that the boys brought to slumber parties. SpongeBob SquarePants and Buzz Lightyear. He unzipped them flat, intending to sleep sandwiched between their layers. Good thing. They were so short and narrow that one wouldn't have contained half of him.

As it was, his feet and shoulders stuck out of each end. But it was enough. He was warmed by being able to gaze on the small cottage that housed his four children and his wife. Flat on his belly, he toed off his shoes and stacked his hands to support his chin as he watched No. 8 through the tent flap.

The low lights coming from the windows wavered in his vision. He was exhausted. Early to work, late to work out, followed by the grinding quiet of the empty house

meant he'd slept little since Tess and his children had
left him.

In his dream, he was swimming in the ocean. Two
seals floated close, their bodies pressing against his. He
put an arm around each, riding alongside them toward
shore, as happy as he'd ever been in his life. As happy as
he'd been from the day he'd met his wife until the morning he'd turned forty years old.

Then something kicked him in the nuts. He awoke with
a jerk and a curse. What the…?

"Knock knock," his brother-in-law's voice said from
outside the tent.

"Griffin?" David craned his neck to peer out the flap.
There he saw the other man, flat on his back on the sand,
staring up at the sky. "What's going on?"

"Just a little stargazing."

It was then that David realized the "seals" he'd dreamed
of were instead his middle children, Duncan and Oliver.
At some point during his doze, he'd turned over. One of
his little guys was plastered against his right, the other
his left. The knee to his nuts had to have come via Oliver,
who'd been a restless sleeper since the womb.

Tess had despaired during the pregnancy that he was
going to be one of those kids who could never sit still.
But while Oliver was all boy and as fidgety as the rest of
his gender, he became even more active in sleep. When
off in the Land of Nod, he twisted and turned and flipped
and flopped. His rowdy nocturnal gymnastics were what
she'd experienced while he'd grown in her belly.

When Oliver crawled into bed with his parents following a nightmare, they'd learned to stuff pillows around
him. David didn't have any such protection now.

"How come they're here?" he whispered to Griffin,

even as he tightened the arms he'd placed around his sons while dreaming.

"Tess and your daughter are at a movie. Jane—" the way Griffin said the word held a wealth more information than four letters should allow "—said we would watch your boys. Russ is snoozing back at the house with her, but these dudes were still squirrelly. We went for a walk, saw the tent, and while I thought you might be a vagrant, they recognized the sleeping bags."

"Ah." David hesitated. "You're probably wondering what's going on."

"Actually," Griffin answered, "I'd rather not know. Keep it your business."

His avowed disinterest surprised David. Maybe his brother-in-law had his own surfeit of problems. "This Jane…"

The ensuing quiet spoke yet another volume. Finally, Griffin broke the silence. "She's worried about Rebecca."

"'She'? Your Jane—"

"Not *my* Jane."

"But she's worried about my daughter." David drew his boys a bit closer. "Why?"

"Jane says girls of Rebecca's age are prone to rebellion. Your teenager is threatening to get pregnant out of boredom."

It surprised a laugh out of him. "Tess wouldn't let that happen."

"You sure?"

Of course there were no absolute guarantees, but his wife had her reasons to be on the watch for unexpected babies. And as for his daughter… "Girls of Rebecca's age are prone to dramatic statements too."

Griffin made a sound of assent. "Christ, they grow up too fast."

"Yeah." David felt that familiar claw tearing at his insides. His little girl was a teenager! They were talking about college, and she was talking about pregnancy, and if he blinked a time or two more, both would be real. He was on the verge of losing one of the precious jewels in his life, and finding a way to survive the idea of that kind of loss was why he'd taken to staying late at the office and racking up marathons on his bike in spin class.

"It seems like a second ago that she was as small as Russ," Griffin said.

Russ. So small and so dependent. David squeezed his eyes at the raking pain in his gut.

"Dad." A sleepy Duncan squirmed in his hold. "You're hurting."

"Yeah, buddy," he murmured.

"You're hurting *me*." He wriggled again.

David loosened the arm that was clutching his oldest son. "Sorry."

"Watcha doing out here?" He butted his head against David's ribs.

"I wanted some fresh air," he said. "Can we keep that our secret? Not tell Mom?"

"Sure." Duncan's voice slowed. "Have a secret too, with Unc' Griff."

David didn't think he was awake enough to share what it was. "Okay, son," he said.

"We been peeing in the ocean." Oliver popped up.

"You're awake too?" David said, glancing down at his second boy.

"Nope. Jus' wanted to tell you our secret. Our man secret." As he settled back down, Oliver kicked David in the shins.

Wincing, he said, "Is that right?"

"Unc' Griff says there's stuff we don't tell girls."

"Peeing in the ocean seems to qualify," David agreed aloud, though from Oliver's sudden bonelessness, he figured the boy had drifted back to dreamland.

"For the record, there's also been some burping and armpit farting," Griffin confessed. "We had a contest."

"Sure you did," David said, unsurprised. "You and Gage never do anything without making it a competition."

"Yeah." Griffin sounded unhappy about it.

"Hey. I'm sorry. I didn't mean—"

"No apology necessary." Griffin stirred. "You want me to leave them with you?"

"I wish you wouldn't," David said. "And I also wish..."

"Another man secret, I get it. I won't tell your wife where you were tonight."

"It doesn't matter," Tess's voice said. In the moonlight he could see her bare, elegant feet. She was standing just beyond Griffin. "Because your wife already knows."

TESS SAT ON THE sand outside David's tent as Griffin carried Duncan and Oliver to No. 8. He'd promised to tuck them in and tell Rebecca she was in charge until Tess returned to the house. Why David was camping on her doorstep she didn't yet know, but she was going to get to the bottom of it. Her avoidance of speaking with him about any serious subjects had merely postponed the inevitable. Tonight she was going to strip every pretense away.

The half-moon cast cool light on the beach, but her husband was little more than a dark shadow inside the confines of the small tent. She nodded at it. "Where'd you get that thing?"

"Borrowed it from the Kearneys across the street," he said. Then he started crawling toward the open flap. "I should take it back to them."

"We should talk first." Tess shifted closer so that he'd

have to push her out of the way in order to get out. He froze, as she expected he would. He'd been avoiding touching her for weeks.

"Fine." His sigh was audible. Then he started speaking in a conversational tone. "What did you and Rebecca see at the movies tonight?"

"I don't know. My mind was elsewhere."

"While I ate dinner, I watched an interesting program on the Nature Channel."

"Really?" She stared at him. Married for thirteen years, separated for several days, and he wanted to engage in small talk?

"Really."

"No, I mean you really want to talk about fauna or flora instead of our family?"

"It was on solar variation—which is neither animal nor vegetable, of course."

David had a dry sense of humor that some people mistook for dullness. She didn't. She knew exactly what he was up to, and it was all about dodging important matters. If she was going to get him on point, he was forcing her to flat-out ask him the tough questions.

Suddenly she felt cold, and she rubbed at the bare skin of her arms beneath her short sleeves. Though she wore jeans, she was shoeless, and she crossed one set of chilled toes over the other. She tried peering into the tent. "Do you have a jacket in there?"

"No." But then he moved, and she could just make out him stripping off his sweatshirt. He scooted closer to the tent entrance to pass it to her, and the moonlight revealed his bare skin.

The material was warm from his body heat. "But you—"

"I'm fine." He drew folds of SpongeBob SquarePants around his torso. "Put it on."

It was a mistake. Once she slipped the sweatshirt over her head, the scent of him enveloped her. You'd think she'd be accustomed to it, but thanks to their separation it was both wholly new *and* wholly familiar. She and her daughter had sniffed two dozen scents last Christmas before settling on this one. One day two weeks ago, Russ had gotten into it after his bath, and she'd cried smelling David on her baby's skin.

It was the closest he'd been to his father in months.

Tears stung her eyes now, but she pinched the bridge of her nose to keep them at bay. How could David have done this to her? To them?

She drew up her knees to her chest and wrapped her arms around her shins. Her gaze drifted to the right, and she watched the calm surf spread its white apron across the sand with a soft *shush*. Any other time it would be a comforting sound.

But only the truth would comfort her now. "Are you having an affair?" she blurted out.

His stare poked at her. "What?"

"Are you— No! Don't answer that!" What was she doing, she thought in a panic. A "yes" wouldn't comfort her at all. She drew her legs closer and squeezed shut her eyes. "I can't do this," she muttered against her knees.

"Then don't do it," David urged. "Come back to the house. Move back in with the kids, and it will be just like before."

She lifted her head. "Like it was a week ago? Like it's been for months?"

He hesitated. "I'm a good provider." It sounded defensive. Guarded.

As he'd been since his fortieth birthday.

Then words she hadn't planned tumbled out of her mouth. "I've been thinking of having an affair myself."

"What?" David erupted from the tent, then rocked back, so that he was half in, half out. "Has that bastard Reed Markov been after you?"

"No," Tess said, waving a hand. "Geez, David, he's sleazy."

"You were the one cozying up to him at lunch."

"Because he actually might have work for me. And the sleaze is automatic with him. He puts it on in the morning when he gets up, just like you put on your…your dress shirts, lightly starched."

She thought she heard her husband's teeth grind. "So the other half of this affair you've contemplated is some fantasy man?"

Agreeing to that would be the easy path. But hell, if she wanted no barriers between them, then she couldn't lie. "Tee-Wee—Teague White. He had a crush on me when he was a kid."

"Him and probably three hundred thousand other men thanks to that damn *OM* commercial," David said, his voice tight. "I'm going to kill him."

"You can't do that. He's been a perfect gentleman. As far as I know, I'm the only one with naughty thoughts."

David twitched at that. It drew her gaze, and she could see more of him in the moonlight. The sleeping bag had pooled at his hips to bare his torso. Since all the gym time, she'd only caught glimpses of him as he'd crossed from the shower to his closet. Yes, those fifteen pounds he'd grumbled about were gone, but until now she hadn't made note of what had taken their place.

His chest was chiseled. Slabs of pectoral muscles were situated above rippling abdominals. His shoulders were heavier and wider now, with biceps that bulged when he shifted to lean back on his hands.

Whoever said women weren't aroused by visual stimulus were full of baloney.

Except, she thought, her heart contracting, she'd take her softer, loving David any day over this finely cut stranger who wouldn't look her in the eye or hold their youngest child in his arms. *I'm sorry,* she thought. *I'm sorry that I got pregnant when we weren't planning another.*

Just like they hadn't planned the first.

She wondered now if that was the explanation for the change in him. He'd never expressed feeling trapped into marriage after she'd told him about Rebecca, but maybe when baby Russ arrived those feelings had finally arrived too. Of course it took two to make new life, but she'd hated the pill, and the diaphragm was clearly not as effective when it came to them. After both unplanned pregnancies, she'd had the guilty yet pleasurable notion that their exciting, vigorous sex was to blame.

"So you've been having thoughts about another man," David ground out.

She shrugged. "You haven't denied thinking about women."

"Oh, I've had plenty of carnal thoughts, Tess."

Her heart squeezed.

"About one woman in particular."

Her lungs contracted.

The stranger who had once been her husband spoke again. "I'm going to get my hands on her."

Dying on the beach might be all right. The tide would come in and sweep her and her pain away.

"I'm going to get my hands on her *right now.*" And

then he had her in his grip and was tugging her into the tent before she could comprehend his meaning.

It was just sinking in as his mouth latched onto hers. Without thinking, her palms slid over those pumped biceps and those new, heavy shoulders. If the recently acquired muscles made him look like a stranger, touching them only enhanced the unfamiliarity. Then she curled her fingers in the short, velvet nap of his hair at the back of his head, and her pulse settled a little. This was recognizable. And so were his lips, the sure thrust of his tongue, the taste of the kiss.

It spun her away from the present.

She was nineteen again, her birthday just the week before. She'd had one lover before him, the summer after senior year, the king of the prom who'd bumbled his way through her virginity. But David was a man, and he was the steady, mature kind who didn't feel it was an ego blow to ask for directions.

Do you like this? he'd whispered in her ear, pinching her nipples just hard enough to make her gasp. His hand had traveled lower. *Shall I rub light and fast or hard and slow?* Just the words had enflamed her.

Now her husband reached for the zipper of the tent, and she heard him draw it down, prohibiting all light. It only drew her further into the past. He'd shared a two-bedroom house in the valley with a guy who was working in the financial district, both of them saving their paychecks. David's room had held a queen bed, a side table and a narrow window. With the curtains drawn it was a dark, intimate space where a girl could hold her guy's head to her breast and not worry that he'd see the embarrassing ecstasy on her face as he sucked her nipple deep.

She wanted that now. She wanted it so badly that she yanked both the sweatshirt and T-shirt over her head in one move. David was already working on her bra, and she felt her skin flush hot as the silky fabric brushed the taut tips when he tossed it away.

Her bare torso rubbed against his. He was hard where she was soft, and he grunted when she ran her hand down the front of his pants and cupped him over his jeans. Nineteen-year-old Tess had done that too, bold as could be in the darkness, but she wouldn't have dared to attack the fastenings.

She did now, though, and another distinctive *vriiip* of a zipper sounded over their heavy breathing. His erection nudged the palm of her hand, and she squeezed it in greeting, eliciting a half groan, half moan from David. He went for her zipper then too, but she didn't release her prize; instead she caressed it with the C of her fingers, stroking up and down until she felt a drop of wetness meet her thumb. She smeared it over the crown, and he cursed, rolling away from her touch.

Her protest died as he yanked at the legs of her jeans. The denim hit the side of the tent with a *thwap*. Her white panties rose like a feather in the air. She didn't see them fall because her eyes squeezed shut as David crouched between her spread thighs.

He'd done that same thing in the sex cave in the valley. *Let me,* he'd said then. *Don't be embarrassed. You'll like it. Don't keep me out. Don't push me away. Never not let me have you, Tess.*

Now, as she had at nineteen, she allowed him to hold her steady, his palms on her inner thighs, his thumbs peeling her open like an exotic fruit he was intent on savoring. A blush burned over her skin. The prom king had probably not even known about the part of her body that David found so easily with the tip of his tongue.

Just the tip. Just the tiniest flick.

The sound she made now was louder than the one she'd made then. At nineteen, she'd swallowed back as best she could those passion noises that had crawled up her throat. David had praised the small moans and whimpers. "Yes, baby," he'd said against her wet flesh. "Show me that you like it. Let me hear how good it is for you."

The numbers guy was nimble in so many other ways.

Just when she thought he'd nudge her over the precipice with the edge of his teeth, he'd flipped her onto her belly. The nineteen-year-old hadn't known this would become her favorite position.

But David had discovered it almost from the first. She could still remember her hot cheek against the cool surface of his sheet. He'd pushed her long hair off her neck and kissed her nape, then pressed a flight of butterfly kisses against the skin of her back, crossing her shoulders and dipping down her spine. Imagine her shock when he'd bit her bottom!

He did it now too, but she didn't squeak as she'd done then. Instead, she lifted into the sting-and-suck of that carnal kiss and felt the throb of it everywhere, at the tips of her breasts, in the pulse points of her wrists, as an insistent ache between her thighs.

She was too empty there. "David…" she heard herself moan.

He ran his thumb along the seam between her cheeks, brushing past a tiny indent that made her skin break out into goose bumps, until he dipped just the pad against the wet, aching well where she wanted his erection.

"Please, David…"

"You're so ready for me."

"I am. I am *so* ready."

He laughed at the urgent note in her voice, the laugh

of a man who knew his way around a woman's body. At nineteen she'd been only grateful for it.

She was still thankful. "Come inside." The Tess of the present was bold enough to wiggle her butt at him.

He caressed her hip with one large hand. He had calluses that were new, and they made her skin prickle in reaction. She rubbed her tight nipples against the sleeping bag beneath her. After this, SpongeBob and Buzz Lightyear were going to have to be replaced by brand-new cartoon characters.

Thoughts of the kids intruded. *Oh, God.* What was she doing? She started to rise, but David's hand clamped hard on her hip bone. His other pressed between her shoulder blades, holding her in place.

His body curled over hers, and his mouth kissed her ear, his hot breath tickling the whorls. "Don't keep me out. Don't push me away. Never not let me have you, Tess."

She let desire spin her back again. She was nineteen, in the capable hands of an incredible lover. Of a real man, a mature man, who caressed her cheek with his mouth as his thick, solid shaft tunneled inside her. She arched, trying to force him deeper, faster, but David was chuckling again, that dark, confident chuckle that had her twisting to abrade her stiff nipples on the surface below her. His hands found hers, and he twined their fingers, gripping tight as he took her that last inch.

They both made satisfied noises and went still.

He was throbbing in her channel, and she tightened it around him, squeezed him as she'd done with her hand. He groaned. "You're so good, baby."

The nineteen-year-old had thrilled to that. She'd done it again, and then he'd started thrusting, helpless, she'd thought, against her wiles.

Now she knew better. Nothing about David was helpless when it came to bedding her. He moved deliberately, pulsing deep, thrusting shallowly, driving her mad by not giving her the vigorous pounding rhythm that would get her off. "David," she said and craned her neck to take his mouth in a kiss.

He sucked on her tongue, and she arched into his next stroke. "Please." She pushed her bottom higher.

His fingers slid free of her right hand. Still thrusting, he passed his hand over her shoulder, down her spine, around her hip. Then two fingers slid between her softness to brush the hard bundle of sensation. A shudder rolled through her. He circled her there with the wet tips, tight, tight orbits that didn't let up even as he plunged inside her with more force.

Still, his movements were controlled, each one designed to propel her to orgasm. Her knees slipped against the sleeping bag, and so she wouldn't flatten, she reared back. It upset the rhythm.

And brought him root-deep.

They both froze again. His heart was pounding against her spine. Their harsh breaths echoed off the nylon walls. She squeezed the fingers of his left hand, and he moved again, withdrawing to drive inside her once more. His right hand went back to its work too.

And Tess let the final pleasure begin to wind inside her. With every turn, her body tensed, until she was tight like a violin string, vibrating at her own personal pitch of bliss. "David…" she moaned again.

"Yeah," he said, her suave lover finally losing his power of speech. "Yeah, yeah, yeah." And on that last word he started shuddering. Her body caught hold and used those tremors and the firming touch of his fingers to take her away.…

"To infinity and beyond," David muttered as he

dropped atop one sleeping bag, flinging his forearm over his eyes.

Tess lay beside him, quiet, reveling in the renewed closeness. Then reality struck, leaving her appalled.

"David." Her voice was faint. "God, David, we didn't use anything." They'd *never* been this irresponsible. Those two unplanned pregnancies had been due to birth control failure, not the failure to use birth control.

"It's all right," he said.

A hot tear slipped out of the corner of her eye and dripped to her temple. "Positive thinking in this regard has never worked well for us."

"I was snipped two months ago."

The sentence didn't make sense. "'Snipped'?"

"I had a vasectomy. And I've been tested since. When I ejaculate? No swimmers."

She stared in his direction, even though she couldn't see him any better in the dark now than she had before. "You…you did that without consulting me?"

His quick gesture she could only sense. "We didn't want any more kids, right?"

They hadn't planned on the fourth. A second hot tear escaped her eye. Without another word, she started feeling around for her clothes. The tent was so small they were easy to discover, and the wife in her even neatly piled David's when she encountered them.

That's who she was, of course. A wife. They might have briefly recaptured the initial excitement of their early relationship, but she wasn't nineteen any longer. No matter what happened when they were skin-to-skin, it didn't alter how *he'd* changed either.

She was the mother of four, and she'd gotten exactly what she'd come for. She'd stripped every pretense away to discover that David wasn't the same husband and father that he'd been in the past. He was unwilling, Tess understood now, to be that same man.

Where that left her, she didn't yet know.

CHAPTER TEN

GRIFFIN DECIDED the only redeeming feature of his new home office and the requisite laptop computer inside of it was that his mind-numbing solitaire hands dealt themselves. He'd put up with Jane bustling about the small space all morning, chattering about outlines, marking a whiteboard with a time line, setting up an internet cloud account so they could share the chapters she expected him to produce. All the while he'd tuned her out by pretending to reread the articles he'd written during his embed year.

He'd merely stared at the black squiggles on the white pages.

When the noon hour hit, he'd banished her.

Through the office's open window he could still hear her, though. Twelve feet away, she was sitting at the table on the deck with his sister and Skye. The three women were sharing a platter of fruit and cheese and watching over the small hoodlums who were his middle nephews. Rebecca, apparently, was still at summer school, and Russ was curled on his mother's lap.

"Oh! Look at that." Jane's voice rose over the *whoosh* of the waves spreading over the sand. "They're going up the cliff."

Worry tried to clutch at Griffin's gut, but he pushed it away along with the urge to rush to the window. It wasn't his problem if those damn kids of Tess's got into trouble.

They weren't his concern. He clicked on an ace, moving it to the top row on the screen.

"I still think it's a peculiar thing to do," Jane added. "Somebody could get hurt."

"I'm going to post warning signs," Skye said. "It's really not safe."

"They're big boys," Tess replied, her tone complacent.

Complacent! With Duncan and Oliver scrambling up those sharp rocks? Griffin tried breathing through his sudden agitation, but then he gave up and leaped to the window for a view of the bluff. *Oh*. It wasn't his nephews climbing after all. It was Tee-Wee White and his firefighting compadres.

"*Very* big boys." Jane might have sighed a little.

Through the window screen, he sent her a sharp look. Her expression was impossible to discern beneath that straw hat once again sitting low on her forehead. He already knew what she was wearing: a sleeveless, tailored dress in ribbon-candy stripes and another pair of her ridiculously feminine shoes. They were high-heeled and toe-revealing, with little froufrou flowers made of matching leather stuck all over them. It was as if she'd strolled through a field, and the wildflowers had walked out with her.

Ridiculous. And she smelled like those wildflowers too. The faint scent still lingered in the office.

She lingered in his mind, damn it. That absurd way she gave herself to his kiss. Feisty, prickly Jane was stubborn as hell until he got his mouth on her. Cool as could be until he put his hand between her thighs. There he found her as hot and sweet as melted candy. As addictive.

A man could get used to pleasing a woman who came so damn easy and so damn hard. Hell. It was only a small leap of thought to those pink panties he'd tucked away in a drawer. He needed to return them—or better yet, throw them into a fire. Somehow he needed to neutralize the spell they'd cast, the one that had made him obsessed with all that Jane hid beneath her buttons and bows.

"I still don't get the lure," she said now, on the deck outside the window. "What's the point of daring death like that?"

Griffin glanced at the firefighters and almost laughed. They weren't daring anything. They were prepping to jump from approximately one-third the distance that was the cove record. The record that belonged to Griffin.

"For the adrenaline rush," Tess said. "At least that's what Gage told me once. He said it's powerful enough to numb pain."

This time he was sure Jane sighed. "And anesthetize emotion? That would explain why Griffin made his latest leap after hearing about his soldier friend's accident."

"'Epic leap,'" Tess corrected. "Said that surfer dude who hangs out around here."

"Remembering makes my stomach hurt," Jane murmured. "Let's not talk about it anymore."

Perfect, Griffin thought. He didn't need his sister and the governess psychoanalyzing him about cliff-jumping or about Brian. The other man was on the mend; they'd spoken just yesterday. Bent on returning to solitaire and dismissing the women from his mind, Griffin stepped over Private, sprawled in the patch of sunshine on the hardwood floor.

"Let's talk about Ian Stone instead," Skye put in, an excited note in her voice. "Tess, did you know that Jane worked with the famous author? That she's his acknowledged muse?"

Griffin's head swiveled back to the window. Ian Stone? The writer responsible for romantic dramas that hit the top of the bestseller lists and stayed there? He'd never read one—women were the intended audience, he surmised—but he couldn't miss the guy's name as he passed through airport sundry stores. The foil letters were four inches high on glossy dust jackets featuring bucolic, color-saturated scenes.

"No kidding?" Tess said.

Skye answered instead of Jane. "The last three books are dedicated to her. It's in black-and-white. 'For my muse, the lovely and generous Jane Pearson.'"

"Wow." Tess was clearly impressed.

Griffin, not so much. If Jane had worked with the man, then she'd likely hounded him into writing those words. She'd probably added the line herself when the author wasn't looking.

"I can't believe you know him. What's Ian Stone really like?" Tess asked, an annoying trace of celebrity worship in her voice.

She should know better, Griffin thought. Hadn't chewing gum made hers a household face?

"Norm Scrogman."

"Huh?"

"You didn't hear this from me," Jane said, "but his real name is Norm Scrogman."

"No. No way." Skye sounded put out. "A guy who looks like that can't be a Norm Scrogman. A Norm Scrogman doesn't have burnished gold hair and dreamy green eyes and the kind of smile that hits a woman right where... well, you know."

Griffin found himself standing at the window again, and he could see his sister staring at the younger woman. "I didn't know *you* knew, Skye. From what I hear, as far as you're concerned, Crescent Cove might as well be Celibacy Cove."

Mumbling, Skye slid lower in her seat. "Ian Stone's a gorgeous literary superstar. I'm not made of ice."

A tickle on the back of his neck made Griffin switch his gaze to Jane. She was paying careful attention to a handful of green grapes. Did she find Ian Stone gorgeous? And what exactly was there to this muse business?

It pissed him off that he was even posing the questions. Though he tolerated her dallying in his office, he was working at getting Jane off his mind. He'd made clear he didn't want her in his bed, hadn't he?

He saw her glance up at the cliff again. "Hey, look! Another firefighter's going to jump."

It seemed a clear attempt at redirecting the conversation. Tess took the bait. "Teague," she said.

A sly little grin overtook Skye's face. As had been her usual uniform this summer, she was dressed in shapeless clothes that might have come from a much larger male cousin, but the brightness of her smile reminded Griffin of how very pretty she was. He wondered what Gage would think of his pen pal if he ever left the danger zone long enough to meet her man-to-woman. "Does his crush go both ways now, Tess?" Skye asked.

Griffin swallowed his groan. Was this the direction the wind blew? Not that he wanted to be bothered with the ins and outs of his sister's relationships, but Deadly Dull David wasn't a bad guy—he wasn't even that dull, and finding his brother-in-law camping on the beach told him that the other man wasn't altogether the absent husband and father his sister believed. But if she was interested in Tee-Wee…

The best part of evading entanglement with a woman, Griffin decided, was that it kept him clear of being at the mercy of someone else's emotions. Jealousy had to sting.

Wanting someone for oneself when they pined over another was a condition he planned to avoid his entire life.

"I'm married," his sister said with a little sigh. "Which leaves the admittedly attractive Teague up for grabs. Have you thought of asking him out, Skye?"

"No!" Skye tempered the tone of her voice. "I mean, no. I'm not really, um, looking for a relationship at the moment."

"Who's talking about a relationship?" Tess replied. "You can get…satisfaction without getting ensnared in coupledom."

Ensnared. His sister was sounding more like him by the minute. Poor David.

"Huh," Jane said. "That doesn't sound bad."

Skye straightened in her chair. "Are you telling me that muse plus superstar author doesn't equal one happy pairing?"

"There's nothing between me and Ian," Jane murmured, looking toward the cliff again. Teague White was braced against the rocks, and though in Griffin's mind's eye he was still the scrawny tagalong of childhood summers, he had to admit the guy had gained inches and pounds. He glanced back at the governess and saw her take off her hat.

The expression on her face was speculative. "I might be due some satisfaction," she said.

He frowned. She certainly was not! Hadn't he doled out some satisfaction to her just the other night? Sure, it had been quick and they'd both remained on their feet, but that wasn't his fault, was it? If she'd been a little more patient, he'd have taken her to his room—

But he'd told her he didn't want her in his bed.

And he didn't.

"Could be I'd benefit from getting some kinks worked out of my system…."

Kinks! Tee-Wee White wasn't owed Librarian Jane's kinks. Griffin was the one who had to put up with her demands and with her maddening perfume and her crazy-making footwear. For God's sake, he should be the one who deserved any kinks that rose to the surface.

And what did anyone really know about Tee-Wee, anyway? He used an ax on the job, didn't he? He could be an ax murderer. Or just plain lousy in the sack. Griffin could practically guarantee that.

"If Skye's hesitating, I guess that means you can have him, Jane." Tess glanced over her shoulder at the window where Griffin lurked.

He jerked back. Had she known he was eavesdropping?

Jane gnawed at the bottom lip of her puffy mouth. "It's not really my nature to be the aggressor in this sort of situation…"

Didn't Griffin know it? *Be still,* he'd said, and she'd done just that. He'd kissed her and she'd been made bone-less. She shouldn't just go around asking men to melt her, because that's what she'd done under his hands and under his mouth—and she seemed to be aware of that. Blowing out a breath, he relaxed.

"…but I suppose nothing ventured, nothing gained."

His spine snapped straight. What? Had she actually said that? The same woman who'd also once repeated "Failure is not an option"?

Nobody knew better than he how determined the woman could be.

And Tee-Wee White was an ax murderer.

Tess shifted Russ from her lap to her shoulder. The baby snuggled into his mom's body, as peaceful as Griffin suddenly wasn't. "I know," his sister said. "You could ask Teague to Captain Crow's tomorrow night. On Sundays they have a special menu, live music, dancing. It's a lot of fun."

A little burn kindled in Griffin's gut. He remembered Jane that second night she'd ventured into Party Central. There'd been music then too. Dancing. She'd been dressed in a bikini top and exposing an ungoverness-like amount of naked skin. What she'd run into hadn't been fun.

Hell, he thought, scowling. Something had to be done to occupy her Sunday night. Of course, he didn't *want* the responsibility to fall to him, but he was the one with the means and opportunity.

Three quick steps took him to his laptop and he xed out solitaire to peruse another program instead. He'd cursed the return of email to his life, but now he was happy to scroll down the list of correspondence he'd trashed after barely glancing at it.

There.

It took but a moment to compose a quick RSVP. Griffin Lowell plus guest.

The women were still in their seats when he strode onto the deck. His businesslike footsteps caused the wooden surface to vibrate, but not even his sister looked his way. The trio continued their avid perusal of the half-naked firefighters on another scramble over the rocks.

For a second he considered running over there and showing the rookies how it was really done, but he had another item on his agenda. He sailed a paper airplane toward the book doctor. The breeze caught it, and it nearly flew over her head. But at the last moment the wind died, and the folded sheet dropped, landing on the table right in front of her.

Jane glanced up.

So sweet and innocent she looked, with those wide-set eyes and that soft mouth. "Do you need something?" she asked.

"Yeah." He reminded himself that she was a favorite of his agent. He owed the man, which just made this rescue more imperative. Frank would never forgive him if he let Jane find trouble here at Crescent Cove. "I require your assistance."

"Now?" She made to rise.

He shook his head. "Tomorrow night. We leave in the morning. Pack a bag. Put in a party dress." It struck him as he said it how rarely he'd left the beach house. See what she was making him do! But still he was determined to take her away. Save her from herself.

She arched a brow. "I told Tess I'd babysit."

"Look at it that way, if you want," he said with a shrug. "In any case, I need a date."

LONGNECK BEER in hand, Griffin leaned against the wall of the California Pioneer Heritage Museum near L.A.'s Griffith Park. "How are you?" he murmured to a passing guest when their gazes briefly caught.

"Great. You?" the other man answered, without pausing for Griffin's answer.

"Smug," he murmured to the guy's retreating back. The evening was working out better than he'd planned. Not only had it given him a legitimate excuse to avoid writing, but it was restful to disappear in the crowd. His original motivation still stood, however. He'd accepted the invitation to the book launch party—another of Frank's clients was making a big splash with a literary mystery set during L.A.'s Spanish Era—in order to save Governess Jane from making a romantic misstep. She might say she was interested in "satisfaction" and not a relationship, but that didn't add up to Griffin. With her prim appearance and rule-bound nature, he figured she was ripe for throwing her heart into the wrong ring.

Griffin had learned the lesson about honesty when it came to women, but there was no guarantee that Teague White was the kind of man who would be up-front with her. He might take what she offered without being straightforward about his own intentions. By insisting she leave the cove tonight, Griffin figured he'd prevented Jane from being hurt.

Though why he was going all hero about this, he wasn't quite sure. Maybe she was starting to feel like a little sister to him.

He ran his gaze around the room, trying to catch sight of her. They'd checked in to a nearby hotel earlier in the day, a few hours before leaving for the party. While he'd gone for a run, she'd borrowed his car to swing by her place for some clothing.

Her apartment was an hour from the party and she'd made noises about staying there overnight, but he wasn't having it. The suite he'd booked had two bedrooms, and that way there'd be no concerns about drinking and driving. Upon her return, they'd ordered room service for an early dinner and then she'd retired to her room to change.

She'd come out in a deep violet dress of some swishy fabric that fluttered and swirled a few inches above her knees. The neckline skimmed her throat, and she had a matching long-sleeved, waist-length jacket on top of it. Her shoes were Jane all the way, lavender-colored and ultrafeminine, the wide straps across the toes and the tops of her feet securing her onto a provocative tiptoe.

He should keep tabs on her for those chichi high heels alone, he thought, continuing to survey the room. As practical as Jane's nature might be, her choice of footwear meant the slightest stumble could take her down. It played out in his mind's eye, a small slip, a tumble to the ground, her skirt flying up to reveal a pair of panties. What would they be this time—

Stop. He clamped down on the mental movie reel. She was a little sister to him.

Or something like that.

To his left, he caught a flash of color among a small knot of dark leather dress shoes and black stilettos. Pushing off from the wall, he ambled toward the bright spot, then froze as her feet shifted, and he caught a glimpse of the backs of her shoes.

Hell. Before, he hadn't seen them from behind. Now that he could, he noticed that each heel bore a distinctive, one-and-a-half-inch brass zipper. You'd have to unzip her to get her out of them! His mind made an instant leap to nakedness. Jane's nakedness, of course. Before he could control the urge, his gaze traced from those fascinating shoe fastenings to the backs of Jane's bare calves. After her days at the beach, her legs had a tinge of creamy gold tan, a color repeated where the dress revealed a slice of skin right over her spine.

More nakedness.

She'd taken off the jacket. It dangled from her fingers, and its removal showed him another rear view that he'd missed when she'd been covered up. While the dress was beyond modest from the front, in the back it was open from neck to waist. The sleeveless top of the garment was held up by—what else?—a long-tailed bow, its ends trailing to tickle her delicate vertebrae.

He hoped he wasn't doing something stupid like drooling. As if she sensed his regard, Jane's head suddenly turned over her bare shoulder. Her silvery eyes picked up the deep hue of the dress, and his breath hitched. He dropped his gaze to the prissy, plump mouth that she'd glossed the color of a ripe plum, but that didn't help.

The whole package made him so hungry he could barely breathe.

Christ, he'd insisted on the party to save her, but who the hell was going to resuscitate him?

She didn't look away from him as he started forward with some vague plan of getting her out of here. Then getting her out of those clothes— No! Well, yes, getting her out of those provocative clothes and into something dull and Skye-sloppy. Following that, they'd repair to their individual rooms, where she would study grammar and he would take a subzero shower.

Otherwise he couldn't be held responsible for the consequences.

Upon reaching her, he stroked the back of her slender arm, and then he had to curse himself and her for the little shiver he watched roll down her naked back. She pulled her elbow close to her body and held it there with her opposite hand. "What?" she asked, sounding truculent.

"We should go."

Her brows pinched together. "We just got here. And I haven't had a chance to say hello to Frank."

"I know." Griffin glanced toward a corner of the room where he could see the agent. The literary mystery had already been optioned and Frank was huddled with movie types. You could pick them out by their watches and their overwhitened teeth. "We'll have to talk with him another time."

"This entire excursion was your idea. I'm sure you just want to avoid explaining your nonprogress to him."

He ignored both her points. "Look, we can spend the evening studying Strunk and White's *Elements of Style*."

In separate corners of their spacious suite. "Won't that make you happy?"

She leaned close enough for him to breathe in her flower fragrance. Her brows came together. "Is there an actual problem?"

"A gut feeling," he lied. "We need to go."

Jane's hint-of-violet eyes studied his face for a long moment. Then she shrugged. "All right." At her half turn, her small nose just missed the chest of a man on fast approach.

She stumbled—Griffin knew those shoes were trouble—and he steadied her with a hand on each shoulder, pulling her back to his front. "Ian!" Jane exclaimed.

Ian? Could the man before them be *Ian Stone?*

Griffin figured it had to be him, because Skye's description matched. There was the gold hair, the green eyes, the smile—though to him it looked more smarmy than seductive. His precise haircut, tailored clothes and overshouldered physique screamed a guy who'd spent too many years as the pip-squeak in prep school and now sweated too many mornings with his Bowflex machine in a mirrored home gym to make up for it.

"Jane," Ian replied, his gaze running from her mouth to her bare toes, then back to her mouth. Leaning forward, he went for a kiss, but because Griffin didn't release his clasp, Jane couldn't meet him halfway. The guy ended up sort of smooching the air.

It wouldn't be polite to snicker.

But maybe he made some kind of sound, because the other man glanced at Griffin's hands on Jane's smooth skin, then at Griffin himself. "I don't think we've met," he said.

Jane's posture was stiff, her voice only more so. "Ian Stone, this is Griffin Lowell. Griffin, Ian."

Their right hands met in the required shake, but he kept his left on the librarian. Tension was humming through her, so he gave her shoulder a reassuring squeeze. "Are you ready to go?" He pretended to smile at Ian. "We were just on our way out."

"Oh, but Jane and I haven't been able to catch up yet," he protested. "And we were so very…close for those happy productive years." His gaze transferred back to her, and he made another almost-rude inspection. "But now you look different. I've never seen your hair appear so…unruly."

Wearing a small frown, she raised a self-conscious hand to it. "I'm living by the ocean," she said, touching the soft waves.

Griffin loved her hair. It was natural-looking, the half-tousled strands reflecting every color of sand from wet to dry. Here and there glinted highlights the sun of his cove had coaxed out.

"You don't like it at the beach. You're afraid of the ocean."

"I'm afraid to *swim* in the ocean."

It was Griffin's turn to frown. He couldn't imagine the governess being afraid of anything. But it was true he hadn't seen her set a toe in the water.

Now Ian's eyes flicked upward once again, taking Griffin's measure. "I didn't know you were seeing someone."

"He's a client," she said, her voice clipped.

"A client!" Ian's brows rose.

Jane's tone was icy. "Yes, I managed to find another one. So I'm pretty busy these days." And then her voice turned scary-sweet. "How's your latest book coming?"

Ian Stone ignored the question to address Griffin.

"She's a treasure, Janie is. But slippery. We worked so well together, then one day...poof!"

Griffin wished he and his gut had hustled her out of the party sooner. The undercurrents between his librarian and this other man were murky, and he didn't want the dirt getting anywhere near her or her pretty shoes. *Janie,* the man had called her. *We were so very...close for those happy productive years.* Christ, she'd been more than the author's muse.

Much more.

"And here I didn't think you'd miss me at all," Jane said, the edge in her voice sharp. She tilted her head to look beyond Ian. "You were so busy with... I don't think I ever learned your name."

She was addressing a woman that Griffin now realized was standing slightly behind the bestselling author. The man brought her forward with a small flourish, as if presenting a prize. "Deandra."

Apparently Deandra didn't require a last name, or it had slipped Ian Stone's mind. The lady was red-haired, brown-eyed and so thin you could slip her between a door and its jamb, then wiggle her like a credit card to jimmy the lock. Griffin reached out to acknowledge the introduction, and it was like shaking hands with a skeleton.

She might be perfectly nice, but Griffin didn't care to find out either way because Jane's body was finely trembling again. Her skin was cool, too cool under his palm, and he wished they were back at Crescent Cove.

Tee-Wee White couldn't hurt her there, Griffin realized now. Because Jane was romantically wounded already, injured by none other than this arrogant, irritating "literary superstar." Damn! While he'd been smugly congratulating himself on saving her by commanding her to come to this party, he'd managed instead to bring her face-to-face with the man who'd apparently broken her heart.

Jane was going to kill him.

The tense silence that followed seemed to reinforce the idea. But someone had to end the standoff, and so he broke the quiet by announcing they were leaving. Jane didn't protest, but clutched his forearm as they made the short walk to their hotel situated across the street from the museum. Her body seemed to go more brittle with each step and Griffin eyed her with concern. Would she make it back to their suite before she fell apart?

Yes, he could leave her to deal with the aftermath alone, but tonight's event had been his idea. So he resigned himself to doling out tissues and considered offering a drink to combat an emotional collapse. What kind of booze mixed well with tears?

At the door to their rooms, he let go of her to reach for the key card. On his first try, he fumbled it. Jane snatched it out of his hand. Uh-oh, he thought, she was clearly eager to commence the weeping.

In another second they were inside. Wary, he walked backward into the living room, watching her as he braced for the first whimper.

She stood against the door, her palms flattened on the wooden surface. Her gaze hopped and skipped around the room, then finally settled on his face. "What do you have on hand that I can use as a murder weapon?"

CHAPTER ELEVEN

JANE SAW GRIFFIN flinch, but in her hot and bothered state she didn't try interpreting the reaction. As she stalked into the room, he kept a cautious eye on her. "I'm really sorry," he said as she passed him by to head for the desk placed against the far wall.

"Huh? Only be sorry if you can't find me a way to maim him." Yanking open the drawer, she scooped up a letter opener and brandished it. She needed some way to work off her terrible temper. "Will this do?"

"Maim *him?* Not, uh, maim me?"

She turned to look at Griffin. "What are you talking about?"

"Attending the party was my idea." He shoved his hands into the elegant, angled front pockets of vanilla-colored trousers. He wore them with a vertical-pleated Mexican wedding shirt in pale turquoise linen and gleaming leather loafers. At the cove, she'd seen him in nothing other than shorts or jeans and ragged Hawaiian shirts or tees. If she'd had to guess, she would have claimed his best pair of shoes had a swoosh on their sides.

She wasn't sure this cleaned-up stranger was any more attractive than the bronzed guy at the beach, however. For whatever reason, both managed to ring her sexual bell. Yet he was confusing her now, looking at her in a strange way that she couldn't decipher.

"Why don't you put down your instrument of death,"

Griffin suggested, crossing to her. He placed gentle hands on her shoulders, just as he had at the party. "Let me take your jacket."

Leaving the book launch, she'd shrugged it on, but she was happy to shed it now. The mad she'd worked up on the way back to the hotel was like a fire under her skin. Griffin hung the garment over a chair, taking an extra moment to straighten the lapels.

Aware he was usually a flinger, her eyebrows rose at his uncharacteristic fastidiousness. He was operating with the slow, careful movements of someone defusing a bomb. From the corners of his eyes, he sent her a sidelong glance. "Can I get you a drink?"

She'd sipped at a quarter glass of champagne before Ian had arrived, and the liquid had soured in her belly after their meeting. "I have a rule against raiding the minibar."

Griffin gave a smile. "Sure you do. But lucky enough, at times our moral codes take quite divergent paths. White wine?"

"All right." However, she'd lay the blame for her lapse not at Griffin's door, but Ian's. He made her so angry she just barely resisted stomping a foot—because she'd missed her opportunity to kick him with it where it counted. "Are you going to have something too?"

"Definitely." She saw him withdraw a bottle of wine from the mini fridge. For himself he poured some sort of amber liquid in a glass, neat. Then he crossed to the couch, setting down the two glasses on the nearby table. As he took a seat on the cushions, he grabbed up a box of tissues.

She frowned. "Are you okay?"

"Sure." He patted the place beside him. "I'm ready."

For what? But before she could voice the question,

he patted the cushion again and sent her an encouraging smile.

She couldn't figure him out. Sitting wasn't exactly appealing at the moment, not when she needed to work off some righteous anger. Call her silly and emotional, but seeing Ian had brought up a roiling combination of insult, disappointment and humiliation.

She would *never* fall in love again. Look what could happen.

"Those shoes must be killing you," Griffin said with another encouraging smile. "Though they're sexy as hell."

The compliment took her ire down a tick, so she made her way to the place beside him. Once she sank onto the seat, he reached for one shoe and brought it to his lap. His fingers found the zipper tab at the heel of the sandal and tugged it down. "Very sexy," he murmured, slipping it off.

He left that foot on his hard thigh and bent for the other. With the same tender care, he removed the shoe. With one big hand draped over the tops of her feet, he reached for a handful of tissues that he then offered to her, the odd expression back on his face. "Go ahead, honey-pie. It was my fault we were there tonight. I guess it's fair that you cry on my shoulder."

Cry on his shoulder? The tissues slipped from her hand as Jane stared at him. Then the pieces came together—his tender consideration, his careful movements, that look on his face that was part kindness, part resignation and part pity. For a moment she went speechless, then her anger started to boil again.

"You think I still care about that…that…"

"Norm Scrogman?" Griffin suggested.

How Griffin knew Ian's real name, she couldn't say. But it was as good a pejorative as any. "I despise him."

"Sure you do."

He didn't believe her. Jane slid her feet from his lap and gave him the evil eye. "Listen to me. The man is a selfish, egotistical, unabashed and unashamed user."

Maybe he mistook her tight voice for a tear-clogged throat. He picked up the tissue box and pressed it into her hands. "Go ahead. Get it all out."

She threw the cardboard carton at him. He ducked, and it bounced off the cushion and fell to the floor. "Hey!" he protested.

"Just be glad I'm not holding the letter opener," she said. "Don't you get it? I won't cry over that man. Any man." Ever again.

"Still, you're shaking."

"From rage. Do you know what he did to me?"

"I'm pretty curious now, I must admit."

Jane swiped up her wineglass and took a healthy swallow. Griffin, his gaze still wary, reached for his own beverage. "Let's agree not to throw anything else, okay?"

"I'm just so mad!" Jane declared. "Seeing him again brought it all back. I feel as if I've swallowed a balloon and it's inflating inside me."

He made a go-ahead gesture with his glass. "Then by all means let out some of the pressure, Jane. Though I find the idea of you exploding…uh, never mind."

More heat shot over her skin and she glared at him. "Did you have to bring that up now?"

"I probably shouldn't," he admitted. "It's just that you're kind of red-faced and your breath is coming too fast and—"

He broke off as she half cocked her wineglass. "—and I'm going to be very quiet now and let you get your feelings off your chest—" his glance dropped to her heaving breasts and then jerked back to her face "—I mean off your, um, mind."

Her gaze narrowed on him. "I think you're trying to distract me. Tease me out of my temper."

"A little. Is it working?"

His semihopeful and too-charming smile didn't move her. "No. Because that means you're still feeling sorry for me."

"Shouldn't I? Apparently the two of you had something going, some sort of…understanding and then he was a jerk to you."

"Jerk doesn't cover it," she muttered. "Have you ever read one of his books?"

"Not really my thing. I was on a plane or two when the movie adaptations played, but though I usually slept or read through them, I caught the gist." Griffin looked down at his drink, then back up. "I admit I heard Skye mention his name, so I checked out his website. I read some reviews of his books."

Jane tilted her head. "What'd you think?"

"That you might have guessed your association wasn't going to be happy-ever-after when the romantic relationship in every one of his novels ends in death by lingering disease or natural disaster."

Despite herself, Jane laughed. "Now I feel an even bigger fool."

He frowned. "I didn't mean to rub salt in the wound."

"You're not listening. I'm past being wounded when it comes to Ian." She took another swallow of wine. "He called me his muse, you know. In print."

"Three times."

She cocked an eyebrow.

"You can learn a lot online."

"He was my client for almost three years. His output was amazing, but he needed someone to help keep things straight. He usually had two or more books going at a time, and he'd bounce ideas off me every morning. We'd polish the pages he'd written every evening."

"Was he your only client?"

She shrugged. "He took up most of my time the last two years we were together. Evening work sessions turned into dinners. We started getting together weekends too. Then all indications were that we were headed for…"

"An ending unlike those in his bestselling novels."

"Yes." Like her father never failed to mention, she had been that silly and emotional. "He said such pretty things—and knew exactly when to say them. I'm annoyed to admit I soaked it all up."

"Why shouldn't you—"

"Because I should have been smarter. More wary." But the male attention and approval had been heady. "Looking back, I realize it was just too…studied."

Griffin frowned. "Meaning?"

"I think it was kind of a first draft. That Ian was working out relationship moves to use in a future book."

"Oh, God." Griffin looked away.

"Maybe he finally got all he needed from me. I only know that one day he said he wanted to start working on something new. And work on it in a different way—this time he was going to write without my assistance."

Griffin groaned. "I can see where this is going."

"I didn't suspect a thing. I even thought it was a good idea—good for our personal relationship—as a matter of fact." Her jaw tightened. "A couple of mornings later, when he'd told me he was going to be at a meeting, I let myself into his house because I'd left some papers I needed beside his computer. That's when I encountered a woman…Deandra. She was wearing the long cardigan sweater I left there for chilly mornings."

"And nothing else, I presume."

It came back to her now, the other woman's startled excuse, her own initial and ridiculous inclination to disbelieve her lying eyes. Then cold had washed over her, followed by an unnatural heat burning outward from her chest. "Ian was stepping into his pants when I walked into his office."

Griffin tossed back the rest of the liquid in his glass. "His reaction?"

"In two words: somewhat sheepish." She was reliving her own reaction now, the curdling contents of her stomach, the dizzying speed of her pulse, the taste of metal in her mouth.

"He asked that I come back at four that afternoon." Her fingers curled into fists. "I was leaching dignity by the second, so I agreed. I assumed we'd made the appointment to give me time to pack up my things—I had books there, my extra laptop—"

"Your favorite cardigan."

"You can't imagine I'd want *that* back." He shook his head and she picked up the story. "When I returned later, he was sitting at his desk, and he proceeded as if nothing had happened. He thought now that the truth was out, we could continue working together as before. Though he needed a new romantic muse, he still appreciated my professional skills."

"Jesus." Griffin laughed. "Even I know there are rules."

"Yes. The fact that he wrote bestsellers didn't give him a pass on lying and cheating. I told him so."

He nodded. "Of course you did. Followed up, I assume, by a dramatic rending of his manuscript-in-progress."

Shocked, Jane blinked, then set the wineglass on the table with a firm clack. "No. *That* would be against the rules too."

"Jane," Griffin said on a sigh.

"Huh?" Closing her eyes, she flopped back to the cushions. How she wished she could pluck that piece of her past out of her head and toss it away, she thought, forking her hands through her hair. Her muscles tight with tension, she stretched for the table with her bare toes, extending her legs as long as they would go. The hem of her dress tickled the top of her thighs as it rose. "He made me feel so naive. So needy."

The air suddenly shifted, and she felt Griffin rear off the couch. She opened her eyes to see him stalking toward the windows, a beautiful male figure in his stylish clothes. His shoulders looked a mile wide as he placed the inner surface of one forearm against the glass and stared into the night. "Maybe we should go to b—I mean to sleep."

"Are you kidding?" Her gaze idly ran down the length of his spine. She was accustomed to seeing him shirtless, and she imagined him that way now—that bronze swath of skin that stretched from neck to hips, the shallow valley of his spine, the play of muscles as he pulled himself up the cliff at the lower tip of the cove. "I'm too wound up for sleep."

He swung around. That laser gaze of his fixed on her face, and she felt herself going hot. Had he sensed her checking him out? She shot straight in her seat, yanking down the hem of her dress as far as it would go. Her gaze shifted aside and caught on her reflection in a mirror across the room. Her hair was tousled and wild. Remembering her conversation with Ian all over again, she touched the disordered waves.

"Why wasn't he honest with me back then?" she asked the woman in the glass as she yanked her fingers through the curling locks. "Tonight he didn't have trouble communicating this new hair wasn't to his taste. Why couldn't he have talked to me before humiliating me by fooling around behind my back?"

Griffin started back across the room, and she shifted to address him. He'd unfastened the top two buttons on his shirt, and her eyes stalled on the wedge of revealed skin. She cleared her throat and lifted her gaze to his face. "Couldn't he have said, 'Jane, it's been nice, but we're over'?"

When her companion didn't answer, a frisson of concern tickled her neck. She licked her lips and pressed farther into the cushions and then found herself talking again, as she always did when she was nervous. "Or he could have left a message on my phone." Her voice lowered, and she tried intoning in an Ian-serious imitation. "'Jane, I'm sorry, but it's time I move on.'"

A still-silent Griffin was standing over her now, the fierce expression on his face making him seem more pirate than that afternoon when she'd found him in eye patches and an earring. Her brain seemed to be stuck on babble. "Even a text would have—"

"Jane," Griffin interrupted, voice tight and matter-of-fact. "I'm sorry, but I'm having one of those inexplicable man-lust moments. Meaning if you don't get behind a locked door in the next seven seconds, I'm going to be all over you like coconut oil at a nudist colony."

At that, the heat in his gaze evaporated her thoughts. It seemed to evaporate the air too, because she went breathless as desire surged, then raced pell-mell through her bloodstream, flushing her skin like a fever. Ian Stone was cleared from her mind, his past betrayal suddenly wiped away by the big, tempting display of muscled male looming so close she could feel his sexual intent radiating outward to press against her skin.

She'd wanted to work off her temper, but now she couldn't remember what she'd been so mad about.

Other than Griffin.

Clearly, she was mad for him, she admitted to herself, because when he'd ordered her to be his party date, there'd been no other reason to agree. Oh, she'd told herself she'd gone along to support his interest in mingling with other writer types. That she wanted to witness him making professional progress. But that had been as good an excuse as any. Fact: she found him fascinating. Fact: despite all the reasons why she shouldn't be alone in a hotel room with him, she was. Fact: he'd been cold-hot-cold when it came to her, and it seemed as if he was running hot again.

Why not take advantage of that? She had those kinks she claimed she wanted to work out.

There was no need to get all uptight about their bubbling chemistry. It was merely the biological imperative to have sex, she told herself. Those irresistible feelings of desire that were near impossible to overcome or explain—so why overanalyze? She'd done research for an author once and learned why historically there were so many rules governing marriage—they were developed to constrain these primitive urges that all men and women experience from time to time.

But there were her own rules, Jane reminded herself. Griffin was her client, and Ian had been her client too, remember? That should prove why she shouldn't cross the line again.

But the devil on her shoulder whispered she'd learned her lesson about love. And Griffin wasn't Ian. Griffin wouldn't pretend pretty feelings he didn't have, and Griffin was so, so attractive, with his straight nose, his perfect high cheekbones, those eyes a fiery aqua-blue beneath the dark stripes of his brows.

She wanted him. Yes, she did. And sometimes even the librarian had to talk aloud among the stacks of books. Sometimes the governess had to break the rules, didn't she? She had to go after what she yearned for, or else there would never be any Gothic fiction.

And if Jane didn't think of herself first, no one else was going to.

THE GOVERNESS SHOULD really get moving, Griffin thought. He wasn't kidding about what he wanted.

And what he didn't want.

He couldn't listen to her for another moment. It got to him, the way that Ian Stone had disappointed her. And it hit just a little too close to home too. Not that he'd ever been a two-timer—banging a woman when seeing another was not his style—but he'd not always come clean about his feelings. Or lack thereof. Particularly the lack thereof. More often he'd kept silent, telling himself he didn't want to let down a lady, when the bald truth was that keeping his own counsel was for his own convenience.

"Five seconds," he warned Jane.

She slowly rose to her feet.

He didn't call the sensation sluicing through him disappointment. He'd made the offer—ultimatum, whatever—and was happy to abide by her decision. Hell, he'd *counted* on her stalking off. It was just as effective a way to prevent her Jane-tentacles from attaching to him as a tumble in his bed. See, every word that came out of her lush mouth made him almost want to care—and, hell, he knew he was incapable of doing more than a shallow imitation of that. Focusing on her body in bed would keep her out of his head.

Having her go to her own bed would work almost as well.

She had to brush by him to get to her room. As she moved, her sweet scent stroked him first. He cleared his throat. "Good ni—"

Her lips muffled the rest of what he'd meant to say.

Surprise slammed his heart against his ribs throughout the kiss. It kept him frozen too, until she stepped back and looked up at him. Her mouth opened.

He braced for whatever was going to come out of it.

"Have you ever been to a nudist colony?"

His jaw dropped. He shook his head. "Where the hell did that come from? Are you working on a Wikipedia article now?"

"You brought it up. It made me curious."

This was what was wrong with her. This was what made her dangerous. She unbalanced him. When he tried to scare her off or push her away, she stood her ground. And then she demanded disturbing things—*I had to help him include the emotion,* she'd said. *You'll have to do that too*—or asked odd, irrelevant questions like this one. He barely restrained himself from wringing her neck. "No, Jane, I've never been to a nudist colony."

She nodded. "Because you'd think they'd use sunscreen instead of coconut oil."

Now it was his turn to stare. "Your brain is too damn busy."

"I've heard that before," she said, looking down. Then she peeped up at him through the screen of her lashes. "Want to try quieting my wild mind?"

As if he was his sister's *OM* chewing gum. Jesus! This wasn't turning out how he'd expected. Which should be exactly as he expected when it came to Jane. Still, he couldn't move.

"First, I want to make clear this has nothing to do with

our working relationship. Instead, let's think of it like this," she said. "Right now, we're in a place out of time."

"Out of time," he echoed.

"This isn't the real world." She gestured with one arcing arm.

He followed the movement and found himself looking out the window at the lights of Los Angeles. He was a native. Jane was also a Los Angeleno. This *was* their real world.

"We've escaped, just for the night. A single night."

Escaped Crescent Cove. Beach House No. 9. The place that had *been* his escape.

That is, until Jane arrived, with her talk, her hair, her pretty eyes and even prettier mouth. Her crazy-making stubbornness.

"So what happens here—"

"—stays here," he finished for her, surrendering to the inevitable. And then he pounced.

With an arm at her back, he dragged her onto her tiptoes, melding their bodies together as he took her mouth. This time, he fell back into the aggressor role, and Jane fell into that only-when-he-was-kissing-her pliancy. Her head dropped back, and he caught it in one hand, his fingers twisting in her glorious, sun-brightened hair as his tongue went to work.

A tremor wiggled up her spine, snaking from the small of her back, and he felt it against the forearm he had pressed against the bare skin of her shoulder blades.

Which reminded him… He tugged on one end of that maddening bow at the back of her neck. The bodice of her dress fell to her waist.

Her arm came up to cover her bared body, but he grabbed both wrists and held them at her sides as he stepped back. Breath soughed in and out of his lungs as if he'd been sprinting as he stared at her naked torso.

His eyes closed for a moment as he imprinted the sight on his memory. Small, high breasts. Pale pink nipples. The thin skin at her throat thrumming with the same rapid beat he felt beneath his fingers.

He needed more nakedness.

Transferring both wrists to one of his hands, he reached around to the small of her back and sought the tab of a zipper. Jane made a helpless little noise as his fingers met her flesh, and then she went still as the metallic teeth parted with a hiss of sound.

The dress dropped from her hips and pooled at her bare feet.

Need surged to his groin, and he staggered back, still holding on to her arms. His cock went fully hard as his gaze took in the scrap of sheer undergarment wrapped low at her hips. "Good God," he murmured. Two halves of delicate violet fabric covered her there, laced together at the center with a narrow satin ribbon of a darker amethyst shade that was fashioned into a bow three inches below her shallow belly button.

Swallowing hard, he stepped forward again and deliberately placed her left wrist at her left side, then he did the same with the other wrist. "Don't move," he said, his voice hoarse. "Don't move a single inch."

Her breasts were trembling. He could see the sweet little nipples tightening as he focused on them. The panties were going to have to wait a minute until he could get his spiking lust under control. With one hand on her shoulder, he flattened his other palm against her ribs, then slid it up to cradle the underside of her breast.

She made to break, he sensed it, and he shot his gaze to hers. "Not a single inch, Jane."

His head bent. He rubbed his cheek against the tip of her nipple, knowing his evening stubble would lightly abrade the sensitive point. Her heartbeat sounded loud in his ear. Her hand touched his hair, and he stepped back again. "Not an inch, Jane," he reminded her.

She'd tortured him for days. Now it was his turn.

Her hand dropped, and he rewarded her with a tiny kiss to her nipple. She made another of those yearning noises, and he obliged her by pressing another one on the other bud. When the yearning turned into a low growl of sound, he grinned against her soft flesh and then relented, drawing the jutting nub into the heat of his mouth.

She bowed into the sensation, and he saw her fingers curl into fists. It was so damn gratifying to have her at his mercy. Her body, he quickly amended. He had her body, which was all that he wanted of her.

Her nipple hardened against his tongue. Lust tightened his muscles, and his cock twitched against the constraints of his clothes. He sucked on her, a sweet little tug, and then he thought of those decadent panties and his mouth tightened, his tongue pushing that bud against the roof of his mouth.

Jane's flower scent imbued the air. She was heating up, her skin burning everywhere he touched her. He switched to her other breast, and his fingers toyed with the one already wet. His tongue circled her areola, then lapped at the nipple, teasing her with the lightest of caresses. He sensed the growing rigidity of her muscles, and just when he gave her the smallest bite, she cracked.

One hand jerked to his head, holding him against her; the other reached for the fastening of his pants. Griffin pulled away, leaving her chest heaving and her eyes flashing silver fire. "No," she said, sounding gratifyingly desperate.

Little darling. With a smile, he wagged a finger at her. "Jane," he said, mock-stern. "I call the shots. I'm doing this just for you, you know."

Framed by curling tendrils of hair, her cheeks were flushed. "If you want to do something for me, take off your clothes."

Keeping his clothes on was keeping this business somewhat sane. The minute they were naked-to-naked the pace would pick up, and it would be a race to the finish. He wanted to savor the foreplay, enjoy their place out of time. As if she read his imminent refusal on his face, she spoke up again. "Just the shirt. Start with the shirt."

Yeah, that desperation was a definitely sweet payback. Taking pity on her, he brought his fingers to his shirt buttons. With her gaze glued to his moving hand, her own touched the center of her body, right between her breasts. As he unfastened his shirt, her thumb drew down her own skin, reflecting his movement. Touching on herself the same inches of skin he bared.

Jesus. It was the most unconsciously erotic sight in his memory. Her skin reacted to her own caress, goose bumps rising on her flesh in the wake of that trailing thumb. When he reached the last button, her hand had fallen to the band of those scandalous panties, and her fingers toyed with the ribbon.

"Don't you dare," he said, shrugging off his shirt.

"Dare what?" Her eyes didn't leave his chest.

"Those are *my* panties."

Frowning, her gaze lifted. "I'm not giving up a second pair."

We'll see about that. Instead of answering, he crooked a finger at her. Apparently forgetting her underwear alarm, she flew into his arms. The silken skin of her breasts met his chest.

Oh, hell. *His* alarms went off. The time for slow was over.

His mouth fastened on hers, his tongue thrust, his palms slid under fabric to cup the curves of her ass. She tilted her hips, her body rubbing against the urgent rigidity of his cock. He groaned, kneading the flesh in his palms as she pressed harder, clearly pleasuring herself.

When it was his job to pleasure her. Damn it! Why wouldn't she wait for him to provide that? Didn't she trust him to take her all the way?

But the questions put her in his head again. He couldn't have that. Bodies were what this was about. Bodies were the matter of the moment.

She was sucking on his tongue, her hips making tight little circles. He felt the tension in her bones and the burn of her skin. He knew the infuriating woman was close. Too damn close.

Breaking their kiss, Griffin slid his hands to her waist and lifted her away from his body. As he swung her into his arms, her mouth, swollen and red from his, turned sulky. "No!"

Ignoring her protest, he strode for the closest bedroom. A lamp was on low, the covers were turned back. He tossed her onto the mattress, then followed her down, their bare torsos meeting again. Immediately, she tried wiggling underneath him, but he knew her game.

She was trying, once more, to get herself off.

He threw one leg over the top of her thighs to keep her still and bent his head to her breasts. Jane moaned as he took her into his mouth. When he sucked at her nipple, she bucked against the weight of the thigh he had over hers but he held firm. "You'll take what I give you," he said on the way to her other breast. "You won't give yourself any more."

Her nipples had gone to a dark, fevered pink. He was fascinated by them and used his tongue to bathe them until they glistened in the lamplight. Jane had her hands in his hair, and her touch mimicked his. When his tongue caressed, she caressed. When he bit down, teasing her with the edge of his teeth, her fingernails sank into his scalp.

Then she made a new, urgent sound, and his head shot up. Her eyes were half-closed, her plush mouth pursed, her body rigid, as if she was poised on a precipice. *Sweet God.*

"Are you about to come?" he demanded. With just his play at her breasts?

Her fingers had dropped to the sheets, and now they curled into the fabric. "I'm…working on it."

"That's it," he muttered, rearing up from the bed. "You wait," he said, pointing a finger at her. "You just better damn well wait." Next he stripped off the rest of his clothes and tossed the condom he carried in his wallet on the bedside table.

Then he dropped back to the mattress and crawled between her legs, pushing them apart as he drew closer to her outrageous undergarment. With an elbow on either side of her hips, he stared down at that pretty ribbon lacing up the two halves of fabric. The panties were a metaphor for Jane herself, he decided. There were two sides to her: the steely governess and the soft woman. Both laced together and tied off with a sturdy yet feminine bow. The whole shielding the vulnerable, unknown heart of her.

Then Griffin groaned, realizing he was intellectualizing again. Once more he was letting Jane into his head and under his skin when he only wanted her *against* his skin. When he only wanted inside her body. "Get ready," he said in a dark voice as he gave a ruthless pull to the ribbon. "I'm going to make you see stars."

Her hair was soft here too. When he opened her with his thumbs, he discovered her pretty flesh went from shell- to fever-pink as well. He stared down at her as he traced the petaled contours and then circled the wet opening he'd explore next.

"Griffin," she said, sounding strangled.

"Hush." He toyed gently with her clit and heard her breathing hitch. "Patience," he said. "I'm getting there."

Still wanting to tease her, his thumb pressed the little button again. Then he placed two fingertips just inside the entrance to her channel. And Jane, stubborn, intractable, infuriating Jane, shoved her body down the sheets and took those fingers deeper. Took him to the palm.

Like that, took her own orgasm.

He watched her face as she rode it out, the sweet surrender to bliss that caused her dark lashes to sweep across her cheeks and her tender mouth to tremble. Then her body calmed, and he watched her eyes open. "Hey," she said.

His mouth was too dry to speak. With one hand she stroked his shoulder. With the other, she reached for the condom. He swiped it away from her. Then he kissed her, thinking that maybe this was the answer. Maybe he shouldn't go forward. Maybe it should be good-night now, and he wouldn't let this go any further.

But her hands were insistent and her mouth greedy on his. He found himself donning the rubber, then sliding inside her. "Aaah." God. Soft. Hot. Sweet.

Her legs clamped over his hips. He let his weight drive him deeper into her, and she tilted her hips again. He knew where this was going. He knew what she was doing.

But he didn't object this time. He just swept her up into the rhythm, and when he felt her reaching, when he was hanging on by a single thread, he put his hand between their bodies and found hers already there instead. It was her own touch that nudged her over before he could protest.

As she contracted around him, he felt the pleasure gather in his belly. Just as he took off, he lifted his head to take in Jane's flushed cheeks, swollen mouth, silver eyes. Then his squeezed shut as release pulsed, pulsed, pulsed through him.

When he came back to himself, he was flat on his back. A boneless Jane was lying across his chest. He didn't shift away, even though he generally didn't like being tangled with a woman in the aftermath. He always figured it was because of the nine months he'd shared the confined space of a womb with his twin.

He lifted his head from the pillow to see if Jane was sleeping. She must have felt his movement because she turned her cheek, their gazes meeting. Her eyes were sleepy. "Thank you," she said, her voice drowsy. "That was nice."

Nice? "Oh, yeah?"

"Mmm." Her lashes drifted toward her cheeks. "Nobody's ever tried to put me first."

On a soundless groan, he dropped his head to the pillow. Nobody had ever tried to put her first.

Would he ever get that—*her*—out of his head?

CHAPTER TWELVE

Sipping at room service coffee, Griffin listened to the sound of the shower and calculated how long before he'd be back to real life—his other real life—in Beach House No. 9. If Jane didn't stop to dry her hair and he put her own caffeine in a to-go cup, they could be in secure environs in approximately seventy minutes, he guessed.

He couldn't get out of the hotel suite soon enough.

His glance caught on the tumbled pair of sandals he'd slipped off Jane the night before. Pooled just a few inches away was the silky fabric of her dress. From there it was just another heartbeat before a memory of those ribbon-and-wishes panties made his palms itch.

"God," he murmured to himself, then strode over to the discarded articles and snatched them off the floor. The shoes he placed on a small table beside the door leading to the bedroom. The dress didn't cooperate as well, but he managed to fold it into a slithery bundle that he balanced on top of the sandals. "All tidied up," he told himself.

Could it be that easy?

We've escaped, just for the night. A single night, she'd said. Now that it was morning, could they return to their previous relationship? Which was no relationship at all, he hurriedly assured himself.

There was a knock on the suite's outer door.

On the other side, he discovered, stood his agent, Frank De Luca. The man was dressed in a coat and tie and car-

ried a supersize manila envelope that rivaled his belly in
the bulging department.

"Uh, hey," Griffin said and had a sudden image of Jane
walking out of the bedroom clad only in a towel, or maybe
even less. With a glance over his shoulder, he stepped to
block the gap in the door. "What are you doing here?"

"I got a text this morning," Frank replied, his gray
brows beetling over his pudgy boxer's nose. He was half
Irish and half Italian, which made him a perfect advocate
for his clients. He loved to fight. "From Janie."

"Janie? You call her Janie?" Ian Stone had called her
Janie.

The other man waved a hand. "I've known her since
she was a kid. Her dad was a client of mine at one time.
Aren't you going to let me in?"

Letting Frank in could complicate matters. And also
postpone Griffin's return to the cove. He glanced at the
envelope. "If that's for her, you can hand it over and be
on your way. I'll make sure she gets it."

"This is yours," Frank said. "And I'm here to talk with
you too."

What could he do but open the door? "I thought you
said Jane sent you a text," he muttered as the other man
passed him on his way inside.

"To say she was sorry she missed me last night. But
when I found out you were both still in town, I decided
to drop by."

"Wonderful. Terrific. Always a pleasure," Griffin
lied. Thank God he'd picked up Jane's fallen clothes. He
wouldn't have wanted to explain them away, he thought,
watching the other man toss the envelope onto the table
in front of the couch. "What's that?"

"Stuff the magazine was holding for you. They for-
warded it to me since you went missing."

"If I went missing, how come the book doctor, my sister and my agent all find me so damn easily?"

"Why are you so damn set on being hard to find?" Frank countered.

Griffin pasted on a smile. "How are the wife and kids?"

Frank hitched up his pants at the thighs and then settled into one of the room's armchairs. "Spending about twenty-three hours of the day in the pool. Raeanne is teaching Tim how to dive. Amy can almost swim one whole length underwater."

Pride puffed Frank's chest so that it nearly matched his belly. Still, since marrying Raeanne, he'd dropped about twenty pounds and his face wasn't quite so unhealthily florid. "Have you been watching your blood pressure and eating better?" Griffin asked, sitting on the couch across from the older man.

"Sure. Raeanne insists on all that organic age-free crap."

Griffin bit down on his smile. "I believe you mean free-range."

"Free-range, age-free, what's the difference? She made something for dinner last night with tutu."

"Tofu."

"It wasn't sirloin, that's all I know. But it makes her happy, so…" He shrugged. "She's been good to me. Marriage has been good to me. I highly recommend it."

Griffin thought of Tess, who'd run from her husband to the cove. Of David, sleeping in his kids' sleeping bags on the beach. "Glad to hear it."

"You know what I'm not glad to hear?" Frank asked, crossing one ankle over his knee. "Janie says you're not making much progress."

Shit. "There's an office. Whiteboards. Sharpened pencils."

Frank just looked at him.

Double shit. "I've never missed a deadline. You know that."

And still Frank looked at him.

Griffin shifted his gaze. Outside the window, the sky was that flat blue of summer, as if it had been ironed by the heat. This time of year in Afghanistan, the temperature was brutally hot, matching the increasing violence as insurgents climbed over the mountain passes to engage the troops. It was a deadly season that might only be mitigated if the previous year's lousy crop yield forced the other side's fighters to focus more on growing poppies and wheat than killing their enemies.

It was the kind of detail that belonged in his book. And if it was just a succession of those kind of details, he'd have racked up the pages by now. But Jane was insisting on emotions too, which meant writing about Erica and Randolph and all the other young and innocent cherries who'd stepped off the Chinooks as rookies and had been exposed to death within thirty seconds.

Which made them feel so damn alive. So damn alive until they went home…or weren't alive at all anymore.

If he wrote about all that, would his calm last?

Maybe he should raise the idea of not completing the project, Griffin thought. Though it was true that he'd never missed a deadline and he didn't want to start now, when each morning came, he couldn't dredge up a shred of motivation. Backing out was going to be a pain in the ass, and he wasn't happy about how it might affect him professionally, but waiting for the will to begin work became less viable an option with every passing day.

Torn, he pushed both hands through his hair. "Look,

Frank. I've not completely made up my mind, but I need to tell you I'm considering—"

"You should cut Jane loose if you're not going to get serious," Frank said.

Grimacing, he leaned forward on the cushion. "I said I'm only considering—"

"This is about her, Griff, not about you."

Griffin stared at the other man. Then he glanced toward the bedroom door, not sure if he wanted Jane to step out and interrupt the conversation or if he wanted Frank to finish. "I—" he started, then stopped, resigned. "What are you getting at?"

"Ian Stone."

The name made him want to spit, even though Ian Stone was exactly why Jane had ended up in bed with Griffin last night. Knowing she was still hung up on her literary superstar had made it safe for him to even consider sex. And it was clear why she'd accepted—she'd been willing to take her night out of time because a little self-esteem boosting had been in order after coming face-to-face with that ass and the other woman.

"I know about all that," Griffin said.

Frank raised an eyebrow. "Then you'll understand me when I say it's not right to fuck with her."

Griffin twitched. Jesus! Did it show on him? Was there a sign on his forehead that read I Boffed Jane? He frowned at his agent. "I don't think it's right to call it fucking, either."

That word implied callousness. He hadn't been uncaring. To the contrary, he'd *wanted* to pleasure her. Was it his fault that she hadn't trusted him to make that happen? His own ego had taken the blow last night, but next time he was going to tie her up—

No, of course there wasn't going to be a next time.

"That's what it will be, though," Frank said, "if it gets around that you reneged on your obligation when you were working with Jane."

The words took a minute to sink in, because Griffin's mind had spun away on images of Jane bound by soft rope. Blinking, he came out of his brief reverie to focus on Frank once again. "I'm not sure I'm following you."

The agent narrowed his eyes. "She told you about working with Ian?"

"Yeah. Heard all about that."

"And that she left him?"

"Because he two-timed her," Griffin protested. "Hell, any thinking person would walk away."

"Ian Stone hasn't turned in a book since. He'd been a blockbuster well, and without Jane it dried up."

"Serves him right." He was supposed to feel sympathy?

"But the blame has fallen on Jane's shoulders. Ian claims to any who'll listen that it's her fault. That her defection eroded his confidence."

"What a pussy," Griffin said, disgusted.

"But a talkative, loud one. Loud enough that she hasn't been able to find more work. He's dragged her good name through the mud. Spread it around that she's willing to leave a writer in the lurch."

Griffin froze. While he'd been loath to ditch his deadline because of the ding to his rep, he could see how much harder Jane would take the professional hit. He heard her voice in his head on the day she went to visit her father: *success is the only option.*

"You said you know her dad?"

"Brilliant guy. Cold as a fish."

His legs suddenly restless, Griffin popped up from the couch, crossing to the window, then circling the room.

There on the table were those girlie shoes, that slithery dress, the evidence that he'd held a naked Jane in his arms.

Nobody's ever tried to put me first.

"So you see, Griffin, if you're not going to get serious on this project, you need to cut her loose, quick, so she can find another client. Have a real success. Reputation and word of mouth are everything in her line of work."

The information tumbled through his brain and roiled his belly. Before he could answer Frank, before he knew *how* he would answer Frank, the bedroom door snicked open. Carrying her small duffel bag, Jane wore a straight khaki skirt, a white T-shirt made like mummy bandages and a pair of glossy flat shoes the color of new money. Her color was high, and her mouth was swollen. If you looked closely—he did and found himself shifting forward before he stopped himself—you could see that the edges of her lips were blurred by the slight burn his stubble had left behind. Her glance flicked to Frank and then transferred to Griffin.

Their gazes locked. This could end now, he thought. Right this moment he could tell Jane he wasn't going to write the book, and Frank would pack her up and take her away. He would never have to see her again, not those too-clear eyes, not her crazy shoes. Never again would he have to wonder what decadent underwear she wore.

Never let himself think that if he hadn't been a part of ruining her career, he sure as hell hadn't been involved in saving it either.

Nobody's ever tried to put me first.

He crossed to her and snatched her small bag out of her hand. His decision had been made. Self-aware enough to acknowledge the ice inside him had been compromised and what came next would risk further damage, he gritted his teeth as he stalked toward the door. He didn't

know how he was going to do it without getting scream-
ing ugly, but real life back at the cove meant writing that
goddamn memoir. "Let's go, honey-pie. We've got work
to do at Beach House No. 9."

JANE AND GRIFFIN were stuck in traffic on an infamous
stretch of the 405 freeway, but she finally felt as if she'd
made some progress. Things were going her way professionally. And on the personal side, her Ian-related demons had been banished. Last night's escapade between
the sheets had been good for her ego.

Only two things kept her from bouncing in her seat.
One, she was a little tender in certain places, and two, she
didn't think her driver shared her good mood. He sat, silent and still, behind the wheel of his boxy vintage BMW.

Nevertheless, it appeared the tide had turned in her
favor. When she'd ventured from the bedroom this morning—a little uncertain, she'd admit, since she'd woken
alone and the only evidence he was still in the suite was
the scent of fresh coffee—he'd been standing on the other
side of the door, an unreadable expression on his face.
"We've got work to do," he'd said, and she might have dis-
believed the seriousness of the statement if Frank hadn't
been in the room as well. Griffin wouldn't have made
the declaration in front of his agent unless he meant it.

Darling Frank.

"He looked good," she mused aloud, then darted a
glance to her left. "Frank, I mean."

Griffin grunted. "He told me he's been eating tutu."

"Huh?"

A smile hitched the corner of his mouth. "Tofu."

She laughed, even as she stared at that small curve of
his lips. He hadn't shaved, and dark whiskers peppered

his jaw and chin. It would have made for a prickly kiss if he'd woken her with one.

She wouldn't have turned away from it.

No, no! She *would* have turned away from it. That was their agreement, right? They'd decided that what happened that night in the hotel room would stay in that hotel room. Meaning she wouldn't have let it happen again this morning.

She wouldn't let it happen again, period.

He looked toward her as if he'd heard her little sigh. "You know Frank's wife, Raeanne?"

"Sure. I've babysat for Tim and Amy on occasion."

"Nice of you." His attention turned out the windshield as the line of cars started to move.

"Nice of them," she said, her voice light. "I needed the extra cash."

Griffin muttered darkly.

"What's that?"

His gaze slid right again, and she felt it like a touch. Then, as the cars in front of them came to a stop, he did just that, he touched her, his hand sliding beneath her hair to cup the nape of her neck. His thumb stroked her cheek, and her belly clenched. Between her thighs there was an instant swelling heat. Tingling.

She held her breath, trying to disguise her reaction. But when his thumb moved again, a shivery chill ran down her neck and made her nipples tighten against the cups of her bra. Surely he couldn't miss the flush blossoming over her skin.

"Jane." His fingers gave her neck a little squeeze. "About last night…"

No! Were there three words a person wanted less to hear? Her annoyed glance bounced off him, and she squirmed against the soft leather. Did he think he needed to reiterate theirs was a one-night thing? Didn't she know that? It had been a great one-night thing—she hoped for him too—but she'd set the terms herself.

Nobody knew better than Jane that going any deeper could lead to professional and personal disaster. A woman had to protect herself from that.

Just as she opened her mouth to make clear she knew the score, a deafening noise blasted. A blur of movement raced past her window. With a little shriek, Jane jumped, dislodging Griffin's hand.

"Damn motorcycle," he said, glaring out the windshield.

Her startled heart settled as she realized what had happened. A guy on a wicked-looking two-wheeled vehicle was weaving through the traffic ahead, using the space between automobiles to create his own lane. Blowing out a breath of air, she noted Griffin continued to glower in that direction.

Then he shook himself and cast a quick glance at her. "Where were we?"

No place they needed to return to, Jane decided, and grasped for a different subject. "You don't like motorcycles?" she asked.

"Hate 'em."

Weird. "I thought men had a thing for those kind of machines—something about all that horsepower between their thighs…." The instant the words left her mouth her mind tumbled back to the night before. Griffin on top of her, his body driving into hers, her legs wrapped around his hips. It had been so long for her that her inner flesh could still feel his imprint. Her face went hot again.

"Jane?" Griffin sounded amused. "What's going through your head?"

As if she'd tell. "I'm just curious," she said, holding

tight to this new thread of conversation. "A risk taker like yourself, an open road, a Harley-Davidson. Is there no appeal whatsoever?"

"Zero." He ran a hand over his hair. It was longer now, long enough for her to see the crisp darkness was thick and straight. "We had a couple of trail bikes as kids. Riding them almost killed my brother. *I* almost killed my brother."

She stared at him when he didn't elaborate. "You can't leave it at that."

The traffic had slowed again, and as he braked he threw her a look. "Did anyone ever tell you you're way *too* curious?"

She supposed she was. Another woman, knowing there was nothing for her beyond a one-night stand, would have curtailed any further thoughts about being in Griffin's bed. To daydream about what it would be like to be there again, to be able to stroke those lean muscles and lick at his hard mouth and run her palm down his erection to see if she could make him tremble as she had when he'd placed that first light kiss to her nipple. That kiss and every other had ignited a fire in her, and she'd been desperate to experience the burn.

"My brother's the real risk taker," Griffin said now.

"Oh, right," she scoffed, hoping he wouldn't notice the hoarse note to her voice. "And you're Safety Sam."

He shrugged. "More so than Gage, anyway. He was the one always issuing challenges."

She glanced over, surprised and a little gratified. It looked as if he might actually open up. "Challenges like what?"

"When we were young it was typical kid stuff. Who could hold a handstand the longest. Which one of us could catch the first lizard. Who could eat the most Oreo cookie middles."

Jane sniffed. "This is what makes males unfathomable to me. Clearly the chocolate wafers are the only reason an Oreo's worth eating."

He tossed her a smile that made her heart stumble. She gave it a moment to stabilize, then prodded him again. "So if Gage was always the challenger, who was usually the winner?"

His smile died. "Gage…Gage would do just about anything to win, and he usually did, except for the day I dared him to race those stupid motorcycles."

"Because…?"

He sent her a wry glance. "It was one of the few things I was better at."

"So what happened?" she asked, her tone neutral.

"We were visiting the mountains. There was a trail that led away from the house, that ran for, I don't know—three or four miles? Off we went."

"With you in the lead?"

"Oh, yeah. Adrenaline was pumping through my blood and I was running as fast and hot as that damn bike. I felt like a million bucks when I got to the turnaround point without a sign of Gage behind me. But then I went cold, my twin-sense telling me something bad had happened."

Jane felt her mouth go dry. Griffin seemed lost in thought, his gaze trained out the windshield but his focus clearly on the past. "But your brother's all right," she heard herself say. Of course he was all right.

"I turned around, revving the bike even faster. Gage was about a mile back, his own bike on the ground. He was struggling to get it righted. That's when I saw that his chest was bleeding. He'd lost control and run into a tree. The sharp end of a broken limb had stabbed him in the chest."

Oh, God. She could see it. She heard the echo of fear in Griffin's voice.

"I got him on the back of my seat. He didn't seem to notice anything was wrong, but I screamed at him to wrap his arms around my waist. I threw one arm behind me to make sure he didn't fall. It seemed to take hours to get back to the house, and the whole time I felt his blood pumping in spurts against my back. And I kept thinking, I goaded him to do this. I'm going to have to tell our parents it's my fault he's dead. I've killed my twin."

"You didn't goad—"

"But I did. He hadn't wanted to race, but I called him every name one brother will call another until he got mad enough to go along." Griffin ran his hand over his hair again, and his voice was so quiet she thought he was talking to himself and not to her. "I'm the older brother. It's up to me to keep everybody safe."

She didn't like the dark note in his voice. This was supposed to be her happy day! But she appreciated the insight into his personality. He felt so responsible for people. "That must have been scary," she said. "Was the recovery difficult?"

"Sometimes I think it was harder for me than him. He took full advantage of my guilt. The video-game challenges I lost!" And then he grinned.

It was as if that white smile had the power to break up the traffic as well as the tension in the car. They started moving again, and she flipped on the radio and found a station dedicated to surf music from the 1960s. "Little Deuce Coupe" and "Surfer Girl." Nobody could be unhappy hearing those songs. They were the perfect antidote to any lingering down mood.

In a few minutes she caught him tapping out the beat on the steering wheel. He saw her looking at him and smiling about that. "What?" he asked.

As if she'd point out he was humming. "Just thinking about how well we'd share a package of cookies," she said, determined to keep things light. "I'd take all the crispy wafers—"

"Leaving me the sweet creamy centers," he finished, capping it off with a leering wiggle of his eyebrows. "You know how good I am with those."

She whacked him on the shoulder, pretending outrage when she was actually delighted by the teasing turn of the conversation. They were almost back at Beach House No. 9, and they'd managed to sidestep all the potential land mines left by their interlude between the sheets the night before.

The car tires crunched over the shells, and Jane unrolled her window to take in the scent of the cove, all warm summer day spiced with salt and balanced by the tang of the eucalyptus trees. A shaft of sunlight hit her straight in the eyes, and she closed them, breathing deep of the magic. In the distance the waves threw themselves onto the shore, no holding back.

He pulled into the driveway at the rear of the house. As they stepped from the car, Private came racing from Tess's place, where he'd had a sleepover with her kids. He ran to Griffin first, carrying a well-bitten Frisbee. But he paused for only a short head rub before he rushed to Jane.

Her mood only rose higher. The plastic toy was more than a little slimy, and Griffin snickered at her lame excuse for a toss, but who wouldn't be charmed by the canine's exuberant greeting? "Good dog," she said as Private raced back.

She might have even skipped a little. Good day.

"Hey, can you get that manila envelope?" Griffin asked. "I'll bring in the bags."

She held the bulky thing in two hands as she followed him into the cottage. The memory of her first visit rose in her mind as she scuffed her feet on the welcome mat that advised the visitor to abandon hope. Take that, she thought, scraping her soles against the words All Ye Who Enter Here a second time for good measure.

He carried their bags toward the bedrooms. Jane headed for the office. The lousy Frisbee toss should have been forewarning, but she didn't think of it as she paused in the doorway to lob the envelope at the desk. It slid straight across the unencumbered surface to fall to the floor, some of the contents spilling.

Grumbling to herself, she crossed the sisal area rug. Everything had landed upside down. She crouched to gather a sheaf of papers. Underneath them was a dozen photographs. Their subject matter caught her off guard, her hand going lax so the pictures scattered across the floor in an array of images.

A shadow loomed in the doorway. Griffin stood there, with Private at his side. She glanced toward him as his gaze trained on the glossy paper. All expression on his handsome face was wiped clean and his fingers curled in the dog's dark fur.

"Erica and I had been embedded about six months when they sent a photographer," he said. His expression remained closed off, but his voice was matter-of-fact. "Believe it or not, we'd had a chance to clean up when those were snapped. Still look a little worse for wear."

Jane gazed back at the photos. Some were posed, some were candid. In each, Griffin and his colleague were front and center. You couldn't miss the effects of their half a year at war. They were both thinner than the "On Our Way" image. Their clothes were ragged.

One shot pictured Griffin from behind. He stood on the edge of a ravine, his arm around Erica's shoulders. Her face was turned in profile, her expression clearly one of...

Love.

There was no doubt in Jane's mind that the woman reporter had been in love with Griffin. Glancing at him now, taking in his tense pose and rigid expression, she realized he must have reciprocated her feelings. Jane didn't know why she hadn't come to this conclusion before...it made perfect sense. Two intelligent, good-looking people with common interests and a common goal. Add to that the intense atmosphere of war, and falling in love seemed inevitable. Ernest Hemingway was famous for a novel with similar elements.

From the beginning, Jane had known Griffin's memoir would include stories of people he'd lived and breathed beside. Some who had been wounded. Some who had died. From the beginning, Jane had known the project would be difficult for him.

A chill washed over her skin as all her happy mood dissipated. She didn't want to think it had anything to do with this new revelation regarding Griffin's heart. They didn't have feelings for each other, after all. They'd been clear about the boundaries. It must be that the fog was returning to the beach early.

But as the room went darker, for the first time Jane was forced to recognize that—even without any particular attachment to Griffin—his project might also be tough on her.

CHAPTER THIRTEEN

AFTER THAT INTERLUDE in the pop-up tent, David had hoped that he and Tess had reached a turning point. The point where she turned around and moved back home. But she'd remained at Crescent Cove, and he remained stymied.

It seemed apropos that he was once again slowed by sand filling his shoes as he trudged behind Duncan and Oliver on their way to the beach bungalow. Soccer practice had finished early, but the boys were still red-faced, and their hair was sweaty around the edges. Racing toward the surf, they shed shirts, shoes, long socks and shin guards. "No going into the water unless your mom is watching," he cautioned them, bending down to swipe up the discards.

Ahead was the patch of sand where he'd pitched the tent. She'd busted him that night. First, by discovering him on his secret mission. Then she'd shattered his vow to keep distant with her talk about sleeping with someone else. But he'd thought the resulting fiery act might have put some points on his side of the scoreboard. She couldn't deny how good they were together in bed, and he'd hoped that reminder might bring her home to him.

Of course, in the preceding months, he hadn't been available between the sheets, either. But that he could change, he decided. Men separated lovemaking from emotion all the time. His pace picked up as he approached No. 8 with new hope. He'd find them some privacy. He'd promise regular sex. Would that get her home by nightfall?

But privacy wasn't an immediate option. As he neared the house from the rear, he caught sight of three pairs of feminine legs propped on the porch railing. The boys, now dressed only in nylon sports shorts, were tussling in the sand at the bottom of the steps, distracted from their initial plan for a wade in the ocean by a rubber ball they both wanted to claim. Just out of sight of his wife and the others, David paused, listening to the women's conversation.

Rebecca was brainstorming ideas for her final assignment for the history seminar she was taking. It apparently included an in-class presentation. "One of my friends can trace her lineage back to the *Mayflower,* and she has a family tree all mapped out. This other boy is going to talk about slavery. He's going to bring in the scrap of a dress an ancestor wore when she was auctioned at eight years old. In comparison, everything I've thought of is boring." With an agitated movement, she crossed and uncrossed her legs, the ankle bracelet they'd bought her for her thirteenth birthday winking in the sunlight.

David shook his head. How could she be a teenager already? But she was; even her voice sounded nearly adult to him now. She'd be moving on from their family so soon. And before that, moving on to high school in the fall, where they could lose her in other insidious ways.

The thought tightened a vise around his chest, and he couldn't catch his breath. His tongue felt thick, and there were black spots at the edges of his vision. It felt like a heart attack, it felt just like that morning on his fortieth birthday when his across-the-street neighbor, Mac Kearney, had called his cell phone. *Breathe,* David ordered himself now. *Breathe.* If he keeled over in the soft sand, no one would hear him fall.

As he tried sucking in air, another voice started talking. It belonged to the woman who was giving Griffin trouble. Jane. "Can your project cover more modern history?"

"I guess," said Rebecca, in the tones of a teen beleaguered.

David's vision cleared as more oxygen infused his bloodstream. His anxiety ratcheted down a notch, and he leaned against the side of the house, clutching the soccer apparatus to his gut.

"How about World War Two?" Jane was suggesting. "You could interview Mr. Monroe. Find out what it was like to be a foreign correspondent. Maybe as part of your presentation he could come speak to your class."

"Hmm…" David's daughter was mulling it over. "Okay. And what if…" her voice gained enthusiasm "…what if Uncle Griff could do the same about Afghanistan?"

"I don't know if that's such a good idea," Tess put in.

Rebecca was standing now, ignoring her mother. "I'm going to ask."

"Let's start with Mr. Monroe first," Jane said. "Can I take Russ along?" As she also came to her feet, David could see she had his youngest son on her hip.

It was only Tess who remained on the porch as the two other females trekked off, Duncan and Oliver on their heels like puppies sniffing out new amusement.

Even though he now had his wife alone, David hesitated, staying hidden from her. There was still a residual aching pressure in his chest, and he wasn't sure that his dry tongue could convincingly promise great sex. He wasn't sure it was even a wonderful idea any longer. Damn it! Though he wanted his family back at the house, he couldn't risk getting too close to any of them.

"Did you have something you wanted to say to me?" Tess pitched her voice in his direction.

Shaking his head, he gave up on lurking and moved around the corner to mount the porch steps. When it came to the kids, she always had a sixth sense, instantly aware if one was about to catch them wrapping the Santa gifts or if another was two steps from interrupting foreplay. Apparently that ability extended to him too. He settled onto a porch chair, leaving an empty one between himself and his wife. The boys' soccer stuff he dropped at his feet.

Glancing over, he felt yet another pang. He thought she might be thinner than before, but her skin had a light tan revealed by her tank top and sporty miniskirt. It had matching attached shorts, and she wore that kind of thing when she took the baby out for a jog in the stroller. Her hair was tied back in a ponytail, the ends brushing the spot between her shoulder blades he'd kissed the other night after he'd mounted her from behind.

His cock went half-hard at the memory, and he could almost feel the sleek skin of her hips against his palms. Why was he having second thoughts? Great sex was a stupendous idea.

Except Tess didn't seem to be much concerned with David at all. Her beautiful blue eyes were trained on the small band of their children as they ambled up the beach. He followed her gaze, and the silence between them grew longer and more uncomfortable. Finally, he cleared his throat. "History, huh?" he said, referring to Rebecca's project.

Her head turned to him, the bones of her face elegant. And the expression so serious. "Our history, encapsulated right there. From Rebecca to Russ."

The vise cinched down again. David plucked at the front of his dress shirt. He'd taken off the tie as he'd left work, but now he went after the buttons. It didn't make it much easier to breathe. It didn't prevent him from glancing again at the kids, receding in the distance.

Over Jane's shoulder, little Russ suddenly looked at him. He raised one chubby arm and executed a baby wave, the kind where the fingers and thumb met a few times like a tiny duck quacking.

A sharp pain shot down David's right arm as he found himself waving back. Was this a heart attack for real, then? Or was the warning sign pain in the left arm? He let his hand fall to his lap but kept his eyes on his smallest son.

Damn it. Why wasn't he turning into his dad? Why wasn't the whole distance thing working? The old man had been as remote as an outer planet. If he'd ever worried over his children or suffered for the love of them, he'd managed to hide it very well.

When his father's youngest child—David's little brother, the first Russ—had died of leukemia, Lawrence Quincy had left the hospital and gone right back to his desk at the water authority. There'd been a funeral. David had been six and his mother had dressed him up in a cousin's hand-me-down suit that had smelled like mothballs. His father had probably taken off work to attend, but there'd been no other vestige of mourning. Lawrence had never mentioned the dead child's name again.

It seemed such a smart way to be now! Stoic and untouchable. That morning when he'd made that stupid, stupid mistake and almost lost his own Russ, all David could think about was the horror he would have felt if it had really happened. All he could do afterward was find some way to protect himself from possible future pain.

He just couldn't, couldn't love them all so damn much.

"David?" Tess's voice grew urgent with concern. "David, what is it?"

Her sixth sense at work again. He ran a hand over his face, wiping away a cold sweat. "It goes by so fast, doesn't it?" His gaze cut to her, then back to the kids, who were almost out of sight around the bend toward the house where the World War Two reporter lived. "That old guy they're going to visit was at our wedding reception, right? And it seems just like yesterday, but it was a lifetime ago. Four lifetimes."

"So that's it, then?" Tess asked.

The sharp note in her voice had him staring back at her, suddenly wary. "That's what?"

"You feel as if your good days are gone."

"No! I was just…" He threw up a hand, not wanting to get into it. Wasn't he here to promise great sex? His voice lowered, he hoped, to a seductive rasp. "I had a good night, a very, very good night, right here on this beach not long ago."

It only took a second for him to realize it was the exact wrong tactic. Her eyes narrowed, and while her face flushed a little, it looked more angry than aroused. "Throwing that…that…purely physical response in my face is not helping matters."

"Damn it," he said, disgusted with himself. "You know I'm no good at this kind of thing. I was never the charming ladies'-man type and I don't know why I'd think I'd start being that way now. You should have married one of those guys in your acting classes if you wanted smoothly scripted lines."

"Just start being honest!" she said. "You talk about time going by fast, about four lifetimes. I don't know what you mean by it."

"I don't mean anything. I was being nostalgic, Tess."

Or an idiot, because she didn't appear placated. "I was thinking about the fact that I'm the father of four. I never saw—"

"You never saw yourself as being stuck with them, I get it. Well, Rebecca and Russell you can claim were oops babies, but you wanted Duncan and Oliver. You were a completely active and informed participant in the conception of them both."

He couldn't believe she was seriously going down this route, so he tried taking the emotion down a notch or two with a small smile. "And really, Tess, what were we thinking? I'm not sure they're actually human children. Have you seen them feeding themselves Cheetos with their toes?"

Amused or appalled. Those were the two emotions he'd been going for. Instead she just stared at him, all expression leaving her face. "That's the answer, then. You wish we didn't have the children."

"No!" Christ, he didn't wish them away. That wasn't it at all. "Tess, you've got to believe me. The kids…" His tongue was the size and consistency of one of those loofahs she used to smooth her skin in the shower.

"You got a vasectomy without telling me."

"I…" His stomach knotted. More cold sweat broke over his skin. Fuck, he could see her point about that. "In my defense, I really thought we had agreed that four was our limit."

"I have to know…" Her voice went very quiet. "I have to know if you're fine with having those four."

Oh, Tess. She was killing him here. "Of course. Good God, of course."

She stood up, her gaze steady on his face. "It's me, then. You don't want me."

"No!" He stood too, reaching out for her as she rushed

to the steps, but he stumbled over Duncan and Oliver's soccer paraphernalia, his foot catching in a loop of a shin guard's stretchy strap. Before he could get himself untangled, she was running off down the sand.

Frustrated, he watched her retreating figure. What was he going to do now? How could he get her back without losing her by telling the truth? How would he get them all back without being crushed by the weight of loving them?

YESTERDAY, FOLLOWING their return from L.A., Jane had spent the rest of the afternoon with Tess and her kids. By tacit agreement, she and Griffin had put off getting down to work until the following morning. She'd even managed to convince Rebecca to delay her request of his help on her history project, not wanting to immerse him in thoughts of Afghanistan too soon. But it had to be done today. Stalling was over.

She'd been up since five, finally giving up on rest when all her dreams took her back to the night before. That single night she should be putting from her mind. He'd yet to stir from his bedroom, and it was closing in on eight. When she heard his door pop open, she wiped her hands on her jeans and gave a quick glance around the office. The manila envelope that Frank had passed to Griffin held a few more surprises that she'd arranged in readiness for him.

She heard him in the kitchen getting coffee. Next, his footsteps sounded in the hallway. Outside the beach house, the surf was up, because its *shush shush shush* was loud in her ears. Or maybe it was just the triple-timing beat of her heart, expressing the nervousness she felt about how she'd find his temperament today. The anxiety was ridiculous, really. She'd seen him in so many moods already:

grim, gruff, teasing, kind. Dispassionate. Passionate. The whole gamut, actually.

More than she'd experienced with any other man, she thought. She was beginning to know Griffin very well.

So her apprehension was probably because this was *her* first real day on the job. It was her time to get down to work, and that's just what she'd do. As a book doctor, beyond brainstorming, editing and fact-checking, another of her responsibilities was to keep the client in a creative mood and upbeat about the current project. So she turned to the office's doorway and smiled as he crossed the threshold.

"Good morning," she said. "Ready to get started?"

He stood, steaming mug in hand. Today he wore a pair of battered jeans and a short-sleeved shirt that was missing a button or two. His hair seemed to have grown inches overnight, and its gleaming darkness only made the blue of his eyes appear more intense. Without saying a word, his gaze roamed about the room.

Jane cleared her throat. "I used surface-safe double-sided tape."

He looked at her, one eyebrow raised.

"For the photos," she clarified. In the packet Frank had delivered had been a second set of photographs—shots of the platoon soldiers at work and at rest. She'd posted them about the room in hopes they'd help Griffin excavate his memories. "I wouldn't take a chance on them peeling off any paint."

"Of course you wouldn't," he murmured.

She walked to the desk and lifted a thick stack of papers. "And there was this, Griffin. You have a little over two hundred manuscript pages of the memoir already written."

He looked at the bundle of white pages as if he'd never seen them before. "I do?"

She ruffled them with one hand. "From the date on the header, you were working on them the last couple of months you were in Afghanistan."

He blinked. "I'd forgotten. Completely put it from my mind." His short laugh didn't sound all that amused. "I dumped the laptop and the memory sticks I used over there after…before I came back."

Once Erica had been killed? It made sense that he'd take such action after losing the person he loved. She remembered him saying, *It's up to me to keep everybody safe,* and realized just how shattering the loss must have been to a man who believed that. Jane swallowed. "But not before you emailed what you had to your publisher. There's a lot to be done in the next couple of weeks, but if you can get this polished and put into shape, you'll make your deadline."

"The next couple of weeks?"

Oh, boy. He really had been sticking his head in the sand. "That's what you have, Griffin, remember? Two more weeks before the first half of your memoir is due. Two more weeks with me at the beach house."

He ran a hand over his hair. "I've lost track of time."

With the whole dispassionate thing going on now, he strolled farther into the room, surveying the fifty or so photos she'd arranged. Most of them were five-by-sevens or eight-by-tens. They showed soldiers tussling, sleeping, eating. Walking on patrol, shooting weapons, standing guard. From across the room, he glanced over at Jane. "You didn't include any of Erica."

Yeah. Well. She'd been trying to spare his feelings, of course. "It's because—"

"She's dead?" he suggested, cool as you please.

The chill ran down Jane's spine as she shrugged.

Griffin turned back to the photos. After another moment's study, he reached out and yanked one from the wall. The kid in it was sitting on his bunk, playing a guitar. "So's he. Dead." In two steps he was before another. This young man was flexing his bicep, showing off a vicious tattoo. "Him too."

Oh, God.

Another step. "Also gone." He snatched away an image of a soldier mugging for the camera.

More cold trickled down Jane's back as she stared at his hand clutching the pictures. His shoulders were stiff, and she could feel the tension emanating from him. She hadn't seen this side of him before, and it made her want to both exit the room and enfold him in a comforting embrace. But her feet seemed rooted to the floor, and she couldn't imagine he'd allow her to touch him now. It wouldn't be what he wanted.

She didn't have, she thought, anything he needed.

Feeling helpless, she saw him on the move again. "Griffin—"

"Lost an arm." Another photo ripped away. "Shot in the stomach. This officer—" he indicated a photo of a dusty figure, distinguishing features hidden by helmet, flak jacket and sunglasses "—I heard was shot and killed a month ago. A full-bird colonel. I'd told him all about the cove before I left Afghanistan. He loved the sound of the place and booked No. 9 for himself and his daughter, Layla, in July."

"Oh, the poor girl," Jane murmured.

"This guy's bringing her instead." Griffin moved to stand before another picture, this one of a golden-haired man whose vivid blue eyes stood out in a sweat- and dirt-stained face. "Vance Smith, our combat medic. We bonded over the crazy shit we did as kids."

Jane took a step closer, because this sounded like someone who had been close to Griffin. Vance Smith looked older than some of the other soldiers, near thirty, and she could see a hint of recklessness in his grin. But his gaze was steady, and she could imagine he was re-assuring in a crisis. "He knows the colonel's daughter?"

"The colonel was dying in Vance's arms when he made him promise to bring Layla to Crescent Cove. They were both shot in an ambush, and Vance has injuries of his own that need to heal."

Injuries on the outside, Jane thought, while Griffin's wounds were hidden away. Her chest aching, she watched him move on, then pause again. His back to her, his breathing turned heavy. He stared at the photo of another young man hefting a futuristic-looking gun that would have been right at home in a video game. He stared at it a long time. "Then there's Whitman."

Jane swallowed again. Since it had been her great idea to tape these images around the room, she supposed she couldn't duck the consequences, however much she cursed herself for the stupid notion now. "Whitman?"

"Cocky asshole stole the supply of Twinkies I'd brought from home."

Whitman looked like a prankster, Jane decided, his expression unabashedly mischievous. Her heart turned to lead in her chest. "What happened to him?"

"Oh, I got revenge." Griffin didn't look toward her, but there was a new note in his voice. "He had a much beloved stash of raunchy porn magazines that I 'acciden-tally' dropped into the latrine."

She stared at Griffin's back, trying to interpret the new facet to his current frame of mind. "He…he didn't die?"

Griffin shook his head. "No. He did, however, insti-gate a series of petty burglaries between us that lasted the rest of the deployment." Then he started to laugh—really laugh, from the belly. "You should have seen his face when he realized the fate of his *Raunchy Babes Collector's Edition.* Never knew a man could cry over bleached blondes in bustiers and dog collars."

As he continued chuckling, Jane thought *she* might cry. But she fluttered her lashes to blink back the mois-ture, standing where she was while Griffin approached the desk and the waiting laptop. He placed the photos of the dead and wounded in a drawer. Only then did she step close enough to slide the manuscript pages onto the surface.

His hand caught her shoulder as she started to move away. "Jane." There was still a faint smile on his face. He reached up with his other hand to cup her cheek. "Thank you for bringing back other memories."

When he kissed the tip of her nose, blinking couldn't hold back the new sting of tears. So she turned away to the workstation she'd set up for herself by the office's love seat. "You're welcome," she managed to choke out, as if he were just any client, one who was writing a treatise on racehorses, say, or a fictional account of lovers doomed by an incoming tornado. "Now let's get to work."

They came up with a plan. As he read through each page he'd written before, he handed it off to Jane, his thoughts and corrections jotted in the margins. She made her own on sticky notes. Though they stopped for lunch, Jane figured he had to be about as cross-eyed and muscle-cramped as she was by four in the afternoon.

That was when he reached over his head to stretch his arms, groaning. "I'm out of gas for the day." He stood, then stretched again.

She let her lashes fall to half-mast as she checked out the slice of taut abs revealed by the rising hem of his shirt.

"None of that," he said, crossing the floor to grab her hand.

"None of what?" she replied, aware of her guilty flush as he tugged her to her feet.

"You were starting to fall asleep on me. Let's go for a walk on the beach."

She didn't tell him any different. While it was part of her job to keep up the client's spirits, she didn't believe she needed to feed his ego. And anyway, Griffin hadn't made a sexual move on her since their return to the beach house. It was as if what had happened in the hotel suite hadn't happened at all. Which was fine. Preferable. Her own idea. *A place out of time.*

But as they stepped onto the sand, the fresh air seemed to bring out some honesty in her. They were strolling away from their end of the cove and the beach was dotted with a sand architect here and there, building everything from a rudimentary igloo to a multilevel castle. But she and Griffin stuck to the damp sand near the shoreline so that the crash of the incoming waves muffled all the voices but their own.

She slid him a sidelong look. "You don't really need me, you know." It was her reputation that needed the work, and that thought just made her feel more guilty. It seemed only right to be truthful. "I'm serious. Before, I didn't know you had any kind of draft."

He didn't answer. His hands were in the pockets of his jeans, and the lowering sun limned his handsome profile. He looked gorgeous edged in gold.

"I'm reading what you have, and it's good," she continued. He had a knack for delivering telling details. She could taste the pasty corn-bread stuffing that came with the Mediterranean Chicken MRE, hear the rattle of gunfire across the sunbaked valley and smell the coming winter snow. The various relationships between the platoon brothers breathed on the page. "I can do the editing, which you claim to despise, catch a grammar mistake or two. But—"

"I won't do it without you, Jane."

"Griffin—"

"That's final. You told me from the first you were here to provide me with everything I need. Everything I ask for."

Had she gone that far? "I know I said—"

"So I want you working with me on the book. And answering the questions I ask."

Her relief—yes, her rep needed this job!—made it take a moment for his second sentence to sink in. "Wait. What questions?"

"You know a hell of a lot about me from reading those pages, wouldn't you say?"

"It's a memoir, after all." Early in the book he talked about his initial excitement over the assignment, the tempering trepidation once he'd been handed body armor and a combat medical pack, his keen interest in what drove the young men around him to risk their lives as they did. There'd been no mention, as yet, of the bloodshed she knew was coming. "You *are* telling it in first person."

"Exactly. And I find myself uncomfortable that my 'doctor' knows more about me than I know about her. So I think you should tell me about the person who is Jane. Turnabout is fair play."

She frowned at him. "You know about her. It's all there in the four letters. J-A-N-E."

"We're both aware there's more to you than that."

Not many had chosen to discover it. She couldn't recall

anyone just asking about her like this, and it worried her
a little. "I don't get where you're going here."

"We only have two more weeks at the cove. Two more
weeks as collaborators. And I don't see how we can collaborate when it's so one-sided."

Okay, this was yet another of his moods she didn't
know. He was being stubborn and unreasonable and she
couldn't figure out what he wanted from her. "Griffin—"

"I'm curious. Are you really scared of the ocean,
Jane?" he asked, halting to face her.

She froze, the question catching her by surprise. It
made her wary again too, because, though it seemed like
such a small thing to admit, her father had taught her to
conceal her weaknesses. *Don't be so soft, Jane,* he'd say,
when she was seven years old and trembling at the idea
of swimming in such a big body of water. *People will
take advantage of your fears. Use your brain to get beyond them.*

Her silence hung between them until Griffin scooped
her up in his arms. "Wha—" she began, startled.

"Will you really be afraid if I wade into the surf?"

"Yes." She clung to his neck, for a moment that second-
grader again. "I mean no."

His pant legs had to be wet as he strode farther into
the ocean. It swirled around them, a mix of green water
and white foam and golden sand. "We've got to mine the
emotions, honey-pie," he said, and that ridiculous endear-
ment told her he was attempting to be playful.

Playful. She did her best to mimic the tone. "Chili-
dog..." Then her breath disappeared as he swung her away
from his body in preparation for tossing her in.

"No!" she shrieked, clinging tighter. She buried her
head in his neck, panic rising like an incoming tide. *"No."*

A second later they were on drier, higher ground. Jane

found herself sitting on the soft sand, Griffin's arms enclosing her from behind, his legs on either side of hers. "I'm sorry," he said, his mouth against her ear. "God, I'm sorry. I didn't think you were really afraid. I didn't think you actually were afraid of anything."

It was still embarrassing to admit she was. "I *can* swim. I'm fine in a pool. It's just... My father always says I'm silly and emotional, but this ocean phobia I would like to blame on my brothers."

"Then we definitely should."

She sighed. "Byron told me that the foamy stuff on the waves was whale snot. Phillip said the sea is green due to the sun's reflection off the scales of giant, lurking eels. It was that scientific sound bite that made it all the more believable, of course. But frankly, it wasn't really them. I always had the kind of imagination that could turn an oven mitt into a monster paw. They were just enjoying getting a rise out of me."

His arms tightened around her. It shouldn't please her so much. She shouldn't lean back against his chest, as she was doing. He made another sound in her ear—suspiciously like a muffled curse.

"What?" she asked him.

"You told me nobody has ever put you first. I can't get that out of my mind."

Another flush of heat ran over her body. How embarrassing! She'd forgotten confessing such a thing, and it meant he knew her better than anyone. She shivered. Ever.

His breath was hot on her ear. "You so tempt me to do something about that, Jane. For the next fourteen days."

CHAPTER FOURTEEN

THE MORNING AFTER the embarrassing scene on the beach, Griffin showed up in the office and began work without incident—and without reference to his little "tempt me" remark. She began to think she might have imagined it altogether. When they finished for the day, they took another walk on the shore, this time Griffin keeping himself between Jane and the surf, which she found absurdly sweet and completely unnecessary. When she mentioned that to him, he ruffled her hair and said when it came to lurking green-scaled eels, you could never be too careful.

The touch, though casual, somehow struck her heart, like a mallet to a gong. Her insides quivered for a moment, then the vibrato quieted to a hum that kept her nerve endings alert. Aware. That alert awareness didn't go away.

The day following that, the walls surrounding them seemed too close. Every squeak of Griffin's office chair had her jumping out of her skin. She caught herself staring at him as he kicked back, his bare feet on the desktop, his computer in his lap. There was a spot on the back of his neck, just below the edge of his hairline, that fascinated her.

She imagined herself licking it.

Griffin suddenly turned his head, his gaze finding her over his shoulder. "What are you doing back there?"

"Uh." She squirmed, her linen cropped pants abrading her too-sensitive flesh.

He narrowed his eyes at her. "Jane?"

"I'm...uh...lost in thought." Lost in lust. Oh, God, and it wasn't getting any better when she was looking at his face. He was all blue eyes and dark stubble, and she had the intense urge to take a bite out of his lower lip. She found herself on her feet.

"Where are you going?"

Her gesture was vague, verging on wild. "Out...away. Be back soon." She scrambled from the room and headed for fresh air. It was only when she was standing in the sand that she realized the entire day had passed. The sun was heading for the horizon, and she couldn't remember accomplishing anything beyond not nipping Griffin's bottom lip.

That wasn't good.

"Jane!" She looked toward the sound of her name and saw Tess and Skye sitting on the front porch of No. 8. Griffin's sister waved. "Come talk to us."

It was as good an excuse as any to avoid returning to the office. She refused the offer of a cold drink and took the empty chair. A little fresh air, a little girl talk, could clear the dangerous images from her mind. She'd cut herself off from friends for much too long, she realized, relaxing into her seat.

Skye, in boyish chinos and a short-sleeved sweatshirt with a kangaroo pouch pocket, sent her a smile. "I haven't seen you around much."

"Sorry. Doing work."

"Me too," the other woman said. She drew out some mail from the oversize pocket. "Want to save me a delivery?"

A postcard. Jane reached for it. "For Griffin?" The back was covered in a slapdash of dark-inked handwriting.

Skye nodded. "From Gage. Everybody got mail from him today."

"Including you?" Tess asked the younger woman, looking up from a sheet of paper in her lap, covered in the same distinctive lettering.

Her face turned pink. "That's right. You know we correspond." She worried the ribbing on the hem of her sweatshirt, then turned to Jane. "It's really nice of him to answer my letters."

Tess snorted. "Nice? Skye, Gage is not a nice man."

"Of course he is!" Skye protested. "I mean, well, he's nice to me."

"He's a reckless daredevil who cares about his next adventure more than any woman in his life."

"I'm not just any woman in his life," Skye said, then her face went redder. "What I'm trying to say is that I'm not a woman in his eyes. I'm a friend from home, that's all."

"You keep reminding yourself of that, okay? The Lowell boys are not good romantic bets." Tess's gaze touched Jane. "Isn't that right?"

Especially the Lowell boy who was in love with a dead woman. Jane lowered her eyes. "You know Griffin better than I do."

"And I know my romantic bets gone wrong too," Tess muttered. "It's men that I don't understand at all. Do you know my sons have been practicing eating Cheetos with their toes? Why would they want to do that?"

"Maybe for some reason we don't understand." Jane's gaze moved to the cliff at the end of the cove. Jumping from it had seemed inexplicable to her until she'd been told that the resulting adrenaline shot had an anesthetic effect. It made some sense now. "Though Griffin tells me that the best part of an Oreo is the white stuff in the middle, which does not compute and never will."

It gratified her that the other two women concurred. The female companionship calmed her, and she was able to relax a little and think about something other than dark hair and broad shoulders. She sighed.

Tess glanced over. "Uh-oh. From the sound of that, do I take it that my bro is still evading the task at hand?"

Jane wished she hadn't used that word. It made her think of Griffin's hands. All day, she'd been watching them move on the laptop, the long, nimble fingers working the keyboard like a piano. It reminded her of his fingers playing along her skin, stroking her hips and opening her thighs. She swallowed a little whimper and remembered the question hanging in the air. "He's actually knuckling—"

Grr. She stopped herself, plagued by more images. She remembered him running the back of his hand along her cheek. One of his curled fingers stroking the slope of her nose.

"He would never talk about it with me, you know," Tess said. "That year in Afghanistan."

Jane looked over. "Somehow I'm not surprised."

"Since he came back he's avoided his entire family, which I don't like at all. David and I tried to get him over a dozen times when he first returned, but he's given excuse after excuse. Mom and Dad are living in Hawaii, yet he's resisted even a short tropical visit." She glanced down at the letter in her lap. "I've been thinking of sending an SOS to Gage. Getting him to the cove for some kind of intervention."

"Don't," Skye said quickly. Then she jumped to her feet, clearly flustered. "Sorry. It's none of my business. I have to go."

Tess frowned. "Skye?"

"He can't see me," she said, lifting a hand. Then, distress in every tense line of her slender body, she rushed away.

They stared after her, the too-loose clothes flapping around her as she ran up the beach. "What was that about?" asked Jane.

Tess looked grim. "I hate to think it's another woman who's fallen for the wrong man." She slumped in her chair, her hands draped over its arms, her long legs splayed. "What a summer. Disaster abounds."

Considering she was still living at the cove with her kids and without her husband, Jane assumed the other woman included her marriage in that gloomy statement. "It's not all bad," she said. "Your daughter's more consumed with her history project than pregnancy these days. Duncan and Oliver may have discovered a marketable skill."

"How so? You think there's money in monkey imitation?"

Smiling, Jane shrugged. "In ten years' time, who knows?"

"I'm developing a dislike of annoying glass-half-full types."

Jane cast a look at her. "Something tells me that's *your* usual type."

Tess sighed. "Give me more to put in my glass, then."

"It's summer. We're sitting beachside. We have a pretty view of the sun setting on the Pacific." Jane crossed her feet at the ankles. "Now you go."

The other woman groaned. "The mosquitoes aren't out. Yet."

"You're not even trying."

"Fine. Russ is too little for Cheetos."

"You *are* in bad shape."

"Don't fall in love, Jane. That's all I can tell you."

The warning only brought to mind a white grin, a big hand tousling her hair, a pair of reporter's eyes that looked at her and seemed to see something beyond four plain letters. *We're both aware there's more to you than that.*

"That's a suspicious silence." Tess groaned again. "Don't say it. Don't tell me you and Griffin—"

"I didn't say it," Jane said, breaking in. There was no "she and Griffin." "I mean, before, I meant to tell you that he's actually working on the memoir."

Tess straightened. "Truth?"

"Truth. He's over there right now, productive as you please."

"Well, that's good news."

"Very good," Jane agreed. The only bad had been her silly self, which allowed her brain to head off on useless tangents. It had been a night out of time! "And it was good I came over here too, because now I can go back, refreshed. Thanks for the conversation."

As she headed for No. 9, dusk was falling. Tess's voice came to her from the now-shadowy porch, a quiet warning. "Jane, just remember. That you… That Griffin—"

"It's all good," Jane said firmly, repeating the word. "Everything's under control."

She let herself into the house and set the postcard from Gage on the coffee table. No lamps were lit in the living room or the kitchen, so she turned them on as she went by, then trod down the hall to the office. Nearing the doorway, she noted there wasn't any sign of life in there either—and she had to shake off the sinister feel of it.

Then she heard Private whine, and she knew man and dog were inside the room. Still, her hand trembled as she reached for the light switch.

"Don't," a voice said. It was gritty and dark and almost unrecognizable as Griffin's.

It took a moment to make him out. He was stretched on the floor like a corpse—except in a mirror of the first time they'd met, he balanced a bottle of beer on his midriff. Three empties lay beside him, knocked over like bowling pins. Private was nearby, attentive to his master's needs.

Whatever they might be. Jane didn't have a clue.

"What happened?" she asked, in her library voice.

He was silent so long she worried he might have passed out on her. Just when she thought she should check, he lifted his head to take another draw from his beer. It was so quiet she heard him swallow. Then his skull clunked against the wood floor, and Jane winced. Griffin didn't seem to notice.

"Nothing. I've been working, just like I'm supposed to, honey-pie. I was going through the notes."

Something else had been in that big envelope: several small notebooks Griffin had used during his embedded year. They were dog-eared and dirty, but each was labeled with their dates of use and bound with a rubber band. She'd assumed that at some point he'd sent back a batch of them for safekeeping.

Private whined again. *Exactly,* Jane thought.

"Maybe we should get you something to eat," she suggested. "Or drink. Coffee. A soda."

"Beer's fine," Griffin said. "Beer's making me drunk." He didn't sound drunk.

"Beer's helping me *mine my emotions,* honey-pie."

Now he sounded angry, and just a little bit mean.

Her stomach clenched, and her first instinct was to run back to Tess's. But there he was on the floor, her dark pirate, looking just as alone as he'd been that first afternoon with the raucous Party Central all around him. His sister had said he'd declined invitations to be with family and refused to talk about his experience. Had he reached a place and time where he could finally tell someone about it?

"What about the notes?" she asked, her voice soft. "Why did they bother you?"

"You don't want to know."

That's when she saw it. A slip of paper crumpled on the floor beside him, a tiny ball that she guessed had packed enough punch to knock over those beer bottles—and knock Griffin off his feet. Without thinking, she bent to pick it up, then flattened it out with her fingers.

It was impossible to read in the dim room.

"Always signed her name the same, goddamn it." His voice was harsh. "Like a fucking fourth-grader. An *E* surrounded by a heart."

Jane's heart gave a little lurch at the image. "This is from Erica?"

Once again he lifted his head to swig his beer. "She would write messages on scraps of paper when we were embedded. Leave them on my bunk."

Jane could guess what kind of notes they were. *An* E *surrounded by a heart.*

When he didn't say any more, she found herself filling the silence. "I know it's hard." If only she could get him started, maybe he could express his grief and find a way past it. Find a way to…to someone else.

She bit her lip, guilty at the thought, and forced herself to go on. "I can't fathom how hard. Loving someone and losing them like that…"

Now his silence seemed to grow, expanding until it pressed against the walls, a black blob that made the room more murky, the atmosphere almost threatening. Private whined again, and his furry head dipped to his front paws.

Jane's throat went dry. Light, she decided. They needed some light. A little warmth, a little glow, would take the menace out of the place. Maybe out of the man.

Griffin lay between her and the lamp on the desk. Urged by an odd panic, she darted for it. Halfway there, his hand snaked out and grabbed her ankle.

She yelped.

"Is that where your sappy, overactive oven-mitt imagination has led you, Jane? You think I'm in a mood because I loved her?"

His fingers were hot, and they bit into her skin, staying just on the not-quite side of pain. Despite that and the billowing tension in the room, Jane felt herself reacting to his touch. Hot chills arrowed up the inside of her leg, a straight shot that pierced her belly and then her heart.

A feeling that was very bad indeed.

GRIFFIN TIGHTENED his hold on Jane's leg. His fingertips met his thumb, she was so delicate, but that didn't encourage him to be gentle. She'd brought him to this emotional place, damn it, and she was going to pay.

"Sit down," he said, releasing her ankle. "Sit down right here."

His eyes were used to the dark, and he could see the wary expression on her face as she obeyed. She was wearing another of her maddening little dresses. Fussy and demure, its full skirt swirled around her thighs as she sank to the floor. In full Lady Jane mode, she sat with her legs folded to one side. A prim-and-proper woman waiting to be served a picnic.

What a meal he had ready to dish out.

He shoved himself up, his fourth beer still half-full. Tipping his hand, he drained the bottle, then let it drop with a clunk.

Jane jumped.

"Nervous now? Thinking about all those eels that are lurking in the corners of my soul?"

Her head moved from side to side, though her eyes didn't leave his. "I'm not nervous. I'm not scared of you."

Those fucking eels, he thought, swiping a hand over his face. He couldn't get them out of his head. The memory was there, Jane in his arms, the way she'd clung to him as he'd almost tossed her to her greatest fear.

Her pretty wavy hair, tickling his chin as they sat together on the beach. He didn't think she'd realized that a little tremor had run down her spine when she'd confessed her phobia. He'd been holding her that close to his heart. It had made him want to be a better brother to her than her own. It had made him want to be her hero.

Her brother. Her hero. What a crock.

He could never be anyone's hero, and he didn't feel brotherly toward her in the least. He'd been dying to fuck her again since that night in L.A. By God, she was going to understand that by the time he was through. Then she'd stop looking at him with those beautiful eyes filled with compassion.

"I didn't love Erica," he said. "I didn't love her, and the fact of that drove her to her death."

"Griffin…"

"Don't take that placating tone with me. You want the facts, don't you? And the emotions, right? That's what you've been asking for. That's what you want on the page."

"I—" She hesitated, and he thought she might bolt. But then she clasped her hands together like a little girl at Sunday school. "Okay. I want it all."

He pushed to his feet and threw himself into his desk chair, which screeched as he swiveled to face her. It arrested him a moment, the sight of Jane at his feet, her expression expectant.

Innocent.

Could he tell her and ruin whatever pretty story she'd made up in her head? But it was his dishonesty that had been the beginning of Erica's end.

"Erica and I were…together before we left the States. We met through the assignment, hit it off, so to speak, started seeing each other as we prepared for Afghanistan."

He rubbed his face again. "I thought it was all fun and games, but she…"

"Wanted more."

"I didn't lead her on." Hell, why he wanted Jane to believe that, he didn't know. "At least I didn't intend to."

"But then she started leaving you little notes."

"After the first couple of weeks in Afghanistan, I realized her feelings had turned serious. I should have been honest with her immediately, but Christ, we'd agreed to be embedded with thirty guys for the next twelve months, and I didn't want that kind of awkwardness in the mix."

"Makes sense."

"Makes me an effing idiot. The close quarters meant we weren't having sex—at least I can claim some nobility there—but we were going out every day, getting shot at, being mortared…. It was pretty intense."

In his mind, Griffin heard the high whine of an incoming mortar round, then its thunder-boom and sharp jolt of impact. The smell of it was in his nostrils and on his tongue, rotten eggs mixed with cordite and red dirt. "You never knew if the thing you were doing—eating, on patrol, taking a leak—was the last thing you'd ever do. So I think for Erica, the last man she might ever be with became the man she had to love. The danger gave me a little shine."

"Because clearly you were pretty dull without that."

He waved Jane's dry comment away. "When we first started dating in L.A., I tried telling her how it was. That I wasn't looking for anything serious. I don't do serious with women, never have. But she didn't listen. She didn't listen to anyone about anything."

"You told me what happened to her—the ambush. That wasn't your fault, Griffin."

"She wanted to impress me," he said, his temples beginning to ache. He needed another beer. "That's why she went with the guys that morning, even though I had told her not to do it. Everyone had told her not to do it. *I* wouldn't have done it. But she went anyway to prove something to me."

"Who said?"

He thought of the note he'd woken to find in his hand. Jane was holding it now. He nodded at it. "She wrote 'You'll see.'"

"You'll see…what? You'll see leprechauns? You'll see *Firefly* shouldn't have been canceled? You'll see that the coffee stain will come out of your khakis?"

She was being deliberately obtuse, and it made the knocking at his temples intensify. "You'll see I'm good enough to love. You'll see that I'm fearless enough to love. I don't know exactly."

In a quick move, Jane stood. Before he could stop her, she leaned over to turn on the desk lamp. Though the bulb was low wattage, it still felt like an interrogator's tool. He blinked against the light, one hand shading his eyes.

"That's certainly an interesting interpretation," she said.

His hand dropped, and he squinted at her face. The lamplight caught the gold tips of her eyelashes. He looked away from them. "What the hell do you mean by that?"

"Maybe there's another meaning to her note."

"Like what?"

"Have you considered that she was saying 'I'll land this story'? Have you thought for just a teeny, tiny second, Mr. Ego, that maybe she wasn't taking risks for you, but for her job. For her career. For herself."

Mr. Ego. His head pounded harder. "Nice spin."

"Why are you so sure it's spin?"

The annoyed note in her voice pissed him off. "Mr. Ego" pissed him off. There was a cup of pens and pencils on the desktop, and he swiped at it, sending the Bics and No. 2s flying. "Damn it, I don't know!"

Private rushed to his side. Griffin felt like shit for scaring the dog. He stroked his soft fur as the Lab pressed hard against his legs.

Jane crossed to his side too, and knelt on the other side of his knees. "I'm sorry, Griffin. I know that whatever her motivation, it was a horrible event. A tragedy for her family and something that hurts you terribly."

He drew back, blinking at her. "Jane," he began, then shook his head. "Jane, you're wrong. I don't know if it's my reporter training or just a tic of my particular personality, but I don't feel anything close to terrible."

A moment of silence passed, and then he dropped the truth on her. "Ninety-nine percent of the time I don't feel anything at all."

CHAPTER FIFTEEN

TESS SANK ONTO the couch in the small, low-lit living room at Beach House No. 8 and watched the flames lick the Pres-to-Log she'd put a match to before checking on the boys. It wasn't cold, really; she was dressed warmly enough in a pair of yoga pants and matching top with long sleeves and a collar that she'd zipped to a point above her cleavage. But she'd decided the fire would be nice company for the night. Rebecca was sleeping over at a friend's, and her sons had slipped into dreamland not long after dark. An inflatable canvas raft had occupied Duncan and Oliver all afternoon. Riding the small waves near the shoreline had so worn them out that they'd almost been asleep before Russ.

She propped her bare feet on the coffee table, bumping the framed photo of the kids that she'd brought from home. With the four either asleep or absent, it was time to think of herself. It was time to decide what she wanted to do with her life.

A knock on the front door startled her. Griffin or Jane, she supposed, needing to borrow a cup of sugar or something similar. But it was Teague White standing in the dim glow of the porch light, his athletic build nearly filling the opening. He smiled, a flash of white in his tan face that struck her somewhere below her heart.

She placed her hand there. "Hi."

He glanced over his shoulder. "I was at Captain

Crow's…and then I thought of you. Would you like to share a drink with me?"

Oh, to be so free! She couldn't remember the last time she'd been able to take off for a drink or anything else without making plans and backup plans and backup for the backup plans. Was that what she wanted for herself? she wondered. More freedom? She had divorced friends and knew it was an unexpected by-product of shared custody. When the kids were with Dad, Mom had hours and hours of alone time.

"Tess?"

"Oh." She laughed. "Sorry, took a hike on a mind trail."

"Mind trail?"

Her next laugh wasn't as amused. It was a phrase that she and David had coined long ago. One of those private codes that came out of a long marriage. "I was daydreaming." She took a breath. "But as to your offer—I'm sorry, I can't go anywhere. The boys are asleep and—"

"Even if I brought the drink to you?" He held up a chilled six-pack of Mexican beer.

Her favorite brand. She hesitated only a second, then held open the door. "I have limes."

As he stepped inside, she hurried to turn on another lamp. She didn't want to send the wrong message with a romantic ambience. In the kitchen, she sliced a Mexican lime into quarters and placed them on a small plate that she set on a tray beside a basket of tortilla chips and a bowl of mango salsa.

"You didn't have to go to all this trouble," Teague said as she slid the items onto the coffee table.

Embarrassed heat washed up her neck. Was he thinking she'd misread the situation? That she considered it some kind of date?

"But now that you did," he said, giving her another of his easy grins, "thanks."

From their opposite corners of the short couch, they both slipped a wedge of lime into their golden brew. Then their gazes met, and with tacit agreement they held out the longneck bottles. It seemed a natural thing to do. But at the click of glass against glass, it suddenly felt datelike. Another wash of heat climbed up her neck, but Tess ignored it and forced herself to relax against the cushions. *Try this out,* she told herself. *Your life could be like this. A romantic evening. A different man.*

More of her tension dissipated as beer was sipped. Small talk was exchanged.

"I ran into your brother earlier today," Teague said. "He didn't look very happy to find me talking to Jane."

"You know Jane?"

"Know all the pretty girls on the beach," he said, tipping his bottle at Tess. "Always looking to end my bachelor status."

"Right," she scoffed. "You and all the other handsome firefighters are on the endless search for your better halves."

He appeared to consider her remark seriously. "Can't speak for everyone else, but I do know what *I* want."

Tess could only feel envy. "What's that?" *Maybe I can co-opt your same wish.*

"You…"

Her swallow of beer almost went down wrong.

"…or should I say, what you have."

She coughed now, clearing her throat as well as clearing her mind of any unbidden image that might be trying to form. "And what do I have that you want?" she asked, trying for rueful. "A crying baby, a rebellious teen, two little boys that… Never mind, just don't ask me about Cheetos."

He laughed. "All of the above…except maybe not the Cheetos since I don't know where that's going. But I grew up in a very lonely house without brothers or sisters."

She thought of the quiet little kid he'd been, trailing after Griffin and Gage.

"I want the whole big, messy family."

"We're that, all right," Tess said with a wry smile. Child clutter was everywhere, from the pairs of rubber thongs jumbled by the front door to the action figures locked in mortal combat by the built-in bookshelves. Surely there was a lurking plastic block or two somewhere, ready to wield brutal pain on an unsuspecting sole.

Teague settled into the corner of the couch. He wore ancient jeans, a Hawaiian shirt he could have stolen from Griffin's closet and leather flip-flops. He looked a little lazy and a lot male, and she felt another small ping of awareness below her breastbone. Heat gathered where her hairline met the nape of her neck.

His eyes on her, Teague took a slow pull from his beer, and his swallow moved along the tan column of his neck. He settled more comfortably on the cushions, and as he stretched out one long leg, the edge of his sandal met the side of Tess's bare heel, the contact as light as a butterfly kiss.

She froze, her gaze dropping to the label of the beer she held, though her peripheral vision didn't miss their tiny point of connection. Did he know they were touching? It wasn't flesh-on-flesh or anything, but wouldn't a normal person pull back from even that small invasion of personal space?

Maybe he didn't notice.

Maybe he was asking a question with that near-nudge.

She'd given him the answer before, though, hadn't she? That first day on the beach she'd explained she was the mother of four. Married.

But how true was the married thing? And wasn't she more than a mother? She was supposed to be figuring that out. Tonight.

Now the heat at her nape traveled around and down, and she automatically pressed the cold beer bottle to the thin skin below her collarbone, bared by the stretchy yoga top. She glanced over at Teague, found him staring.

A sheepish grin curved his mouth. "I told you about that crush, right?"

Another opening. She wasn't such a wife and mother that she didn't know it. The woman in her recognized that she could make a move of her own right now, twitch a toe, find something flirtatious to say, and this moment could possibly turn into something different.

Could turn into someone different.

Tess opened her mouth—

—and heard Russ begin to cry. She was up so quickly she stepped on Teague's foot. But the contact barely registered as she hurried in the direction of the hall. "He's been fussy," she said over her shoulder. "I think he may be getting another tooth." ·

Her guest was rising from the couch. "I should go?" But then Russ squawked again, and Teague answered his own question. "I should go."

She didn't bother seeing him out. It took twenty minutes to soothe her baby. Humming under her breath, she held his head against her shoulder and rocked back and forth, standing outside the room he shared with Duncan and Oliver. Once he was down again, she pulled a light-weight throw over his sailboat-printed jammies and arranged his special blanket under one arm. He reflexively gathered it close to his chest.

David used to do that to her when they were in bed.

David hadn't touched her in bed in months.

Back in the living room, she cleaned up the bottles and snack and then returned to her original place on the couch. She stared at the photo of the kids in front of her. Her foot twitched, remembering that brief connection with Teague. Maybe she should have asked him to stay. Start that new life with a bang.

The stupid pun made her groan.

Over her own low-throated sound she heard another knock on the door. Her heart lurched. He'd come back!

Tess couldn't pretend she wasn't home. She also couldn't pretend that her pulse wasn't racing at a chance for...another bite of the apple.

Oh, God, she was full of wordplay tonight.

And nerves.

Her palms were so wet, her hand slipped on the doorknob. When she opened it, her breath caught.

Not Teague, but David. Her husband, David, carrying a carton, one of those portable file boxes. "I have something to show you," he said.

She couldn't help but compare him to her other visitor of the evening. Instead of being casually dressed, David appeared to have come straight from the office. His shirt was white, his slacks pale taupe, he wore the loafers she'd had resoled six weeks ago. She'd given him the paisley tie for his birthday. When everything had changed.

"Can I come in?"

She moved aside and watched, bemused, as he transferred the framed photograph to a corner of the coffee table, then removed file folders from the box. His long-fingered hands laid them on the flat surface, one after the other, until they were all on display. With a satisfied air, he stepped back.

Curiosity piqued, she came closer, trying to understand the point of his exhibit. It wasn't immediately apparent, and he didn't immediately offer up an explanation.

She glanced at his profile. He had a strong, masculine nose, and his lips were set in a serious line. There was a shadow of whiskers along his jaw that her fingers suddenly itched to stroke. His short hair was ruffled on top, and she knew he'd been forking his fingers through it, a gesture he made when he was in deep concentration or worried.

They stood without speaking, and she listened to him breathe, one of the dearest rhythms of her life. Tears pricked the corners of her eyes as a heavy understanding settled over her. Familiar didn't equal dull, she thought. New and different was not that big a draw.

At least not for her.

"What's all this?" she finally asked, gesturing at the folders.

"I wanted you to look over our financials," he said.

Her heart seized for a moment, then restarted at a dizzying pace. Look over their financials! That sounded like predivorce business. Though...maybe not. One of her friends had been given the divorce talk by her husband— but only after the bastard had siphoned off most of their accounts.

David wouldn't do it like that, she assured herself. If she and David divorced, he would be excruciatingly fair.

If she and David divorced... There would be dates. A different man.

She pressed the heel of her hand to her forehead. "I'm looking them over," she said, her voice weary. "What about the financials should I be seeing?"

He took a seat on the sofa and tapped a finger on the front of each manila folder. "Statements for all our bank accounts. Your 401(k), my 401(k). College funds for the kids. Current mortgage statement. I had the house appraised yesterday and this is the report. We own the cars outright, but I have estimates for their value in this file. See? I've labeled it Big-Ticket Items."

She stared at him. "What, no credit report?"

He slid out a folder from under another. "Right here."

A few years back, new neighbors had moved in, and she and David had invited them to their New Year's Eve party. The husband of the couple insisted on a midnight tradition: "Throw all the change in your pockets onto the street!" It was supposed to bring good fortune for the coming year, according to the man.

David had gone along with a smile.

Before breakfast the next morning, he'd re-collected every coin.

At least some things about him hadn't changed—he was still careful about each penny. Looking into the face of the man she'd loved and married, while remembering that New Year's, made her sure of something else that was unchanged as well.

Tess herself was still the same. *I still love my husband, my life as his partner. My work as the mother of our children.* That was what she wanted. The knowledge of it settled in her chest, a puzzle piece being reseated where it belonged. She could move away from the house she and David shared together, but that didn't mean she could leave behind her love for him. The thoughts about dates and different men were passing fancies. A match flare compared to the steady light and heat that were her feelings for her husband.

She sighed and gestured to the table. "What's all this mean, David?"

"It's our net worth. What we've accumulated in the last almost fourteen years."

She shook her head. "I don't understand."

"You thought I didn't want you. Of course I do. I'm showing you what we've done together. What we've built." He huffed out an impatient breath. "I'm trying to convince you to come home. To stay."

"Do you want me or my 401(k)?"

He looked at her as if she was speaking in Russ's babbling baby language. "Both. They go together. Your plan is in your name."

He refused to understand. Instead of talking to her about what was going on with him and why he'd altered, he was trotting out paperwork. Exhausted, she dropped into the armchair adjacent to the sofa. "I don't know, David…."

He rose, his expression panicked. "What? Tess, don't you get it? Don't you see?"

"See what?"

He threw a hand in the direction of the files. "This is what I have to offer," he said. "This is what is on the table."

But instead of the columns of numbers and the neatly compiled accounting of what David thought summed up their worth—his worth—Tess only saw that photograph. Their four beautiful, beloved children. The family that he had somehow reduced to file folders and appraisal forms. Rising, she picked up the frame and held it with both hands so he could see.

"*This* is what's on the table." With tears pricking at the corners of her eyes, she stalked toward her bedroom. "This is what you have to find a way to value."

He didn't follow, and she didn't expect him to. In her bedroom, she closed the door and leaned against it, holding her children's picture against her heart. Was it any good knowing who you were and where you wanted to be in your life, she thought, if the person with whom you wanted to share that life wouldn't share himself?

JANE WATCHED Griffin hand the sleeping baby to his sister. Then Tess glanced toward Duncan and Oliver, crashed on the couch at No. 9, their heads together and their bodies lax, like a pair of rag dolls put down for the day.

Following her gaze, Griffin sighed. "Fine, I'll carry one next door."

Jane raised her hand. "I'll get the other."

"I can do it," Rebecca offered. "We left you with the s'mores mess."

Griffin gave Jane a look. "Yeah. You stay here and clean up. Get ready."

The look, the ominous note in his voice, tripped a shiver down her spine. Get ready for what? But Jane thought she knew, so she reined in her imagination and gathered up the marshmallow bag, the graham cracker box, the straightened wire clothes hangers and took them into the kitchen. Back by the dying fire in the living room, she found the last square of chocolate and popped it into her mouth.

She was licking a sweet trace from her thumb when Griffin stalked back inside. The door slammed behind him. His gaze snapped to her face, and she froze, her lips still sucking her flesh.

"What do you think you're doing?"

With a slow movement, she released her finger and let her hand fall to her side. Her palm pressed against the cream-colored lace of the swingy shorts she wore with a tennis sweater she'd found one day thrown over a chair. She supposed it was Griffin's—well, she knew it was, because the cotton cable-knit held his smell, that dry sage and lemon scent that was starting to pervade her dreams. If he had a problem with her co-opting his clothing, he'd kept it to himself.

"You don't like s'mores?" she asked. "I think you had at least three."

"I don't like turning into my sister's go-to babysitter," he said. "Those kids should stay on their side of the fence."

"It was one evening so your sister could visit with her girlfriend," Jane said, waving away his complaint. "They're your niece and nephews."

"I've got enough to worry about," he muttered. "Now, I'm talking to Rebecca's history class with that crabby coot next door."

Jane managed not to smile. "That was very kind of you to agree."

"Have you ever tried saying no to a thirteen-year-old drama queen?"

Now she grinned and clasped her hands together, holding them over her heart. "Please, Uncle Griff," she said in a theatrical tone. "If you don't say yes I won't pass the class. I won't get into a good college. I'll be forced into selling makeup at the MAC counter until I'm sixty-two when they'll turn me out to the Estée Lauder pasture." It had gone something like that.

"Plus," he said darkly, "I'm never going to look at a Cheeto the same way again."

"You're just jealous of Duncan and Oliver's new talent." She dared to move closer and poked him in the ribs covered by the ragged T-shirt he wore with jeans. "Admit they're adorable."

He narrowed his eyes until they were mere slices of summer sky. "I know what you're doing, Jane."

"Then why did you bother asking me what it was?" Even though the fire was nearly out, her body seemed to heat up under the weight of his gaze. Her skin prickled against her clothes, and her scalp felt flushed. She took a few steps back. "There's nothing wrong with some relaxation with family at the end of a long workday."

He followed her. "Relaxation? Is that what you think I need?"

"Sure." She gave a casual shrug, though there were flutters in her belly now, teasing and twirling. The way he was looking at her, the way he was stalking her, caused a fraying of her nerves. "Everyone does." Though he'd not had another outburst after that night she'd found him on the floor in the dark, she was aware working on the memoir was wearing on him. By evening he was as tense as barbed wire strung between two posts.

"You too?"

She shrugged again. This wasn't about her.

"Because you're right, being cooped up all day with you is…hard on me, Jane."

Her mouth went dry. He gave that word *hard* a distinct sexual edge. Clearing her throat, she looked away. "I'm sorry, but you'll remember it was you who insisted we collaborate. And I try to give you space. I don't mean to be intrusive."

"I know you don't. But there you are, with your shoes. Every day, the shoes."

Puzzled, she glanced down. They were flat thong sandals she'd bought at a flea market. On top, striped ribbon was folded into a flower, its center made up of multicolor, shiny beads. They were feminine and mostly sweet, nothing that should put that burning intensity in his eyes. As she looked up, that gaze seemed to trap her.

His voice softened. "And the mouth, Jane, the mouth is making me feel…"

"I thought you didn't feel anything," she whispered. It was what had appalled her that night in the office. It was what had motivated her to get the kids over this evening. Because of course he felt things. She didn't know precisely how the self-delusion was serving him, but she did think he needed to find a way to connect with the emotions he'd walled off.

"Ninety-nine percent of the time," he reminded her. "But that remaining one percent is all about you."

Her shoulder blades clipped the edge of the aperture leading to the hallway. She'd been in retreat, she realized, but Griffin had kept pace. He was still as close as before, his breath hot on her temple, stirring her hair.

"I think we should relax my way, Jane."

Now the flush spread across her body in one hot rush. His delicious smell surrounded her, his hard rangy body was tempting her from just inches away. She could rub herself against it again. Kiss him. Touch him. Mold herself to his long muscles and hair-roughened skin.

"Oh, I don't think that's a good idea," she told both of them.

"But we have so few days left to…relax together, Jane. How could this single time hurt?"

True, she thought hazily, though the logic felt a little wobbly. Then his big hand cupped her cheek and his thumb brushed across her mouth. *She* went wobbly and, just like that, knew it was the first caress of the night.

Because she was going to give in, of course. Maybe another woman would resist a man who said *I don't do serious with women, never have,* but after her last romantic disaster she wasn't in danger of going silly and emotional with another unavailable male. Been there, done that, got the trampled heart.

But that didn't mean she would walk away now.

He was studying her face, his thumb dragging slowly and deliberately across her bottom lip. It had been leading to this since that night in L.A. Since before then... since that first afternoon when she'd walked into Party Central and found a dangerous pirate alone in the crowd.

It wouldn't last. Of course it wouldn't last. Nobody expected a commitment from a pirate. You knew he would steal, though. Your breath, your good sense, your ability to make more token protests, or your insistence on negotiating some favorable terms. Still, she hesitated another moment.

Griffin was as persuasive in his own way as Rebecca had been in hers. "You need to give me what I want, Jane." He slid one arm around the small of her back even as his thumb kept up that slow back-and-forth. "You need to give it to me the way I want."

Seduction dripped from the low-voiced words. Jane swayed toward him, and when he made yet another pass across her mouth, she dipped her chin and sucked his thumb inside. His breath hitched, and the reflexive twitch of his arm jerked her closer against him.

He was aroused. The bulge in his jeans was hard against her, and she couldn't help the way her hips pressed into it.

"Oh, no, you don't." He tucked his fingers in the waistband of her shorts and tugged, canting back her hips. "What part of the 'way I want' don't you understand?"

In answer, she ran her tongue over the pad of his thumb. He grunted, then popped it free of her clinging lips. He placed his own on hers and kissed her, that help-less heat washing over her again. Her fingers curled in the sides of his shirt, and she hung on to him as his tongue plunged inside her, possessing her, plundering, as only a pirate could.

With his hand still fisted in her shorts, he walked her backward, she retreating as directed by the forward press of his hard thighs. On the hallway runner, she stumbled, and he was forced to yank her close to keep her upright. She moaned as they were pressed together, and she ground her pelvis against his, needy for deeper contact.

His mouth lifted and he cursed. "You stop," he said, his eyes boring into hers. "*I'm* going to make it good for you."

"It is good," she said. Her hands slid up his sides and curled around his neck. "Kiss me again."

He succumbed to her demand for a moment, but broke this kiss too soon. His hands grabbed her wrists and he unwrapped her arms, then spun her around so she faced forward. Still holding on to her, he herded her down the hall to his room.

Inside it was dimly lit and smelled of Griffin, layers of citrus and sage, peppered by temper. He hadn't made his bed, and its sheets lay rumpled and wild, just like the man himself. As well she knew, he didn't sleep much… and she realized that tonight his insomnia might keep her up too. She trembled.

"That's right, honey-pie," he said, his breath blowing hot against her ear. "We're gonna get you all shivery." His hands went to the hem of the sweater, and he lifted it, sliding the thick material along her body. It brushed against her braless breasts, catching on the already-stiff jut of her nipples.

Griffin groaned as he tossed the garment away with one hand, widening the fingers of the other over her chest.

His long fingers were able to reach each sensitive peak. He nuzzled her neck, his mouth hot against the tender skin.

Jane writhed, rubbing her backside against his groin. Then he threw off his own shirt, and she moaned as his chest crowded her back. His fingers plucked at her nipples, and her head lolled against his shoulder. She tilted her face. "Please, Griffin." His mouth covered hers.

Again, he plundered. Again, she pushed back, wiggling against him. He muttered, breaking the kiss so he could turn her around. They looked at each other, their pants coming fast and heavy, the sound louder than the ever-present breath of the ocean outside.

He bent his head, nipped her bottom lip. Jane's womb clenched at the little pain, her nipples curled tighter. She ran her palms up his sides, her thumbs riding the rippling muscles. He grunted into their kiss, and then he slanted his head for another fit. When she sucked on his tongue, his hands found the soft lace of her shorts and he yanked.

They fell to her ankles.

Griffin stepped back. There was a flush across the bridge of his nose. His mouth was wet, his gaze intensely blue in the half-light of the room. "You wore that underwear for me," he said.

How could she have? How could she have known he would choose tonight to undress her? They were more lace, a stretch of pale pink that sat low on her hip bones and was banded by flirty black ruffles.

"Admit it," he said, his voice rough.

She started to shake her head, but then—oh, God, she realized he was right. All her big talk about one-night stands had been just big talk. Without conscious awareness of it, she'd been hoping for this. Planning for this. She'd been wearing her prettiest panties every day.

Because of him.

"Let's get you to bed," he said, moving close again.

But when she tried stepping back, her feet tangled in the pooled fabric of her shorts. She lost her balance, and Griffin tried stabilizing her. His grab was just a fraction too late, and she landed on her knees…right in front of that tempting bulge of denim. Another shiver rolled down her spine, and she looked up. Griffin was staring at her, his chest moving like a bellows as her fingers rose to the top button of his jeans.

He was hard—everywhere—as she tugged down the tab of the zipper. Glancing up again, she peeled the heavy fabric and his soft cotton boxers away from his hips. His hand sifted through her hair as she leaned forward and drew a line on his shaft with the tip of her tongue.

With the flat of it, she rolled over the crown, wetting the plum-soft skin before drawing it into the cavern of her mouth. His soft groan ratcheted her arousal. Her nipples tightened again, the points tingling as she swallowed more of him. She curled her fingers around the root of his shaft and balanced herself with her other hand on his steely thigh. Her mouth set up a languid yet steady rhythm, and she breathed along with it, her pulse thrumming loud in her ears.

It was carnal and beyond hot, and she imagined herself on the deck of his pirate ship, the Jolly Roger fluttering in the breeze above her head as she was captive to his desires. Her imagination had always been her most seductive partner, and it worked again for her now. Her panties were wet, and she took her hand from his thigh to reach inside them and touch—

"Damn it!" Griffin suddenly yanked her to her feet.

"What? What?" She was dizzy as he lifted her from the floor and half carried, half tossed her onto the bed.

Then he was on the mattress too, and he stilled, taking in her body splayed on his sheets, wearing only the pink-and-black panties and the girlie sandals. "What's wrong?" she asked.

Her voice seemed to shake him from his stupor. He slipped her shoes off her feet, dropping one and then the other over the side of the bed. His fingers played with the waistband of her panties. "I'm the captain of this orgasm," he said, as if he'd been privy to her little fantasy. "This time *I'm* the one who's going to give it to you."

He slid the last piece of her clothing free, and she watched him tuck the little ball of fabric in his bedside table drawer. "You only get them back if you let me give you your climax. Take it yourself, and I take the underwear."

Panty ransom? She would have laughed, but he was giving her a burning, smoldering, serious look. So she stifled her little nervous giggle. "Okay."

He stacked a couple of pillows against the wood-slat headboard. Next, he pushed her up against them, propping her there. "It'll give you a good view," he said. "Now put your hands here and here." He moved them himself, making her curl her fingers around a slat on either side of her head.

It was Jane who was breathing hard now. Her breasts trembled with each inhale and exhale. Still wearing his unfastened pants, he swung a leg over her body to straddle her, his head at the level of her stiffened nipples. "You hold still," he instructed, and then he bent his head to them.

She bowed into the wet heat, the avid tugs. Griffin tightened his knees against her legs, keeping her thighs pressed close together as he sucked her into his mouth. At first it was just the taut bead of the nipple, then he widened to take in more of her breast, then he drew his mouth away, letting the soft mound slide out until his teeth caught only the tight nub. She cried out at the little sting and then cried again when he lifted completely away. But he only moved to the other breast, performing the same salacious, delicious acts on it as one hand played with the already wet nipple.

Desire flowed outward from his touch. Her fingers tightened on the slats as he continued working over her breasts. Holding still became impossible. She twisted her torso, her lower half still caught by his powerful thighs. Then he was scooting down, trailing kisses toward her navel. He insinuated a leg between her knees, and then he was grasping her there, one in each hand, opening her to his gaze.

Chills raced over her body. He looked at her soft, swollen center. "Pretty," he said, his nostrils flaring, his blue eyes blazing. One finger swiped through the drenched tissues and he brought it to his mouth. Sucked.

Jane's breath seized.

"Tasty," Griffin said, then slid lower.

Oh, God. She understood his intention, and instantly shifted her legs, trying to bar him access.

He glanced up, one eyebrow raised.

"I don't… I've never…" She couldn't get out the words.

"Well, I do," Griffin said. "And there won't be any 'never' about this." Then he slid his palms from her knees to her inner thighs, widening her body, opening the delicate folds of flesh.

She really was the captive of a pirate. Because he was plundering again, his mouth taking her prisoner. The wet thrust of his tongue had her making a high, keening noise. Then it took a short excursion north, where he worried her clitoris with the tip, lashing it with tiny, measured strokes of pleasure.

He dipped low again, penetrating her with a firm wet thrust, then back up to the knot of nerves that now was pulsing with its own demand. Over and over, down and up, back and forth, in and out. Jane's muscles went tense, started a fine tremble, and she could only hold fast as she watched his dark head move between the paleness of her thighs.

The view, as he'd known, only took her higher.

Each of her short pants ended in a moan. He glanced up, and she saw it all, his hot blue eyes, his extended tongue, his mouth glazed from her own wetness. It twisted her arousal tighter, and then he went after her clitoris again, sucking it into his mouth as two fingers speared her body.

His impalement tossed her overboard and into wave after wave of orgasmic bliss. She pitched and rolled with pleasure, wanting to ride them forever. Griffin stayed with her, his mouth easing as the seas calmed. On her final shudder, though, he still possessed her, his fingers deep inside of her.

She opened her eyes to find him watching her face.

"*That's* putting you first, Jane," he said.

In the haze of postclimax bliss, the words didn't register. She only knew that she needed more of him. She protested as he slid his fingers from her and caught at his arm as he moved across the bed.

He laughed, low and smug. "I'm only getting a condom."

It took too long. But finally he was over her, inside her, filling her again, and her inner tissues twitched as he worked her with his penis, finding the last twitches of the orgasm still waiting for him there.

His thrusts were heavy and decisive, and she opened wide in every way to accept him. His mouth found hers, and she opened there too, taking in the thrust of his tongue. She twisted against his chest, her sensitive nipples abraded by his hair.

"Can you go again?" he said, his voice breathless.

"What?" Her brain wasn't working; only her body made sense to her now. Her body and his.

Instead of answering, he reached between them and found her clitoris once more. He stroked it gently, an irresistible counterpoint to the intense driving rhythm of his shaft. She lifted into both, her hips rolling upward, and then she was shuddering and Griffin was pushing deep, deep, deeper, drowning them both in sharp, sweet bliss.

When she came to herself, he was sliding back into the bed. He had a warm washcloth that he drew over her face and neck, down her midsection, and finally to the still-throbbing place between her thighs. He held it there.

She felt drugged by sex and intimacy. He used the intoxication to worm yet more out of her. "You think I should relax, Jane? Then fine, we're going to be relaxing like this a lot. Until we leave Beach House No. 9, I'm saving all my one percent for you."

Drowsy and pliant, she could only murmur. "Yes, sir. Aye, aye."

CHAPTER SIXTEEN

GRIFFIN FOUND Jane standing at the shoreline, her toes being teased by the foamy outermost hem of the incoming surf. Approaching her from behind, he sighed a little at how very *Jane* she looked in a lemon-colored two-piece bathing suit. Petal-like ruffles cut high on her tush, and he knew there were matching ones edging the deep vee of the halter-style top. She looked both sweet and tart, like a lemonade Popsicle.

She made him hungry.

He slid one arm around her waist, and she squealed. He growled in her ear as he pulled her back against him. "The eels have landed."

With a twist, she squirmed out of his hold. "You scared me!" But before he could respond, she clutched his arm with one hand and pointed with the other. "But I'm glad you're here. You need to rescue the boys."

Duncan and Oliver stood in the surf, the water swirling around the flapping hems of their hibiscus-print swim trunks. They were tan despite the sunscreen his sister slathered on them. Oliver, the fairer of the two miscreants, had a white triangle of goop on his nose. Between them they held an inflatable raft, but they were having trouble keeping it steady. Every time they tried to throw themselves on it, belly down, it popped free of their weight and dumped them in the shallow water.

"Sweetheart, they're fine." The breeze blew a piece

of her golden-hued hair across her face, and he caught it with his hand and tucked it behind her ear. "Where's your lotion? Your nose is turning pink again."

She cast another anxious look toward the water. "Are you sure? I told Tess I'd keep an eye on them while she gets Russ some juice. The baby's been very fussy today."

"You have to stop involving yourself with my sister's kids." He crossed his arms over his chest. "Thanks to you, I had to suffer through an hour-long meeting with Old Man Monroe about the presentation to Rebecca's class. He was so cantankerous I let Private dig for bones in his flower beds before we left."

Not only had the antique been his usual curmudgeonly self, he'd been his usual *nosy* curmudgeonly self. "What's changed?" he'd demanded. "You look rested, son, like you might actually be sleeping."

Griffin had shrugged a shoulder. "You're my worst nightmare. Guess I'm just getting used to you being next door."

The coot had slapped one age-speckled hand on the tabletop. "It's that pretty woman. She's smart, so I don't know what she can see in you, but Jane's doing you some good."

He hadn't denied it. Jane was smoothing some of his rough spots, and he wasn't going to feel guilty about it either. They both understood the situation was temporary. Though very satisfying.

"Hell's bells, boy," Rex had said, his mouth dropping open. "You're smiling."

"So?" he'd countered, not even bothering to scowl.

"So don't screw this up," the old man had cautioned. "You've got a good reason to beat back that darkness inside you now. Don't use it to shove her away instead."

"Griffin?"

Jane's voice jerked him back to the present. "What?"

"The boys," she said, "I'm worried about your nephews."

"You need to stop that," he said, putting Rex and his ramblings from his head. "I'm going to make a rule. No more contact between you and the devil's minions."

"You and your rules," she scoffed, with a little flounce that fluttered the ruffles at her ass.

"Don't you forget them, either," he said, enjoying the way her cheeks went as pink as her nose as he pointed his finger at her. They'd come to an understanding three days before, and he didn't mind mentioning it again because it always made her blush and shiver. "You must be the first to get naked. You must be the first to—"

"I get it, I get it."

He grinned. "So you do, honey-pie. Each and every time, by my hand or my mouth or by my—"

She clapped a hand over his lips. "Stop."

"Not gonna," he said against her palm. Then he grabbed her wrist and drew it low, twisting it so her body was brought flush to his. "Not as long as we're living together at Beach House No. 9."

His kiss took the sass out of her, and he reveled in her pliant warmth. His free hand cupped the back of her head as he took the kiss deeper.

She broke away, breathing hard.

He grinned at her and the hard points of her nipples that were pressing against her swimsuit. "Oh," she said, glancing down. Clearly flustered, she crossed her arms over her chest. They covered the little buds but plumped the tantalizing curves of her cleavage.

"That meeting with the old man still has me all wound up," he lied. "Think we could go inside and find some way to take the edge off? I'm pretty certain I need to relax."

"No." Her head tilted toward the surf. "Little boys? Unpredictable surf?"

"Whale snot. Green-scaled eels." When she frowned at him, he caught her hand and carried it to his mouth. The woman had given him hours of pleasure in bed. "Sorry. I shouldn't tease you."

"I shouldn't be so easy to tease."

They both watched Duncan and Oliver for a few more minutes, and when they finally got a good ride into shore, Jane clapped her hands. The boys grinned at her, then dashed back into the water.

"They make my fear seem even more ridiculous," she murmured.

"Do you want to get over it?"

She raised an eyebrow at him, her expression suspicious.

It was the cutest damn thing. "Honey-pie…" He'd forgotten what he meant to say.

"Chili-dog?"

He was never going to think of that menu item without thinking of Jane. The governess had changed him and he wanted to return the favor. His fingers tightened on hers, and he stepped toward the water. "Come in with me, sweetheart."

Biting her lip, she dug her heels in the sand. "I don't know."

"I won't let go of you, I promise."

Her head wagged back and forth. "Your kind always lets go. That's how I learned to stay afloat in the first place. My father carried me out in the deep end of the pool. When we were far from where I could stand up, he released me. I had my arms around his neck, and he just went under, slipping out of my grasp. So it was up to me alone. Sink or swim."

Griffin had to look away from her earnest, unsmiling face. When his temper had cooled a little, he tugged her toward him again. "Trust me, Jane. We won't go too far. When you're done, you say so and I'll get you right back to shore." It was suddenly important to him that he do this, that he be different than the others of his "kind."

She hesitated another moment, then took a step forward, wincing when the Pacific washed over the top of her foot. "Cold."

"Bracing," he said, walking backward. "Now don't forget to do the stingray shuffle."

"Stingray shuffle?"

"They bury themselves in the sand and if you step directly on them, they'll strike with their tail. So you do the stingray shuffle to avoid the less dignified—and pretty painful—stingray hop."

Doubt creased her forehead and she eyed the water around her. "Maybe my brothers weren't so wrong."

"The eels are much farther offshore."

She stuck her tongue out at him.

He laughed, once again tugging on her hand. "Come closer and say that to me."

To his satisfaction, she kept pace as he waded backward into the surf, checking over his shoulder every so often to make sure a wave wouldn't catch him unawares. They made it past shins and knees, and were approaching the tops of her thighs when she froze up. She peered into the water around her. "Something touched me. This is why I don't like the ocean. There are things in here with me."

"Probably a piece of kelp," he said, his voice soothing. The sound of an approaching wave had him glancing back again. It was tall enough to hit her belly. "Heads up."

She did the girlie shriek when the water struck her midsection. "It's freezing."

"Bracing," he repeated.

They were getting in deep enough water that she could float, if she wanted, and hold on to him. When he suggested it, she hesitated a moment, then took a breath and went prone on the water, stroking toward him. He caught her, and she circled her arms around his neck. He drew in her silky legs so they wound his waist.

He gave a maniacal laugh. "You fell right in with my plot." Then he hitched her closer and kissed her. In contrast to their ocean-cooled skin, their mouths burned. Griffin slipped one of the hands propping up her bottom beneath the elastic of her swimsuit. He palmed the round cheek, and she wiggled closer. The kiss turned feverish.

Then Jane jerked her mouth away. "We forgot the boys!"

"They're fine," he said, quarter-turning their twined bodies so she could see them on the shore, engaged in some kind of behavior that was likely preparing them for a life of crime. Really, those two little kids made him nervous.

With a wet hand, she brushed back his hair. "Thank you," she said.

"No, thank *you*." He grinned at her and bent his head, intent on another kiss. "Now where were we?"

Before lip met lip, they were tossed over by a wave. Damn, he thought as she tumbled out of his grip. Then a second wave struck, and he was submerged again.

Eyes open, he looked for Jane in the swirling green world of rising bubbles and undulating seaweed. He saw something yellow, but it was a garibaldi fish and not Jane's swimsuit. *Hope she has her eyes closed,* he thought. Then he popped up, and immediately began surveying the surface of the water. "Jane?" he called as he regained his footing.

Alarm squeezed his chest. *"Jane?"*

Then, a few feet away, thrashing arms and legs rose from the water. He rushed toward her, hampered by yet another, smaller wave. When he caught hold of one of her arms, the other smacked him in the shoulder.

"Sweetheart." Her eyes were tightly closed, and she didn't seem to hear him. "Honey-pie!"

Her wet lashes blinked open. He yanked her against him, and she latched onto his body. "You're okay," he said, keeping her close. "You're fine."

"I almost died!" she said, in Rebecca-like tones.

"Not even close." Her hair was sodden, and he finger combed it off her forehead.

Her breath was sawing in and out, and he just held her, waiting for her to calm as he kept one eye on the incoming waves. Finally, she shuddered, and her head dipped, her forehead against his chin. "I feel like an idiot."

"It was my fault," he said, moving a little closer to shore, Jane still in his arms. "I wasn't paying attention."

"I was thrashing."

"More like floundering."

Her head lifted. "Gee, thanks, I feel so much better now."

"It's no big deal."

"I don't like looking foolish," she said. *"You* didn't panic."

Only when I thought I might have lost you. He shook the words out of his head. "You don't have to corner the market on competence, Jane."

"Funny you should say that." She wrinkled her nose, then her pretty, clear eyes gazed past his shoulder at the horizon. "My father told me not long ago it was better to be competent than lovable."

"Jesus," he muttered, then he drew her head to his shoulder, holding her cheek to his salty skin. "You're a pain in the ass, Jane, you know that? But somebody's going to find that lovable about you. Somebody's coming along real soon and you'll know just how lovable you are."

She was still for a moment, her mouth touching his wet shoulder, pressing it there in the semblance of a kiss.

The water, the world, swirled about them for a quiet few moments. Then Griffin cleared his throat. "Want to go any farther, Jane?"

"No." She had begun to shiver, but he didn't think it was from the sixty-eight-degree water. "I'm afraid I'm already out of my depth."

EVERY PARENT KNEW the worst day in a normal family household was the day when all the kids were hit with the flu at the same time—and then the mom was struck down too. Tess tried telling herself that wasn't happening, though. It was the washing out of the barf bowl for the tenth time that was making her nauseous. She was only burning up one moment, then shivering with cold the next because one minute she was running to her room where she'd placed the two middle boys in her own bed, and the next she was sitting with the baby on her shoulder, trying to console his unhappy whimpers.

She and Russ were the only ones who hadn't disgorged the contents of their stomachs. But she had a terrible feeling it was only a matter of time.

The sounds of retching reached her. Duncan or Oliver—too sick to be counted on to make it to the bathroom—was making use of the big plastic bowl that she planned to never see again once this was over. Closing her eyes, Tess willed her legs to move. When they didn't obey, she raised her voice. "Rebecca, do you think you could—"

The remainder of her sentence was drowned out by the pitter-patter of her daughter's feet on a mad dash from her "bower of death"—the teen's own words—to the bathroom across the hall.

There would be no help there.

She pushed off with her bare feet and managed to stand. A short spin of her head later, she stumbled toward her needy children. *Women manage alone all the time,* she reminded herself. *It's good preparation for your life ahead.*

Tears gathered, but she blinked them away. She needed to be clear-eyed to wash the despicable bowl. Next she wiped down Duncan's and Oliver's faces with a cool, wet cloth. When she asked them if they could take a sip of water, they didn't bother answering. She was a little more forceful about offering the pediatric drink that she tried to foist off as "juice," but they both turned their faces away.

In a last-ditch effort, she dangled the image of cold cola—a rare treat—and it was testament to how ill they felt that neither gave a twitch.

Rebecca's footsteps sounded zombielike as she moved from the bathroom back to her bed. Tess wet another washcloth and bathed her daughter's face as she lay sprawled on the mattress. The cell phone on the small table beside Rebecca's pillow started a little dance. Things were serious when the teenager didn't even reach for the device to check the sender of the text.

"I want Daddy," Rebecca moaned, her eyes squeezed shut.

Things were serious indeed. Her daughter hadn't called her father "Daddy" since her thirteenth birthday. *David,*

Tess thought, then pinched off the fruitless longing. He was somewhere pushing pedals in circles or lifting a weight that wasn't the weight of their family's situation.

She stood over her daughter, rocking the baby back and forth. Perhaps the movement would counterbalance the seasick feeling in her stomach. Her decision-making process felt just as unbalanced as she pondered her options. "Maybe I should call Uncle Griff," she said.

One of Rebecca's eyes opened. "You called Uncle Griff. He said he was rushing right over…to put a quarantine sign on the door."

"I didn't tell him we needed help." That had been eight hours ago, when she'd thought the kids were suffering from a mild tummy bug.

"If you call next door again," Rebecca said, "ask for Jane. Men aren't any good at caretaking."

More tears burned behind Tess's eyes. Her lovely, sweet, trusting little girl had already been disappointed enough to internalize that message. *Men aren't any good at caretaking.* Hadn't her father given up on that job during the past few months?

Anger added itself to Tess's mix of sickness and sadness. David had done this! David had fractured Rebecca's faith. The thought put a bit of steel in her spine, and she sought to reassure her teenager. "I'm here to take care of us. We don't need anyone but me."

One-handed, she pulled up the covers around Rebecca's neck while the other hand balanced Russ, draped over her shoulder. Then she put the drowsing baby down in his crib and ignored her own queasiness to gather the clothes and towels strewn around the house. She filled the washing machine and pressed Start, just as she heard yet another round of retching.

Duncan or Oliver or possibly both had missed the bowl.

Standing in the doorway of her bedroom, holding on to the jamb to keep herself upright, she stared at the miserable children and the messed sheets. For just a moment she envisioned that other life she'd stopped fantasizing about the night David had dropped by with his carton of files. It beckoned more seductively than before. Shared custody—and they'd be sick on David's watch. Hours of blissful alone time. A different man with whom she could play on the beach while her children were someone else's responsibility.

"Mommy," Duncan whispered.

The plaintive word broke her heart. She hurried toward her little guy. "Mommy's here," she assured him, as she moved forward to tackle the task of changing sheets and pajamas. "Mommy will always be here."

A couple of hours later a knock roused her. She'd been half-asleep on the living room couch, the baby slumbering on her chest. Her movement woke him, and he started to cry a little.

Tess just managed not to join him as she pulled open the door. Her brother stood on the doorstep. "Plague over?" he asked. "I've brought provisions for you and the minions." He waved a greasy bag in her face that was branded with the golden arches.

The smell of the burgers and fries—usually one of her favorites in the whole world—wafted in on a briny breeze.

Tess felt herself go green. Then, Russ still in her arms, she slammed the door in Griffin's face and ran to the kitchen sink where she left the contents of her stomach and entered the eighth circle of hell. According to Dante, the eighth circle was the provenance of Fraud, which made perfect sense because she'd have brief moments of elated good health following a trip to the bathroom before queasiness rose up once again.

Now she was glad she was alone with the kids because she couldn't imagine wanting anyone to see her like this: worn down, lank-haired and sweaty around the edges.

There wasn't a name for the next level of hell, the one in which the baby finally caught up with the rest of them and started throwing up too. It was his first experience with the oh-so-unpleasant activity, and clearly it frightened him, even though Tess had been prepared enough to unearth another plastic bowl.

He cried through the whole procedure.

Sitting on the living room couch, she cried afterward, silently though, so as not to frighten the kids. *Mom needs to be strong,* she reminded herself. *Mom can go it alone.* While Russ kept up a low whimper, she half dozed and held him close to her heart, the bowl in her lap at the ready.

When the baby's weight lifted from her chest, she thought the sudden change was part of a dream. Since David's fortieth birthday, rarely had anyone taken Russ from her when he was fussy—and she'd asked for help even more rarely. An almost-fatherless baby shouldn't have his mommy pass him off too.

Time passed. Minutes probably as she drifted into the dream where there was a male voice murmuring and a male presence moving about the small house. Occasionally a note of a child's voice would spike through her slumber, but that couldn't be real either, because there was no one home to take that responsible *shh-shh* tone of voice. She allowed herself to fall into sleep because she knew she needed her strength. And because she knew that her kids would make a riot if Mom was really needed. They only had her.

Then a new sound poked her into wakefulness. Baby Russ was retching again, and her hands registered he wasn't with her. And that his bowl still lay in her lap. *What?*

Tess lurched from her sprawl on the couch. Her eyes opened as she stood and there was a figure in front of her. She blinked a few times to put it into focus. Her husband. David. He was holding her baby.

She might think it was still a dream, but little Russ's body was moving, undulating in that way—

"The bowl," she said, holding it out.

But David ignored her, murmuring to their baby and cradling him close as their smallest son puked all over David's favorite high-tech, fancy-fiber, sweat-wicking spin shirt.

She stared. "The bowl."

"It's all right. He's not so scared when I'm holding him like this."

Another moment passed, then she heard sounds from her bedroom. With her hand on one wall, she made her way to her other sons. Looking more bright-eyed, Duncan and Oliver were propped up on pillows and watching cartoons on the flat-screen TV across the room. Each had a glass of what looked to be water in hand, a bent straw ready for a small mouth.

Oliver noticed her, sketched a wave. "Mommy."

She echoed the movement. "Sweet boy."

Duncan sipped his water and then glanced over. "Daddy's home."

"I see that," she said. Then a wave of sickness slammed into her, and she ran for relief.

Bout over, she checked in on Rebecca. There was a glass of water and a bent straw beside her cell phone. The teenager was sleeping. The sound of a shower running drew her to the end of the hall. Through the half-open door, she saw her husband holding her youngest in the shower, both of them fully dressed.

"What are you doing?" she croaked out. But she realized he couldn't hear her over the rushing water and his own crooning voice as he sang to their son.

"'Hush little baby don't say a word, Daddy's goin' to buy you a mockingbird.'" David had sung to all their children when they were small. A story, a song, and then good-night. Once Rebecca had begged for "A Hundred Bottles of Root Beer on the Wall," and she'd made it to twenty-seven remaining before dozing off. He'd never fallen for that again.

Watching him now, Tess was absolutely positive she'd never fall for anyone else besides him.

She pushed open the door the whole way as he stepped onto the bath mat in his dripping clothes. "Give me Russ," she said, reaching for a towel.

David shook his head and took the terry cloth out of her hand. "I've got him."

With her energy at an all-time low, she could only watch as he stripped himself and the baby out of their wet clothes. Then, with a towel around his waist, he found the boys' room and quickly diapered Russ and put him in a soft onesie. Russ's eyes closed. Tess watched from the doorway. "He's almost asleep. You can put him in the crib."

"Think I'll hold him awhile," David said over his shoulder. "You're almost asleep too. Go lie down."

The suggestion was nearly irresistible. Nearly. "You'll stay with the kids?"

He hesitated. "I'm staying with all of you. Always."

It was enough to get her moving in the direction of an empty bed, even though the stranger of the past few months wasn't a man she'd want with them for always. If that was who was in the house, then once she was better, he'd just have to leave again.

CHAPTER SEVENTEEN

IT WAS EVENING and the kids had all kept down water, chicken noodle soup and soda crackers for hours by the time David saw his wife peek into the living room where the older boys and Rebecca were crowded together watching a Disney movie. He'd had time to dry his clothes, and though he was holding Russ again, he managed to pour her a mug of the soup he'd kept warm. "Drink this," he said, crossing to her, "and then go take a shower."

"Thank you." Her hand trembled a little as she reached for it.

Seeing her like this made him want to kick his own ass all over again. In using distance to try to save himself, he'd allowed Tess to get overtired and sick. If Griffin hadn't called him...

His wife took a tentative sip from the mug, then seemed to think it was going to stay down and so took another. "Rebecca, are you kids okay?"

"Yeah." She didn't take her gaze from the screen. "Daddy handled things."

Tess glanced over at him, her expression unreadable. "Will you be all right with Russ while I take a shower?"

"Yes." That she felt she had to ask twisted his gut. "Take your time."

When she next appeared in the living room, the four kids were in bed asleep. Tess's hair was still slightly damp, and she was dressed in a pair of plaid flannel pants and a sweatshirt proclaiming Happy Mom from Eaglewood Elementary. There was a little more color in her cheeks, but her blue eyes still stood out too brightly against her pale features.

He reached in the oven. "Hungry? I made mac and cheese."

Her gaze jumped to his. "You made your mom's mac and cheese?"

"My specialty." He smiled a little. "That and hot dogs."

She sat gingerly in a chair at the kitchen table, as if maybe her bones hurt. As he placed a plate and glass of water in front of her, he wanted to lift her from its hard surface and cuddle her on his lap, whispering promises that he would always cushion her, that he would always be what she needed.

But when he'd shown her the cushion of their financial situation, she'd thrown it back in his face. And as to always being what she needed…if he'd done that she wouldn't be sitting in that chair, shivering.

"I'll light a fire," he said, though the pressed-sawdust log wouldn't give off much heat. On his way back toward the kitchen alcove, he grabbed a small blanket hanging over the arm of the sofa. He draped it over her shoulders while she sat staring at the steaming mound of pasta.

"Would you rather I put it away?" he asked. "I can make you something else."

She shook her head and managed to eat a few bites. Then she downed the entire glass of water. It revived her a little, and when he thought she was through, he encouraged her to stretch out on the sofa.

He tucked the blanket around her.

"Thank you," she said.

So polite again. He sat on the coffee table in front of her, his elbows on his knees, his hands dangling between them. Now that they had privacy and time, he couldn't seem to get his tongue to wrap around the words he'd been planning since walking into the house and finding his family looking like ghosts.

Tess pushed at her hair, her wary gaze on him. "David—"

"Come home." The words burst from his mouth. "Please, come home. I'll step up. Change more diapers. Make more mac and cheese. When Russ wakes up in the night, I'll get up with him."

"He sleeps through the night, now. He's slept through the night for months."

"I knew that." Not exactly. "I just meant…if he has nightmares or…" David looked away, scrubbed a hand through his hair, faced his wife again. "I'll do just about anything to have you all home again."

"'Just about anything,'" his smart and beautiful wife echoed.

"That's right." He tried blustering his way through the qualifier. "You name it."

"I won't go home to the man you've been lately, David." She dropped her gaze to pick at some lint on the blanket. "That man made me doubt myself. I thought maybe I wasn't enough because I don't have a degree or because I 'only' take care of our kids. But I loved that life we had before. I enjoyed being the woman who lived it, and I thought we were very happy. Maybe I can't have it back. Maybe I'll have to go to work or go to college because we're not going to be together anymore."

Her words sent those dull knives digging into him again. What he'd done, the pulling away, it hadn't been about any failing of hers. "Tess…"

"But I know I deserve a man like the one you were

before you turned forty, and I'm not going to settle for anything less."

David jumped to his feet and paced to the window, staring out over the sand to the ocean that looked like a black hole in the night. The same as what would be inside him if he lost what he and Tess had together. He didn't know how to stop that from happening, and he felt as if he was drowning in all that darkness already. The cold seemed to be overtaking him, dragging him deep, deep, deep.

He rested his forehead against the cool glass. "I love all of you so much, Tess. Too much."

Behind him, he sensed her sitting up on the sofa. "We love you too. Why is this a problem?"

His hand flailed wildly. "Rebecca is a teenager, for God's sake!"

"Yes, well," his wife said, her voice dry, "after the past couple of weeks I think I'm a little bit more aware of that than you."

"And Russ..." He couldn't finish the thought because it had a stranglehold on his throat.

"What is it about Russ?" Tess asked. "I've been racking and racking my brain trying to understand why you've treated him differently than the other babies."

She stood now and came closer to him. "Do you...do you have some doubts that you're his father?"

Startled, David turned. "What?"

Her hands were in the kangaroo pocket of her sweatshirt. There was a paint stain on it, the pale sky color of their youngest child's room. He remembered her up on a ladder with a roller, her pregnant belly round under the cotton fleece. He'd lifted it from her taut skin, his kiss for her and their growing baby boy.

Tess smoothed her hair. "I just thought maybe that's why you're so cool to him."

"Of course I know he's mine! And not just because I know it, but because—" David shoved his hands in his own pockets and transferred his gaze to his shoes "—he has my ear."

"What? You mumbled that last bit."

"He has my ear."

"Your *ear?*"

David felt the back of his neck go hot and he lifted one shoulder. "The rim of my right ear is not the same as the rim of my left. It's thicker. Larger."

Tess stomped right up to him then and took his jaw in her cool hands. She turned his head this way and that. "You're right. I've known you for fourteen years and I never noticed that before."

"I didn't want you to notice. I used to get teased about it when I was a kid. It was worse then, but it's still a…a flaw."

"You have a lot worse flaws than that," Tess informed him, then she hurried out of the room.

He looked after her, unsure of her purpose until she came back, wearing a bemused expression. "You're right. Russ does have your ear."

"I talked to the pediatrician about it," David muttered. "I asked about plastic surgery."

Her arms slammed across her chest. "No one is changing a hair on my little baby's body. You're crazy."

"That's pretty close to what Dr. Gomez said."

There were roses in her cheeks now, and she looked as if her health had returned with her indignation. Her blue eyes blazed at him, and he found her so beautiful that he felt that tightening in his chest again, that vise constricting his ribs. Or maybe the pressure was coming from the inside, because his heart felt as if it was swelling, its beat banging hard against his bones.

Tess's brows drew together. "Are you all right? Are you feeling sick now?" Her face showing clear concern, she came toward him and put her arm around his waist. "Come sit down."

Put yet another black mark on his side of the record books because he didn't tell her it wasn't the flu that was affecting him. Instead, he slid his arm around her shoulders and made sure she sat beside him on the sofa. But there was still worry in her eyes when she turned to him. "David, is there something wrong with your health? Is that what you've been keeping from me?"

"No, no." He drew her hand to his mouth and kissed it. "It's not about me."

Her fingers tightened on his as her eyes searched his face. "You're lying to me. That's why you've been exercising. That's why—"

"Tess, it's not my health. It's…everything. Rebecca growing up. All the kids moving out into the world where things…things can happen to them. I've tried to separate from all of you because of how much that could hurt me."

She shook her head. "What kind of things are you talking about?"

"What if we lost Russ?" Again, the words just burst out of him. They tasted bitter on his tongue, and he hated that he'd said them, as if they could pollute the air with the ugliness of the idea.

Tess's hand trembled in his. She sat back in the cushions, her other hand rising to her throat. "Why would you say such a thing?"

"The other Russ, my brother…"

Her gasp was loud in the room. Then his wife drew

closer, her arms circling him. His arms closed around her. It felt so good. So right.

"My love," she said against his pounding heart. "Oh, my love."

Then she pulled back, relief written all over her face. "This is what it's about. Your little brother dying of leukemia. You're afraid to be hurt that way again."

"I loved him so much, Tess," he said, his voice hoarse. "I made promises and avoided cracks and took all my favorite toys and put them on his bed and he still didn't come home from the hospital."

"I'm so sorry," she said, pressing herself to him again.

He squeezed his eyes against the burn behind them. His hand cupped her head, and he pressed his mouth against her hair. It smelled of baby shampoo. "He was a good little kid. He never did anything wrong."

"And neither did you," his wife said.

His body gave him away. He stiffened as the horror of that morning came to him again. Panic flushed through his blood at the memory, and he sharply inhaled as if it might be the last oxygen his lungs would ever take in.

Tess moved back, wary once more.

"I need to tell you…I did do something wrong," he said, feeling as if each word was pulled from his throat. "On the morning of my fortieth birthday."

She swallowed. "I was out shopping for the party we were throwing that night. You took the kids to the park."

"The Gordon kids from next door wanted to come with us. All three of them and their bikes. No, the oldest had his skateboard."

"Rebecca was still at her friend Marcy's…"

"Right. And as we were getting ready to head out, the Gordons' cousins showed up, so I said I'd take them too."

"So you had—what?—eight kids with you?"

David, knowing he would never be the same in her eyes, shook his head. "Seven. I left one behind, sitting in his stroller on the sidewalk in front of our house. I left Russ."

She shot back on the cushions until she was pressed against the sofa's arm. "But you turned back...you remembered...."

He was still shaking his head. "We'd been gone fifteen or so minutes when Mac Kearney from across the street called my cell. Mary Hampton—from the PTA?—was at the park, and I asked her to watch my pack until I got back. I ran, Tess, God, I ran as fast as I could, and it was then that I realized what those stupid fifteen flabby pounds might cost me."

"Surely Mac..."

He nodded now. "He stayed with Russ, but I wasn't going to be able to breathe again until I could see our baby."

She sat silent now, one hand over her eyes. David didn't believe he had organs or blood or bones anymore. He felt like a husk of himself and maybe it wasn't so bad, because perhaps he'd finally reached that place he'd been striving for...where he felt nothing. Where he could be that distant and unfeeling man like his father.

Then Tess's hand dropped, and he saw that she was crying and the tears caused everything to come flooding back: his panic, his shame, his absolute terror and the certain knowledge that he didn't deserve the beautiful creatures that had been entrusted to him. He saw his wife reach for the box of tissues on the side table, and she grabbed a fistful that she passed to him.

Because he was crying too. He mopped up the wetness as best he could, while avoiding her eyes. He didn't know what he wanted to see less: her condemnation or her abhorrence of his weakness.

"You once told me," Tess said, "that accountants never cried…"

"…unless there's an audit," he finished with her, his voice a rough croak. But that's what this was, wasn't it? An examination of his accounts. His records were completely open now. The numbers laid bare.

But it was all revealed for him as well. What a fool he'd been to try to separate his heart from her, from those who sprang from what they had together.

You couldn't duck love. It was the nature of being human to want the connections. And it was his own nature to hold close to his family with everything he had.

He dried the final dampness on his cheek with the heel of his hand, then got down on his knees, shoving aside the coffee table to make room for himself. "I love you. Forgive me for what I did that morning and for how I've been since then. Stay married to me. I promise I'll do better."

"You won't go back to the way you've been?"

He shook his head. "I won't be that stupid."

Her hand came out to brush his face. More tears overflowed the most beautiful eyes in the world. His *OM* girl who hadn't quieted his wild mind but who'd brought light and life to his tame world. "You can't get rid of me so easily," she said.

No, you can't duck love.

Relief unbalanced his heart, and a supreme sense of rightness steadied it again. "Thank you," he said, dropping his head so his cheek pressed against her knee. "Thank you for being my wife and their mother."

Tess tugged on his arms then, bringing him to the cushions beside her. They embraced, but she resisted his kiss. "Germs," she said.

"Are you kidding? Russ barfed all over me. If I'm going to get it, I'm going to get it."

The argument persuaded her, and they kissed until she claimed to be dizzy from it. And knowing what she'd just been through, he didn't insist, instead drawing her against his chest and cuddling with her, their gazes on the fire.

He idly ran his fingers through her hair, and her contented sigh released the last knot of his tension. "I'm sorry I had the vasectomy without telling you about the appointment."

She shook her head. "We had agreed. It was just another sign of your distance that I objected to."

He pressed a kiss to her head. "Did you really want more children?"

"After the past two days? No. Or maybe it's the whole Cheetos thing." She tilted her head to send him a wry look. "I'm counting on you to train that out of the boys."

And that's how he knew they were going to be good again, because she was smiling and because she'd said *I'm counting on you.* It was the single most important job they had, he realized now…to be the person the other could depend upon.

And David Quincy, forty-plus years old, no longer feared the passage of time. Because age had wrought wisdom.

JANE HADN'T LIVED with anyone since graduating from college. Even during those years she'd rarely had time to socialize with her various roommates. She'd been a full-time student and a part-time nanny. The mother of the children she'd overseen had been head writer for a top-rated TV show. When the woman wrote a book on screenwriting, she'd asked English-major Jane to beta-read a draft…and a career had been born.

So waking up with a roommate who was also a work-mate in your—his—own bed should have been a shock.

It was shockingly easy.

She rolled her head on the pillow and gazed at Griffin. He was lying on his stomach, and his face was turned toward hers. He didn't look little-boy in his sleep. The stubble of his dark beard was too harsh for that. But he appeared rested, and she thought it good that his TV-all-night habit had been broken since she'd started sleeping in the room.

One midnight she'd awoken to find him absent from the bed. Her bare feet hadn't made a sound on the floor, but he wouldn't have heard her, anyway. When she'd found him lying on the recliner in the living room, he'd been clad only in boxers and had had an iPod lying on his bare belly, its buds tucked into his ears. He must have felt her gaze, because he'd opened his eyes.

There'd been weariness in them and a bleakness that she couldn't address with words. So she'd thrown off the T-shirt of his that she'd been wearing, shifted the iPod to the arm of the chair and crawled into his lap. She'd figured he was listening to music that was hard rock or heavy metal and her touch was the antithesis to that. Every kiss gentle, every movement languid, the rhythm when she took him inside her mouth had been slow and measured. All meant to conquer the beast that wouldn't let him sleep.

He'd never left her in the middle of the night since.

Jane was no idiot. She knew that there was danger in their compatibility and propinquity, though he continued to tease her and get annoyed with her and sometimes became mad enough to stomp out of the office. But underlying it all, she thought they had an understanding of each other that she'd never expected to find with a man. She told herself that she was lucky. With a set end point to the relationship, that understanding could never be ruined.

When she left Beach House No. 9, she would leave the laughing, the arguing, the sex, behind. But she could retain it, she hoped, like a little snow globe in her mind. A tableau that she could shake up and revisit: the sand, the cottage, a palm tree and two little figures that were she and Griffin, forever caught in a together moment.

"Jane," Griffin murmured now, his eyes still closed. "Did you know that I can feel your mind at work from here? It's irritating."

His growl chased away the little melancholy that was edging into her thoughts. "Some of us can rub two brain cells together before sixteen ounces of coffee."

"Then if you're so all-powerful, why don't you get up and make that coffee, or, better yet—" he suddenly reached out and grabbed her "—let's find some other kind of cells to rub together."

Squealing, she pretended to fight him off, turning her mouth away from his with a breathless complaint about his morning beard.

He gave an evil laugh. "All the better to make you burn, honey-pie."

"Chili-dog—"

A banging on the front door had them halting midtussle. When the sound came again, Griffin groaned. "I'd know that rat-tat-a-tat-tat anywhere. It's the minions."

The way he said "the minions" in his gloomiest voice made her giggle. "The Cheeto minions?"

"Definitely the Cheeto minions." He was already rolling from the bed, one hand reaching for a pair of shorts he'd left on the floor.

She watched him head for the door, shirtless, and the play of muscles in his back made her sigh. "Griffin…"

He glanced over his shoulder, then his feet stopped moving and his gaze softened. "What do you need, sweetheart?"

More memories for her snow globe. "You," she said. Since it was just for a little while more, she could say it aloud.

"Then let me get those damn kids out of No. 9."

When he didn't return right away, though, she got curious. Pulling on her bathing suit and a beach cover-up, she headed in the direction of the kitchen, from which came the smell of coffee and the sound of male voices. Inside she found Tess's husband at the table with Griffin, who sent her an apologetic look. "David and the boys came over to borrow some milk and…"

And it looked as if the two men were having a serious talk. She could see Duncan and Oliver on the deck outside, still dressed in their pj's and tossing the plastic jug of milk back and forth. "Why don't I see that the beverage gets safely next door," she said. "I'll take the boys with me."

On her way past him, Griffin caught her hand. Slanting her a brief smile, he pressed her fingers, then let her go. *Sorry…and thank you.* That brief and silent communication between them was as intimate as any kiss.

She was smiling as she followed Duncan and Oliver into No. 8, where she found Tess standing over a bowl of pancake mix and cracked eggs. "Looking for this?" she asked, handing over the milk.

"Yes, thanks." She scattered some Cheerios on the tray of Russ's high chair at the same time that she instructed the bigger boys to turn down the volume on the TV.

"You guys got over your flu?"

Tess smiled. There was no doubt she'd always been a striking beauty, but now there was a serene glow about her. She'd lost the brittleness that she'd shown the past couple of weeks. "We got over a lot of things."

"David's next door," Jane said.

"He was here last night. Was the real deal when we needed him."

Jane nodded. "I wanted to come, but Griffin insisted on calling him. According to your brother, your husband made a land-speed record from your house to here."

A little smile crossed the other woman's face. "He's a by-the-book sort of man, but if his family's threatened..." She poured milk into the mixing bowl and began stirring the contents with a wooden spoon.

"I'm happy for you, Tess. It sounds as if you two worked things out."

"The cove has a way of making good things happen." Duncan and Oliver came clomping into the kitchen, swim fins on their feet. They were out of their pajamas and into swim trunks, mask-and-snorkel combinations perched on the tops of their heads. Tess easily dodged them as one chased the other, Frankenstein-style, arms reaching. "Despite David's and my troubles, the kids have had a great time here."

Jane had to grin at the small boys. She ruffled Duncan's hair as he staggered past her. The touch stopped him. "Hey," he said, as if a lightbulb had gone off.

"Hey back," she said, still smiling. Griffin claimed they were destined for a life of crime due to their unceasing energy and incessant curiosity, but she figured they were more likely headed for careers of adventure and excitement like their uncles. With their dark hair and blue eyes, Tess's boys were prototypes of the children that Griffin might have someday.

"Don't be sad," Duncan said.

She realized she'd dropped her smile. With effort, she pinned another back on. "Okay."

"'Cuz I'm going to make you happy today." He hitched up his board shorts in a move that looked just like his uncle's. "You said you'd love to."

"Hmm." She mentally walked back through her memory. "I said I'd love to…what?"

"Get buried in the sand." His voice lowered. "Me 'n' Oliver are going to bury you alive from your crumpy bitty toes to your scrawny chicken neck."

The words sounded like something from a story, but his tone was so bloodthirsty that Jane wondered if Griffin might be right about their criminal tendencies. "I remember that now. It's going to be today?"

"Has to be today," Duncan said. "'Cuz we go home this afternoon."

"Oh." She glanced over at Tess for confirmation.

"Yep. I have flower beds that have been neglected, and it's easier for the kids to do all their activities from our regular home base. Rebecca's ecstatic at the idea of closer proximity to her friends."

"I'll…I'll miss you," Jane said, realizing how true it was. The other woman had become a friend in the days they'd been neighbors.

"Me too," Tess said. "But we can get together beyond the cove too, you know."

Could they? Because once Jane left here and ended her working relationship with Griffin, she didn't know how it would be to see his sister on a regular basis. Would it be weird or even…painful?

From the onset, she'd settled in her mind that the period to all this was the day she left Beach House No. 9. Without speaking, she watched Tess pour circles of batter into a heated frying pan and then retreated toward a corner to keep out of the way when she called Rebecca to set the table. "I should be going."

"Stay for breakfast," Tess offered. "We're going to make it a leisurely one, and then we'll get serious about packing for home. Which reminds me...I found a few of your things when I started doing some organizing this morning. Will you want to bring them next door or should I leave them here?"

Jane froze. That's right. When Tess and company headed home, that would free up this cottage. Her original purpose for moving in with Griffin had been to give his sister and family the space they needed. After today, there wouldn't be any good reason for her to remain in No. 9.

Tess frowned. "Jane, are you—" She broke off as David entered the house.

"Honey," he called. "Gage is on Griffin's cell. Why don't you go over and get your chance to talk with him."

"Oh!" She reached around her waist to untie her apron. "Can you flip the pancakes?"

"Sure." He kissed her cheek as she handed over the spatula.

As if struck by a sudden thought, Tess touched her husband's arm. "Is Gage all right? Everything's okay?"

"Seems so. He's got some new assignment he's stoked about. Wants Griffin to meet up with him so they can work together in faraway Somewhere-istan."

Tess slid a look at Jane. "When?"

"Sounds like he wants him on the first plane out."

Jane put a hand to her suddenly still heart. Was the idyll over just like that? Her snow globe filled with all the memories it would ever have? An emptiness opened in her belly, and cold loneliness swamped her like a Pacific wave. She hadn't seen it coming so soon, but if Griffin headed to his brother, there wasn't any reason for her to stay in Crescent Cove—or at Beach House No. 9.

CHAPTER EIGHTEEN

JANE HAD DISAPPEARED on him. Griffin tried tamping down his annoyance but hell! That mouth of hers was always flapping about deadlines and work to be done and then she was nowhere to be seen when he was ready to get to it. He'd ended his call with Gage twenty minutes ago, and she'd done a complete Houdini.

Of course he didn't need her to be nearby for him to continue with the memoir. But her presence made it easier to confront those photos she'd taped around the office. His gaze would catch on a face, and something odd would pop into his head. He'd remember that person's blood type, for example, because it was posted on them from head to toe: A POS, on helmet, vest, boots. Griffin could have taken the images down, but Jane was right, they helped him taste the flavor of the dirt, smell the stench of the men's sweat after combat, remember the incongruously blissed-out look of a bleeding soldier sucking on a fentanyl lollipop to block the pain.

Good times.

So he didn't want to do any of that without Jane in the room. When it got to be too much, he'd look over at her wacky shoes or her pouty mouth, and find himself centered in the present. He'd think about *her* center, and instead of wallowing in the past he'd be dreaming up ways to get her into bed and the ways he'd take her once he did.

After wandering around No. 9 for a few minutes, he

ventured next door. His sister was the calm in the middle of chaos, as there were piles of kid crap on each bed and pretty much everywhere else. He leaned on a doorjamb, watching her pack up clothes while discussing with Russ the merits of cutting his beloved blankie in half. "Think of it, my sweetness—then if we did the unthinkable and lost it somewhere, we'd have an extra at home."

"Why don't you just buy the baby another one?"

Her head turned to him. "It's a comfort object. You can't just buy another one, because they're not interchangeable. It wouldn't smell the same, feel the same, *be* the same."

"Creepy. You're making it sound like Russ has a relationship with a square of fabric."

"And it's probably more meaningful than the ones you have with the people in your life," she retorted. "Russ doesn't hesitate to become attached."

He blinked. "Hostile."

"I'm not hostile, I'm being honest. And honestly, Griffin, you need to be careful or people are going to get hurt."

He retreated from the doorway.

Tess pointed at him. "That's exactly what I'm talking about. You back off when things get a little too real."

"I don't know what you mean."

"Let me be clear." She huffed out a sigh. "It's going to hurt Jane when she sees how easily you can walk away from her."

The back of his neck felt hot. "We're colleagues. Professional colleagues."

His sister skewered him with a look that she'd learned from their mother. A look only the female half of the population could deliver. "Cut the crap, brother dear."

"Fine," he said, defensive. "But it's just sex."

"And I suppose you'll tell me Jane sees it exactly like that," Tess replied, a wealth of doubt in her tone.

"Of course she does." He'd told her from the beginning that he didn't have anything more to offer than temporary fun and games. Besides, it was pretty clear from their recent encounter with Ian Stone that Jane was still hung up on her ex, though Griffin didn't know why the thought bothered him so much.

Tess shook her head. "Then I suppose it's best. Go chase after the carrot that Gage dangled in front of you. If you're going to get out of Jane's life, then you should do it now—the sooner the better."

He refused to let her older-sibling act unleash his hold on his temper. It was a beautiful day, he'd heard his brother's voice so he knew Gage was safe, and Bossy Big Sister and her minions would be out of his hair by the afternoon. He should be able to get a lot of work done today if he could just locate the missing governess.

He stomped out of No. 8 and surveyed the beach, scanning the sand for her. When she'd left their place that morning she'd had a lacy white cover-up over that yellow swimsuit. A slender piece of lemon meringue should be easy to spot.

The only figures in the vicinity were Private and the munchkin mafia. Duncan and Oliver were on their knees, their expressions intent as they...

A little chill ran down Griffin's spine. What were they doing? They both held short shovels that weren't the customary plasticware that kids used at play. These had wooden handles and metal blades and looked exactly like what a hit man would have in his trunk in order to bury the evidence.

Griffin drew closer, then stopped, gaping. "What the hell?"

Jane's head, the only part of her that hadn't been laid to rest—so to speak—turned toward him. "Don't use that word in front of the boys."

"Yeah," Duncan said. "'Cuz me or Oliver will say it by mistake at school and then get sent to the principal's office."

Griffin figured that wouldn't be a new experience for them. "Sorry, boys. What the *heck* are you doing?"

Oliver cackled as he upended a plastic bucket of sand over the mound that covered Jane's body. "We's burying her alive from her crumpy bitty toes to her scrawny chicken neck."

The kid was wigging him out. Seriously. "Uh, Jane?"

"I think it's from a book," she said. "At least I hope it's from a book."

Oliver nodded. "A book about a pirate."

"And buried treasure," Duncan added.

"And dead bodies," Oliver said in a sinister voice. Then he turned to his brother. "You know what we need, Dunc?"

The older boy appeared puzzled, then his eyes sparked and his face split into a gap-toothed smile. "I know exactly what we need," he said, raising both fists to tap them against Oliver's. They followed that up by taking a running leap at each other to bump scrawny chests, yelled "Crabs!" in unison, then swooped up their buckets to race toward the surf. Barking in happy abandon, Private followed in their wake.

Shaking his head, Griffin crossed his arms over his chest and returned his gaze to the librarian's head. She bit her lip, her eyes darting from Griffin to the boys and back again. "Crabs? Maybe you should help me out from under here."

"Having a problem with your crumpy bitty toes?"

"No. I'm just not sure I like the idea of being pinned under here when the minions come back with crabs." She bit her lip again. "I actually loathe the idea of being pinned under here when the minions come back with crabs."

Griffin sat cross-legged beside the Jane-sized mound of sand and grinned at her. "There's something about you being restrained like this that I kinda like. Later, we'll get in the bathtub, and I'll help you get the sand out of all those pesky places it's sure to be hiding, like from between your crumpy toes and from between your—"

"I get it, I get it," she said hastily. Then her gaze shifted away, and her voice turned casual. "I heard you got a call from Gage this morning."

"Yeah." Probably his Big Mouth Big Sister had let it be known, just as she'd told his twin about Griffin's involvement with Jane. "It was good to hear his voice."

Though his brother had gone bossy on him too. Gage thought he should cut the strings with Jane, and pronto. *It doesn't sound like you, bro, shacking up with some chick.*

Jane was not some chick, damn it!

You breaking more hearts, bro?

He and Jane had an understanding, not that his siblings could comprehend that. Everybody just assumed he was on his way to harming the smartest, sexiest—

"Gage's offer sounds perfect for you. You should take him up on it."

—most annoying and most troublesome woman in the world. "What the hell do you know about it?" he demanded.

Inside her sand tomb he could discern her shrug. "I picked up bits and pieces. David said it's an in-depth piece on a new rebel training camp in Somewhere-istan."

"Somewhere-istan," Griffin muttered. "Everybody's a comedian."

"It sounds right up your alley. And it's a chance to work with your brother."

"I've already got work," he said. What was wrong with her? Didn't she remember that this project was necessary to recoup her reputation? "Not to mention a dog."

"Tess and family would take Private. I will, if it comes to that."

"Tess's minions keep her busy enough. And I can't leave him with a talking head."

She just looked at him. "Griffin—"

"And Rebecca's presentation. You think I can skip out on that? The old man will live another twenty-five years just so he can tweak me about it."

"Be serious," she said. "For this, you can probably get an extension on your deadline. Maybe you can work the new assignment into the memoir. Or just finish it while you're on the road. You know you can do it."

Without her. That's what she was saying. *Go ahead, go on and go about your life.*

He stared at Jane. She'd forgotten sunscreen again, and her nose was going to peel if she kept this up. Tess and Gage had been worried he was on his way to quashing her romantic dreams while the clear-eyed, pouty-mouthed book doctor was intent on sweeping him away without the smallest sign of hesitation or regret. Why did everyone, including Jane, assume he'd snatch up the first opportunity to ditch her? What kind of man did they think he was?

Besides the kind he'd professed to be from the very beginning, a mocking voice in his head answered. *I don't do serious with women, never have.*

The thought turned up his temper, which had been simmering since the munchkin mafia interrupted his morning nooky, to a boil.

He jumped to his feet. "Why does everyone think they know what's best for me? Nobody goddamn knows me at all, and that includes my sister, my twin and you. *Especially you.*"

JANE FELT THE WEIGHT of the sand on her chest long after Duncan and Oliver returned—crabless, thank God—and dug her out. She walked down the beach to the outdoor shower near the entrance to Captain Crow's and rinsed off. Then, even though she didn't have any money on her, she was able to smile a glass of iced tea out of the guy behind the beachside bar.

Nobody goddamn knows me at all.

She supposed Griffin was right, despite her earlier claims that they had an understanding. After that call from Gage, she'd expected to find him packing a bag and double-checking the expiration date on his passport. She'd promised herself she'd be happy for him. Shouldn't she be happy for him?

But now, well... Private was going to be thrilled that the man was sticking around.

Later she wandered back down the beach. Tess's Mercedes station wagon was stuffed to the gills, and it looked iffy that there'd be room for all the kids in David's SUV. While Griffin was working with his brother-in-law to find places for the stroller, two skimboards and a mountain of beach towels, Jane slipped into No. 9 and quickly collected most of her clothes and personal items. Whatever she left behind could be retrieved later, since he'd decreed they'd still be working together on the memoir.

Not fifteen minutes later, she was smiling and waving as the Quincy clan exited the cove. "I'm going to the office," Griffin said.

"I'll be there in a little bit," she remarked to his retreating back. When the door to No. 9 shut behind him, she located her stashed suitcases and reached into her pocket for the key to the cottage next door that Tess had handed over. When she turned the knob, she pushed one bag across the threshold with her foot. The other she deposited on the narrow bench that stood in the small entry.

A gust of air blew through the open door, and she left it standing, allowing the salt-tinged breeze to mix with the mingled scents of crayon, baby powder and nail polish. It was so quiet without the minions.

Which was why she heard the footsteps behind her. Startled, she whirled around, only to see a stone-faced Griffin stalk through the entrance. He brushed past her to grip one suitcase and then the other bag. Without a word, he turned back toward No. 9.

"What are you doing?" she said, hurrying to keep up with him.

"Do you think I'm blind? I passed by the laundry room, and the first thing I noticed is that your filmy bits of sexual torture are missing."

Her lingerie. She'd hand washed a batch the day before and hung it on the drying rack. Of course she'd collected the garments as part of her packing process.

"This is kind of high-handed, you know," she said, as he walked through the door of No. 9 without even looking to see if she still followed.

"Pot, meet kettle," he muttered.

She trailed after him on his way down the hall. "Maybe I want some alone time."

"So take an hour next door when you need it. The rest of your days and nights you're with me." Then he dropped her belongings on the floor of the master bedroom and took her in his arms, making sure she knew exactly what he meant by "with me." And Jane, seduced by that long, strong body enclosing hers, pressed her cheek into the delicious, heated skin of his throat and abandoned any more thoughts of escape.

DESPITE HER DECISION to remain at No. 9, Jane realized over the next few days that things didn't go back to the way they'd been. He wasn't the same Griffin as before. Though he was at turns teasing and seductive and brooding, there were times when he went even quieter now, as if every part of him stilled. Like a body submerging in deep waters, he would sink inside himself to a place that was unreachable.

Nobody goddamn knows me.

She kept coming back to that, and as more time went on, she acknowledged it was true. Though she read the pages of his memoir and thought she understood something of his experience while embedded in Afghanistan, there seemed to be a link missing in the connection between herself and Griffin. Between him and the world he lived in now. He wasn't tethered to it in any meaningful way, and he didn't seem in any hurry to make the essential attachment.

She also began to suspect he was using sex as he'd previously used the television and his iPod and his solitaire games. It was a way to occupy his body without his brain actually being engaged.

After a short while with this newly distant man, she longed for the distraction of Tess and the minions.

She saw them not long after they'd left the cove, however, on the day that Griffin and Rex Monroe gave their talk to Rebecca's history seminar as part of her final project. To accommodate working parents, the presentations were scheduled in the late afternoon. The entire Quincy family was there, though Duncan and Oliver were allowed to play on the grass just outside the classroom door. David held baby Russ in one arm as he and Tess sat together, fingers enmeshed. Skye attended as well, and she was in the car with Jane, Rex and Griffin as they headed back to Crescent Cove once the war reporters' talk was over.

Unsurprisingly, the men traded insults the entire return trip.

"Your ugly mug frightened the kids," Rex said from his place riding shotgun.

Griffin's hands tightened on the steering wheel as he glanced over at his nemesis. "Give it up, you old crank. They looked scared because they never thought they'd meet a man who handed out prunes on Halloween."

"You shouldn't have told them that."

"They were yawning," Griffin said. "Your stuff was putting them to sleep."

The conversation continued in that vein despite how affecting their discussion had been. Rex's experiences as a combat journalist in World War Two echoed Griffin's sixty-odd years later. They'd both described surviving brutal temperatures, the tense boredom of waiting for action and the bonds of brotherhood between the soldiers. War was war, their accounts made clear to the teenagers, no matter what the weapons, the era, the prize to be won.

A young man had raised his hand, wanting to know if war wasn't also exciting. They'd glanced at each other, and then Rex had admitted that it was. "It's not do or die," he'd said. "Combat is die or live."

"Nothing will get your heart pumping more than that," Griffin had added. "The adrenaline sharpens your senses in a way that can save you when you're taking fire." His voice had hushed, and he'd looked at Rex. "Civilian life can seem lackluster after war. Almost colorless."

The words had jolted Jane then, and they gave her another unpleasant shake remembering them now. Jerked back to the present, she listened to the two reporters continuing their exchange of insults.

Skye spoke up for the first time, interrupting them. "I'd like to point out that forty summer-schooled teenagers gave you a standing ovation."

"That was for me," the two men said together.

Jane couldn't help but laugh.

Back at Beach House No. 9, she watched Griffin aid Rex up the path to his cottage. He said it was to make sure that the "crusty coot" didn't try stealing his half of the photos they'd mounted on a display board that Griffin carried tucked beneath his arm.

Though she couldn't hear his voice, his tone carried. More verbal abuse. And yet his steps were slow and his hand steady on the older man's elbow.

Nobody goddamn knows me.

But she knew enough, Jane suddenly thought, her blood starting to pulse in anxious chugs through her veins. Oh, God help her, she knew enough.

How many times had she seen the contradiction of Griffin's attitude and his actions? Complaining about the minions and yet brushing a kiss on a nephew's hair. His arms swooping to toss her into the ocean, then holding her close to calm her fears. Those "rules" he'd established about their sex life that were all for her ungovernable pleasure. Despite all his tough talk he'd always been so… caring.

Beside her, Skye sighed. "Look at that," she said, gesturing toward the pair of reporters. "Sweet, huh?"

Sweet? Disastrous. Jane's face went hot, and she

couldn't feel her feet. There was a high whine of panic in her ears, and her fingers, when she knotted them together, were tense and cold.

She'd done it, she thought, feeling sick. She'd done the very thing she'd vowed to avoid. Silly and emotional Jane had fallen in love with a man she understood well enough to know he would never love her back.

CHAPTER NINETEEN

GRIFFIN ROLLED HIS shoulders as he left Rex's place, the
heat of the sun baking the last of the tension from his
muscles. The speaking gig he'd been dreading was over.
He'd managed to talk of his experience without choking
on the words or running from the room.

It had gotten easier after the first couple of minutes.
There'd been a water bottle at hand to alleviate the dry-
ness of his mouth, and the kids had been fascinated with
his description of the primitive conditions at the outpost.
They hadn't skipped the hard questions. He'd been obliged
to acknowledge witnessing death and grave injury—but
he'd avoided going into much detail.

Still, a gloomy darkness had welled at the mention of
it, and he'd been forced to focus on Rex's gnarled knuckles and take a few slow breaths. Maybe the other reporter
had sensed his disquiet. When the classroom had begun
to fade in his vision, the curmudgeon had jumped in,
his loud voice bringing Griffin back to whiteboards and
textbooks.

So now he was here at the cove, safe and sound, and
he found he could even smile at his Lab trotting ahead,
as eager as he to get back to Beach House No. 9. Private
likely hoped he could sweet-look Jane into giving him a
treat. She was easy that way. A total pushover for the dog.

Maybe Griffin could sweet-talk her into bed.

His sense of well-being grew, pushing out the edginess that had been growing the past few days as he came to the end of the manuscript pages he'd written. He remembered now working on the book in Afghanistan— and he didn't like recalling the day he'd set it aside. That particular memory loomed in the corner of his mind all the time, and more than once it had reached out with its claws to yank him low. Now, though, it seemed that the beast had retreated. At least for the moment.

Jane and Skye were sitting in chairs overlooking the beach. As his footsteps clapped against the wooden deck, Skye glanced over, then stood. The dress she'd worn for the day's event was as shapeless as the rest of her wardrobe. She'd pulled on an extra-large hoodie as insurance—against the ocean breeze, Griffin supposed. "Mail," she said, as he came closer.

She handed him one of Gage's postcards. The image was full color and arresting, as so much of his twin's work was. It was a close-up shot of a young boy's face. His hair was close-cropped and topped with an earth-toned woven cap. His ears stuck out, and he held a bright pink flower to his nose with a grubby hand. But it was the eyes that caught Griffin's attention. Ringed with spiky lashes, they were the same silvery gray as Jane's.

He cut his gaze to her, but he only had a view of the back of her head as she stared out to sea. Flipping the postcard, he glanced down at the message. *Still breathing.*

That was good. Even though he'd talked to Gage just days before and the postcard had likely been mailed a week before that, seeing his brother's handwriting and touching the card stock that had been handled by him made his twin's security seem more assured. *Still breathing.*

Weird, though, that he wasn't certain the same could be said about the librarian. He glanced over at her again, puzzled, and then shifted his focus to Skye, sending her a silent question. *What's with Jane?* But the other woman only shrugged and said she had to be on her way.

Jane gave her a wave but otherwise didn't move.

Griffin didn't like her uncharacteristic preoccupation. "What's up, Jane?"

"Nothing."

He frowned. "Are you mad at me?"

She seemed to consider this, her head tilting, her gaze not leaving the surf. "Yes."

Sighing, he threw himself into the chair that Skye had vacated. "All right, let me have it."

"I don't think I will," Jane said after a moment. "I think instead I'll get up and start chopping. Remember we have Rex coming for dinner tonight to celebrate your mutual success. I'm making shish kebab."

He craned his neck to watch her cross the deck. She wore a dress that was nothing more than a figure-skimming, knee-length T-shirt. But it was made of blocks of color—yellow on top, pumpkin in the middle, black on the bottom—and she wore it with matching pumpkin shoes that had a dozen or two straps wrapping her small feet.

As she walked away, the breeze plastered the knit fabric to her, and it molded her body so sweetly that he could see the cleft of her pert ass. It got him thinking of her underwear again—always a cheerful notion.

The legs of his chair scraped as he pushed out of it. She didn't glance back, but he saw her shoulders stiffen as he stalked her into the house. Still, she ignored him, even when she whirled from the refrigerator, her hands full of vegetable bags, to find him standing right in front of her.

When she made to step around him, he stepped too, blocking her path. Then he took the bags out of her grasp and placed them on the counter. His hands he placed on her waist.

"You're bringing me down, Jane," he said. "I was feeling pretty good until you started staring out at the surf doing the whole pensive thing. Face it, moody is what *I* do. So tell me what's wrong, so we can get past it."

She hesitated.

"Is this going to require force?" he asked, mock-serious. "Because I'm prepared to take your panties hostage." His hands slid to her hips. "And I mean the ones you're wearing, by the way. I have to know…bows on the side or bow in the front? Is it the pair with those cute zippers at your hip bones?"

Her eyes narrowed to silver slits. "Is it all about the sex with you?"

"Yes," he said promptly. "Right now it's all about the sex."

She looked away, sighed. "At least he's honest," she murmured. Then her gaze returned to his, and her spine straightened. "You're right, moody is your domain. So I'm officially over it."

Suspicious, he tightened his fingers on her curves. "'It' what?"

Pursing her pouty mouth, she shook her head and slipped out of his grasp. As she made for the countertop and the waiting vegetables, she gave him a hot little glance over her shoulder that caused his cock to twitch.

"I'm wearing a pair you've never seen before," she said. "Fishnet triangle in the front and the back…"

Fishnet triangle? Blood screamed southward as he imagined it, and his mouth went dry. "And the back?"

"Crisscrossed strings, kind of like a cage," she said. "I believe they're crotchless."

Crotchless. He fell back a step. "No. Now you're just playing with me, Jane."

From the butcher's block she pulled a shiny, sharp knife. "Maybe I am, maybe I'm not."

"Let's find out." He took a step toward her.

She spun, putting the counter at her back and the knife between them. "Nuh-uh-uh. No time for that. We have a guest coming for dinner."

"Just another reason why I can't stand that cantankerous grouchy grump."

"You resemble that remark, Griffin."

"So I do," he agreed, backing away. "But I'm coming after you tonight, baby, and you'll be giving up all your panty secrets and every other one besides."

Her wide eyes and sudden frown signaled that threat seemed to worry her a little, so he turned around and left the kitchen, enjoying the upper hand. He even heard himself whistling as he headed for the beach. A twenty-minute walk would cool him off and give Jane time to stew over what he'd promised.

Ha. The day was only getting better.

At the appointed hour, he was whistling again when he and Private jumped over the fence on their way to collect Rex. Sure the old guy could make it to No. 9 on his own, but there was no reason Griffin couldn't lend a hand. They'd return via the longer route that didn't involve fence-climbing, and he could rib the old guy some more about their presentation.

Rex had done a good job, not that Griffin would let him know he thought so. And the more he considered his own part in it, the more he realized it had been a bit of a…relief to talk about that year. Like releasing steam from the boiling kettle that was his work on the memoir.

Maybe that was why he was whistling.

He glanced over his shoulder, looking back at his house. Jane was in there, bustling around in her efficient way while wearing her naughty underwear. Later tonight he'd tease her out of them and tease her into confessing what had been bothering her out on the deck. Whatever it was, he'd make it disappear, like magic. He was feeling so great he was starting to believe in such a thing. Maybe Beach House No. 9 *was* the magic.

At Rex's front door, he rapped briskly. When there was no response, he tried again, aware the old man wore hearing aids. Maybe he'd removed them and so didn't know Griffin had arrived.

That thought had him trying the doorknob. It turned. "Monroe?" he called, not wanting to startle him. "Rex?"

Griffin glanced in the den, the living room, then headed toward the kitchen. His eyes fixed on an unexpected sight and his feet stuttered to a halt, but it took his brain a second or two longer to process. A body lay crumpled on the floor. There was a puddle of red blood, a pool of the bright stuff, and it made a dark stain on Rex's khaki-colored shirt…which in Griffin's mind became a younger man's camouflage BDUs.

The world turns dark, because there's dirt covering the windshield of the Humvee carrying him and four other guys. There's a ringing in his ears, left over from the percussive blast of the IED. Their vehicle has flipped, but he doesn't remember the tumble, only the aftermath, when he's lying in the wreckage, pinned by he doesn't know what yet, and wondering why his heart rate has barely registered that they've been bombed.

Erica had died three days before, and lying there, he supposes it might be his turn. If he isn't dead already, he's going to have to get out of the vehicle and run through a hail of bullets in order to survive. In this moment, he's not sure it's worth the effort. Getting shot's probably going to hurt.

Something wet touches his hand. He starts. More blood? But it's Private. His dog is in... No, he's not in Afghanistan, he's in the States.

Lurching back to the present, Griffin pulled his cell phone from his pocket with sweaty, shaking hands. His fingers fumbled as he called for the paramedics to come to Crescent Cove.

Where all the magic was gone.

Upon their return from the hospital, Jane wanted to escape Griffin and the tension that was radiating off him in a constant buzz of dark energy. But worried about leaving him alone right away, she found herself agreeing to a glass of wine, sipping at it as he downed his second beer, then his third. He sank low in the kitchen chair, and so did her spirits. They'd already taken a panicky dip when Griffin burst into No. 9 and explained that Rex was injured. The two of them had followed the ambulance to the hospital and stayed there until the elderly reporter was stabilized. There were tests still to be run, but the doctor didn't believe he'd experienced a heart attack or stroke. He'd fallen as he had a few weeks before, but this time he'd hit his head on the kitchen counter and shed a lot of blood.

"We'll have to encourage him to get one of those devices," Jane said. "The kind you press if you've fallen and you can't get up."

Griffin flicked her a glance, the blue of his eyes washing over her like the brief pass of a strobe lamp. "He wasn't conscious. He couldn't press anything."

"Right," Jane said, grimacing.

With a sudden shove, Griffin jerked away from the

table and stalked toward the office. Private followed. Jane looked at the door, looked down the hallway. She cast a glance to the countertop, where a dish held the key to No. 8. Then with a sigh, she trailed in the wake of the man and the dog.

When she breached the doorway, she found Griffin studying the photos. Then he spun toward her, his face set. His voice tight. "I lied. Remember Whitman?"

The soldier who had stolen Griffin's Twinkies and gotten his porn purloined in return. "Yes."

Griffin's eyes blazed with too much heat, and his hand was rubbing a spot on his denim-covered thigh, over and over. "There are other memories, beyond death and blood and stink and boredom, but there's no good memories. I shouldn't ever say any of them are good."

"You didn't say 'good' the first time," Jane said, her voice set on soothe. "You said that very thing, 'other memories.'"

He paced around the small room. She didn't think he was actually seeing his surroundings, or Private, or her. Which meant she could go, right? Ever since realizing she'd fallen for him this afternoon, she'd known distance was the only way to ensure he'd never guess the truth.

Dangling from his fingers was the half-full beer. Tipping back his head, he drained the brew, then reached for another that she hadn't noticed he'd carried in. It sat on the desk beside the original pages of the manuscript. The sheets were marked with blue pencil by him. Her comments were on yellow sticky notes.

The latest beer was half consumed in less than a minute. Considering they'd missed dinner for a run to the hospital, she gave a look to the bottle in his hand. "Don't you think you should slow down?"

He stilled and his eyes slid to her. They hadn't cooled

any, but the expression in them made her shiver. "Are you my mother? Oh, no, that's right, you think of yourself as my governess."

"I'm your friend," she told him.

"Well, then as *your* friend, let me tell *you* something." He set the half-full beer back on the desk in the very precise way of the getting-drunk and leaned against it. "You can't slow down, Jane. You gotta fill all the moments with everything you can—with booze, with sex, with whatever gives you pleasure—because this moment might be the Very. Last. One."

Then he straightened, and she could read the intent in his eyes. "No," she said, putting out a hand and stepping back at the same time. "I don't want to go to bed with you right now." Everything was too raw. The state of her heart, his state of mind.

He stared at her a moment, then shrugged and went back to leaning on the edge of the desk. His hand reached for his beer, but it found the manuscript instead. The pages spilled to the floor. "Ah, look at that," he said.

Jane came forward.

"I've got it," he said. He bent for the papers, taking them up in his hands. "I know exactly what to do." And then, to her shock, he began tearing great hunks of the pages, ripping them in half, in quarters, rending them into unrecognizable shapes only to let them flutter from his hands to fall to the floor like snow. Like tears.

"Griffin, no," she said, but she was too stupefied to stop him. And maybe a little afraid.

So he tore more. He tore again and again and again until all their hard work was a mound of ragged confetti scattered by his feet.

Private whined, and the sound woke her from her stupor. She looked up from the wreck of pages to Griffin, remembering that she'd told him that rending a manuscript out of temper would be against the rules.

With a nonchalant little gesture, he retrieved his beer and toasted it in her direction.

It was the implied fuck-you in the motion that lit her own fuse. She wasn't his enemy, but that was clearly the role he wanted her to play this time. Librarian, governess, foe. Just another way to diminish her. To dismiss her. To not see *her*.

And to think that for half a day she'd considered—

"Well, Jane?" He stirred the pile of scraps with his toe. "What do you have to say?"

"I have to say thank you," she replied in a cold, clear voice, enjoying the surprise that wiped away his expression of smug anger. "Thank you very much. For a few hours I was worried…but now I realize it was just some dumb and sappy overreaction of mine. Because there's no way in the world I could…could…care for such a stupid, stupid man as you." Then, with a crisp spin on her heel, she headed for that key in the kitchen and the beach house next door.

Her escape didn't last as long as she expected. An hour later, after she'd showered and put on pajama pants and a tank top that either Rebecca or Tess had left behind, she heard a knock on the door of No. 8. Her mind leaped. *Griffin.* But the sound was too polite. Tentative. Not angry and demanding. Not arrogant and sexy.

There was no peephole, so she had to peer through the inches revealed by the chain lock. The Beach Boy, the one with the curly blond hair and surfer's body, stood there, an anxious expression on his face. "Ted?" she said, remembering that was his name. "Can I help you?"

"Uh." He made a vague gesture over his shoulder.

"He's going for another record. At least that's what he says. I don't think he should be going anywhere."

She shook her head. "Huh?"

"Captain Crow's. We were at the bar. Then he got it in his head to jump off the cliff."

Now she understood, and the realization had her rushing out the door. Griffin had been drinking before, and if he'd had more after she left, then he was too drunk to attempt a leap off the cliff in the dark. "Where is he?"

Ted took her hand and led her down to the sand and along the moonlit beach. "This way."

Sure enough, Griffin stood at the base of the cliff, staring up and swaying a little. Jane groaned to herself, then hurried forward to tuck her hand in the crook of his elbow. He looked at her, blinked, then gave her a broad, drunk grin. "Jane!" he said, as if he was glad to see her. As if he'd forgotten completely what he'd done in the office.

Really, she so could not love an idiot like this.

"C'mon," she said, tugging on him. "We have to go."

"What?" His eyebrows drew together. "Why? I…" He made a broad gesture with his free arm that almost spun them both around.

She tightened her hold. "We have that thing, remember?"

"Thing?"

"Yes." A push, a prod, and she had him turned in the direction of No. 9. "The thing about the thing." Someday she'd laugh about this. Or perhaps even ten minutes from now, when she was safely alone again.

His head turned this way and that, until he spotted Ted. He squinted at the other man. "The thing about the thing, Ted?"

"You got it, buddy. Gotta do that thing."

"'S'okay."

His feet moved in tandem with Jane's, though he was not very steady on them. She tried to control his lurching movements by sliding her arm around his waist and holding him tight against her. He grinned down at her, his smile fond. *"Jane,"* he said.

Clearly, the man was too much trouble to love. She couldn't wait to pour him into his bed and return to her own cottage. "Keep moving, chili-dog," she muttered. Ted was a few feet behind them, and she thought of handing Griffin over to him, but she'd been taught since birth to see a job through to the end. The only time she'd done different was with Ian, and that debacle had led to this one.

Her stick-to-it-iveness almost ended up killing her. Because when they were still a dozen feet from No. 9's deck, Griffin tripped on the smooth, soft sand. The both of them started to go down, and she figured she'd be smushed under his one-hundred-eighty pounds of lean muscle and drunken idiocy, but at the last second he twisted and it was his back that hit first. She landed flat on top of him.

There was a moment of stunned quiet.

Then Griffin's hands ran unsteadily over her body. "Jane," he said, his voice suddenly urgent. Anxious. "Jesus, Jane." He sounded panicked, and his hands kept rushing along her skin, feeling her from head to toe. Then his arms dropped to the sand, limp. "Jesus. For a second…"

Her breath had been knocked out of her. It took another moment to inhale a decent lungful of air, then she coughed it back out. "For a second what?" she asked huskily, rolling off of him.

He was staring upward at the million pinpricks of stars tossed like glitter across dark sky. "When our Humvee was bombed," he said, his voice slurred, "it was Jackal who landed on me. Jackson was his last name, but we called him Jackal. Little guy, not much bigger than Duncan. I said to him, to Jackal, 'You all right, kid? Are you all right?' 'Yeah,' he said. He said he was good, just that effing ringing in his ears. So he shifted off of me…and that's when I realized I was all wet, wet with his blood, and when he'd moved he'd left one of his legs behind."

Oh, God.

Oh, God.

She had no idea how to respond to that. Call her a coward, but the story only made her more eager to get back to her own cottage. Ted didn't seem any braver than she. Though he helped Jane draw Griffin to his feet, he left them both at the door of No. 9, mumbling something about a girl back at the bar.

Griffin allowed her to steer him to his bedroom. It was dark except for the glow from a small lamp on the dresser. She had plans to shove him into bed and then beat a hasty retreat. He, naturally, resisted. "Gonna take a shower," he said, brushing off her hands and heading for the bathroom. The door shut with a definitive click.

Jane paced back and forth as she listened for the rush of water. He didn't appear sober enough to leave safely alone. She had visions of him falling on the slick tile and hitting his head or breaking a limb. *I realized I was all wet, wet with his blood, and when he'd moved he'd left one of his legs behind.*

A shiver rolled down her back, quickly followed by another and another. She was trembling with cold or with reaction to what he'd shared. When Griffin got out of the shower, she'd see him under the blankets and then go bury herself beneath her own set next door. Probably pull them right over her head.

Five minutes later, he emerged, naked except for a pair of ratty jeans that hung low on his hips. She kept her gaze trained on his face. He looked exhausted and not quite so drunk, if you didn't count the bloodshot eyes and the disheveled hair. It was wet, and she could smell the shampoo from across the room, but it was long enough to need a comb now, and he hadn't bothered.

Did he realize she was here? He leaned against the wall, then pressed the heels of his hands to his eyes. "Rex?" he asked, his voice low and rough. "Any news?"

"No change." She'd called the nurses' station about a half hour ago.

"Good. That's good."

"Yes." She could leave now.

"About before…" His gesture could encompass a host of things.

"It doesn't matter. We'll figure it out tomorrow."

"No." He pushed away from the wall. With erratic strides he left the room and headed down the hallway.

"What are you doing?"

He didn't answer. When the light blazed in the office, he took a half step back, his hand shielding his eyes, but then he moved in, determined steps taking him to the desk. The pile of shredded manuscript was inches from his bare feet, but he didn't disturb it as he started going through the drawers.

"What are you doing?" she repeated.

"I'm going to fix it. Right now." One hand pointed to the mess on the floor, while the other continued rifling through pencils and pens. "I'm going to fix this for you, Jane."

Oh. *Oh, God.*

"As soon as I find the tape, I'll put it back together."

Jane closed her eyes. His movements were suddenly frantic and so was her pulse rate. The pirate wanted to make amends…and yet there was no way to repair all that was wrong. As she watched him become increasingly frenzied, she knew her brief bout of self-delusion was over. No retreat was going to change the truth. No lie to herself would paper over the deep hole into which she'd fallen.

Fallen in love with Griffin.

I'm going to fix this for you, Jane.

Her heart hurt so bad, she couldn't breathe again. Despite her good sense and her past experiences, there was no denying that she'd gone ahead and written her very own Ian Stone love story. No one was going to get a disease or succumb to drowning, but just like in those bestsellers there wasn't going to be a lasting happy ending.

"Shit!"

At Griffin's sharp exclamation, she opened her eyes. All the drawers were half-open and he was down on his knees, bending low to peer beneath the desk. *"Shit!"* he said again.

"Griff—"

"I give up." He pivoted to look at her, his gaze hot, his expression filled with misery and frustration. "Why the fuck should I care about a missing tape dispenser? How *can* I care about a missing tape dispenser? How does that fucking compare to a fucking missing leg or a fucking finished life?"

His despair drew her close. Without thinking twice, Jane brushed his damp hair back with her hand. "I don't know," she said, her voice as soft as she could make it. "I don't fucking know."

"Nothing's ever going to be the same," he said, his eyes as blue as the center of a flame. *"I'll* never be the same." Then he made an inarticulate sound and clamped his arms around her hips, snatching her close to bury his face against her stomach.

His skin was burning, and even his half-wet hair held heat. She caressed his head again, and he made another deep-throated noise. His mouth moved, finding space between her low-slung pajama pants and her tank top. He kissed her on her bare skin just to the right of her belly button, and she jerked into it as he nipped her there, then sucked the flesh, his tongue sliding over the little sting.

"I've got to have you," he said, his mouth moving on her. "Let me have you." And before she could speak, he'd pulled her down to the scratchy sisal carpet and was on top of her, his heavy weight pushing open her thighs.

"Please, Jane. Please."

Oh, God, she thought, her hands in his hair, her body already softening. If only this would fix things for him.

"Jane?" he said, sounding desperate.

"Yes," she whispered, eyes stinging. "Yes."

His mouth latched onto the curve where her neck and shoulder met. He bit her there too, then kissed the place and inhaled deeply, as if he was trying to breathe her in. Jane ran her palms on his naked back, feeling the play of tense muscles as he moved over her collarbone, neck, jawline, delivering more of those greedy, consuming kisses.

She arched up, offering herself to him and his hungry mouth. One of his hands gripped the hem of her skinny-strapped tank, and he yanked it over her head, only to immediately take in her nipple. There was no sweet lick of welcome or gentle teasing pull. No, he sucked greedily on the tightening nub, one big hand plumping the soft tissue of her breast to feed himself more of her. Chills swept over her skin, and she moaned, the sound deepening as he bit down. When he shifted to do the same on the other side, her fingernails scored his back, the coiling twist of arousal inside her needing an outlet of its own.

His free hand slid into her pants, the movement hitching a little when he realized she was naked beneath them. But then his palm slid lower, cupping her so his long fingers could play in the wet, pleated layers. The heel of his hand ground against her clitoris as he took her nipple deeper, rhythmic pulls that mimicked the throbbing ache growing inside her.

"Griffin," Jane said and drew one hand around the curve of his ribs to his lightly furred chest. She rolled the edge of her thumb over his nipple, teasing it to a small point that she could pinch between her thumb and forefinger.

He grunted, his big body twitching against her, and she did it again. Griffin released her breast, rearing up to hover over her on his hands and knees. His eyes were wild, his breathing rough. Jane's heart was thumping so hard she was sure he could hear it. She thought the whole cove might hear it, the sound taking over for the ceaseless *shush shush shush* of the surf.

Then he was standing, and he yanked her to her feet, already pulling her in the direction of the bedroom. They tumbled onto the mattress and he was tugging and shoving at her flannel pants; she tried to help, scissoring her legs to kick out of them, and when they flew off he grabbed her half-lifted leg and used it to flip her to her belly.

She lay there, just a little worried about the vulnerability of this position. Though she was naked, he was still wearing his jeans, and the soft denim pressed against the insides of her thighs as he nudged them open with his knees. But then he brushed his fingers along her shoulders and down her spine. "The carpet," he mumbled, his voice slurry again, almost drugged, "it scratched what's mine."

It was lust she heard in his words. Lust and possession fueled by all the emotions dredged up that day. As his mouth traced over her, she moved, sinuous and slow against the cool sheets, her own arousal fueled by the tickle of his tongue tracing the ladder of her spine.

His hands bracketed her hips, holding her still as his lips reached the small of her back. He pulled her to her knees, her bottom canting high, and he went greedy again, his teeth scraping against the soft curves, his mouth taking sucking kisses. The whiskered stubble along his chin and jaw only added another layer of throbbing sensation to her flesh, and she pressed her hot face into the sleek pillowcase.

"Griffin," she moaned. She was wet and needy and if he'd just give her the slightest touch… Her hand moved, but he caught her fingers and pressed them to the mattress, his palm flattened over her wrist.

She struggled a little, and he brought his mouth to her ear. *"No."* His other hand fumbled at the fastening of his jeans, his knuckles bumping against her where she was swollen and full blossom-ready for him. The drawer to the bedside table squeaked as he jerked it open. Panting, she watched him reach for a condom, and the anticipation made her pulse flutter in her throat. Then he was over her and the thick knob of him was at her entrance, his hand guiding him to her.

He pushed, grunting at the first breach. Jane gasped, her belly hollowing out as he drove slowly forward, the angle, the position, making him feel impossibly large. "No," she moaned, even as she lifted her hips toward the intrusion, impaling herself on his thickness.

Denim abraded her whisker-burned bottom, and she realized he was still half-dressed. She reached back, wanting to touch him somewhere, but he caught that hand too. He placed it like the other; palm to the sheet, his hand flattened over her wrist.

"Griffin…"

"Shh shh shh." His mouth was against her ear, his breath hot, his chest bowed over her back. "Relax now. Stay open for me. Let me in. Let me have it. Give it to me. Give me everything I need."

Every lust-laden word in his dark, sexy voice added more kindling to her own fire. She wiggled back, trying to take more, trying to incite a riot in him, because she was going to become violent if he didn't move.

And then he did. His movements were aggressive, a powerful rhythm of retreat-and-thrust that instantly made her wetter. "Yeah," he whispered, clearly aware she was slicker than before. "Like that. Yeah."

Griffin didn't sound like himself. This wasn't the charming lover, the playmate-in-the-sheets. At this moment, she thought, he might not even know her name. This was the male animal using sex, taking her to take himself away, an elemental act to avoid an entanglement of feelings.

And, God help her, she loved it.

If it brought him some relief from the pain of his memories, she'd be on her knees every night.

He started grunting with each new thrust, and she pushed back to take him to the root. His breath was soughing in her ear, fast and hard, and sweat dripped from his face onto her shoulder. She wiggled her going-numb fingers, and he noticed, adjusting her arms for a little more blood flow, yet still keeping her pinned with his hands.

His movements became rougher, his breath more jerky, and she braced herself, thinking, *Go ahead, my love. Let go*.

On the next retreat, though, he pulled free.

"Wha—" Jane spit out, but then she was flipped to her

back. Griffin was on her in an instant, his tongue penetrating her mouth, his shaft once more pumping inside her. Her hands came up, flailing around his shoulders. He grabbed them once again and entwined their fingers. Lifting his mouth, he stared down at her, his gaze going as deep inside her as his body.

His eyes on her, he continued pumping. Another excruciating round of chills broke over Jane's flesh. This wasn't the pirate crouched over her. They weren't honey-pie and chili-dog. In this bed in this moment there was no librarian or governess. No friends or foes.

Again, she suspected he didn't know who he was with, that she was just the female he needed to his male. Tonight's yin for his yang.

His eyes glittered as he released one of her hands. He slid his palm between them, brought his fingers to her clitoris. "You first," he said.

You first. Tears stung her eyes. She'd been wrong. He knew her. He knew so very much about her that even now, even under this duress, she was on his mind. And it was that, as much as his sure touch, that detonated her explosion. The pleasure twisted tight, then released, whipping outward in circles until her entire body was shaking with the strength of it. She arched back, pushing up to take more of him, and he went still and deep, his arms shaking, as he came with short, jabbing pulses.

Then he fell to the mattress, half on her, still in her. They were both breathing hard, and she stroked a light hand through his hair.

"I'm sorry," he said finally, his head turned away from hers. "I was rough."

"It's fine. It's all right," she said, feeling her face go red.

He turned to look at her. "Are you sure?"

"Everything we did—I loved it. Griffin, I—" She stopped herself just in time.

He was already going tense, however, and she knew he'd heard her unspoken words. *I love you.*

Damn, she thought, as he withdrew and headed for the bathroom. But she was too tired and sexually replete to devise a fallback position. Shifting on the bed, she allowed herself a little wince as she twinged where she had never twinged before. Still waiting for him to return, she drifted off.

It couldn't have been a long while later that she awoke. Alone. She could feel he wasn't in the house, and she padded through the quiet rooms to confirm it. Private was gone as well. As she passed through the kitchen, she caught a glimpse of the next-door cottage through the window. There were lights on in No. 8, lights she hadn't left burning. A blue flicker told her the TV was on as well.

It was Griffin who had made his escape, not Jane.

CHAPTER TWENTY

THE NEXT MORNING, Jane left the cove to run a few errands, which included visiting a quickly recovering Rex at the hospital. If she was also using the time to steer clear of Griffin, that was nobody's business but hers. Upon her return in the late afternoon, she approached the door to Beach House No. 9, steeling her spine to face the man inside. Everything between them was a tangled mess: the ruined book, his brutal memories of war, last night's unbridled sex, her unspoken words.

She adjusted her denim-blue linen pants and squared her shoulders beneath the tissue-thin white tee. She was wearing the same espadrilles she'd had on the day she'd brought him coffee, and now she wished she had something like that to occupy her hands.

Glancing down, she noted the mat under her feet. *Abandon Hope All Ye Who Enter Here.* How many times had the words and Griffin himself warned her away? And yet she'd pushed forward, pushed him, and her reward was falling for a prickly loner who felt things so deeply he had to pretend he felt nothing at all.

Images of him flashed through her mind. In one he raced up the cliff, in another he steadied Rex on the short stroll to his home. She remembered him playing tag with his nephews on the sand and holding Private like a big furry baby on his lap. His voice whispered in her head.

I didn't think you were actually afraid of anything.

Somebody's coming along real soon, and you'll know just how lovable you are.

You first.

Shaking off the memories, she twisted the doorknob and strode over the threshold. Private gave one loud bark and rushed to her in exuberant greeting. "Hey, boy," she said, rubbing his silky head. "Can always count on you being happy to see me."

Griffin came into view from the direction of the bedroom and glanced at her as he moved toward the deck. In jeans and his favorite Hawaiian shirt, he carried a pair of well-worn hiking boots and had the pinched look of someone suffering from a headache. "Jane."

"Griffin." She followed him outside.

"I guess we can safely say we remember each other's names." He flicked a glance at her again as he held the boots upside down and tapped the toes together. "I don't know if you were as drunk as me—"

"I wasn't."

"Well, that's good. Because I'm a bit hazy on the particulars past, oh, the third beer or so."

Liar. She stared at him as he bumped the shoes together again. He was pretending to not remember, so they wouldn't have to honestly address what had occurred the night before. Could he really keep this up? Crossing her arms over her chest, she watched him set the pair of shoes on the picnic table and inspect them like a doctor might a patient, up to and including looking under their tongues.

"Habit," he said, as if she'd asked him what he was doing. "In Afghanistan, the tarantulas would climb into our boots. I wouldn't want to bring any stowaways with me on the trip."

Her gaze snapped to his face. "Are you saying—"

"I feel sure I have some apologies to make, Jane." He

was still focusing on the shoes, making a big show of working on the laces, slipping them free of the grommets then reworking them through the small holes. "I saw the chaos in the office."

"About that—"

"I talked to Ted. He said you came onto the beach and collected me last night."

Did he really not recall it? "You told me about Jackal—Jackson."

Griffin winced. "Sorry to put that in your head."

But it was in *his* head, and letting it fester there was poisonous. "What happened to him after the explosion?"

"He made it. Has a prosthesis, and gets around quite well, considering."

"Have you talked with him, then?"

Griffin was working over the second boot. "A couple of times."

It made Jane think of the soldier who'd traveled from Philly to see him. "What about your friend who visited here—the one who had the car accident?"

"Hernandez. He's okay too, finally getting some counseling at the VA."

They had services like that for soldiers who'd been in war. Places and people who were trained in helping them manage the aftermath of their injuries and of what they'd seen and done. The guilt that they'd survived when their buddies had not.

But who was helping Griffin? Who was there for the observers who were witnesses to fear and horror and heroism?

"You should talk to someone too," she said.

He stiffened.

"You're smart. You've got to realize you're exhibiting some of the classic symptoms of—"

"I'm handling everything just fine. Christ, Jane, I was a reporter—lucky me got to come home while the soldiers are still serving their country. Even when I was with them, I carried a pen, not a gun."

"I think if you end up covered in blood and holding someone's blown-off limb, the distinction is pretty moot." She realized she was sounding slightly tense herself when Private whined and came over to lick her hand.

"That's a funny word, isn't it? Moot."

"In this case it means without or with little practical value—" She broke off, realizing she'd fallen into the trap he'd set. Always trying to distract her. "Griffin," she ground out.

"Jane." He flicked her a glance. "Look at that, we're still good with the names."

Frustrated, she looked toward the horizon, seeing the line where the steely-gray of the ocean met the turquoise-blue of the sky. The wind ruffled her hair, sending a swath of it across her face. Before she could brush it away, Griffin was beside her, his touch light as he caught the strands and tucked them behind her ear. It was a tender gesture, and she read something in it. Apology. Regret. Farewell.

"You changed your mind," she said. "You're going to Gage."

He nodded.

"Is this your competitive streak coming out?" she asked, the words knife-edged. It felt as if he was cracking open her ribs and reaching in to squeeze her heart with his bare hand. He'd survived bullets and bombings before, but would he again? How many times could one man tempt fate? "Is it that you can't stand letting your brother be somewhere dangerous when you're not?"

"I don't know what else to do with myself." He rubbed a thumb over her cheek. "Jane…"

She jerked her face away. "Yeah. I get it. You still know my name."

"About the memoir." Griffin shoved his hands into the pockets of his jeans. "I'll call Frank and make sure he's clear that missing the deadline is all my fault. It does not reflect on you. And, please, feel free to use me as a reference. As a matter of fact, I insist on it."

"Oh, as if you'll be so easy to reach at some remote location in Somewhere-istan." Her hair blew across her eyes again, but she shoved it away before he could touch her a second time. "Why don't you at least finish the half of the book that's due before you go?"

His eyebrows rose. "Last night—"

"As if I would let that be the only copy," she scoffed, shaking her head in disgust. "I typed it into a word processing file shortly after you got it from Frank and have added both our comments to it on a daily basis. There's a copy in the cloud, on my laptop, and on three separate memory sticks." She was a little anal about stuff like that.

He looked bemused. "Efficient Jane."

"So you see, you can finish it."

Now he was shaking his head. "I can't. I really can't."

Meaning he really couldn't face coming to terms with the experience. She saw the truth of that on his face, and she had to look away. "All right. But it doesn't mean you need to take off for another war-torn country."

There was a long silence.

"Gage will let me be me. The way I am now," Griffin finally said, so quiet that she could hardly hear him over the surf. "No questions, no expectations, no…" He shrugged.

No Jane and the love she felt for him.

Seagulls were wheeling and diving, their movements a large-scale imitation of what the butterflies were doing in her stomach. Maybe he didn't like facing what had happened between them, but she couldn't pretend things away like he could. She took a deep breath, determined to be straight with him. "If this is about what I didn't say last night…"

"Jane, I don't want you—"

A man's voice, coming from the direction of the sand, interrupted. "That works out well, then, because I do."

Her head whipped toward the newcomer, Griffin's following suit. Ian Stone, looking urbane and completely at ease, stood on the sand below the deck, wearing pressed khakis and a short-sleeve button-down shirt. "Hello, Jane," he said, with his made-for-TV-interviews smile.

She gaped at him. "How did you know where I was?"

"Your father told me." He smiled again. "I've come with an offer you shouldn't refuse—which, by the way, was his message to you."

And with that, the snarled mess that was her current situation took on yet another twist.

GRIFFIN WAITED AT No. 9 for Jane to return. She'd let The Author Ian Stone—for some reason, he'd started imagining the guy would introduce himself that way—take her down the beach to Captain Crow's for a drink and conversation. He checked his dive watch, then addressed his dog. "How long could it take to say, 'Hell, no'?"

Private didn't reply, and Griffin's patience wore thinner. He had things he wanted to say to the librarian—as well as subjects he wanted to avoid. On the To Say list: *Thank you for being kind to my dog and my elderly neighbor. You did good with Tess and the minions. Not anybody else in the universe could have gotten me to touch a single page of that book.* On the Subjects to Avoid list was just one item: Last Night.

Despite what he'd told Jane, he remembered everything about it. Well, there was a little missing between having drinks with Ted and falling on the sand with Jane. The impact had knocked him near sober, and the shower had made him even more clearheaded. What happened after…

The memory made him hard. He threw himself into the lounge chair and stared at the ocean, willing thoughts of it away. But they were like the surf, drawing back for a moment but then charging back in. And in. And in. Jesus. He threw his arm over his eyes as if that could prevent the image of a naked, delectable Jane as she'd been last night in his bed. High on her knees, her sweet hips in his hands as he took her with everything he had. He was dimly aware of Private settling on the deck beside him with a thump and a canine sigh.

"I was about to confess I'm a dog," he said, reaching out to stroke the Lab's fur, "but that would be an insult to you, my friend."

He'd been hard on Jane. Used her as a way to empty himself. It made him no better, he thought, than that asshole, The Author Ian Stone. But she hadn't complained, had she? *Everything we did—I loved it.*

Because she thought she was in love with him. Jane hadn't said the words out loud. She'd stopped herself, and yet the truth of it was written all over her face for anyone who knew her as well as he did.

Her "I love you" had hovered between them in the sex-scented air. It had horrified him then and made him sick to recall now. His intention had never been to engage her heart—he didn't deserve it, and he was sure she wasn't thrilled about it either—but those big silver eyes of hers couldn't lie.

Yeah, she was in love with him, and that's what he really didn't want to talk about.

Just thinking about it made him restless. He sat up. "I'm going," he told the dog. "If Stone's not taking no for an answer, then I can provide Jane some backup. I'll be happy to see him on his way."

Griffin considered putting on nicer clothes. The Asshole Author Ian Stone had looked as if he was ready for a photo shoot. But then Griffin shrugged. His ragged jeans and soft shirt printed with pineapples and naked wahines might have seen better days, but, hell, so had he. It took a moment to slip into his second-best flip-flops and then he was ambling down the sand toward the restaurant.

"She'll be grateful," Griffin said aloud, addressing a seagull picking at a mound of drying kelp. "It'll be my small attempt at paying her back." For the way she made him laugh, for that annoyed little squint of her eyes when he was teasing her, for those ridiculously frilly shoes and fascinatingly plump mouth.

For the great sex.

Yeah, he owed her a lot for that.

It was conch-shell time at Captain Crow's. From his Party Central days, he recognized most of those crowded on the beach saluting the martini flag. As they all climbed back up the steps to their tables and drinks, he joined them, and was immediately tugged into a free chair.

A beer was shoved in his hand. A girl in a bikini plopped onto his lap and slid an arm around his neck.

A month ago, life wouldn't have been any better than this, but now he could only think of Jane. He slid out from under the pretty girl and surveyed the deck for *his* pretty girl. Yeah, she wasn't really his, of course, but she certainly didn't belong to The Smug Author Ian Stone.

That's exactly how he looked too, gazing on Jane as if he knew all her buttons and exactly how to push them. Griffin would bet a billion bucks that the other man didn't know how Jane took her coffee—one dollop of half-and-half and a stingy sprinkle of real sugar—how she liked her pencils—sharpened to the point of battle-readiness—how sweet she looked in the morning wearing only the perfume of lovemaking and a pillow crease.

He stalked to their corner table. Without looking at the other man, he addressed Jane. "Hey, I've been waiting for you back at No. 9."

Her expression was cool. "I thought you'd be busy packing."

"And we're busy having a private conversation," The Annoying Asshole Author Ian Stone put in.

Griffin showed him his teeth. He didn't believe either of them would call it a smile. "Let me make it a much shorter conversation. She said no. Goodbye."

"I want to work with her again," the other man started. "It's a good offer."

"And I'm considering it," Jane put in.

Griffin stared at her. "Are you kidding me? This guy's a smarmy hack who treated you like crap when he had you."

"That's number one *New York Times* bestselling hack to you," Stone said in his snobby voice.

"This isn't about what you write, okay? This is about Jane." He narrowed his eyes at her. "Is this because your father gave him some sort of endorsement?"

She waved that away with a sour look on her face.

Griffin's stomach was sour. Sour with the idea of Jane working with this man. He'd once thought she was still in love with Ian Stone, but of course Jane wouldn't love someone who had the looks of a bowl of oatmeal and the kind of mind that imagined every great love affair meant someone had to end up weeping on the last page. Who would think up shit like that?

He pointed at the other man, the churning burn in his stomach turning to fire in his blood. "He's a pessimist, you know that, don't you, Jane? How can you think of working with someone who is…who is…"

"Kind of like you?"

That hurt. He pulled over a chair and slammed into it, turning his back on Ian Stone to focus exclusively on the librarian who was looking at him as if she wished she had a ruler or, better, one of her lethal pencils. "I'm not a pessimist, Jane."

"I'm not one either," That Asshole Author put in.

Griffin ignored him. "Jane…"

Her gray eyes were calm, and when she crossed one leg over the other, he couldn't help but notice the funky shoes, so Jane with their cork wedge and leather-and-rope straps. Over the toes was a matching bow. Ian Stone probably didn't even realize she had a most unique and arousing taste in footwear.

"He didn't appreciate you before. He won't appreciate you now," Griffin said.

"I have to work. And personal history aside, there's merit to the idea. Another success with him will recoup my reputation."

The one that Griffin had failed to improve. He put the heels of his hands to his suddenly throbbing temples. "I still say this is about your father. You're thinking if you do this, Daddy'll be happy. His seal of approval on the job makes you think you'll have his approval for yourself."

"Stop," she said. "Stop talking."

He wouldn't. She'd flapped her mouth at him plenty of times, hadn't she? "But your father's opinion is not worth the hot air it rides on, Jane. He should know how special, how special and lovable you are. Success is not a necessity to make that happen. And neither is working with Dumb-ass." His thumb jerked toward Stone.

The other man's chair scraped back. "Who are you calling Dumb-ass?" he asked, leaping to his feet.

"You." Griffin flicked him a careless glance. "Christ, man, you have to know that already. You're the one who stepped out on Jane. You're the one who lost her and then went out of your way to hurt her in the aftermath. Just another idiot who doesn't know a real treasure when he has one."

He must have touched a nerve, because The Asshole Author Ian Stone wrapped his fingers around the back of Griffin's collar and tried to yank him from his seat. Of course, he was too short and Griffin too solid to budge. Still, it added another layer of pissed-offness to what was turning into a really shitty day. Grabbing the other man's wrist, he jerked his hand free of his shirt.

The old fabric ripped. "I love this shirt," he said from between his teeth. Then he shoved out of his seat.

"Griffin," Jane said. "Calm down."

"As soon as I beat the crap out of this guy." It suddenly seemed like a great idea. A real problem-solver. He turned to confront the man and gave the classic gimme gesture.

Face going red, the author charged him like a bull.

Griffin shoved him aside, then went after him with his right. Ian Stone got a good crack at his jaw before getting punched in the face. The pretty boy stumbled back, falling into a chair.

Someone whooped, "Bar fight!" and his Party Central buddies gathered round. All that free booze he'd offered up in the past bought him a lot of goodwill. They started up a chant: "Griffin! Griffin! Griffin!"

The Asshole Author Ian Stone shook his head. Then he placed his palms on the arms of the chair, getting ready for another go. When he stood, Griffin allowed him to start a second charge. Then he swept his leg, sending the clown flat on his ass. He'd learned the move from a twenty-year-old native of Kansas City on a freezing day when practicing fight moves seemed a finer way to keep warm than huddling by the diesel-powered heaters.

The kid had later lost an eye to a Taliban bullet.

And remembering, Griffin wanted to hit someone all over again. "Get up," he said to Ian Stone, feeling his temper redoubling, shooting fire into his blood and hardening his fists into blocks of cement. "Get the hell up."

A hand touched his elbow, and he spun toward the new threat, his right arm lifting, ready to swing. At Jane. He froze, his arm cocked to attack.

The world went still. Sound and light and everything dropped away but his fist, set to strike her face. Jane's beautiful face. He couldn't breathe.

How could this happen? He'd almost hurt her, his Jane, with the soft hair and tender mouth and clear-as-mirrors eyes.

In them he saw the bastard that was himself.

Lurching back, he bounced off a table. The rebound brought him near to her again, and she flinched. At the sight, he thought he might throw up. "I'm sorry," he said, his voice hoarse and ugly. "I would never hurt you."

But of course he had.

The crowd around them was silent now, and two bikini girls scuttled out of his way when he made to leave. Leaping off the top step, he landed in the sand and wished he could get a hundred miles away a hundred times faster. He wished he wouldn't be taking himself when he got to wherever he was going.

Jane caught up with him before he'd made it back to

the beach house. She must have run, because she was breathless and her cheeks were red. "Griffin, stop. Wait."

Shoving his hands into his pockets, he halted without looking at her. He couldn't look at her. "What is it?"

"It's what I wanted to talk about before Ian showed up."

His stomach roiled again. "I don't want to hear it, Jane."

"Well, too damn bad. Not ten minutes ago you were telling me how lovable I am. I just wanted to return the favor."

"Ha." It was a bitter laugh. "I almost punched you."

"Almost."

"And last night…" Oh, shit. Just where he didn't want this conversation to go. He pressed his temples between his palms and sent her a glance. "You give too much."

"I might never see you again. You're going someplace dangerous, and who knows what might happen there?" Tears clogged her voice. "So I think I have to tell you—"

"Don't be silly and emotional, Jane," he said, desperate to stop her.

Her hurt expression made clear the verbal punch had done its work.

He started walking again.

Still, she kept talking. "I won't apologize for falling in love with you."

Griffin jerked at the words. She'd said them, damn her, and they seemed to strip away a layer of his skin. How could she do this to him? He'd never set out to hurt her, and now there was no way to escape it.

"I won't be sorry for being silly and emotional because now I realize the alternative," Jane continued, pitching her voice louder. "And that's being cold and alone like my father."

Another beat went by; he distanced himself a few more feet. But then she spoke again. "Cold and alone like you."

He kept moving.

"It's no strings attached, Griffin, I just wanted you to know. I get that you don't love me—"

"You don't get it at all!" He whirled to face her. "I don't *want* to love you. I don't want to ever love anybody."

CHAPTER TWENTY-ONE

GRIFFIN DIDN'T KNOW what to do with himself, so he drove to visit Rex during the hospital's evening visiting hours. Anything to occupy himself since he couldn't find his iPod, and nothing on television—not even 24/7 news— was working as a tranquilizer. He ran into his sister near the bank of elevators on her way to see the old man too. "David took the kids out for pizza to give me a break," Tess said.

Even in the shittiest mood of all time, he could attempt some social niceties. "How are the minions?"

"Great. Happy to be home with a happy mom and dad."

"Listen, you gotta do something about Duncan and Oliver." He might not get another chance to tell her before he left the States. "That Cheeto thing just creeps me out."

"David's working on it," Tess said. "Why don't you come home with me after our visit and give him some opinions on how to best do that? I made a cake for dessert."

Griffin stepped back. "No." He'd just gotten the tribe of them out of his life. "I don't feel much like cake."

"That's the thousandth time you've refused to do a family thing with us since you returned from Afghanistan. If I hadn't come to the cove, would we have seen you at all this summer?"

He ignored the question. "A thousand is an overstatement. And I just don't have a big interest in cake."

Unexpected tears glittered in his sister's eyes. He groaned. "What is it now, Tessie? What's wrong?"

She held the back of her hand to her nose. "I heard what you said in Rebecca's class. That the civilian world is dull after coming back from war."

He shrugged, not following her thought.

"You think *we're* dull. Is that why you won't come over for dessert? Is that why Gage never visits? The two of you are too busy on your never-ending quest for the next adrenaline high?"

Why hadn't he stayed home and pushed pins beneath his fingernails? His sister looked ready to bawl.

"I can't speak for Gage," he said. "It's just…I'm sorry." He shrugged again.

Tess stepped forward. He held out his arms, exhorting himself to give her a comforting hug. Instead she whacked him on the shoulder with her purse. "Ow!" he said. She carried one of those bags big enough to hold a circus. Including the elephant. She lifted it again, and he put up his hands. "What's gotten into you?"

"You're so dumb, that's what!" She put her fists on her hips. "How do you think you find meaning in our mundane world? You come to your family—you find your purpose with them."

"What purpose is that?" he asked, half bemused and half bewildered by her diatribe.

She made a wild gesture that had her purse swinging. "Teach your nephews how to catch a ball—David's got the bicycle down, but he hates baseball. Get to work glaring at your niece's first dates. Tickle Baby Russ's belly."

"Tess—"

"And then find a woman who you can value and love every day."

"Tess—"

"Which bring me to Jane," his sister said.

His expression must have made some sort of statement.

His sister groaned. "Griffin. Tell me you haven't ruined what you had with her."

"We didn't have anything." Just the greatest sex, the best laughs, the kind of connection he'd never found with another woman. The elevator arrived with a ping. "Get off my back, Tess."

They stepped into the empty metal box. "I thought there was some magic at the cove," Tess said. "Seeing you and Jane, I had high hopes, and with Gage exchanging letters with Skye, for a moment I even thought…"

He stared at his sister. "Gage and *Skye?*"

Tess waved a hand. "Forget it. Now I wouldn't wish you and your twin on any woman."

Magic at the cove, Griffin mused, as the elevator chugged upward. What a crock. And to think he'd sold Colonel Parker on the idea. Colonel Parker, who wouldn't be bringing his darling daughter to No. 9 after all. He thought of Vance Smith, the combat medic who always kept his cool. Could that last during the month at the cove he'd promised to a fatherless girl? Still recuperating from his own wounds, he'd be at the beach house in mere days.

Which got him thinking about the email he'd received that very morning. Vance himself, touching base. Griffin was still confused by it. The man seemed to be operating under the impression that the colonel's daughter, Layla, was a child, when Griffin knew for a fact she was in her mid-twenties—all grown up. *Must be me who misunderstood Vance,* he decided. Still, he sent the other man a silent message. *Good luck, buddy.*

When Griffin and his sister found the coot's room, Tess was still muttering about her twin brothers' lack of intelligence, common sense and general good manners.

"That's rich, coming from you," he told her. "We never ate food with our feet."

She ignored him to greet the elderly reporter with a kiss on the cheek, and Griffin could tell she was trying to be cheerful for the invalid's sake. Rex looked pretty damn lively for someone ancient enough to be a first cousin to God, and Griffin told him so.

"They're letting me go home tomorrow," the elderly man said. "After fourteen tests and being prodded and poked more than a rodeo clown, they say it was likely dehydration."

"Well, drink some more water, you irascible antique!" But the news solidified a hazy idea Griffin had. "Listen, Rex…I'm going overseas and could use somebody to look after Private. Are you up to it?"

"Me? And that flea-bitten, mannerless, mangy canine that either pees on my bushes or tries to dig them up?"

Griffin lifted a shoulder. "If you're not interested—"

"I didn't say I wasn't interested. Someone has to take charge of that dog. I'll bet I can teach him a little courtesy."

"You manage that, you should tackle Duncan and Oliver next."

He realized his sister was giving him a dirty look. "Hey," he said, defending himself, "the curmudgeon scared the shit out of me when I was their age. It could work."

"It's not about my boys," she said. "It's about this new plan of yours to go overseas. This is about Gage's offer, I presume? You're taking him up on it after all, and that's why you had the falling-out with Jane."

"We haven't had a falling-out." There'd almost been a knockout, and the thought of it still sickened him—

and only confirmed how necessary it was for him to get away from her.

Suddenly that memory was front and center. Even the chatter between Tess and Monroe couldn't prevent what was recurring in blazing Technicolor in his head. In one quick breath, it stopped being something he recalled and became something he was reliving.

He's on the deck at Captain Crow's. Rage is a ball of fire in his belly. Ian Stone is a smug prick who thinks he's going to get Jane back into his life and back into his bed. Griffin doesn't want to allow him to have another chance to chip away at her confidence. Jane might seem to stand ten feet tall, but a lot of that is wedge heel and ribbon bows. She should be with a man who cherishes her, who will nurture her can-do attitude and spoil her on the days when she's feeling blue.

Ian Stone is not that man. And as Griffin waits for the jerk to get back up and come at him, his fists clench tighter.

Then there's that quick touch. He spins, his arm cocking back.

Jane's sweet face. Her little jerk of fear. The thudding crash his heart makes when it falls to the pit of his belly.

He came back to the present and realized that Tess was gone and he was alone in the hospital room with his neighbor. Surprised, he looked around him. "I…"

"She had to get back home to her husband and family. You answered when she said goodbye, but I didn't think you were all here." Rex waited a beat, then asked a casual question. "Flashback?"

Griffin stared at the old man.

"You think PTSD is new? We called it something different, but…"

"I don't have that." Griffin paced to look out the window. It was nearing dark. "I wasn't at war. I was reporting on war."

"In my time, I talked to a lot of soldiers and I talked to a lot of other combat journalists. Believe me, Griffin, we're all affected by the things we've seen. I've told you before, you need to describe how that changed you."

"I put it away. It's better to keep it distant." And he'd managed that fairly well until Jane insisted he look at the photos and write the words.

He's on the deck at Captain Crow's, and then he isn't. Instead he's in the Humvee, his ears ringing and Jackal's leg...he can feel it right now in his hands, the weight of it, the bloody warmth....

"Sit down, son," Rex said, his voice sharp. "Griffin, sit down."

The vinyl cushion wasn't soft, but at least the chair supported his weight. He rested his elbows on his knees and put his head in his hands. "I'll leave in a minute," he mumbled. "I have packing to do."

"There's no place far enough away," the old man said. "No place you can go that those memories won't find you."

"I feel like I'm going crazy," he heard himself mutter.

"Finish the memoir," Rex urged. "Stay stateside and finish before thinking of traveling again."

"I don't care about the book."

The coot sighed. "Do I have to remind you that a life unexamined is a life not worth living?"

"What?" Griffin said. "Did you read that on the bottom of a bubble-gum wrapper?"

"Socrates, which I'm sure you know." The old man was silent a moment, then his voice turned softer, kinder. "Son, you need to deal with your experience. When you put down the ugly memories on the page, you defuse them of their power."

"Rex—"

"Put them down like you would put Private down if he was sick and he was hurting. Out of kindness, Griffin. Out of love."

Before he could spit out some pithy and clever retort like "Fuck you," which was the first that came to mind, a nurse arrived and shooed Griffin away. A doctor was coming in for late rounds. Griffin was damn glad to walk away from the crabby codger and his amateur psycho-analysis.

The fact that the guy was ninety-four years old didn't mean he knew squat about anything.

Truth was, it wasn't the memories that were sick and hurting. It was Griffin himself.

On the way down in the elevator, he had company. A couple were talking in low tones to each other. The man of the pair had a little girl's hand in his. Maybe…three, four years old? She had dirty-blond hair in pigtails tied with red ribbons. Her white dress was dotted with red cherries, and the poofy skirt belled around her knees as she swung her body back and forth. On her feet were white socks and little red patent leather shoes that were tied on with more ribbon.

Jane would have loved the outfit.

Jane would have looked just like this when she was a kid.

This kid noticed Griffin staring at her, compelling him to make a stab at conversation. "Uh, you have very pretty shoes," he said, feeling awkward.

She responded to the compliment by lifting the hand not clutching her dad's. Four tiny fingers waved in his direction. "I'm this many."

He nodded, acknowledging the unsolicited intel. Then the elevator stopped, the door opening with a ping. With a gesture, he indicated the family should precede him. As the little kid crossed into the lobby, she glanced over her shoulder at Griffin. "It's my birfday."

The three words shot through him like an arrow. It froze him for a moment, thinking of Jane's recent birthday, of all the birthdays he'd miss of hers. Another sharp-edged ache. The elevator doors started to close, and it galvanized him to move, but there was still the hurt.

And an idea. He wasn't any good for Jane, true, but he couldn't leave without first letting her know she'd meant something to him. That he wouldn't forget her, even though he couldn't love her as she deserved.

MOONLIGHT POURED OVER the cove, and at her place on the cliff just south of Beach House No. 9, Jane watched a series of incoming waves ripple forward, as if someone on the horizon had snapped an immense gray sheet. The night was warm, the breeze mild, and she let the calming sound of the water wash over her. With the seabirds asleep, there were no raucous high notes to nature tonight, just the constant wet wash that, while not unchanging, was unceasing. A reminder to take the next breath. To put your next foot forward.

To toughen up and get on with your life.

She'd been doing that ever since the final confrontation with Griffin on the beach that afternoon. Even with his "I don't want to ever love anybody" still echoing in her ears, she'd marched back to Captain Crow's and given Ian Stone the big heave-ho in no uncertain terms.

"For the record," she told him, standing beside his table, her arms folded over her chest, "I'm not now and not ever going to work with you again."

He'd blinked at her, looking bewildered behind the blossoming facial bruises. "But…but it sounded like you were considering my offer."

She'd been goading Griffin was what she'd been doing. And maybe giving Ian some momentary false hope in the process, because she was a little mean that way. "I don't work with cheaters. And I don't work with people who try to blame their failures on someone else."

"What am I supposed to do now?" he asked, like a kid who finally had to do his own homework. "I haven't written a word since we've been apart!"

"Not my problem, Norm," she'd said, then strolled away.

His career could stay flatlined, for all she cared. As for her…she'd find another author to work with, or a new line of work if it came to that. She had great confidence in her ability to overcome—even with her heart broken, she was still breathing, wasn't she?

And though a certain blue-eyed reporter might be out of her life, he'd left her with something. When he'd taunted her about trying to please her father, it had been the boot she needed to get her butt to Corbett Pearson's place again. Once there, she'd ticked off three points on her fingers. One, never give her personal information to anyone; two, never get involved in her professional life again; and three, she loved him despite what she considered to be *his* faults and she expected him to do the same when it came to her. No more interfering and disapproval or no more daughter Jane!

Her dad had stuttered, he'd stumbled, he'd even managed to give her an awkward pat on the back. Progress.

Yes, she thought, closing her eyes, her life would move forward too.

The sound of her name startled her, and her eyes flew

open. But no, she was mistaken, she must be, because she'd come up here to be alone for her goodbye and there weren't any others on the bluff. Below, though light shone in some of the Crescent Cove bungalow windows and far- ther off was the glow from Captain Crow's, the nearest dwellings were dark. She'd packed and put her belong- ings in her car and closed up No. 8. Beach House No. 9 still appeared deserted.

Yet something caused the downy hairs on the back of her neck to rise. Rubbing her nape, she edged closer to the rim of her jutting promontory. This protrusion was nowhere near the bluff's highest point, but it seemed a long twelve feet to where the water swirled and lifted in white tufts against the jagged edges of rock below. She shivered and took a wary step back, then her gaze shifted left and caught on the sight of a dark figure scaling the cliff. Swift and sure, he swung up arm-over-arm, some- thing—a bag?—caught in the grip of his teeth, just like a pirate clenching a dagger, climbing the riggings of an unsuspecting ship.

Jane retreated two more steps, until her back pressed against the rough surface of the bluff's face. It still left little room for the buccaneer who reached her ledge and tore the paper from his mouth to address her in a raspy, breathless voice. "What the hell are you doing?"

It wasn't fair, she thought. She'd come up here to gain perspective. To begin the process, finally, of abandon- ing hope when it came to her and Griffin. But seeing him again, even wearing a grim expression and with his chest heaving with jerky breaths, made her skin feel ten- der and her heart soften with exquisite yearning, both painful and sweet.

"Well?" he prompted, clearly agitated.

Shoving her hands into the pockets of her jeans, she met his gaze in stubborn silence.

"It's dangerous up here," he said. "You shouldn't risk it."

"That's rich coming from you," she said, then managed a little smile. "Hey. Irony again."

The line of his mouth flattened. "Let's go, Jane." He held out his hand to her. "I'll help you down."

She shook her head, shuffling away from his touch. "I don't need your help. I got up here just fine on my own, though by an admittedly tamer route than yours."

"Yeah, well." He shrugged. "I took a shortcut when I spotted you. I was worried…"

"Worried about what?"

His gaze cut away from hers, and she suddenly knew what had gone through his mind.

"No," she said, a laugh escaping. "You thought I was going to do myself in? All because you don't love me?"

"No. I don't know. Not exactly." He still wouldn't look at her. "Go ahead, call me Mr. Ego again."

Except the idea of jumping in *had* crossed her mind. Not because she wanted to end it all—yes, Mr. Ego indeed—but because she wanted a temporary end to her current unhappiness. Griffin wasn't in love with her. He was going toward danger, and she might never see him alive again.

According to Tess, the jolt of jumping off could offer some reprieve. It had a numbing power.

Jane moistened her lips. "Does adrenaline really get rid of the pain?"

His glance was wary.

"Is that why you're going to Gage? To get away from what's hurting you here?"

He made a dismissive gesture, drawing both their attention to the bag he was holding.

"Look," he said. "I brought you presents. Come down and you can have them."

"Presents?" Jane frowned and crossed her arms over her chest. Gifts to appease his conscience? "I don't need anything from you."

"I missed your birthday," Griffin said.

"For heaven's sake…" Couldn't he just go away? The shelf of rock was so small that she could feel his body heat from here. It pressed against her breastbone, making it hard to breathe. Putting stress on her already battered heart.

"Come on down," he coaxed again.

"I won't," Jane said. She'd depart on her own terms. Alone, just the way she'd arrived that day when she'd foolishly disregarded the skull and crossbones, scoffing at the idea of danger.

He sighed, apparently accepting her stubbornness. "Fine, then," he said, his tone disgruntled. Then he rummaged in the bag. "I was at the mercy of that convenience store a couple of miles away, you understand."

"If it's one of those icky beef sticks, I'm tossing it over the cliff," she warned.

"You just stay where you are," Griffin said. With a little flourish, he presented her with a slender plastic-and-cardboard package.

Jane stared down at the item in her hands. The bright moon was as good as a flashlight. "A toothbrush?"

"Are you aware you hum when you brush your teeth, honey-pie?"

"The 'Happy Birthday' song. Twice. Dentists recommend brushing the length of time that takes for optimum cleaning."

He quickly averted his head, but it didn't hide the swift grin.

"Don't laugh at me!"

"It's either that or kiss you, Jane."

She took a half step away from him. "None of that, either."

Still smiling, he pointed to her gift. "This one's special. You can record any song you like, then listen to your favorite while keeping your dentist happy morning and night."

"Oh." Jane regarded it with more interest. "Clever."

His hand dipped back in the bag. "Here."

Out came a small square of cardboard threaded with a pair of earrings. Pink with purple polka dots, they were probably intended for a child, given the color combination.

"They're bows," Griffin said. "You always wear bows."

She looked up at him. His amazing eyes were focused on her, as if he was trying to read her thoughts. Her feet moved again, taking another step away from him and his piercing gaze. "Th-thank you," she said, her voice unsteady.

No man had ever seen so much about her.

He shrugged and then rummaged in the bag. "Last one." His hand stilled inside the paper, and he locked eyes with her. "No matter what happens, Jane, I want you to know…" And then the daredevil reporter seemed to run out of words. Instead of handing over the final gift, he pushed the bag into her hands.

Feeling both curious and oddly cautious, Jane tucked the toothbrush and the earrings into the pockets of her jeans, then reached inside the sack for the next present. Her fingers curled around something plastic and mostly round. Her breath caught in her throat as she drew it out.

A snow globe.

How had he known?

A cheap tourist trinket, it had probably been made thousands and thousands of miles from here but was stamped "Crescent Cove" on the base. Clutching the bag in one hand, Jane let the globe sit on the shelf of her other palm, ignoring how it trembled. Inside the bubble was a dab of blue ocean and a painted beach. On that sat a little grass shack beside two palm trees and strung between them was a tiny hammock, upon which reclined an even tinier woman in a yellow bikini.

Griffin gestured at the plastic capsule. "You have a suit just that color. So it's as if you'll always be here. Forever."

A prickle ran across Jane's scalp. Always and forever unable to forget this place or the man she'd fallen in love with. Always and forever wishing for him, worrying about him, wondering if he ever thought of her with regret. Always and forever his, even if he didn't want her. That wasn't any kind of progress.

Panic clutched her throat and wrapped her ribs with heavy bands.

God knew what expression overtook her face, because Griffin suddenly started forward. "Sweetheart…"

But she couldn't be touched by him, she thought in hasty alarm. Not now. Not ever again. Her feet shuffled in retreat and she put out the hand holding the bag to keep him away.

A sudden gust of wind fluttered her hair and caught at the paper. It was torn from her grasp and instinct had her snatching for it. Unsteadied by the sudden move, she took another step back to keep her balance.

Her foot found air. She felt herself going over the ledge.

IN COMBAT, TIME stretched like a child's imagination, allowing in every boogeyman, every monster-under-the-bed, even as one's vision sharpened and dexterity heightened. Griffin's heart knelled like slow thunder as he saw Jane wobble and her body arch over the edge. Fear tasted like ash on his tongue as he lunged for her. Image after image shuffled through his mind as he made the long reach.

Jane plummeting onto sharp rocks, Jane plunging into chilly water and never coming up, Jane falling toward her greatest fear as her body slipped through his hands. She'd go down thinking he'd failed her like every other man in her life.

Your kind always lets go.

But then—miracle!—he caught her upper arm. His fingers closed over her slender biceps, locking them together. Just as he prepared to yank her back to safety, though, he realized that her momentum was too much for him to battle.

In this, the librarian couldn't defy the laws of physics.

They both went over, the ocean a second or two away. But it took a very long time to fall when you'd really rather not.

Enough time for Griffin to realize that Jane wouldn't know to swim away from the rocks to keep from being bashed against them.

Enough time for that thought to plow with the power of an ice-breaking ship through his frozen heart.

Enough time for him to be certain he wouldn't survive one more loss. That he wouldn't survive without her in his life.

Dark, cold water closed over him like a thick shroud. It tried tearing Jane from his grasp, but knowing what was at stake, he hung on to her, kicking powerfully with his legs to take them both away from the dangerous crags. To his surprise, she was kicking too, doing her share, but the unexpected dousing, fully clothed, made it a heavy slog.

For every movement forward, the water washed them back. He'd lost his flip-flops, and he felt the bite of rock on his sole as he pushed off to propel Jane away from danger. "Let…go!" she gasped out, then coughed. "Let. Me. Go!"

Let go? He couldn't let go. He'd never let go.

But then she wrenched free of him, and without the hamper of a second body, she started stroking away. Heart pounding in his ears, he followed behind, matching his arm pulls to hers. It wasn't easy getting away from the surf breaking against the bluff. It still fought to wash them back, just as they fought to break from it. He was breathing hard, anxiety taking its toll, and his panic didn't lessen, even when he realized the shoreline was a straight shot ahead.

People drowned in bathtubs. In puddles. In their own blood.

Those thoughts were still in his mind as their bellies hit sand. They combat crawled and coughed their way onto the beach. Safe.

Lying on the sand beside her, he tried coping with the aftermath of horror and the sharp spike of survival euphoria. And the new sudden yet certain understanding that his life was about to take a drastic turn.

He glanced over when he finally caught his breath. "We have to talk."

Then he jerked upright and put his hand on her shoulder. "Jane!" She was sodden and cold as a corpse, her eyes open and staring straight at the sky. Jesus, was she dead? *"Jane."*

"I'm right here," she said, sounding slow and drunk. One hand flopped on the sand like a fish. "Right. Here."

"Oh, thank God." He pulled her into his lap, curled his chilled and wet body over her chilled and wet body. Pressing his cheek to hers, he rocked them a little. He couldn't lose her now.

His arms tightened. "I was terrified, damn you," he said, his voice rough. "Beyond terrified. And if anything had happened to you, I would have killed you!"

She reached up to pat his dripping hair as she would Private. "Calm down."

"I am calm. I'm always calm!"

Her hand gave him another pat. "No, you're not. You throw things—plates, fists, fits. I'm not sure if you're aware, but those aren't really the actions of a ninety-nine-percent no-feelings guy." She allowed that a minute to sink in. "Just saying."

"Jane, I…" But a shiver racked her small frame, and new alarm rushed through him. "We have to get you warm." He picked them both up off the sand and half carried, half led her to Beach House No. 9. Private greeted them with a worried whine and stealthy licks at the salt water running off their bodies.

Griffin escorted her to the guest bath when she insisted on privacy, then hit his own shower. Standing under the spray, his restless mind replayed the event: his alarm upon seeing her on the cliff, his panic when she started to fall, that absolute certainty that he couldn't go on without her.

She'd come to mean so much. And yes, she was right again, damn her. He wasn't a ninety-nine-percent no-feelings guy.

Even as anxiety beat its vulture wings in his belly at the idea, he could no longer hide from the truth. His heart was no longer untouchable. Hell, it was no longer his own. He hadn't wanted this, had never wanted this, but the battle was lost.

Dry and dressed again, he stood outside the bathroom where Jane was cleaning up, overwhelmed by the need to see her and touch her. Each moment that passed ratcheted his tension higher. His hand rubbed a nervous path on the thigh of his jeans, and he had to keep telling himself to unclench his back teeth. Nothing had prepared him for this feeling.

Never had he felt so vulnerable.

And still Jane didn't emerge from the shower.

"It's taking too long," he muttered. Then he banged on the door with his knuckles. "You're wasting water!"

She came out long minutes later, wrapped in a towel and flushed with heat, a pink cast to her cheeks, her shoulders, her chest.

"Are you all right?" he demanded.

"It seems I am," she said, her expression bemused. "I saved myself from the giant eels and the whale snot."

Griffin wanted to claim that he had saved her, but of course it wasn't true. "You did," he acknowledged. "You did."

"I'm sort of an ocean stud now," she added, a satisfied gleam in her eyes.

God, the woman just slayed him. His mouth twitched with a smile. "You are."

"Well, then." She took a quick step. "I have clothes in my car—"

"You don't need clothes," he said brusquely.

Her downy brows came together. "What?"

"Just a minute, just a minute," he muttered, then stalked down the hall, stalked back.

"Griffin?"

"I'm a writer, okay? Give me a second to find the words."

Instead of being patient as he thought she should, she

brushed past him and turned into the master bedroom. There she rummaged through his drawers, filching a pair of boxers and a T-shirt. She went behind another closed bathroom door to put them on.

He found himself rapping on that door too. How long did it take to get dressed? "Hurry up."

Her expression was a little forlorn when she finally emerged. "I lost my new toothbrush."

"I'll buy you another one."

"I don't mind about the earrings. They were designed for a five-year-old."

"Hey, it's the thought that counts," he said, nearly annoyed.

She swallowed, and the new expression overtaking her face was one he couldn't read. "I never want to see that snow globe again."

He frowned at her. "That kind of hurts my feelings."

"Are we back to that?" Now, for the first time since they'd washed up on the beach, she sounded weary. "I thought you were sure you didn't have any."

He hesitated one more moment, and then he saw a shiver work its way up her spine. "You're still cold." Jane should never be cold again.

He reached out, intent on sweeping her to his chest. The maddening librarian stepped back, forcing him to beg for her patience. Which she seemed to like. "Please, Jane. Please give me a moment of your time."

She allowed herself to be towed to the living room, where he wrapped her in a blanket and placed her on the couch. He sat on the coffee table opposite her, staring into her lovely face.

A tense silence developed as he tried to figure out what to tell her.

"I've already showed you the inside of my heart, Griffin," she said in a tight voice. "Can't you leave me alone now?"

"You don't understand," he answered. "I'm trying to see myself in your eyes. I keep thinking they're like mirrors."

She cocked her head, cautious. "What is it you think you should see?"

Griffin took a breath. *A life unexamined is not worth living.* "That final explosion in the Humvee…the one that took Jackal's leg—it splintered me into pieces. One part objective reporter, one part combatant affected—no, injured—by war, one part human being grieving for friends lost and wounded. I've been avoiding putting those three back together."

"You don't say."

"Smart-ass." He scrubbed his hands through his hair. "Separated like that, it seemed I could keep myself from feeling—" Breaking off, he forced himself to breathe.

"But you *are* feeling. You're hurting. That's why you're—"

"Throwing plates, fists and fits." He looked away, looked back. She deserved the truth. "I'm having flashbacks. More all the time."

"Oh, Griffin." Sitting straighter, she leaned toward him. "How frightening."

His mouth was dry. "I'm a mess." He'd been trying to deny it for so long. Refusing to acknowledge what everyone had been telling him.

"You can get help."

"Rex thinks the book will go a long way toward that," he said, then hesitated. "I'm not going to Gage. I'm done with war."

God, what a relief it was to say those words.

Jane's expression was once more inscrutable. "But not

done with the memoir?" she asked. "You're actually going to finish it?"

Here was the critical moment, one that felt more live-or-die than any he'd faced in Afghanistan. He took another deep breath. "If I can get some assistance."

In an abrupt move, she sat back. "Maybe Frank can find you someone."

His gaze caught hers. "I've already found someone."

"Griffin…"

"Look, your reputation doesn't need me. It doesn't need this job. You're incredible at what you do—you're good with the words, you're good with people. You've already made my memoir so much better."

Her face flushed. "Thank you."

"But this isn't about the book. I need you, Jane." He was certain of this. *Find a woman you can value and love every day.* "You're the glue. In your eyes I see me, whole and well. Loved…and loving."

She made to rise off the couch.

He grabbed her knees, holding her down. "I love you, Jane Pearson. I can't run from my memories any longer, and I don't want to distance myself from this either. I am desperately in love with you."

She turned her face away from his. "You're riding the adrenaline rush from the fall. Don't say something you'll regret later."

Griffin hadn't come this far to fail. "Let me be the one who never lets go of you, sweetheart." He caressed her bare legs in soft persuasion. "I know I'm not completely healthy, but I promise—"

"It's not that." She whipped her head toward his, and he could see the tears standing in her eyes. "It's… You've been all over the world. Been in perilous places, taken risks that stop my breath. In comparison to all that, will what we might have…will *I* be enough?"

"Sweetheart…"

"You said my world, this world, is colorless, remember?"

It almost made him laugh. "Honey-pie, when I'm with you, I think of a thousand colors. Your beautiful silvery eyes, your lemon-yellow swimsuit, your pink sunburn, your pumpkin shoes. You're…you're my rainbow." His darling, serious, wonderful, brave, spirited, beautiful, talented Jane. So, so lovable.

He would make it his worthy purpose to assure her of that every day.

But she didn't yet appear entirely convinced, damn it.

"Jane, sweetheart, remember…" His heart felt unmoored in his chest, bumping throat, ribs, belly. Oh, God, he thought, he had to get this right.

He reached for her hands, held tight. "Remember when I told you that during each moment in war, you hold the certain knowledge that what you're doing might be the very last thing you ever do?"

She nodded, and her mouth was trembling.

He pulled her forward, into his arms. His lips found the smooth skin of her cheek. "Jane. Oh, Jane."

Holding her away again, he hoped that there really was magic in Beach House No. 9, because he wasn't too proud to accept enchanted spells and secret love potions if it meant he could convince her. If it meant he could keep her forever. "I want my very last thing to be you."

There was a taut moment of stunned silence. Then she launched herself into his arms, laughing and crying at the same time. "Oh, God. I love you, I love you too."

Their kiss was tender and deep, carnal and exuberant. Needing breath, he finally lifted his head. "Jane—"

"Griffin—" she said at the same time.

They smiled at each other. Her eyes sparkled. "We've still got the name thing down, chili-dog. But this time... you first."

He grinned, and then when he opened his mouth to speak, he found himself reaching for a real future, he found himself believing in it for the first time since he'd left Afghanistan, and he finally felt one hundred percent alive, ready to leap for that silver horizon ahead that was waiting for him in Jane's eyes. "Marry me. Please, honey-pie, marry me."

And then he knew there was indeed magic at Beach House No. 9, because his beloved took her own leap, trusting that he would always be there to catch her, to be the one who never let go. Without another hesitation, she said, "Yes."

* * * * *

Join bestselling authors
Jennifer Crusie,
Victoria Dahl and Shannon Stacey
for three *sexy* stories about finding
the one you love.

Available wherever books are sold!

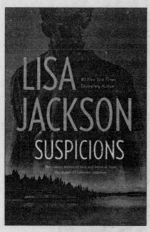

The hunt for justice…and love…begins.

A gripping new romantic suspense from
USA TODAY bestselling author

B.J. DANIELS

Jack French has had two long years of prison-ranch labor to
focus on starting over, cleaning up his act and making things right.
When he comes home to close-knit Beartooth, Montana, he's
bent on leveling the score with the men who set him up.
The one thing he doesn't factor into his plans is spitfire
beauty Kate LaFord.

Available wherever books are sold!

HARLEQUIN® HQN™
www.Harlequin.com

REQUEST YOUR FREE BOOKS!

2 FREE NOVELS
FROM THE ROMANCE COLLECTION
PLUS 2 FREE GIFTS!

YES! Please send me 2 FREE novels from the Romance Collection and my 2 FREE gifts (gifts are worth about $10). After receiving them, if I don't wish to receive any more books, I can return the shipping statement marked "cancel." If I don't cancel, I will receive 4 brand-new novels every month and be billed just $5.99 per book in the U.S. or $6.49 per book in Canada. That's a savings of at least 25% off the cover price. It's quite a bargain! Shipping and handling is just 50¢ per book in the U.S. and 75¢ per book in Canada.* I understand that accepting the 2 free books and gifts places me under no obligation to buy anything. I can always return a shipment and cancel at any time. Even if I never buy another book, the two free books and gifts are mine to keep forever.

194/394 MDN FVU7

Name	(PLEASE PRINT)

Address	Apt. #

City	State/Prov.	Zip/Postal Code

Signature (if under 18, a parent or guardian must sign)

Mail to the Harlequin® Reader Service:
IN U.S.A.: P.O. Box 1867, Buffalo, NY 14240-1867
IN CANADA: P.O. Box 609, Fort Erie, Ontario L2A 5X3

Want to try two free books from another line?
Call 1-800-873-8635 or visit www.ReaderService.com.

* Terms and prices subject to change without notice. Prices do not include applicable taxes. Sales tax applicable in N.Y. Canadian residents will be charged applicable taxes. Offer not valid in Quebec. This offer is limited to one order per household. Not valid for current subscribers to the Romance Collection or the Romance/Suspense Collection. All orders subject to credit approval. Credit or debit balances in a customer's account(s) may be offset by any other outstanding balance owed by or to the customer. Please allow 4 to 6 weeks for delivery. Offer available while quantities last.

Your Privacy—The Harlequin® Reader Service is committed to protecting your privacy. Our Privacy Policy is available online at www.ReaderService.com or upon request from the Harlequin Reader Service.

We make a portion of our mailing list available to reputable third parties that offer products we believe may interest you. If you prefer that we not exchange your name with third parties, or if you wish to clarify or modify your communication preferences, please visit us at www.ReaderService.com/consumerchoice or write to us at Harlequin Reader Service Preference Service, P.O. Box 9062, Buffalo, NY 14269. Include your complete name and address.

New York Times Bestselling Author

CARLA NEGGERS

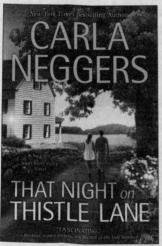

Librarian Phoebe O'Dunn deals in stories, but she knows that happy endings are rare. Her life in Knights Bridge, Massachusetts, is safe and uneventful…until she discovers the hidden room.

Among its secrets is a cache of vintage clothing, including a spectacular gown—perfect for the gala masquerade. In the guise of a princess, Phoebe is captivated by a handsome swashbuckler who's also adopted a more daring persona. Noah Kendrick's wealth has made him wary, especially of women: everybody wants something.

When Noah and Phoebe meet again in Knights Bridge, at first neither recognizes the other. And neither one is sure they can trust the magic of the night they shared—until an unexpected threat prompts them to unmask their truest selves.

Available wherever books are sold.

MCN1420